KILLDOZER!

Theodore Sturgeon, New York City, March 1945.
"No, This isn't the office boy cutting up after the boss left
for lunch. This is Teddy as Copy Director of the
Hudson-American Corporation for two glorious weeks.
Isn't he cute with his little blue pencil?" (written on the back
of the photo by THS, to his sister-in-law)

KILLDOZER!

Volume III:

The Complete Stories of

Theodore Sturgeon

Edited by
Paul Williams

Foreword by
Robert Silverberg

Afterword by
Robert A. Heinlein

North Atlantic Books
Berkeley, California

Killdozer!

Published by
North Atlantic Books
P.O. Box 12327
Berkeley, California 94712

Cover art by Paul Orban
Book design by Paula Morrison
Cover design by Catherine E. Campaigne

Printed in the United States of America

Killdozer! is sponsored by the Society for the Study of Native Arts and Sciences, a nonprofit educational corporation whose goals are to develop an educational and crosscultural perspective linking various scientific, social, and artistic fields; to nurture a holistic view of arts, sciences, humanities, and healing; and to publish and distribute literature on the relationship of mind, body, and nature.

Library of Congress Cataloging-in-Publication Number

Sturgeon, Theodore.
 Killdozer! : the complete stories of Theodore Sturgeon / edited by Paul
Williams : foreword by Robert Silverberg, afterword by Robert A. Heinlein.
  p. cm
  Contents: v. 3 1941–1946
  ISBN 1-55643-327-1 (v. 3)
  I. Williams, Paul. II. Title
PS3569.T875U44 1994
813'.54—dc20   94-38047
                                                                        CIP

 1   2   3   4   5   6   7   8   9 / 03   02   01   00   99

EDITOR'S NOTE

THEODORE HAMILTON STURGEON was born February 26, 1918, and died May 8, 1985. This is the third of a series of volumes that will collect all of his short fiction of all types and all lengths shorter than a novel. The volumes and the stories within the volumes are organized chronologically by order of composition (insofar as it can be determined). This third volume contains stories believed to have been written between 1941 and 1946. Four are being published here for the first time; and two others have never before appeared in a Sturgeon collection.

For invaluable assistance in the preparation of this volume, I would like to thank Noël Sturgeon and the Theodore Sturgeon Literary Trust, Marion Sturgeon, Jayne Williams, Debbie Notkin, Robert Silverberg, Virginia Heinlein, Ralph Vicinanza, Lindy Hough, Richard Grossinger, Tom Whitmore, Frank Robinson, Kyle McAbee, Matt Austern, Donya White, Sue Armitage, Bob Greene, Dixon Chandler, David G. Hartwell, T. V. Reed, Cindy Lee Berryhill, Sam Moskowitz, and all of you who have expressed your interest and support.

CONTENTS

Foreword

by Robert Silverberg

THE STORIES IN this volume are the work of a writer in transition, a writer on the threshold of greatness who has already found his important themes but has not yet—quite—attained his full measure of artistic breadth and technical assurance. The familiar Sturgeon warmth and compassion are there, the concern with the inner workings of the human soul, the narrative ingenuity. What we don't yet have is the soaring poetry, the visionary beauty, of Sturgeon's writing in the great period of his maturity that began about 1950 with the novel *The Dreaming Jewels* and reached its apogee with the 1953 novel *More Than Human* and the myriad short stories and novellas of 1952–1962. But we can see harbingers of it.

The present group of stories come from two very different periods in Sturgeon's life. "Blabbermouth," "Medusa," "The Hag Séleen," "Ghost of a Chance" and "The Bones" were written by 1941, when he was 23 years old. They represent the last outburst of the precocious first phase of his career, the 1939–41 period when he carved a place for himself among the heroes of editor John W. Campbell's Golden Age period with such tales as "Microcosmic God," "It," "Shottle Bop," and "Yesterday Was Monday" in Campbell's magazines *Astounding Science-Fiction* and *Unknown*. The remaining stories in the book were written between the spring of 1944 and the early months of 1946, after three years of silence. That three-year gap is a significant one, and not only because three years is a long time in the development of a prolific writer who is still in his twenties. Those particular three years were the years of World War II, which worked an immense transformation on Ted Sturgeon and on

ix

the world in which he lived. They were a time of challenge and maturity for him; the author of "Memorial" was a very different man from the author of "Medusa," and the problems of 1946 were very different from those of 1941.

The war years were bleak and gray ones for science fiction readers and writers. The war effort itself was all-encompassing. Most of the top writers were involved, either through actual battlefield experience or in some non-combatant role that absorbed most of their energies. In those years magazine publishers were plagued by skyrocketing expenses and paper shortages; many magazines disappeared altogether and those that survived cut back severely on their frequency of publication and number of pages per issue. Magazines then were the only outlet for publication that an American science-fiction writer had: paperback book publishing in the United States had only barely been born, and the orthodox hardcover publishers had scarcely any interest in science fiction. Only in the pulp magazines—gaudy-looking crudely printed entities with names like *Startling Stories, Thrilling Wonder Stories,* and *Astounding Science-Fiction*—could a science fiction writer find readers, and then only at a rate of pay that even then had to be considered a pittance. $50 to $75 was the going price for short stories; a long work, running to 100 manuscript pages or even more, might fetch $200 or so. The shrinkage of the magazine market during those years eliminated any hope that a writer, even one who had not gone to the war, could earn even a modest living from science fiction.

It was in the brief pre-war boom of the pulp magazines that the young Ted Sturgeon, unfettered and experimental-minded, launched his writing career. After some uncertain times writing short-short stories for newspaper syndicates, he turned to fantasy and science fiction in 1939 and clicked almost immediately with John Campbell, the pre-eminent science fiction editor of the day. Throughout 1940 and 1941 he sold Campbell virtually everything he wrote.

Campbell, a ponderous, emotionally awkward man with a background in engineering and gadgetry, found the mercurial, elfin young Sturgeon immensely charming. Isaac Asimov, another of Campbell's discoveries of that era, wrote more than forty years later of how, "little by little, John gathered a stable of writers and learned the trick of keeping us rubbing our noses against the grindstone. One thing he did, in my case, was to tell me what the other members of his stable were doing.

"The one he mentioned with the greatest affection was Theodore Sturgeon. I can see him grinning now as he would hint at the manifold pleasures of something upcoming by Ted.

"How I watched for his stories myself. I remember 'It' and 'Ether Breather' (his first) and 'Shottle Bop' and 'Yesterday was Monday' and 'Killdozer'—and how eagerly I read them and how hopelessly I decided I couldn't match him. And I never could. He had a delicacy of touch that I couldn't duplicate if my fingers were feathers."

Those early stories of Sturgeon's stood out like beacons in the pages of Campbell's two magazines, even against those of Asimov, Robert A. Heinlein, A.E. van Vogt, and the rest of Campbell's galaxy of new stars, because of that magical lightness of touch and the cunning of his narrative strategies, so different from the earnest straightforward storytelling and simple functional prose of most of his contemporaries.

Consider the insinuating, ingratiating charm of the first words of "Microcosmic God"—"Here is a story about a man who had too much power, and a man who took too much, but don't worry; I'm not going political on you." Pulp-magazine writers in 1941 didn't begin stories that way, unless they were Theodore Sturgeon.

Consider the tone of the opening, both disarming and compelling, of "Medusa"—"I wasn't sore at them. I didn't know what they had done to me, exactly—I knew that some of it wasn't so nice, and that I'd probably never be the same again." It is a tone we will hear again in the famous opening lines of *The Dreaming Jewels* a decade later: "They caught the kid doing something disgusting out under the bleachers at the high school stadium, and he was sent home from the grammar school across the street. He was eight years old then. He'd been doing it for years."

Consider the last line of "He Shuttles"—"Perhaps he was never here at all. But this is the story I wrote last night." Sturgeon speaking to the reader in his own voice: confident of his irresistible appeal, smiling and winking as he pulls us through the convolutions of his plots.

It was a new and refreshing way to write science fiction, which until then had, by and large, been straitjacketed by pulp-magazine conventions of plot and narrative mode. What it was, actually, was a compounding of Sturgeon's unique irreverent sensibility and a storytelling manner imported from mainstream fiction, from the broader, more expansive modes common in such magazines as *The Saturday Evening Post,* modes which such writers as F. Scott Fitzgerald had raised in the 1920s from slick commercialism to something approaching art. The slick-magazine stories were primarily *people*-centered rather than *plot*-centered or (as in the best science fiction of the day) *idea*-centered, and their writers allowed themselves considerably more latitude in their narrative methods than pulp editors permitted.

At the beginning of his career in the late 1930s, Sturgeon had had little luck selling the stories that he aimed at such magazines. The best of them, "Bianca's Hands," had to wait until 1947 to see print, and others remained unpublished until collected in the first of these present volumes, *The Ultimate Egoist.* But his application of slick-magazine techniques to a pulp-magazine market made an immediate impact. John Campbell, then engaged in an all-out challenge of science fiction's established modes, which ran heavily to rarefied tales of science on the one hand and slam-bang adventure on the other, welcomed Sturgeon's material eagerly and only occasionally rejected any of it. ("Blabbermouth," one of the weaker Sturgeon stories of the period, probably was intended for *Unknown,* but went unpublished for six years.

His stories still relied heavily on mechanical plot contrivances, and his style was freighted with colloquialisms that now seem archaic; but, thanks to Campbell, Sturgeon quickly found himself selling regularly and developing the self-confidence a professional writer needs.

He was now the head of a family, though, with a host of new responsibilities, and the writing income available to even a successful science-fiction writer in pre-war America was proving insufficient. Sturgeon found a job managing a resort hotel in the British

West Indies in June of 1941 and hoped to go on writing on the side. But the coming of the war brought a swift close to this period of Sturgeon's literary career. Married and the father of a small child, he was safe from the military draft, but the outbreak of war meant the end of his resort job and soon he was serving as assistant chief steward for the U.S. Army at Fort Simonds, where he ran a tractor lubrication center and learned to handle earth-moving machinery. The following year saw him in Puerto Rico at Ensenada Honda, an airfield, drydock, and shipyard, where he had further experience with bulldozers and other heavy-duty equipment, until the end of 1943. After some months doing clerical work for the Navy, he and his family moved to St. Croix in the American Virgin Islands. From the summer of 1941 to the spring of 1944 he wrote no fiction at all. The end of his military employment forced him back to writing in April 1944, and for the first story of this new period he drew on all the considerable knowledge that he had acquired during the war about earth-moving machinery, an unlikely subject, perhaps, for science fiction, but one which brought forth gripping results. In nine days Sturgeon wrote the 31,000–word novella "Killdozer!," his longest and probably most successful work up until then, in which he imbued a fantastic notion with rock-solid specificity of detail to create great conviction and enormous suspense. Campbell, who had been struggling to keep *Astounding* filled with good material during the wartime absence of most of his best contributors, was overjoyed, and rushed the powerful story into print within a few months, in the November, 1944 issue. The magazine's readers responded enthusiastically.

The sale of "Killdozer!" brought Sturgeon a bonus rate of $542.50, the most he had ever received for a story—something like $10,000, or even more, in modern purchasing power. The end of the war seemed in sight, here in mid-1944, and the story's success awakened in him the possibility of reviving his dormant writing career. It was at this time that he wrote "Abreaction," another bulldozer story but this one a psychological fantasy, which perhaps might have sold to Campbell's off-trail magazine *Unknown*; but *Unknown* had vanished in 1943, a victim of wartime paper shortages, and the story went unpublished until the venerable *Weird Tales,* a magazine market of the most marginal kind, printed it in 1948. Once again he attempted an entry into mainstream fiction, too, with "Noon Gun," probably written late in 1944 or early in 1945. But it was a mediocre story at best, and found no takers. (Slightly refurbished, it sold to *Playboy* in 1962, most likely on the strength of Sturgeon's science fiction accomplishments in the intervening years.)

Despite these unpromising early results, Sturgeon persisted in his plans for returning to writing as a profession. A clause in his government contract enabled him to wangle plane fare from St. Croix back to the American mainland, where he attempted to make arrangements for finding a job or a new literary agent and moving his family to New York. But nothing worked out. The literary agents of the era had no use for writers who proposed to earn a living writing stories at a cent or two a word for a single specialized market that consisted only of John Campbell's remaining magazine and five or six low-paying quasi-juvenile competitors. Sturgeon drifted into a period of confusion and despair; what had been intended as a ten-day trip stretched into a futile eight months, during which time he received word from his wife in the Virgin Islands that she wanted a divorce. By late 1945 he found himself alone in New York, penniless, bewildered, and wholly unable to write.

It was Campbell, once again, who rescued him. In December of 1945, Sturgeon was staying as a house guest in Campbell's New Jersey home, and Campbell sat him before a typewriter in his gadget-crowded basement. Out came the story "The Chromium Helmet," which Campbell read as it emerged and accepted instantly. It was the first substantial fiction Sturgeon had managed to write in a year and a half.

"The Chromium Helmet" is marked by slick-magazine cuteness ("Dreams is all fuzzy. But I stinkly *remember* about that doll") and clichéd pulp-magazine slanginess (" 'Don't let me horn in,' I said. 'Only—I've known youse guys for a long time' ") that put it below such masterpieces to come as 1953's "A Saucer of Loneliness" and 1954's "To Here and the Easel." But the intricacy of its high-tech plot showed that Sturgeon's story-constructing skills were undiminished, and the thoroughness of its machine-shop technical background (perhaps inspired by the clutter of electronic gear all about him in Campbell's legendary basement as he worked) is impressive testimony to his unwillingness to fake his material. He works his story out down to the last inductance bridge and oscilloscope, where a lesser writer might have been content to speak vaguely of unspecified "devices" and "gadgets" and let it go at that.

So a new beginning had been made. Sturgeon followed "The Chromium Helmet" with "Memorial," a heavy-handed and implausible vignette written (as so many stories in Campbell's magazine were that year) in an emotional response to the detonation of the first atomic bombs the previous summer, and then with the much stronger "Mewhu's Jet," which anticipates the themes of Stephen Spielberg's movie *E.T.* and much of Sturgeon's own later output by putting a normal American family in contact with a highly abnormal situation and working it not for horror or thrills but for emotional warmth.

The Sturgeon of 1946 is not yet the Sturgeon of the sudden 1950–51 efflorescence ("The Stars are the Styx," "Rule of Three," and the gaudy adventure story "The Incubi of Parallel X,") or of the more profound "Hurricane Trio" and "Bulkhead" and "A Way of Thinking," which will come another few years onward from those. But the man who wrote the splendid stories of his major epoch—that man of such outward tenderness and charm, such inner turbulence and stormy ambition—is recognizably present here, and so are the basic technical skills, however they would develop and blossom later on. Everything is in place for the greatness to come.

Robert Silverberg
March 1996

Blabbermouth

SHE WAS A LOVELY THING, and before either of us knew it my arms were around her and her deep eyes were all tangled up in mine. I held her a little too close a little too long, I guess; she squirmed away, got her balance and brushed me off like so much pretzel-juice.

"Sorry," I lied.

A winged eyebrow went up as two heavy lids went down.

"That's all right," she said in a voice like the sound of a cello whispering in the low register. "But you really ought to signal for a turn." I'd been trying to whip in front of a rotund individual who was about to climb into the taxi I wanted to get, and in doing so had almost knocked the girl off her feet. She turned away just in time to miss the practiced click of my heels as I tipped my hat. I sighed and flagged another cab. I had a lot of friends and knew a lot of glamour, and until this minute I had flattered myself on having a pretty picturesque string of 'em in my little black book. But now— well, I could only wish I had seen her somewhere before. She reminded me of someone I used to know a few years back, when I really was a bigshot. Instead of running an all-night radio program and writing feature articles on the side, I used to be a Power. I was in high school and managed the basketball team. I cut a lot of ice and a lot of corners.

I stepped into the cab and gave the address of the restaurant where I was supposed to meet Sylvia. That was a date I'd worked hard to get, and now for some strange reason, I had little stomach for it. I stared out of the side window as the taxi drew past the girl I'd just run into. She was walking slowly, apparently looking at something beautiful two miles away and two hundred feet up, and there was an entrancing half-smile on her face. Her hair was long and black and it turned under just about where her straight back started to

I

make her waist so slim; I'd never seen hair like that, but there was something about the strong, clean curve of her jaw and the way the inside corners of her eyes were lower than they should be—

"Stop!" I screamed to the cabby. He must have thought that I was about to have some kind of an attack. He was wrong, then. I had already had the attack but it had just now hit me. Anyway, he did a dollar and a half's worth of damage to his brake linings, took the dollar I threw at him as I dived out, and went his unprofitable way.

I ran to her, caught her elbow. "Hey! I—"

"Ah," she contraltoed. "My friend the Juggernaut."

"Amend that," I said quickly. "Your very dear friend Eddie Gretchen."

"Oh?" said her eyebrow, and she said, "And when and where did Eddie Gretchen become my very dear friend?"

"Damfino," I said, and we began walking. By glancing at me without turning her head, she conveyed the general idea that we were walking the same way but not together. "That's for you to figure out," I went on, "and in all sincerity I wish you would. I know you. I used to circulate around you like a bloodstream. But I honestly can't remember when it happened. You're a dream that got broken up by an alarm clock. Come on now—you have my face and you have my name. What do they mean to you?"

"I was never married to you," she said distantly. "So I haven't your name. And I don't want your face."

"With a face like yours," I said, "I can't blame—"

She actually smiled at me. "You haven't changed a bit, Eddie."

I glowed for a second and then realized that she didn't intend to help any. "All right—when was it?"

"The year Covina High beat your Filthy Five 48 to 17."

"It was 48 to 19," I said furiously, "And they were the Fighting Five."

"They were filthy," she said, and laughed richly.

"Fighting," I growled. "And besides, the referees—hey! You're not Underhanded Mazie?"

"I am not! No one knows me well enough to call me that! I'm Maria Undergaard—*Miss* Undergaard to you, Mr. Gretchen."

"Aha! Er—Mazie, m'love, what was it they called the team?"
"The Fighting Five," she acknowledged.
"Okay, Maria." I took her arm happily.
"But they were filthy," she muttered. I let it go at that.

We found a table off the avenue on which to hook our elbows and gab. I don't think I took my eyes from her once in three hours. It was unbelievable. When I had first met her, she'd been a refugee from one of the low countries, in this country about four years. She had, then, an utterly charming clipped accent, which was now replaced by beautifully schooled diction—the pluperfect English achieved only by those who have thoroughly learned it as a strange language. Ah, she'd been a killer-diller in her school days. She'd always had an odd seriousness about her, a deep and unwavering intensity; and my strongest memory of her was the sleepless night I spent after our first—and only—date. It was all wonderment. I wondered what a girl like that would ever develop into. I wondered how in blue hell she had kept me at a respectable distance all evening without using her hands. And most of all I wondered at the overwhelming sense of satisfaction I had got out of it. I never spoiled that satisfaction by asking for another date—it was too complete. For the kind of wild Indian I used to be, that was quite something. And now here she was, telling me how she had inherited a little money after she graduated, had spent four years at a small college up on the Lakes, and had been studying herself myopic ever since.

"Studying what?"

She looked at me oddly. "Spiritism. Psychic manifestations. Possession, more than anything else. I've read a million books and barked up a million wrong trees, but I—think I proved what I thought all along."

"What?"

"That possession is an established fact. That anyone can be possessed. That I myself can be possessed."

"I'd like to be sure of that," I said. She took it the nice way, though her eyes told me that she hadn't missed anything. "Psychic possession is a very strange thing. But it is not strange in the way you might

3

think. I'm sure you've read stories—books, articles—about it. How spirits drift about in and among us, how, as elementals and familiars, they sometimes take possession, causing us to do things completely alien to ourselves. Well, it isn't like that at all. It isn't psychic—it's psychological. I have proof of that." As she spoke her eyes began to wander and her voice to fade and come in strong with her wavering gaze. She seemed to be struggling desperately to keep her attention on what she was saying; but it seemed as if she were being distracted by some conversation inaudible to me. "Did you know that a vibrating string never gives off the fullest tone unless it has a sounding board back of it? The 'spirit' that possesses people is like that. My vibrating string in the analogy is the source of that spirit—a mind emanating suspicion. The sounding board is—" She broke off, looking over her shoulder at the woman who sat alone at the next table. I'd noticed her before, because of the remarkable viciousness of her expression, and the brittle politeness of the man who had sat there with her. They seemed to be a little bit married and finding it quite a strain. Maria half rose, glanced at me, and with an effort sat down again.

"What's the matter—don't you feel well?" I asked.

"Oh no—no, I'm perfectly all—I was just ..." She sipped at her drink, glanced over her shoulder again, took a deep breath, smiled at me.

"Someone you know?" I queried.

She shook her head. "Where was I?"

"You were here with me, looking very lovely, and you had just told me that the possessing spirit is in reality an emanation of suspicion."

"Oh. Well, it has its sounding board in a mind which bears a guilty conscience. Suspicion and guilt; when the two of them combine, they form a very powerful psychological entity, which is actually the thing which possesses a mind opened to it."

"Sounds very involved and not overly important to me," I said, scratching my ear. "Now that you've got it, what's it get you?"

She shrugged. "What good is any knowledge, once achieved? Maybe some day someone cleverer than I will find out how to use what I have learned. As far I'm concerned, I've learned all I—care to about it." She looked at me; there was something behind that statement and the poignant glance that went with it. She was smooth, svelte; the most equable and poised human being I had ever seen; and yet under that knee-action armor she wore was a pleading, little-girl kind of terror at something she couldn't understand. It didn't fit. It didn't make sense. It made me frightened, too, a little, and hugely anxious to share it with her, whatever it was. No matter *what* it was!

She giggled suddenly. I said. "Huh?"

"I just thought of something, Eddie. You were in an awful rush when you swept me off my feet on the Avenue. Whatever became of that appointment you had to keep?"

"Oh, that. Well, I—*holy smoke!*"

I leaped up, a horrible picture of Sylvia sitting in a restaurant for three hours, waiting for me, wafted through my mind. I excused myself to Maria's laughing face and hightailed for a phone. Halfway there it occurred to me that Maria had come out with her little reminder with peculiar suddenness. One phone booth was occupied, I noticed, by the frozen-faced gentleman lately from the table next to ours. He was ogling into the phone with a real genuine sugar-candy ogle. I hate guys like that. I slid into the next booth, dialed. While I was waiting for my connection I glanced back at my table. Maria wasn't there. I froze. This was dandy. Call up one babe to fix a stand-up while another was doing precisely the same thing to me.

I got helloed at through the receiver and asked to have Sylvia paged. Sitting back to wait, I looked out again. I'd been wrong. Maria hadn't gone, she was over at the next table, talking earnestly to the basilisk who sat there. I felt my eyebrows go up. What did she mean by lying to me about not knowing those people? And why lie about it?

I could see even at that distance how the woman's face was lowering and setting as Maria spoke swiftly in her ear. When her countenance had achieved the general lines of the bulbous bow on a battleship, she got up and started over toward the phones. I had an impulse to pop into the next booth and warn the man in there that

5

she was coming, but I didn't want to miss my call. Just as she reached the booths and plastered her ear against the glass, I heard Sylvia's voice in my receiver.

"Hello?"

"Sylvia? This is Eddie Gretchen."

"Ah. Eddie Gretchen. I wish I didn't know you well enough to remember your name. Where have you been? Where are you?"

"It was this way," I said gently. "An old friend of mine is in trouble. I just had to lend a hand—couldn't help myself." That's true enough, I thought, and anyway, she's not listening to me.

"Too bad," she said bitterly. "Meanwhile I've waited for two and a half hours in a restaurant where I'm not known, in which I have eaten a substantial lunch and from which I have secured a pack of expensive cigarettes, and to which I have brought no money. I am to assume that you will not be here?"

"Oh, Sylvia, I can't possibly. About the check, put the manager on. He knows me. I can fix that. And Sylvia—I'm terribly sorry. I—" but she had put down the receiver. In a moment the manager's voice came over. I explained the situation, got his okay, and asked for Sylvia.

"I'm sorry," said the manager. "The lady seemed—well, miffed. Definitely miffed. She said to tell you not to hold your finger down your throat until you hear from her again, because you'll sure digest it off. Heh heh."

"Heh heh," I mimicked, and hung up. I stepped out of the booth into the messiest piece of publicized domesticity I had ever seen. It was the woman Maria had spoken to. She was just in the act of bursting into the next booth. Piling in practically on top of the hapless man inside, she gave vent to her emotions in a screaming falsetto.

"You moth-eaten old billygoat! How dare you leave me sitting alone in a fourth-rate dive while you call up that sleazy little tramp? Take your hand away from the mouthpiece, you crumb. Let her hear me. Here—get away. (into the phone:) Listen, you home-wrecker. If you want my filthy husband you can have him. But you just better think it over. If you want his money, he hasn't any. I haven't had a new dress in six months, although I'll bet you have, you—ah, she

6

hung up." She banged the receiver violently onto its hook and turned to her palsied spouse. "Things have come to a pretty pass," she shrieked, "when total strangers can walk up to me and tell me about your goings-on! You—"

Along about then she began to repeat herself, and my interest dwindled. I pushed my way through the crowd that had collected, and went back to Maria. She sat with her head bowed, and I really don't think she knew I had returned until I was seated and spoke to her.

"Maria—"

"Oh, Eddie—" with a bright, phony smile, "did you get it fixed up all right?"

"Yeh." I sat looking at her somberly. "You did, too."

"What?" all innocence.

"Fixed something up all right. I hate to pry, Mazie, but you just caused a hell of a stink over there. What was the idea of tipping that woman off that her husband was daddying some sugar over the phone? How did you know what he was up to in the first place? And why the devil did you tell me you didn't know those people?"

She was a little panicked. Her eyes went wide, and she reached over and clutched my wrist. She didn't know it, but her touch on my arm clinched any argument, forever and ever. As long as she held me that way, looked at me that way, she was right; I was wrong. "Please don't be angry, Eddie. I hoped you hadn't noticed. No, I didn't lie to you. I never saw them before. How did I know what was going on? I just—knew, Eddie. Please believe me—please don't catechize me! Will you forget it—just this once? I'll try not to let it happen again! Truly I will, Eddie!"

I tried to grin those bright tear-stars out of her eyes. I put one fist under her chin, punched it gently, shaking my head. "Sure, Maria. Sure. Heck—it was nothing. Skip it."

Why I hadn't sense enough to tie the incident up with her theory of possession, I'll never know.

The fourth time I saw her I proposed. That was three hours after the third time, which was one day after the second time, which was five solid weeks after the first time. Yes, it took five weeks for me to persuade her to entrust herself to me for an evening after that occasion in the little bar off the Avenue. Twice she almost cried over the phone, and after that she laughed it off; and when she had run out of reasons for not seeing me she broke down and confessed that it was because she was afraid she would embarrass me the same way again. I had to tell her that in the first place I hadn't been embarrassed and in the second place I didn't give a damn about its happening again; I just wanted to see her. It wasn't until I threatened to walk out of a window at the studio that she finally made that second date. Eighty-seven floors is a long way, and I meant what I said.

She always insisted on going to places where we'd be more or less alone, whether it was in a hansom cab in Central Park or a walk over the Brooklyn Bridge. That suited me so well I didn't bother to wonder about it. But she'd go to any lengths to avoid being with me and strangers at the same time. So it was there in the park, at four o'clock in the afternoon on the day I'd rolled out of bed early to take her to lunch, that I proposed. It was easy. I just held both her hands and felt afraid to look into her eyes when I said,

"Hey. We got to get married."

And she smiled her very own smile and nodded. I kissed her. When a passing cop grinningly broke it up, she straightened her hat, parted the back of my hand and shook her head. "I wouldn't marry you, Eddie," she said quietly. My blood turned to salt water and began to ooze coldly out of my pores. I didn't have to ask her to say it again because she did. Then she stood up. "Let's get out of here, Eddie." One of my arms went up and yanked her back down on the bench. I stared woodenly at some kids who were feeding the ducks down on the lake."

"For a minute I was scared," I said. My voice hurt me. "I thought you said you wouldn't marry me."

"I did, Eddie."

"Yeah." I turned to her and when she saw my face she lifted her hands a little and shrank back. "Why?" I asked. "Single, aren't you?"

She nodded. "It's something that—Eddie, will you take my word for it—just this once?"

"No," I said, "I already took your word for something 'just this once.' Spill it."

"It's—about the things I studied. I spent a month or so by myself up in the mountains not long ago—did I tell you? I didn't see a soul for forty-two days. I was always susceptible to what has been called the psychic. Up there, I studied, and I tried out a lot of things, and experimented a lot. That was when I got on the right track. About possession, I mean. I found out how to open my mind to possession. I went too far. I held it open too long. It—grew that way. I can't close it. I'm a permanent susceptible, Eddie. When I came down from the mountains I was different. I always will be."

"What the hell's this all about?" I snarled. "Do you love me?"

"You don't have to ask me that," she whispered. I looked at her. I didn't have to ask her. I put my arms around her and said, with my teeth on the lobe of her ear, "Tell the rest of that nonsense to your husband on your honeymoon."

The cop came along again. I thumbed at the lake over my shoulder and told him to go jump in it. He went away laughing.

Different she might have been but her only difference was in being better, finer, sweeter than any other woman on earth. That's what I believed after our honeymoon. I believe it now, with an amendment. Then, I thought that what I just said covered everything. Since, I learned a little more. Maria did have a profound difference from other women.

It didn't show up until we came back to the city and I got back on the air again. I had a nice stretch, and she adjusted herself to it gracefully. I m.c.'d an all-night radio program from two to seven in the morning, which meant getting up around four and breakfasting at suppertime. Great stuff. That way you're fresh and ready to go in the evening when everyone else who has to work for a living is tired out from a day's work. Before I got married I had a thousand friends and a thousand places to go every night. Afterward, I couldn't see why Maria shouldn't go to at least five hundred of them with me. She didn't like the idea. Acted afraid of it. I kidded her and swore at her and annoyed her and persuaded her. "A guy like me has to have friends," I said. "Look. My program has sponsors. As long as people wire in requests for phonograph records, the sponsors know that if they're hearing the music they can't very well avoid the plugs. They renew their contracts and that's what gives me nickels and dimes to buy you ice cream cones and automobiles and stuff. You'd be surprised how many people wire in from bars and restaurants, whether they know me personally or not, just because they saw me there during the evening. I got to get around. I can notice the slack-off already, when I've only been off the stem for a couple of weeks. Last night I played fifty-eight minutes of records and transcriptions without getting a single wire. That isn't good, babe."

And she kept saying, "Then go, Eddie. I'll be all right. I won't run away from you if you leave me alone for a few hours. Go see your friends." So I did. But it didn't work out. Those weren't stag parties I was going to. The babes all knew I was married, and when they saw me by myself all the time they got the wrong idea. A little bit of this, and I went home one night and laid down the law.

She didn't like it, but she didn't argue. She took an unconscionably long time to put on her face, but she came without a peep. I didn't expect that meekness. I told her so. She smiled without enthusiasm.

"I've asked you not to force me to come with you," she said sadly. "I guess you've just got to find out for yourself."

We started on West Fifty-second Street and did it up pretty well. The evening netted us four dinner invitations, three pairs of tickets to shows on the stem, and a total of ninety-two telegrams on that night's program. Maria did me proud. There wasn't a lovelier or more charming woman under lights that night, and after the first half hour or so she seemed to be enjoying it. When I tossed her into a cab in front of the studio at one-thirty, she grinned and squeezed my hand. "Maybe I was wrong, Eddie. I hope so anyway. But it was swell."

I went on up to the studio, feeling all warm inside, and it wasn't the highballs either. Jakie Feltner was winding up the "Hits at Home" stretch, two hours of records of bands playing currently in New York spots, with a background of transcribed night-club chatter to make the unwary listener think he was listening to the real thing. He gave me a peculiar look through the plate-glass as I went in, waved his hand toward my table. I threaded my way through the record-stacks and picked up the sheaf of early wires that fed out of the teletype by my microphone. As a favor to me, Jakie used to read off the one-thirty to two wires and stack up the first few releases for me while his own were being played. I gathered that he had come across a wire of particular moment. He had. Among the run-of-the-mill requests was this little gem, marked "Personal":

> HEY EDDIE BETTER KEEP THAT SHEMALE SHERLOCK YOU MARRIED OUT OF POWDER ROOMS OR SHE'LL WIND UP MINUS AN EYE. SHE WENT OVER FIVE WOMEN IN THERE ONE AFTER ANOTHER, TOLD EACH ONE EXACTLY WHAT SHE WANTED TO KNOW. TOLD MY WIFE ABOUT THE RAISE I GOT TWO MONTHS AGO. I GOT TROUBLE SON. YOU LEAVE HER HOME NEXT TIME.
>
> DUKE FROM DUBUQUE.

I read it over three times. The Duke was one of my steadies, who apparently went on a telegram binge every payday. I've seen him send twenty-eight in two hours. I never did find out who he was, though he apparently saw me very often.

"Pretty, huh?" said Jakie, closing the soundproof door into the other section and coming over to me.

"Yeah," I said. "The guy's nuts." He looked over my shoulder at the Duke's wire. "Oh—that one. Could be. Maybe all these are nuts too." He riffled through the pile, tossed out three more wires.

> DEAR EDDIE THERE CAME THE BRIDE AND THERE WENT THE DETAILS OF MY MONKEY-BUSINESS TO THE WAITING EARS OF THE WORLD. IF YOU CAN'T AFFORD A MUZZLE I'LL SEND YOU ONE. PLEASE PLAY "I'LL BE GLAD WHEN YOU'RE DEAD" AND DEDICATE IT TO YOUR WIFE.
>
> A FRIEND.

> HI EDDIE SAW THE NEW MATA HARI ON FIFTY-SECOND STREET AND WAS TOLD SHE BELONGS TO YOU. WHO'D OF THOUGHT YOU'D WED A PUBLICITY ENEMY? PLEASE PLAY "WHISPERING GRASS."
>
> ANN ONYMUS.

EDDIE: DIDN'T HAVE A CHANCE TO TELL YOU AT THE TIME BUT I WISH YOU'D KEEP WHAT I TELL YOU UNDER YOUR HAT. YOUR WIFE TOLD BERGEN ABOUT MY MERGER WITH WILLIAMSON WHICH WAS DUE TOMOR-ROW. THAT WILL COST ME ABOUT EIGHT THOUSAND. GUESS IT WASN'T MARIA'S FAULT BUT YOU SHOULD HAVE TOLD HER TO KEEP QUIET ABOUT IT. HARRY ELLIOTT.

They were all lousy but the last one hurt the most. Harry had been a friend of mine for years. Maria and I had joined his crowd a couple of hours ago at Dave's place. Bergen and his wife were there. Bergen was Harry's A-number-one rival and competitor in the print-ing business. I'd known for quite some time that Harry had a deal coming up with the Williamson concern that would give him weight enough to drive Bergen underground. I gathered that now that the info had leaked out through Maria, Bergen had managed to bear down on Williamson and kill the merger. That was bad enough in itself; but imagine how I felt when I remembered that *I had posi-tively not told Maria one word about Harry Elliot's affairs!*

Jakie said quietly, "Sorry, Eddie."

I looked at him. I felt my jaw flapping foolishly and waved him away. "Go back to your turntables, Jakie. You're on the air— remember?"

"Yeh." He went to the door, turned to give me a long look, and then dashed for the mike as his number played itself out. Jakie was swell. He'd do anything for me, I knew, but there was nothing he could do about this.

How could Maria have done these things? If she had why did she? I could easily see how. Anyone who goes clubbing with me has to spend a lot of time by himself, because I know so damn many people. I'm always hopping from one table to another. While I was making the rounds, I guess Maria had been getting in her work.

"That—stinks," I said.

Long practice had taught me how to maintain a free-and-easy mike style no matter how I felt, no matter how much good luck or bad had piled into me before the show. Jakie put my theme on the table and the red light in front of me flashed on. I sat back mulling over the whole dirty business and when the last chorus of my theme faded, I grabbed the mike around the neck and went to work.

"Top o' the wee sma' to ye, boys and gals. This is the man behind the mike who makes all that talking noise between the music—Eddie Gretchen's the name. We're open for business till the sun comes up and stops us, and if there's any ol' thing you want to hear over the air, drop me a wire and tell me about it. Don't call me up because I haven't the intelligence to use a phone. Before I play you some transcriptions and stuff there's a little something on my mind, viz. and to wit: There's no law yet in this country against sending me personal wires while I'm working. It's fun for you and fun for me. But there's nothing funny about hitting below the belt. I just got a sheaf of that kind of thing and I don't feel so happy about it, boys and gals. I'm not saying to quit sending them, though. Oh no. But when you do, sign your names and addresses. If I find out that the information is phony, I might like to drop around and personally cave in some faces. Think it over while Tony Reddik's swell little band shows you and you how drums are really kicked around in 'Suitcase Shuffle.'" I spun the platter and let it go.

Well, it brought results. During the show I got fourteen more wires of that sort. I think all of that powder room crowd were represented. Some of them were funny and some of them were nasty and some were just hurt about it. I got my names and addresses too. Nine of them were women. It certainly seemed as if Maria had done the most vicious piece of blabbing I'd ever heard of. She told husbands about their wives and wives about their best friends. She broke up business deals and caused fistfights and broke up more than one otherwise happy couple. I couldn't understand where she got all her information, or what on earth possessed her to spill it around. Possessed—possessed . . . the word did something to my brain. That was the thing she was always trying to tell me about. The reason she didn't want to mix with a crowd. I'd seen loose-tongued women before, but this particular woman—damn it! She was so restrained! Her every thought and movement was so perfectly controlled! Well,

I thought sourly, she's going to have her chance to explain it all tonight. Every dirty lousy little bit of it.

She was asleep when I came in. I stood over her, wanting to kiss her, wanting to punch her lovely mouth, wanting to kick her teeth in, wanting to have her put her arms around me so I could cry on her shoulder. She must have sensed me near her. She put up her arms and smiled without opening her eyes. I took the telegrams out of my breast pocket and closed her fingers on them. Without a word I went into the bathroom and shut the door. As I peeled off my clothes and got into pajamas and a robe I heard her start to cry, and then be quiet again. When I went back she was lying with her face buried in the crumpled telegrams.

"I see you beat me to it," I said evenly. She turned her head ever so slightly, so that one dark eye regarded me piteously. "What do you mean?"

"Why, I was going to rub your nose in those wires myself."

She rolled over and sat up. Her face was scared and defiant, and not terribly apologetic. I hadn't expected any of that except the fear. "Don't say I didn't warn you," she said softly. "Don't say I didn't try and try to keep you from taking me to those places. Don't say I didn't try to tell you about it even before we were married."

"My mistake for shutting you up. Go on—you have the floor."

"What do you expect me to say? I'm sorry?"

"Babe, that doesn't begin to cover it." I went over to her. My gums hurt, the way my jaw was clenched, driving the teeth into them. "I want the whole story. I want to know why you are such a lousy little blabbermouth, and how you got the dirt you threw around all night."

"Sit down," she said coolly, "or you'll get a seizure and fall down."

Her eyes were very wide, and that dark something in them that had chilled me on the day we met was there. I crossed the room and sat. She began to talk in a low voice.

"I was possessed last night, Eddie. Not once, but time and time again. Oh, you're so stupid sometimes! I knew this was going to happen—I knew it, but you had to be so bullheaded and—oh, I can't blame it on you, except for not trying to understand. I'll try once more. You can take it or leave it, Eddie. I've known this was coming; I know just what to say. Funny, isn't it?

"Remember what I told you about the entity that is conceived of suspicion and born of guilt? It's a wicked little *poltergeist*—an almost solid embodiment of hate. And I'm a susceptible. Eddie, I can't be in the same room with any two people who bear suspicion and the corresponding sense of guilt! And the world is full of those people— you can't avoid them. Everyone has dozens upon dozens of petty hates and prejudices. Let me give you an example. Suppose you have a racial hatred of, say, Tibetans. You and I are sitting here, and a Tibetan walks in. Now, you know him. He has a very fine mind, or he has done you a favor, or he is a friend of a good friend of yours. You talk for a half hour, politely, and everything's all right. In your heart, though, you're saying, 'I hate your yellow hide, you sniveling filth.' Everything will still be all right as long as he is unconscious of it. But once let this thought flicker into his mind—'He dislikes me because of my race'—and then and there the *poltergeist* is born. The room is full of it, charged with it. It has body and power of its own, completely independent of you or the Tibetan. I am a susceptible. The entity approaches me. I try to avoid it. I make bright remarks. I move around the room, busy myself with some flowers, a book, anything, but it's no use. I can't escape it. I can't fight it away or close my ego to it. Suddenly it has me, completely. I am part of it. It directs me, drives me. Its whole purpose is one hate. It wants to drag your dislike and his suspicion into the light. I am its instrument now. My control is only strong enough to temper the words that burn at my lips. So instead of screaming out 'He hates you, because he hates all of your yellow kind!' I move closer to the man. I stop near him, and say out of the corner of my mouth, 'You'd better go soon. He doesn't like Tibetans and I don't know how long he can keep on being polite.' Once it's said, the *poltergeist* is nullified. The hatred between you is open, no longer secret, and secret hate is the very essence of a *poltergeist*. It dissipates, and I am free; but the damage is done. The most that I can do is to apologize, make a joke of it, say I was trying to be funny. I won't be believed, because my statement, rotten as it was, was true in its very essence and can't be denied. But if I should be believed in my apology, then the seeds of hatred and suspicion are left, and the entity is conceived all over again, and possession takes place once more, then and there. To be spared that, I never deny what I have said, and never apologize for it. It would only make it worse.

"That's how it happens, Eddie, and it can't be changed. I was always susceptible, and I made the condition permanent and acute by my experiments when I was alone in the mountains. I can't change, Eddie. I shouldn't have married you, shouldn't have done this to you. I—guess this is the wind-up. I'll get out." She tried a weak little laugh. "Good thing we haven't been married long enough to have collected a house and a mess of furniture, eh?"

"Yeh," I said. I watched her as she got up, slipped into a house coat, and began to pack. She moved swiftly about the place, collecting the little odds and ends that I had just been learning to expect in my apartment. It had taken some learning, too. Bachelor digs sure get made over when a woman comes into them. After a while I went over and got into the bed. It was still a little warm and smelled nice. I turned my face to the wall, and in a minute I heard her thump a suitcase down beside the others in the middle of the room. She was looking at me; I could feel her eyes on the nape of my neck. I knew she was dressed for the street, all ready to go.

"Maria . . . "

"Yes, Eddie?" She answered a little too quickly to hide the fact that she wasn't as collected as she hoped.

"Wake me up around four, will you? We'll eat us some scrambled eggs and then take that spin around the park like we did when we were single."

There was a thump when she dropped her handbag, and then she was all over me. I put my arms around her and held her until she gasped for breath, and then I ginned at her and got me some sleep.

After that I did my clubbing solo and let Maria build me a home. She loved it. If she missed not seeing people, she didn't complain. I guess she got used to it after a while; I know I did. Things went along beautifully until Ivor Jones, the station manager, called Jakie Felt-ner and me into his office one evening. Neither of us knew what was up, but we both had guesses.

Jones pursed his lips and took off his glasses as we came in. He was a dried-up little man, a stickler for detail but a pretty good man to work for. He told us to sit, handed cigarettes around.

"Boys, I want you to help me. I don't have to tell you how the station is making out. I think we all are satisfied with it, but you know and I know that a small independent broadcasting station can't make as much or pay as much as a big network outlet. Now, one of the network stations here is shutting down. It needs complete new equipment, and the corporation wouldn't mind doing it. But since there are too many stations here already, and since we are equipped up to the hilt with all the latest, I rather think they'd like to take us over. They'd boost our power ten thousand watts. We'd run all their releases and therefore share in their income. You boys, as staff announcers, stand to get a twenty-per-cent raise. How's it sound?"

"Swell," said Jakie. I nodded.

"I'm sold on it," said Jones. "If we could get Shanaman, the general manager of the Eastern Network, to feel the same way, we could come to terms. I've done all I could think of in a business way. But it'll take a little more than that. If I can mellow the old boy down a bit with a swell dinner-party, I might get him to sign the papers then and there. I want you two to come and bring your women. It'll be next Friday night. Shanaman's bringing his wife. My house. You'll be there?"

"Formal?" asked Jakie. Jones nodded.

"I'd rather not, Mr. Jones," I said. "I sort of had an engagement—"

"Break it," Jones said. "Shanaman's interested in meeting you. As a matter of fact, your show is a high spot, a real selling point for the station. You've got to come. And bring that new wife of yours. I want to meet her."

Jakie laughed and got up, slapping me on the back. "I'll persuade him, Mr. Jones. We'll be there, don't worry." He was a big fellow, that Feltnor. He had me rushed out of there before I knew what went on. Cornering me in the corridor, he said, "Come on Eddie—be a sport. Don't queer that party. It means a lot to me. Claire has been acting a little peculiar lately and that party ought to fix the trouble. No kidding, Eddie—you've got to do it."

"I'll see what Maria says," I muttered, and headed for home.

Maria said she didn't like the idea. We had a long argument about it. I pointed out that it was formal, that it was a business affair, that the eight people who were there knew each other very little and had nothing but the broadest interests in common, and that anyway I couldn't avoid it. It was orders. I also mentioned the fact that Jakie wanted me to do it, and I was a good friend of his. Maria's arguments were all old stuff to me, but for one new one. She was afraid that she wouldn't be able to stand it. When she had been in more or less constant contact with people, she was conditioned to the influx of possessions. Now it was different. She feared it. It was months since she had been through it; she was afraid of what it might do to her. But I had my way, and Friday night found us walking into Jones's place in Queens Village.

It was quite a layout. Jones had a nice income and used it. Big house, big rooms, big butler. We were the last to arrive. We got rid of our coats and were shown into the library, where cocktails were being served. I stopped at the door and looked around the room. Over in a corner Jones was talking to a stout old apple who seemed all jowls and boiled shirt. Shanaman, I surmised. Talking uninterestedly with Jones's slightly washed-out wife, was Claire Feltner. I knew her well; she hung around the studio a lot. A nasty thought occurred to me; I noticed Claire there many a time when Jakie was out. Jones always seemed to be around at the time. I began to see why Jakie had been so anxious to bring Claire and Jones into the same room. He wanted to watch them. That was bad.

I rescued Jakie from the voluminous feminine counterpart of Shanaman. The network manager's wife had poor Feltner in a corner and was pounding his ear frighteningly with an account of her husband's metabolism.

Introductions were made all around, and I left Maria with Jakie while I joined Jones and Shanaman. The talk was general and too loud. Just about then I began to wish I hadn't come. That went on all the time I was there. I disliked particularly this business of our being in that big room free to wander from person to person for Lord knows how long until dinner was served. In a matter of minutes Maria could stumble across one of her little *poltergeists,* and then—well, in a matter of minutes Maria did.

Shanaman was building up to a terrific climax in an unfunny story, when I saw Maria across the room from me, looking from Shanaman to Mrs. Jones and back again. There was something about her stance, her eyes, that told me she was fighting the thing. I broke away from Shanaman as fast as I could. Not fast enough. Maria got to Mrs. Jones before I did, sat down beside her, began talking swiftly. As I got there, Mrs. Jones rose, glaring at Shanaman, and went over to her husband.

"What goes on?" I asked anxiously.

"Oh, Eddie, it happened again." She would have cried if I hadn't caught her hands, squeezed them until they hurt. "Shanaman plans to put a network crew in your station if he takes it over. Everyone will lose his job, except you, Eddie!"

"And you told that to Mrs. Jones?"

"Yes—don't you see? She suspected it, and Shanaman knew he was going to do it! I couldn't help myself, Eddie!"

"That's all right, kid," I whispered. "No hair off our necks." I watched the Joneses. It seemed to me that he didn't believe his wife. She was evidently furious with him for his stupidity and said so into his ear. He turned his back on her and went to Claire Feltner. She went over to see if she couldn't pump some information out of Shanaman. Jakie stood near them, glumly watching his wife puckering up to Jones.

"Try to keep away from Jakie," I said, turning back to Maria. But she had slipped away when I was looking at Jones. She was standing by the window behind me, kneading her hands and staring out into the night. I figured it was best to leave her alone as long as she could stand it. Meanwhile, I was going to try to keep the rest of them away from her. I barged in on Shanaman's conversation with Mrs. Jones. It was short and sweet. She was just winding up what must have been quite a scintillating piece of vituperation.

"—and don't think I don't know what you're up to, you old wolf," she was saying. She was hopping mad. Shanaman looked bewilderedly indignant. It was too late to do anything about it.

"My dear lady," he said pompously, "I regret exceedingly that your suspicions should have reached such a state. Ah—Mr. Jones. Will you come here a minute?" Jones looked up, saw what was happening, came rabbiting over. I saw the studio deal flitting out the window when I saw Jones reach out and clip his wife across the mouth. Shanaman held up his hands in horror, then barged across the room to his wife.

Then everything happened at once. Maria popped up from nowhere, nudged Jakie Feltner, whispered in his ear, nodded toward Claire. Jakie roared, reached out, spun Jones around and smeared him with a terrific right hook. Shanaman, fear of publicity plastered all over his fat face, bolted for the door with his wife.

And that was the wind-up of Jones's precious little dinner party. Maria filled in the details for me on the way home. It seemed that Jones had been seeing Jakie's wife, and Maria, possessed, told Jakie how far it had gone, and he punched Jones's mouth. Mrs. Jones's hysterical calling of Shanaman's bluff sprang, I imagine, from jealousy and the desire to hurt Jones. It was an unholy mess, one of those awful things that are awful when they happen and funny afterward. Except for one thing. Jones didn't get up after Jakie knocked him down. He smashed his silly brains out on the brass andiron in the fireplace.

The rest of it was rough. When the trial was over and poor old Feltner got sent up for thirty years on a second-degree murder charge, there wasn't much left for me. Unfavorable publicity pulled a lot of advertising contracts, and anyway, as I said, there are too many radio stations in this town. But the notoriety hadn't finished with me when it took my living away from me. Eddie Gretchen turned out to be the guy with a thousand friends who never heard of him. The radio game was strictly on the receiving end, for me. Old Shanaman's bolting for the door the night of the murder hadn't done him a bit of good; he was subpoenaed and put on the grill with the rest of us. I hadn't liked the way he cried about it—after all, big shots and little, we were all in the same boat—and he got even with me by passing the word around the studios that I wasn't to get so much as an audition. That, after seven years in radio! Yeah, it was rough. I'd always had money and I didn't know how to go about being poor. I learned. Maria had a couple of grand in the cooler but that went quickly, along with what I'd saved, which wasn't a hell of a lot. I hit the jolly old rock-ribbed bottom the day I tried to get a job as a studio page and got well treated until somebody remembered me and I got handed the rush. The smell even reached into publishing houses, and the feature articles I used to sell brought checks every six months instead of every two weeks. I sold a little stuff under a phony name; but for that Maria and I would have starved. We lost our place and our furniture and the car. Bad. But I couldn't lose Maria. She almost left me right after the trial, feeling herself guilty of Jones's murder. I talked her out of that, telling her that he had it coming to him anyway; and then she got morbid and turned on the gas one day. I got there in time, and the police emergency squad brought her around. After that she buckled down like the ace she was, and tried helping instead of hindering. God, when I think of her down on her four bones scrubbing floors, and rubbing her white hands raw on my shirts, I know what they mean when they say "For richer, for poorer"...

I stood out on the sidewalk in front of the radio playhouse and shivered because I had sold my overcoat six weeks before. There was nowhere else to turn to, and I hadn't the gall to go back to Maria so early in the day. Uptown, downtown, crosstown—all the same to me.

A man walked up, looked me over, handed me a slip of paper. It said, "Could you tell me how to get to South Ferry from here?"

I said, "Sure. Take the Seventh Avenue subway—"

He shook his head, pointed to an ear. Deaf. I took the pencil he offered, wrote down the directions. He tipped his hat, went his way. I remember wondering how a guy like that got such a nice warm coat. Some agency, I guessed. I got all my faculties and no overcoat. He's a deaf mute and has an overcoat. I'll take the overcoat.

Then the great idea hit me. I smacked my hands together, whooped like a drunken Indian, and headed at a dead run for the West Side, where Maria was trying to make a home for me out of an eleven-a-month cold water flat. I reached it, flung myself up three flights of stairs, fell gasping and moaning for breath inside the room. Maria didn't know what to make of it, and figured even less when I got wind enough to explain. If she was possessed, I wanted to know, could she keep from tipping anybody off about it *if she wrote the information down?*

"I don't know, Eddie. I never tried it."

"Well, try it, damn it. Try it!"

"H-how?"

I glanced at the ninety-eight cent alarm clock on the stove. "Come on, babe. Get your coat on. We're going to get some money."

She was used to me by this time or she never would have done it. I didn't tell her until we reached the pawnshop that the money was coming from the one thing of value she'd hung onto—the star sapphire I'd given her as an engagement ring the day before we got married. Under the three golden spheres I relieved her of it, shoved an old envelope and a stub of pencil into her hands, and dragged her in.

I knew the broker well by that time. The only Irishman I'd ever seen in a hock shop. "Terry, me lad," I shouted. "I'm about to do you a favor. Hock me this ring for eighty bucks and you can't lose a thing." I gave it to him. He grunted sourly. Maria started forward, about to speak. I shoved her toward a trunk, pointed at the paper and pencil. She grinned and began to write.

"I'll give ye ten," said Terence.

"And I'll take me pathronage ilsewhere," I mocked him.

"Twinty, an' ye're a young thief."

"Sivinty-foive, ye grave-robber."

"Twinty-two an' a half, and be dommed to ye. It's white gold, not platinum."

"Platinum's twenty bucks an ounce on the open market you pernicious old Gael, and gold's thirty-five. Don't blind me with your jeweler's tricks."

And still not an interruption from Maria.

Terence looked at the ring carefully through his glass. "Thirty dollars."

"Will you make that thirty-two fifty?"

"I will that, and there I'm done."

"You're a good business man, Terence, and I'll treat you right. You just went up ten dollars and I can afford to come down ten. That's meeting you halfway at sixty-five dollars." Maria's pencil scribbled busily.

"Fifty dollars to get yez out o' my store," said the broker with a great effort.

"Fifty-seven fifty."

We settled at fifty-five; I signed the book and we left. As soon as we were outside I snatched the envelope. Maria had written no less than twelve times, "Don't be a fool. He only paid sixty for it when it was new."

I kissed her then and there. "It works," I breathed. "It works!"

She looked at the envelope. The truth will out," she grinned. "But Eddie—I didn't want to pawn that ring. I—"

"You dry up and leave it to me, pal," I said. "Come home—I want you to dig up that dress of yours—you know, the black-brown one with the truffles on it."

"Ruffles," she said. "You eat truffles. But it's an evening gown, Eddie. Where—"

"—are we going? West five-two street, babe, and we're going to scrabble up all the dirt from gutter to gutter." I stopped in front of a "Tuxedos to Hire" joint. "I'm going in here. You beat it home and pretty up."

She did, under protest. I got myself a fair-enough dinner jacket, and brought it home. In two hours we looked like a million. I tucked the thin little roll into my pocket, and we started. We took the subway to

Fiftieth and caught a cab there to go to Fifty-second. A thirty-cent cab ride looks just as good as a three-dollar one at the far end of the line. I carried a battery of sharp pencils and Maria had my little black book.

Well, it was a snap, I'd barge into a table, and because I looked it and felt it, the old "friends" thought I was up on top again, and so they were glad to see me. Maria sat quietly with her book in front of her. I told everyone she was gathering material for a novel. Once in a while she would look sharply at a couple of faces and begin to scribble madly. For once in my life I let other people pick up the checks, and we worked practically the whole street. We got out of there with eighteen bucks left, which is something of a record, and I took the lady all the way home in a taxi. We spent the rest of the night poring through the book.

Man! What a haul! There was enough dirt there to resurface the Dust Bowl and ten like it. Advance information on big business deals; messings about with the Stock Exchange; who was seeing who, how long, why, and how much it cost; what book a major studio was going to buy; the truth about that fixed fight at the Garden Monday night. I found Maria an excellent editor. Once the little old *poltergeist* had dissipated, she was quite impersonal about what she found out. We took, out of more than two hundred juicy items, ten that were due to happen within the next twenty-four hours. They were carefully picked to do the least possible harm if they were made public, and they all packed a wallop. There was an act of sabotage, three elopements, a decision on the locale of the premiere of a new picture, two business deals, a diplomatic stroke of genius, a lapse of option on an erstwhile great movie star, and the name and address of a firm which was going to get a government contract for high-pressure boilers on the battlewagons under construction at Boston Navy Yard. I wrote them up, wording them for the most punch, and first thing the next morning I took them up to the newspaper with the largest newsstand circulation in the country. I was in the office for forty minutes, and I walked out with fifty bucks advance. The following day I got a wire to come in and go to work. Every item had come as predicted. Score, one hundred per cent.

So I'm back in the big time again. Yes, I'm the guy they talk about. The one about whom they say, "Did you see his column today? Holy Swiss cheese, where does that man get all his information?" And "I'd like to know how a Broadway columnist gets that radio personality."

Well, I get the first from my wife, who sits quietly, writing in a little black book. She gets her dope from a thousand million little *poltergeisten*. And don't mention radio to me too often. The name of Eddie Gretchen still stinks on the stem, but I don't care. I don't use it any more. You ought to know who I am by this time.

Medusa

I WASN'T SORE at them. I didn't know what they'd done to me, exactly—I knew that some of it wasn't so nice, and that I'd probably never be the same again. But I was a volunteer, wasn't I? I'd asked for it. I'd signed a paper authorizing the department of commerce of the league to use me as they saw fit. When they pulled me out of the fleet for routine examinations, and when they started examinations that were definitely not routine, I didn't kick. When they asked for volunteers for a project they didn't bother to mention by name, I accepted it sight unseen. And now—

"How do you feel, Rip?" old Doc Renn wanted to know. He spoke to me easylike, with his chin on the backs of his hands and his elbows on the table. The greatest name in psychoscience, and he talks to me as if he were my old man. Right up there in front of the whole psycho board, too.

"Fine, sir," I said. I looked around. I knew all the doctors and one or two of the visitors. All the medicos had done one job or another on me in the last three years. Boy, did they put me through the mill. I understood only a fraction of it all—the first color tests, for instance, and the electro-coordination routines. But that torture machine of Grenfell's, and that copper helmet that Winton made me wear for two months—talk about your nightmares! What they were doing to or for me was something I could only guess at. Maybe they were testing me for something. Maybe I was just a guinea pig. Maybe I was in training for something. It was no use asking, either. I volunteered, didn't I?

"Well, Rip," Doc Renn was saying, "it's all over now—the preliminaries, I mean. We're going ahead with the big job."

"Preliminaries?" I goggled. "You mean to tell me that what I've been through for the last three years was all preliminaries?"

Renn nodded, watching me carefully. "You're going on a little trip. It may not be fun, but it'll be interesting."

"Trip? Where to?" This was good news; the repeated drills on spaceship techniques, the refresher courses on astrogation, had given me a good-sized itch to get out into the black again.

"Sealed orders," said Renn, rather sharply. "You'll find out. The important thing for you to remember is that you have a very important role to play." He paused; I could see him grimly ironing the snappiness out of his tone. Why in Canaan did he have to be so careful with *me*? "You will be put aboard a Forfield Super—the latest and best equipped that the league can furnish. Your job is to tend the control machinery, and to act as assistant astrogator no matter what happens. Without doubt you will find your position difficult at times. You are to obey your orders as given, without question, and without the use of force where possible."

This sounded screwy to me. "That's all written up, just about word for word, in the Naval Manual," I reminded him gently, "under 'Duties of Crew.' I've had to do all you said every time I took a ship out. Is there anything special about this one, that it calls for all this underlining?"

He was annoyed, and the board shuffled twenty-two pairs of feet. But his tone was still friendly, half-persuasive when he spoke. "There is definitely something special about this ship, and—its crew. Rip, you've come through everything we could hand you, with flying colors. Frankly, you were subjected to psychic forces that were enough to drive a normal man quite mad. The rest of the crew—it is only fair to tell you—are insane. The nature of this expedition necessitates our manning the ship that way. Your place on the ship is a key position. Your responsibility is a great one."

"Now—hold on, sir," I said. "I'm not questioning your orders, sir, and I consider myself under your disposition. May I ask a few questions?"

He nodded.

"You say the crew is insane. Isn't that a broad way of putting it—" I couldn't help needling him; he was trying so hard to keep calm—"for a psychologist?"

He actually grinned. "It is. To be more specific, they're schizoids—dual personalities. Their primary egos are paranoiac. They're perfectly rational except on the subject of their particular phobia—or mania, as the case may be. The recessive personality is a manic depressive."

Now, as I remembered it, most paranoiacs have delusions of grandeur coupled with a persecution mania. And a manic depressive is the "Yes master" type. They just didn't mix. I took the liberty of saying as much to one of Earth's foremost psychoscientists.

"Of course they don't mix," snapped Renn. "I didn't say they did. There's no interflowing of egos in these cases. They are schizoids. The cleavage is perfect."

I have a mole under my arm that I scratch when I'm thinking hard. I scratched it. "I didn't know anything like that existed," I said. Renn seemed bent on keeping this informal, and I was playing it to the limit. I sensed that this was the last chance I'd have to get any information about the expedition.

"There never were any cases like that until recently," said Renn patiently. "Those men came out of our laboratories."

"Oh. Sort of made-to-order insanity?" He nodded.

"What on earth for, sir?"

"Sealed orders," he said immediately. His manner became abrupt again. "You take off tomorrow. You'll be put aboard tonight. Your commanding officer is Captain William Parks." I grinned delightedly at this. Parks—the horny old fire eater! They used to say of him that he could create sunspots by spitting straight up. But he was a real spaceman—through and through. "And don't forget, Rip," Renn finished. "There is only one sane man aboard that ship. That is all."

I saluted and left.

A Forfield Super is as sweet a ship as anything ever launched. There's none of your great noisy bulk pushed through the ether by a cityful of men, nor is it your completely automatic "Eyehope"—so called because after you slipped your master control tape into the automatic pilot you always said, "you're on your way, you little hunk of tinfoil—I hope!"

With an eight-man crew, a Forfield can outrun and outride anything else in space. No rockets—no celestial helices—no other such clumsy nonsense drives it. It doesn't go places by going—it gets there by standing still. By which I mean that the ship achieves what laymen call "Universal stasis."

The Galaxy is traveling in an orbit about the mythical Dead Center at an almost incredible velocity. A Forfield, with momentum nullified, just stops dead while the Galaxy streams by. When the objective approaches, momentum is resumed, and the ship appears in normal space with only a couple of thousand miles to go. That is possible because the lack of motion builds up a potential in motion; motion, being a relative thing, produces a set of relative values.

Instead of using the terms "action" and "reaction" in speaking of the Forfield drive, we speak of "stasis" and "re-stasis." I'd explain further but I left my spherical slide rule home. Let me add only that a Forfield can achieve stasis in regard to planetary, solar, galactic or universal orbits. Mix 'em in the right proportions, and you get resultants that will take you anywhere, fast.

I was so busy from the instant I hit the deck that I didn't have time to think of all the angles of this more-than-peculiar trip. I had to check and double-check every control and instrument from the milliammeter to the huge compound integrators, and with a twenty-four-hour deadline that was no small task. I also had to take a little instruction from a league master mechanic who had installed a couple of gadgets which had been designed and tested at the last minute expressly for this trip. I paid little attention to what went on round me; I didn't even know the skipper was aboard until I rose from my knees before the integrators, swiveled around on my way to the control board, and all but knocked the old war horse off his feet.

"Rip! I'll be damned!" he howled. "Don't tell me—you're not signed on here?"

"Yup," I said. "Let go my hand, skipper—I got to be able to hold a pair of needle noses for another hour so. Yeah, I heard you were going to captain this barrel. How do you like it?"

"Smooth," he said, looking around, then bringing his grin back to me. He only grinned twice a year because it hurt his face; but when he did, he did it all over. "What do you know about the trip?"

"Nothing except that we have sealed orders."

"Well, I'll bet there's some kind of a honkatonk at the end of the road," said Parks. "You and I've been on ... how many is it? Six? Eight? ... anyway, we've been on plenty of ships together, and we managed to throw a whing-ding ashore every trip. I hope we can get out Aldebaran way. I hear Susie's place is under new management again. Heh! Remember the time we—"

I laughed. "Let's save it, skipper. I've got to finish this check-up, and fast. But, man, it's good to see you again." We stood looking at each other, and then something popped into my head and I felt my smile washing off. What was it that Dr. Renn had said—"Remember there's only one sane man aboard!" Oh, no—they hadn't put Captain Parks through that! Why—

I said, "How do you—feel, cap'n?"

"Swell," he said. He frowned. "Why? You feel all right?"

Not right then, I didn't. Captain Parks batty? That was just a little bit lousy. If Renn was right—and he was always right—then his board had given Parks the works, as well as the rest of the crew. All but me, that is. I *knew* I wasn't crazy. I didn't feel crazy. "I feel fine," I said.

"Well, go ahead then," said Parks, and turned his back.

I went over to the control board, disconnected the power leads from the radioscope, and checked the dials. For maybe five minutes I felt the old boy's eyes drilling into the nape of my neck, but I was too upset to say anything more. It got very quiet in there. Small noises drifted into the control room from other parts of the ship. Finally I heard his shoulder brush the doorpost as he walked out.

How much did the captain know about this trip? Did he know that he had a bunch of graduates from the laughing academy to man his ship? I tried to picture Renn informing Parks that he was a paranoiac and a manic depressive, and I failed miserably. Parks would probably take a swing at the doctor. Aw, it just didn't make sense. It occurred to me that "making sense" was a criterion that we put too much faith in. What do you do when you run across something that isn't even supposed to make sense?

I slapped the casing back on the radioscope, connected the leads, and called it quits. The speaker over the forward post rasped out, "All hands report to control chamber!" I started, stuck my tools into their clips under the chart table, and headed for the door. Then I remembered I was already in the control room, and subsided against the bulkhead.

They straggled in. All hands were in the pink, well fed and eager. I nodded to three of them, shook hands with another. The skipper came in without looking at me—I rather thought he avoided my eyes. He went straight forward, faced about and put his hands low enough on the canted control board so he could sit on them. Seabiscuit, the quartermaster, and an old shipmate of mine, came and stood beside me. There was an embarrassed murmur of voices while we all awaited the last two stragglers.

Seabiscuit whispered to me, "I once said I'd sail clear to Hell if Bill Parks was cap'n of the ship."

I said, out of the side of my face, "So?"

"So it looks like I'm goin' to," said the Biscuit.

The captain called the roll. That crew was microscopically hand picked. I had heard every single one of the names he called in connection with some famous escapade or other. Harry Voight was our chemist. He is the man who kept two hundred passengers alive for a month with little more than a week's supply of air and water to work with, after the liner crossed bows with a meteorite on the Pleione run. Bort Brecht was the engineer, a man who could do three men's work with his artificial hand alone. He lost it in the *Pretoria* disaster. The gunner was Hoch McCoy, the guy who "invented" the bow and arrow and saved his life when he was marooned on an asteroid in the middle of a pack of poison-toothed "Jackrabbits." The mechanics were Phil and Jo Hartley, twins, whose resemblance enabled them to change places time and again during the Insurrection, thus running bales of vital information to the league high command.

"Report," he said to me.

"All's well in the control chamber, sir," I said formally.

"Brecht?"

"All's well back aft, sir."

"Quartermaster?"

"Stores all aboard and stashed away, sir," said the Biscuit.

Parks turned to the control board and threw a lever. The air locks slid shut, the thirty second departure signal began to sound from the oscillator on the hull and from signals here and in the engineer's chamber. Parks raised his voice to be heard over their clamor.

"I don't know where we're goin'," he said, with an odd smile, "but—" the signals stopped, and that was deafening—"we're on our way!"

The master control he had thrown had accomplished all the details of taking off—artificial gravity, "solar" and "planetary" stases, air pumps, humidifiers—everything. Except for the fact that there was suddenly no light streaming in through the portholes any more, there was no slightest change in sensation. Parks reached out and tore the seals off the tape slot on the integrators and from the door of the orders file. He opened the cubbyhole and drew out a thick envelope. There was something in my throat that I couldn't swallow.

He tore it open and pulled out eight envelopes and a few folded sheets of paper. He glanced at the envelopes and, with raised eyebrows, handed them to me. I took them. There was one addressed to each member of the crew. At a nod from the skipper I distributed them. Parks unfolded his orders and looked at them.

"Orders," he read. "By authority of the Solar League, pertaining to destination and operations of Xantippean Expedition No. 1."

Startled glances were batted back and forth. Xantippe! No one had ever been to Xantippe! The weird, cometary planet of Betelgeuse was, and had always been, taboo—and for good reason.

Parks's voice was tight. "Orders to be read to crew by the captain immediately upon taking off." The skipper went to the pilot chair, swiveled it, and sat down. The crew edged closer.

"The league congratulates itself on its choice of a crew for this most important mission. Out of twenty-seven hundred volunteers, these eight men survived the series of tests and conditioning exercises provided by the league.

"General orders are to proceed to Xantippe. Captain and crew have been adequately protected against the field. Object of the expedition is to find the cause of the Xantippe field and to remove it.

"Specific orders for each member of the crew are enclosed under separate sealed covers. The crew is ordered to read these instructions, to memorize them, and to destroy the orders and envelopes. The league desires that these orders be read in strictest secrecy by each member of the crew, and that the individual contents of the envelopes be held as confidential until contrary orders are issued by the league." Parks drew a deep breath and looked around at his crew.

They were a steady lot. There was evidence of excitement, of surprise, and in at least one case, of shock. But there was no fear. Predominantly, there was a kind of exultance in the spaceburned, hard-bitten faces. They bore a common glory, a common hatred. "That isn't sensible," I told myself. "It isn't natural, or normal, or sane, for eight men to face madness, years of it, with that joyous light in their eyes. But then—they're mad already, aren't they? *Aren't they?*"

It was catching, too. I began to hate Xantippe. Which was, I suppose, silly. Xantippe was a planet, of a sort. Xantippe never killed anybody. It drove men mad, that was all. More than mad—it fused their synapses, reduced them to quivering, mindless hulks, drooling, their useless minds turned supercargo in a useless body. Xantippe had snared ship upon ship in the old days; ships bound for the other planets of the great star. The mad planet used to blanket them in its mantle of vibrations, and they were never heard from again. It was years before the league discovered where the ships had gone, and then they sent patrols to investigate. They lost eighteen ships and thirty thousand men that way.

And then came the Forfield drive. In the kind of static hyperspace which these ships inhabited, surely they would pass the field unharmed. There were colonists out there on the other planets, depending on supplies from Sol. There were rich sources of radon, uranium, tantalum, copper. Surely a Forfield ship could—

But they couldn't. They were the first ships to penetrate the field, to come out on the other side. The ships were intact, but their crews could use their brains for absolutely nothing. Sure, I hated Xantippe. Crazy planet with its cometary orbit and its unpredictable complex ecliptic. Xantippe had an enormous plot afoot. It was stalking us— even now it was ready to pounce on us, take us all and drain our minds—

I shook myself and snapped out of it. I was dreaming myself into a case of the purple willies. If I couldn't keep my head on my shoulders aboard this spacegoing padded cell, then who would? Who else could?

The crew filed out, muttering. Parks sat on the pilot's chair, watching them, his bright gaze flitting from face to face. When they had gone he began to watch me. Not look at me. Watch me. It made me sore.

"Well?" he said after a time.

"Well *what?*" I barked, insubordinately.

"Aren't you going to read your bedtime story? I am."

"Bed—oh." I slit the envelope, unfolded my orders. The captain did likewise at the extreme opposite side of the chamber. I read:

"Orders by authority of the Solar League pertaining to course of action to be taken by Harl Ripley, astromechanic on Xantippean Expedition No. 1.

"Said Harl Ripley shall follow the rules and regulations as set forth in the naval regulations, up until such time as the ship engages the Xantippean Field. He is then to follow the orders of the master, except in case of the master's removal from active duty from some unexpected cause. Should such an emergency arise, the command does not necessarily revert to said Harl Ripley, but to the crew member who with the greatest practicability outlines a plan for the following objective: The expedition is to land on Xantippe; if uninhabited, the planet is to be searched until the source of the field is found and destroyed. If inhabited, the procedure of the pro-tem commander must be dictated by events. He is to bear in mind, however, that the primary and only purpose of the expedition is to destroy the Xantippean Field."

That ended the orders; but scrawled across the foot of the page was an almost illegible addendum: "Remember your last board meeting, Rip. And good luck!" The penciled initials were C. Renn, M.Ps.S. That would be Doc Renn.

I was so puzzled that my ears began to buzz. The government had apparently spent a huge pile of money in training us and outfitting the expedition. And yet our orders were as hazy as they could possibly be. And what was the idea of giving separate orders to each crew member? And such orders! "The procedure of the pro-tem commander must be dictated by events." That's what you'd call putting us on our own! It wasn't like the crisp, detailed commands any navy man is used to. It was crazy.

Well, of course it was crazy, come to think of it. What else could you expect with this crew? I began to wish sincerely that the board had driven me nuts along with the rest of them.

I was at the chart table, coding up the hundred-hour log entry preparatory to slipping it into the printer, when I sensed someone behind me. The skipper, of course. He stayed there a long time, and I knew he was watching me.

I sat there until couldn't stand it any longer. "Come on in," I said without moving. Nothing happened. I listened carefully until I could hear his careful breathing. It was short, swift. He was trying to breathe in a whisper. I began to be really edgy. I had a nasty suspicion that if I whirled I would be just in time to catch a bolt from a by-by gun.

Clenching my jaw till my teeth hurt, I rose slowly, and without looking around, went to the power-output telltales and looked at them. I didn't know what was the matter with me. I'd never been this way before—always expecting attack from somewhere. I used to be a pretty nice guy. As a matter of fact, I used to be the nicest guy I knew. I didn't feel that way any more.

Moving to the telltales took me another six or eight feet from the man at the door. Safer for both of us. And this way I had to turn around to get back to the table. I did. It wasn't the skipper. It was the chemist, Harry Voight. We were old shipmates, and I knew him well.

"Hello, Harry. Why the dark companion act?"

He was tense. He was wearing a little mustache of perspiration on his upper lip. His peculiar eyes—the irises were as black as the pupils—were set so far back in his head that I couldn't see them, for the alleyway light was directly over his head. His bald, bulging forehead threw two deep purple shadows, and out of them he watched me.

"Hi, Rip. Busy?"

"Not too busy. Put it in a chair."

He came in and sat down. He turned as he passed me, backed into the pilot's seat. I perched on the chart table. It looked casual, and it kept my weight on one foot. If I had to move in any direction, including up, I was ready to.

After a time he said, "What do you think of this, Rip?" His gesture took in the ship, Xantippe, the league, the board.

"I only work here," I quoted. That was the motto of the navy. Our insignia is the league symbol superimposed on a flaming sun, under which is an ultraradio screen showing the words, "I only work here." The famous phrase expresses the utmost in unquestioning, devoted duty.

Harry smiled a very sickly smile. If ever I saw a man with something eating him, it was Harry Voight. "S'matter," I asked quietly. "Did somebody do you something?"

He looked furtively about him, edged closer. "Rip, I want to tell you something. Will you close the door?"

I started to refuse, and then reflected that regulations could stand a little relaxing in a coffin like this one. I went and pressed the panel and it slid closed. "Make it snappy," I said. "If the skipper comes up here and finds that door closed he'll slap some wrists around here."

As soon as the door closed, Harry visibly slumped. "This is the first time in two days I've felt—comfortable," he said. He looked at me with sudden suspicion. "Rip—when we roomed together in Venus City, what color was that jacket I used to keep my Naval Manual in?"

I frowned. I'd only seen the thing a couple of times— "Blue," I said.

"That's right." He wiped his forehead. "You're O.K." He made a couple of false starts and then said, "Rip, will you keep everything

I say strictly to yourself? Nobody can be trusted here—nobody!" I nodded. "Well," he went on in a strained voice, "I know that this is a screwy trip. I know that the crew is—has been made—sort of—well, not normal—"

He said, with conviction, "The league has its own reasons for sending us, and I don't question them. But something has gone wrong. You think Xantippe is going to get us? Ha! Xantippe is getting us *now!*" He sat back triumphantly.

"You don't say!"

"But I do! I know she's countless thousands of light years away. But I don't have to tell you of the power of Xantippe. For a gigantic power like that, a little project like what they're doing to us is nothing. Any force that can throw out a field three quarters of a billion miles in diameter can play hell with us at a far greater distance."

"Could be," I said. "Just what are they doing?"

"They're studying us," he hissed. "They're watching each of us, our every action, our every mental reflex. And one by one they are—taking us away! They've got the Hartley twins, and Bort Brecht, and soon they'll have me. I don't know about the others, but their turns will come. They are taking away our personalities, and substituting their own. I tell you, those three men—and soon now, I with them—those men are not humans, but Xantippeans!"

"Now wait," I said patiently. "Aren't you going on guesswork? Nobody knows if Xantippe's inhabited. And I doubt that this substitution you speak of can be done."

"You don't think so? For pity's sake, Rip—for your own good, try to believe me! The Xantippean Field is a thought force, isn't it? And listen—I know it if you don't—this crew was picked for its hatred of Xantippe. Don't you see why? The board expects that hatred to act as a mental 'fender'—to partly ward off the field. They think there might be enough left of our minds when we're inside the field to accomplish our objective. They're wrong, Rip—*wrong!* The very existence of our communal hatred is the thing that has given us away. They have been ready for us for days now—and they are already doing their work aboard."

He subsided, and I prodded him with a gentle question.

"How do you know the Xantippeans have taken away those three men?"

"Because I happened to overhear the Hartley twins talking in the messroom two days ago. They were talking about their orders. I know I should not have listened, but I was already suspicious."

"They were talking about their orders? I understood that the orders were confidential."

"They were. But you can't expect the Hartleys to pay much attention to that. Anyway, Jo confided that a footnote on his orders had intimated that there was only one sane man aboard. Phil laughed that off. He said he knew he was sane, and he knew that Jo was sane. Now, I reason this way. Only a crazy man would question the league; a crazy man or an enemy. Now the Hartleys may be unbalanced, but they are still rational. They are still navy men. Therefore, they must be enemies, because navy men never question the league."

I listened to that vague logic spoken in that intense, convincing voice, and I didn't know what to think. "What about Bort Brecht— and yourself?"

"Bort! Ahh!" His lips curled. "I can sense an alien ego when I speak to him. It's overwhelming. I hate Xantippe," he said wildly, "but I hate Bort Brecht more! The only thing I could possibly hate more than Xantippe would be a Xantippean. That proves my point!" He spread his hands. "As for me—Rip, I'm going mad. I feel it. I see things—and when I do, I will be another of them. And then we will all be lost. For there is only one sane man aboard this ship, and that is me, and when I'm turned into a Xantippean, we will be doomed, and I want you to kill me!" He was half hysterical. I let him simmer down.

"And do I look crazy?" I asked. "If you are the only sane man—"

"Not crazy," he said quickly. "A schizoid—but you're perfectly rational. You must be, or you wouldn't have remembered what color my book jacket was."

I got up, reached out a hand to help him to his feet. He drew back. "Don't touch me!" he screamed, and when I recoiled, he tried to smile. "I'm sorry, Rip, but I can't be sure about anything. You may be a Xantippean by now, and touching me might ... I'll be going now ... I—" He went out, his black, burning eyes half closed.

I stood at the door watching him weave down the alleyway. I could guess what was the matter. Paranoia—but bad! There was the characteristic persecution mania, the intensity of expression, the peculiar single-track logic—even delusions of grandeur. Heh! He thought *he* was the one mentally balanced man aboard!

I walked back to the chart table, thinking hard. Harry always had been pretty tight-lipped. He probably wouldn't spread any panic aboard. But I'd better tip the captain off. I was wondering why the Hartley twins and Harry Voight had all been told that all hands but me were batty, when the skipper walked in.

"Rip," he said without preamble. "Did you ever have a fight with Hoch McCoy?"

"Good gosh, no!" I said. "I never saw him in my life until the day we sailed. I've heard of him, of course. Why?"

Parks looked at me oddly. "He just left my quarters. He had the most long-winded and detailed song and dance about how you were well known as an intersolar master saboteur. Gave names and dates. The names I know well. But the dates—well, I can alibi you for half of 'em. I didn't tell him that. But—Lord! He almost had me convinced!"

"Another one!" I breathed. And then I told him about Harry Voight.

"I don't imagine Doc Renn thought they would begin to break so soon," said Parks when I had finished. "These boys were under laboratory conditions for three solid years, you know."

"I didn't know," I said. "I don't know a damn thing that's going on around here and I'd better learn something before I go off my kilter, too!"

"Why, Ripley," he said mockingly. "You're overwrought!" Well, I was. Parks said, "I don't know much more than you do, but that goofy story of Harry Voight's has a couple of pretty shrewd guesses in it. For instance, I think he was right in assuming that the board had done something to the minds of ... ah ... some of the crew as armor against the field. Few men have approached it consciously—those who have were usually scared half to death. It's well known that fear forms the easiest possible entrance for the thing feared—ask any good hypnotist. Hate is something different again. Hate is a psychological block against fear and the thing to be feared. And the kind of hate that these guys have for Xantippe and the field is something extra special. They're mad, but they're not afraid—and that's no accident. When we do hit the field, it's bound to have less effect on us than it had on the crews of poor devils who tried to attack it."

"That sounds reasonable. Er . . . skipper, about this 'one sane man' business. What do you think of that?"

"More armor," said Parks. "But armor against the man himself. Harry, for instance, was made a paranoiac, which is a very sensible kind of nut; but at the same time he was convinced that he alone was sane. If he thought his mind had been actually tampered with instead of just—tested, he'd get all upset about it and, like as not, undo half the Psy Board's work."

Some of that struck frightening chords in my memory. "Cap'n—do you believe that there is one sane, normal man aboard?"

"I do. One." He smiled slowly. "I know what you're thinking. You'd give anything to compare your orders with mine, wouldn't you?"

"I would. But I won't do it. Confidential. I couldn't let myself do it even if you agreed, because—" I paused.

"Well?"

"Because you're an officer and I'm a gentleman."

In my bunk at last, I gave over wishing that we'd get to the field and have it over with, and tried to do some constructive thinking. I tried to remember exactly what Doc Renn had said, and when I did, I was sorry I'd made the effort. "You are sane," and "You have been subjected to psychic forces that are sufficient to drive a normal man quite mad" might easily be totally different things. I'd been cocky enough to assume that they meant the same thing. Well, face it. Was I crazy? I didn't feel crazy. Neither did Harry Voight. He thought he was going crazy, but he was sure he hadn't got there yet. And what was "crazy," anyway? It was normal, on this ship, to hate Xantippe so much that you felt sick and sweated cold when you thought of it. Paranoia—persecution. Did I feel persecuted? Only by the thought of our duty toward Xantippe, and the persecution was Xantippe, not the duty. Did I have delusions of grandeur? Of course not; and yet—hadn't I blandly assumed that Voight had such delusions because he thought *he* was the one sane man aboard?

What was the idea of that, anyway? Why had the board put one sane man aboard—if it had? Perhaps to be sure that one man reacted differently to the others at the field, so that he could command. Perhaps merely to make each man feel that he was sane, even though he wasn't. My poor tired brain gave it up and I slept.

We had two casualties before we reached the field. Harry Voight cut his throat in the washroom, and my gentle old buddy, Seabiscuit, crushed in the back of Hoch McCoy's head. "He was an Insurrectionist spy," he said mildly, time and again, while we were locking him up.

After that we kept away from each other. I don't think I spoke ten words to anyone outside of official business, from that day until we snapped into galactic stasis near Betelgeuse. I was sorry about Hoch, because he was a fine lad. But my sorrow was tempered by the memory of his visit to the captain. There had been a pretty fine chance of his doing that to me!

In normal space once more, we maneuvered our agile little craft into an orbit about the huge sun and threw out our detectors. These wouldn't tell us much when the time came, for their range wasn't much more than the radius of the field.

The mad planet swam up onto the plates and I stared at it as I buzzed for the skipper. Xantippe was a strangely dull planet, even this close to her star. She shone dead silver, like a moonlit corpse's flesh. She was wrinkled and patched, and—perhaps it was an etheric disturbance—she seemed to pulsate slowly from pole to pole. She wasn't quite round; more nearly an ovoid, with the smaller end toward Betelgeuse. She was between two and three times the size of Luna. Gazing at her, I thought of the thousands of men of my own service who had fallen prey to her, and of the fine ships of war that had plunged into the field and disappeared. Had they crashed? Had they been tucked into some weird warp of space? Were they captives of some strange and horrible race?

Xantippe had defied every type of attack so far. She swallowed up atomic mines and torpedoes with no appreciable effect. She was apparently impervious to any rayed vibration known to man; but she was matter, and should be easy meat for an infragun—if you could get an infragun close enough. The gun's twin streams of highly charged particles, positrons on one side, mesatrons on the other, would destroy anything that happened to be where they converged. But an infragun has an effective range of less than five hundred miles. Heretofore, any ship which carried the weapon that close to Xantippe carried also a dead or mindless crew.

Captain Parks called the crew into the control room as soon as he arrived. No one spoke much; they didn't need any more information after they had glanced at the viewplate which formed the forward wall of the chamber. Bort Brecht, the swarthy engineer, wanted to know how soon we'd engage the field.

"In about two hours," said the captain glibly. I got a two-handed grip on myself to keep from yapping. He was a cold-blooded liar— we'd hit it in half an hour or less, the way I figured it. I guessed that he had his own reasons. Perhaps he thought it would be easier on the crew that way.

Parks leaned casually against the integrators and faced the crew. "Well, gentlemen," he said as if he were banqueting on Earth, "we'll soon find out what this is all about. I have instructions from the league to place certain information at your disposal.

"All hands are cautioned to obey the obvious commander once we're inside the field. That commander may or may not be myself. That has been arranged for. Each man must keep in mind the objective—the destruction of the Xantippean Field. One of us will lead the others toward that objective. Should no one seem to be in command a pro-tem captain is to be elected."

Brecht spoke up. "Cap'n, how do we know that this 'commander' that has been arranged for isn't Harry Voight or Hoch McCoy?"

"We don't know," said Parks gravely. "But we will. We will."

Twenty-three minutes after Xantippe showed up on the plates, we engaged her field.

All hands were still in the control room when we plunged in. I remember the sudden weakness of my limbs, and the way all five of the others slipped and slid down to the deck. I remember the Biscuit's quaver, "I tell you it's all a dirty Insurrectionist plot." And then I was down on the deck, too.

Something was hurting me, but I knew exactly where I was. I was under Dr. Grenfell's torture machine; it was tearing into my mind, chilling my brain. I could feel my brains, every last convolution of them. They were getting colder and colder, and bigger and bigger, and pretty soon now they would burst my skull and the laboratory and the building and chill the earth. Inside my chest I was hot, and of course I knew why. I was Betelgeuse, mightiest of suns, and with my own warmth I warmed half a galaxy. Soon I would destroy it, too, and that would be nice.

All the darkness in Great Space came to me.

Leave me alone. I don't care what you want done. I just want to lie here and— But nobody wanted me to do anything. What's all the hollering about, then? Oh. *I* wanted something done. There's something that has to be done, so get up, get up, get—

"He *is* dead. Death is but a sleep and a forgetting, and he's asleep, and he's forgotten everything, so he must be dead!" It was Phil Hartley. He was down on his hunkers beside me, shrieking at the top of his voice, mouthing and pointing like an ape completely caught up in the violence of his argument. Which was odd, because he wasn't arguing with anybody. The skipper was sitting silently in the pilot's chair, tears streaming down his cheeks. Jo Hartley was dead or passed out on the deck. The Biscuit and Bort Brecht were sitting on the deck holding hands like children, staring entranced into the viewplate. It showed a quadrant of Xantippe, filling the screen. The planet's surface did indeed pulsate, and it was a beautiful sight. I wanted to watch it drawing closer and closer, but there was something that had to be done first.

I sat up achingly. "Get me some water," I muttered to Phil Hartley. He looked at me, shrieked, and went and hid under the chart table.

The vision of Xantippe caught and held me again, but I shook it off. It was the most desirable thing I'd ever seen, and it promised me all I could ever want, but there was something I had to do first. Maybe someone could tell me. I shook the skipper's shoulder.

"Go away," he said. I shook him again. He made no response. Fury snapped into my brain. I cuffed him with my open hand, front and back, front and back. He leaped to his feet, screamed, "Leave me alone!" and slumped back into the chair. At the sound Bort Brecht lurched to his feet and came over to us. When he let go Seabiscuit's hand, the Biscuit began to cry quietly.

"I'm giving the orders around here," Bort said.

I was delighted. There had been something, a long time ago, about somebody giving orders. "I have to do something," I said. "Do you know what it is?"

"Come with me." He led the way, swaggering, to the screen. "Look," he commanded, and then sat down beside Seabiscuit and lost himself in contemplation. Seabiscuit kept on crying.

"That's not it," I said doubtfully. "I think you gave me the wrong orders."

"Wrong?" he bellowed. "Wrong? I am never wrong!" He got up, and before I knew what was coming, he hauled off and cracked three knuckles with my jawbone. I hit the deck with a crash and slid up against Jo Hartley. Jo didn't move. He was alive, but he just didn't seem to give a damn. I lay there for a long time before I could get up again. I wanted to kill Bort Brecht, but there was something I had to do first.

I went back to the captain and butted him out of the chair. He snarled at me and went and crouched by the bulkhead, tears still streaming down his cheeks. I slumped into the seat, my fingers wandering idly about the controls without touching them, my eyes desperately trying to avoid the glory of Xantippe.

It seemed to me that I was very near to the thing I was to do. My right hand touched the infragun activator switch, came away, went back to it, came away. I boldly threw another switch; a network of crosshairs and a bright central circle appeared on the screen. This was it, I thought. Bort Brecht yelped like a kicked dog when the crosshairs appeared, but did not move. I activated the gun, and grasped the range lever in one hand and the elevation control in the other. A black-centered ball of flame hovered near the surface of the planet.

This was it! I laughed exultantly and pushed the range lever forward. The ball plunged into the dull-silver mystery, leaving a great blank crater. I pulled and pushed at the elevation control, knowing that my lovely little ball was burning and tearing its inexorable way about in the planet's vitals. I drew it out to the surface, lashed it up and down and right and left, cut and slashed and tore.

Bort Brecht was crouched like an anthropoid, knees bent, knuckles on the deck, fury knotting his features, eyes fixed on the scene of destruction. Behind me Phil Hartley was teetering on tiptoe, little cries of pain struggling out of his lips every time the fireball appeared. Bort spun and was beside me in one great leap. "What's happening? Who's doing that?"

"He is," I said immediately, pointing at Jo Hartley. I knew that this was going to be tough on Jo, but I was doing the thing I had to do, and I knew Bort would try to stop me. Bort leaped on the prone figure, using teeth and nails and fists and feet; and Phil Hartley hesitated only a minute, torn between the vision of Xantippe and something that called to him from what seemed a long, long while ago. Then Jo cried out in agony, and Phil, a human prototype of my fireball, struck Bort amidships. Back and forth, fore and aft, the bloody battle raged, while Seabiscuit whimpered and the skipper, still sunk in his introspective trance, wept silently. And I cut and stabbed and ripped at Xantippe.

I took care now, and cut a long slash almost from pole to pole; and the edges opened away from the wound as if the planet had been wrapped in a paper sheath. Underneath it was an olive-drab color, shot with scarlet. I cut at this incision again and again, sinking my fireball in deeper at each slash. The weakened ovoid tended to press the edges together, but the irresistible ball sheared them away as it passed; and when it had cut nearly all the way through, the whole structure fell in on itself horribly. I had a sudden feeling of lightness, and then unbearable agony. I remember stretching back and back over the chair in the throes of some tremendous attack from inside my body, and then I struck the deck with my head and shoulders, and I was all by myself again in the beautiful black.

There was a succession of lights that hurt, and soothing smells, and the sound of arcs and the sound of falling water. Some of them were weeks apart, some seconds. Sometimes I was conscious and could see people tiptoeing about. Once I thought I heard music.

But at last I awoke quietly, very weak, to a hand on my shoulder. I looked up. It was Dr. Renn. He looked older.

"How do you feel, Rip?"

"Hungry."

He laughed. "That's splendid. Know where you are?"

I shook my head, marveling that it didn't hurt me.

"Earth," he said. "Psy hospital. You've been through the mill, son."

"What happened?"

"Plenty. We got the whole story from the picrecording tapes inside and outside of your ship. You cut Xantippe all to pieces. You incidentally got Bort Brecht started on the Hartley family, which later literally cut *him* to pieces. It cost three lives, but Xantippe is through."

"Then—I destroyed the projector, or whatever it was—"

"You destroyed Xantippe. You—killed Xantippe. The planet was a . . . a thing that I hardly dare think about. You ever see a hydromedusa here on Earth?"

"You mean one of those jellyfish that floats on the surface of the sea and dangles paralyzing tentacles down to catch fish?"

"That's it. Like a Portuguese man-of-war. Well, that was Xantippe, with that strange mind field about her for her tentacles. A space dweller; she swept up anything that came her way, killed what was killable, digested what was digestible to her. Examination of the pictures, incidentally, shows that she was all set to hurl out a great cloud of spores. One more revolution about Betelgeuse and she'd have done it."

46

"How come I went under like that?" I was beginning to remember.

"You weren't as well protected as the others. You see, when we trained that crew we carefully split the personalities; paranoiac hatred enough to carry them through the field and an instant reversion to manic depressive under the influence of the field. So you were the leader—you were delegated to do the job. All we could do to you was implant a desire to destroy Xantippe. You did the rest. But when the psychic weight of the field was lifted from you, your mind collapsed. We had a sweet job rebuilding it, too, let me tell you!"

"Why all that business about 'one sane man'?"

Renn grinned. "That was to keep the rest of the crew fairly sure of themselves, and to keep you from the temptation of taking over before you reached the field, knowing that the rest, including the captain, were not responsible for their actions."

"What about the others, after the field disappeared?"

"They reverted to something like normal. Not quite, though. The quartermaster tied up the rest of the crew just before they reached Earth and handed them over to us as Insurrectionist spies!

"But as for you, there's a command waiting for you if you want it."

"I want it," I said. He clapped me on the shoulder and left. Then they brought me a man-sized dinner.

Ghost of a Chance

SHE SAID, "There's something following me!" in a throttled voice, and started to run.

It sort of got me. Maybe because she was so tiny and her hair was so white. Maybe because, white hair and all, she looked so young and helpless. But mostly, I think, because of what she said. "There's something following me." Not "someone." "Something." So I just naturally hauled out after her.

I caught her at the corner, put my hand on her shoulder. She gasped, and shot away from me. "Take it easy, lady," I panted. "I won't let it get you."

She stopped so suddenly that I almost ran her down. We stood looking at each other. She had great big dark eyes that didn't go with her hair at all. I said, "What makes you go dashing around at three o'clock in the morning?"

"What makes you ask?" Her voice was smooth, musical.

"Now, look—you started this conversation."

She started to speak, and then something over my shoulder caught her eye. She froze for a second; and I was so fascinated by the play of expression on her face that I didn't follow her gaze. Abruptly she brought her eyes back to my face and then slapped it. It was a stinger. I stepped back and swore, and by the time I was finished she was halfway up the block. I stood there rubbing my cheek and let her go.

I met Henry Gade a couple of days later and told him about it. Henry is a practical psychologist. Perhaps I should say his field is practical psychology, because Henry ain't practical. He has theories. He has more damn theories than any man alive. He is thirty and bald and he makes lots of money without doing any work.

"I think she was crazy," I said.

48

"Ah," said Henry, and laid a finger beside his nose. I think the nose was longer. "But did you ask her what *she* thought?"

"No. I only asked her what she was doing running around that time of night."

"The trouble with you, Gus, is that you have no romance in you. What you should have done was to catch her up in your arms and smothered her with kisses."

"She'd have sla—"

"She did, anyway, didn't she?" said Henry, and walked off.

Henry kids a lot. But he sometimes says crazy things like that when he isn't kidding a bit.

I met the girl again three months later. I was in the Duke's beer garden looking at his famous sunflower. The sunflower was twelve feet tall and had crutches to keep it standing up. It grew beside the dirt alley that was the main road of the beer garden. There were ratty-looking flowerbeds all over the place and tables set among them. And Japanese lanterns that had been out in the rain, and a laryngitic colored band. The place was crowded, and I was standing there letting all that noise beat me back and forth, looking at the sunflower. The Duke swore he could fill a No. 6 paper bag with the seeds from that one flower.

And then she said, "Hello. I'm sorry I had to slap your face." She was squinched up against the stem of the sunflower, in amongst all those shadows and leaves.

I said, "Well, if it isn't my pretty little pug. What do you mean, you're sorry you *had* to? You should be just sorry you did."

"Oh, I had to. I wouldn't slap you just for nothing."

"Oh—I did something? I shoulda got slapped?"

"Please," she said. "I am sorry."

I looked at her. She was. "What are you doing in there—hiding?"

She nodded.

"Who are you hiding from?"

She wouldn't say. She just shrugged and said she was just—you know—hiding.

"Is it the same thing you were running away from that night?"

"Yes."

I told her she was being silly. "I looked all around after you left and there wasn't a thing on the street."

"Oh, yes there was!"

"Not that I could see."

"I know that."

I suddenly got the idea that this was a very foolish conversation. "Come out of there and have a beer with me. We'll talk this thing over."

"Oh, I couldn't do that!"

"Sure you could. Easy. Look." I reached in and grabbed her.

"You should know better than that," she said, and then something happened to break the stem of the big sunflower. It tottered and came crashing down like a redwood. The huge flower landed on the tray that Giuseppe, the waiter, was carrying. It held eight long beers, two pitchers and a martini. The beers and a lot of broken glass flew in every direction but up. The martini went back over his head and crashed on the bars of the cage where the Duke kept his trained squirrel. There was some confusion. The girl with the white hair was gone. All the time that the Duke was telling me what a menace I was, I kept staring over his heaving shoulder at the squirrel, which was lapping up the martini that had splashed inside the cage. After the Duke ran out of four-letter words he had me thrown out. We'd been pretty good friends before that, too.

I got hold of Henry as soon as I could. "I saw that girl again," I told him, "and I grabbed her like you said." I told him what had happened. He laughed at me. Henry always laughs at me.

"Don't look so solemn about it, Gus!" he said, and slapped me on the back. "A little excitement is good for the blood. Laugh it off. The Duke didn't sue you, did he?"

"No," I said, "not exactly. But that squirrel of his ate the olive out of that cocktail that fell into his cage and got awful sick. And the Duke went and had the doctor send his bill to me. Stomach pump."

Henry had been eating salted nuts, and when I said that he snorted half a mouthful of chewed nuts up into his nose. I've done that and it hurts. In a way I was glad to see Henry suffer.

"I need some help," I told him after he got his health back. "Maybe that girl's crazy, but I think she's in trouble."

"She most certainly is," said Henry. "But I don't see what you could do about it."

"Oh, I'd figure out something."

"I also don't see why you want to help her out."

"That's a funny thing," I said slowly. "You know me, Henry—I got no use for wimmen unless they leave me alone. Every time one of 'em does something nice, it's because she's figgerin' to pull something lousy a little later."

Henry swallowed some cashews carefully and then laughed. "You've summed up at least seven volumes of male objectivism," he said. "But what has that got to do with your silver-haired Nemesis?"

"Nemesis? I thought maybe she was Polish. Her? Well, she's never done anything to me that wasn't lousy. So I figure maybe she's different. I figure maybe she's going to work it the other way around and pull something nice. And I want to be around when that happens."

"Your logic is labored but dependable." He said something else, about what's the use of being intelligent and educated when all wisdom rests on the lips of a child of nature, but I didn't catch on. "Well, I'm rather interested in whether or not you can do anything for her. Go ahead and stick your neck out."

"I don't know where she lives or nothing."

"Oh—that." He pulled out a little notebook and a silver pencil and wrote down something. "Here," he said, tearing it off and handing it to me. It said, "Iola Harvester, 2336 Dungannon Street."

"Who's this?"

"Your damsel in distress. Your dark-eyed slapper of faces."

"How the devil do you know her name?"

"She was a patient of mine for quite a while."

"She was? Why you son-of-a-gun! Why didn't you tell me?"

"Why didn't you ask me?"

I started for the door, reading over the name and address. "You know what, Henry?"

"What?"

"Iola's a pretty name."

Henry laughed. "Let me know how you make out."

I went up and rang the bell. It was a big apartment house; Iola lived on the fourth floor. The foyer door belched at me and I pushed it open and went in. They had one of those self-service elevators so I went up the stairs. Those things make me nervous.

She was waiting up on her floor to find out who had rung the bell. She was wearing a black housecoat that touched the floor all the way around and was close around her throat. It had a stiff collar that stuck up and out and seemed to sort of cradle her head. There was a zipper all down the front and two silver initials on the left breast. I couldn't get my wind right away and it wasn't the stairs.

"Oh!" she said. "It's you!"

"*Yup!*" I looked at her for a minute. "Gee! I didn't know you were so *tiny!*" There was something about her that made me want to laugh out loud, but not because I saw anything funny. When I said that she got pink.

"I . . . don't know whether I should ask you in," she said. "I don't even know your name."

"My name is Gus. So now you can ask me in."

"You're the only man I have ever met who can be fresh without being fresh," she said, and stood aside. I didn't know what she meant, but I went in, anyway. It was a nice place. Everything in it was delicate and small, like Iola. I stood in the middle of the floor spinning my hat on one finger until she took it away from me. "Sit down," she said. I did and she did, with the room between us. "What brings you here; how did you find out my address; and will you have some coffee or a drink?"

"I came because I think you're in a jam and you might need help. A friend of mine gave me your name and address. I don't want any coffee and what have you got to drink?"

"Sauterne," she said. "Rum, rye and Scotch."

"I never *touch* that stuff."

"What do you drink?"

"Gin." She looked startled. "Or milk. Got any milk?"

She had. She got me a great big glass of it. She even had some herself. She said, "Now, what's on your mind?"

"I told you, Miss Iola. I want to help you."

"There's nothing you can do."

"Oh, yes there is. There must be. If you'll tell me what's both"erin' you, making you hide away in ... in sunflowers and runnin' away from nothing. I'll bet I could fix you up— What are you laughing at?"

"You're so earnest!" she said.

"Everybody's all the time laughing at me," I said sadly. "Well, how about it?"

The smile faded away from her face and she sat for a long time saying nothing. I went and sat beside her and looked at her. I didn't try to touch her at all. Suddenly she nodded and began to talk.

"I might as well tell you. It's tough to keep it to myself. Most people would laugh at me; the one doctor I went to eventually gave me up as a bad job. He said I was kidding myself. He said that what had happened just couldn't happen—I imagined it all. But you—I think I can trust you. I don't know why—

"It started about two years ago. I had a slight crush on a fellow at a summer camp. He took me to a dance one night—one of those country square dances. It was a lot of fun and we danced ourselves tired. Then we went out onto the lake shore and he—well, the moon and all, you know—he put his arms around me. And just then a voice spoke to me. It said, 'If you know what's good for you, you'll keep away from this fellow.' I started back and asked the boy if he had said something. He hadn't. I was scared and ran all the way home. He tried to catch me, but he couldn't. I saw him the next day and tried to apologize but there wasn't very much I could say. I tried to be nice to him, but as time went on he got more and more irritable. And he lost weight. He wound up in the hospital. Almost—died. You see, he couldn't sleep. He was afraid to sleep. He had the most terrible dreams. I heard about one of them. It was awful.

"I didn't realize then that my seeing him had anything to do with his getting sick; but as soon as they had him in the hospital he began to get better, fast, as long as I didn't visit him. Then he would have a relapse. I heard that after he left the camp for good and went back to his home in Chicago, he was quite all right.

"Well, nothing happened for quite a while, and then I began to notice that a counterman at a sandwich bar where I ate every day had begun to act strangely. I saw him every day, but there was absolutely nothing between us. One afternoon while I was eating, he began dropping things. It was nothing at first, but it got very bad. It got so that he couldn't lift so much as a spoon without dropping it. He spilled cup after cup of coffee. He would try to make a sandwich and he'd drop the makings all over the floor and his work table. He couldn't set a place at the counter, he couldn't wait on anybody— *as long as I was there!* At first he kidded about it and called me his jinx girl. But after a week or so of that, he came over to me just as I sat down and said:

"Miss Harvester, I hope you don't mind what I'm going to say, but something's got to be done. I'll lose my job if I don't stop dropping things. But I never do that unless you're here! I don't know why it is, but there you have it. Would you be angry if I asked you not to eat here for a while?" I was astonished, but he was so worried and so polite about it that I never ate there again. And from what I've heard my friends say, he never dropped anything again.

"And from then on it got worse and worse. A traffic cop, a nice old man, that I used to nod to each morning on my way to work, began to *itch!* I could see it, every time I passed him! I'd nod, and he'd nod, and then start to scratch as if he itched so badly he just couldn't help himself. And an office boy who spent a lot of time near my desk began to miss doors! I mean, he just couldn't get through a door without running into the jamb. The poor boy almost went crazy. He'd walk slowly toward a door, aim carefully, and try to go through, but he couldn't do it unless he struck the jamb first. I got so heartsick watching him that I quit my job and got another—which took care of the nice policeman, too. Neither of them were ever troubled again.

"But that's the way it's been ever since. Any man I see regularly starts suffering dreadfully from strange trouble. It's bad enough for the ones who just see me in a routine way. But oh, the poor men who try to take me out to shows and things! When I go out, that strange voice speaks to me again, and tells me to keep away from the man. And if I don't, he gets terribly sick, or he gets blind spells when he crosses any streets, or he does things that cause him to lose his job or his business. Do you see what I'm up against?"

"Don't cry, Miss Iola. Please don't cry."

"I'm n-not crying, Mr. Gus!"

"Just plain Gus!"

"Well then, you call me just plain Iola. Or Miss Harvester. Not Miss Iola."

"I'd have to feel a certain way about you to call you Iola," I said slowly. "And I'd have to feel a certain other way about you to call you Miss Harvester. I'm goin' to call you Miss Iola."

"Oh, Gus," she said, "you're so *cute!*" She smiled and sipped some milk and then went on with her story.

"I work now for a woman who owns a cosmetic business," she said. "I have a woman boss and a woman manager and office force and mostly women customers. And I hate them! I hate all women!"

"Me, too," I said.

She gave me an odd glance, and went on. "Once in a while I'm free of this thing. I can't tell you exactly how I know, but I do. It's a sort of lightening of the pressure. And then I'll be walking along the street and I can feel it trying to catch up with me—just as if it had hunted me out and was following me. Sometimes I can hide and get away from it. Generally I can't."

"Oh—that's why you were running away that night I first saw you! But—why did you slap my face?"

"Because I liked you."

"That's a funny sort of way to show it, Miss Iola."

"Oh, no! The thing, whatever it is, had just caught up with me. It knew I liked you. It would have done some terrible thing to you if I hadn't slapped you to make it think I disliked you. And after I had done it I was so ashamed I ran away."

"Why did you break the stem of the sunflower?"

"Gus, I didn't! The thing did that, to get you in trouble."

"He succeeded."

"Oh, Gus—I'm so sorry."

"What for? Not your fault."

"Not— Gus, you believe me, don't you?"

She kissed me. Just a little one, on the cheek, but it made my heart pop up into the back of my neck and slug me.

"Well," I said as soon as I could make my breathing operate my voice, "whatever this thing is, I'll help you lick it. Ah—what is it, by the way? Got any ideas?"

"Yes," she said quietly. "I certainly have. When I told the doctor this, it convinced him that I was suffering from an overdose of old wives' tales. Doesn't it seem funny to you that after all I've told you about what happens to a man if I so much as talk to him, nothing is happening to you?"

"Come to think of it, it is funny."

"Look, then," she said, pointing. "There, and there, and there!"

I looked. Over the tops of the three doors that opened into the room, and over the two big windows, were strands of—garlic.

"I . . . heard of that," I said. "A ghost, huh?"

"A ghost," said Iola. "A jealous ghost. A dirty, rotten dog-in-the-manger ghost! Why doesn't he leave me alone?"

"I'll tear'm apart," I growled.

She smiled, the saddest, puckered-up little smile I ever did see. "No, Gus, no. You're strong, all right, but that kind of strength won't do me much good with my haunt."

"I'll find some way, Miss Iola," I said. "I will, so help me!"

"You'll try," she said softly. "So help *me!*"

She got my hat and opened the door for me, then closed it with a bang, whirled and stood with her back to it. "Gus!" She was pale, anyway, but now she looked bloodless. "Gus. He's out there! The ghost—he knows you're in here, and he's waiting for you!"

I looked at my hands. "Move on out of the way, then, Miss Iola," I said quietly, "and let me at him."

"No, Gus—no!"

"Now, looky here. It's getting late—too late for you to have my kind in your digs. I'll run along." I walked over to her, took her by the shoulders, and lifted her out of the way. Her forehead was near, so I kissed it before I put her down.

56

"Good night," I said. She didn't answer. She was crying, so I guess she couldn't. Awful scared. I was glad about that because I knew it wasn't herself she was scared for.

I woke up the next morning and thought I was still asleep, in the middle of a foul dream. I was cold—stone-cold, wet-cold. I felt as slimy as an eel in a barrel of oil. I opened my eyes and tried to shake the feeling off. It wouldn't shake. My last night's dinner rolled inside me as I realized that the sliminess was there, all right—my two sheets were coated with it. I could feel the wet, thick mass of it all over me. I could strip it off one arm with the other hand, and throw it— *sclup*—onto the floor.

But I couldn't see it.

I ran, gasping and retching, into the bathroom. My feet seemed to slip on the stuff, and I had trouble turning the doorknob with my slimy fingers. I climbed under the hottest shower I had ever taken, soaped, rinsed, soaped again, rinsed again. And I got out of the tub feeling cold and clammy and slimy as ever.

I tried to put some clothes on, but I couldn't stand the pressure of them; they seemed to drive the thick mass of it into my pores. I threw them off, leaped into bed, and pulled the covers over me, and with a yelp I leaped out again. It was bad enough to have it, but I couldn't bear to wallow in it. The phone rang. Iola.

"Gus, I'm terribly worried about you. Has he ... it ... done anything to you?"

I hesitated. It wouldn't do any good to lie. "Yeah, he's been skylarking around."

"Gus, what has he done?

"Nothin' worth talking about."

"Oh, you won't tell me. It must be something really terrible!"

"Why so?"

"Because I ... I ... well, I— Gus, aren't you going to say it first? Why is that he would you treat you worse than any other man?"

I slowly began to get what she was driving at. "Miss Iola—you don't lo ... care for me or something?"

"Darling!"

I said, "Holy smoke!"

I did some thinking after I hung up. I couldn't let this thing get me down—not now, not after my hearing news like that. I clamped my jaw and got out some clean underwear and socks. I was remembering something my pop told me after my first street fight. "If ye git hurt, me bye, don't let th' other fellow know it. If he thinks he can't hurt ye, ye've got 'im licked."

So I dressed. With my clothes I clasped the chill ooze to me, and when I walked out the door the slime dripped from the creases of my flesh as I moved. I stepped out onto the street with some misgivings, but it was invisible, thank the Powers.

And when I woke the next day the sliminess was gone.

I went to Henry Gade's place and borrowed a pen and paper. I had told him what I'd heard from Iola about her trouble, but nothing else.

"Who are you writing to?" he asked over his pipe, watching me scratching laboriously away at the letter.

"I'm doin' what anyone should do when he's in trouble—consulting an expert," I said, and kept on writing.

"'Miss Beatrice Dix, *The Daily Mail,*'" he read aloud, and roared with laughter. "So you've got trouble along those lines, too, have you? Ha? Beatrice Dix—Advice to the Lovelorn!"

"You tell your little mouth to stop making those noises or it'll get poked," I growled. He went on reading what I had written:

Dear Miss Dix:

I got a problem about a girl I am very serious with. This girl has a fellow who likes her, but she don't like him none at all. He keeps on bothering her and ordering her to keep away from other men, but he never comes to see her or gives her anything or takes her out and on top of that he keeps on doing things to any other man that is interested in her and especially to me because—

"Good heavens, Gus, couldn't you put a full stop in there somewhere?"

—because I am at present her big moment. The things he does are not the kind of things you can get the law on him for. What I want to know is what right has this fellow to be so

*jealous when the girl has no use for him and what can we do
to get rid of him.*

"Either you're an extremely exacting student of literary styling,"
said Henry, "or you actually are the kind of person who writes in
to Beatrice Dix's column. I've always wondered what one of those
nitwits looked like," he added thoughtfully, standing off and regard-
ing me as if I were a museum piece. "Tell me—who's the cutter-inner
in your little romance?"

"A ghost."

"A ghost? Iola's jealous ghost? Gus, Gus, you improve by the
hour. And do you really think you can exorcise him with the aid of
a heart-throb column?"

"He don't need no exercise."

"Get out of here, Gus, you're killing me."

"I will before I do," I said.

The following day Iola's haunt created something new and different for me. But I couldn't brave this one out. I stayed home all
day after phoning the boss that I was very, very ill. Exactly what was
done couldn't be printed.

The answer to my letter came far sooner than I had hoped. I
hadn't asked for a personal reply, and so it was printed, with my letter, thus:

> G.S.:
>
> *You are up against a very difficult problem, if we under-
> stand the situation correctly. We have run up against such cases
> before. The young man who is persecuting the two of you will
> continue to do so just as long as he finds the girl attractive to
> his peculiar type of mind. And what can you do about it?*
>
> *You can ignore him completely.*
>
> *Or you can, together or singly, get the man to talk the whole
> thing out with you.*
>
> *Or you might try to find someone else who would interest
> him.*
>
> *But you must be patient. Please, for your own sakes, do not
> do anything rash.*

I read it over half a dozen times. I figured this Dix woman was a real expert at this racket, and she ought to know what to do. But how to go about it? "Ignore him completely." How can you be married to a woman when you know you're liable to turn slimy at a moment's notice? "Appeal to his better nature—talk it out with him." Catch him first. "Find someone else who would interest him." Catch a lady ghost, huh? And persuade her to vamp him.

I took the paper over to Henry Gade. He's better at thinking things out than I am.

He waved the paper aside as I came in. "I've seen it," he said. "I was looking for it."

"What do you think?"

"I think it's a lovely piece of say-nothing, except that she hit the nail on the head when she said that the guy will keep right on bothering you lovebirds just as long as he finds the girl attractive. I can't get over it!" he exploded, and put his head on one side, watching me. "Good old Gus, in love after all these years!"

"Maybe it hits harder for that," I said, and he stopped his ape-grinning and laid a hand on my shoulder.

"I guess it does. You do reach in and get the truth at times, old man."

The letter from Iola was waiting for me when I got back home.

> *Dearest Gus,*
>
> *This is a rotten thing for me to do, but I've got to do it. I have a suspicion of what you've been going through so bravely; he talked to me last night and told me some of the things he's done to you.*
>
> *So you mustn't write, Gus darling, and you mustn't phone, and above all you must never, never see me again. It's the only way out for both of us, and if it's a painful and a cruel way, then that's the breaks.*
>
> *But, beloved—don't try to get in touch with me. I have bought a little revolver, and if you do that I'll kill myself. That's not idle talk, Gus. I'm not afraid to do it. I've lived through enough pain.*
>
> *Sweet, sweet sweetheart, how my heart bleeds for you!*

I read it over once and tried to read it again because, somehow, I couldn't see so well. Then I dove for the phone, and thought about the revolver, and turned my back on it. Oh, she'd do it—I knew her.

Then I went out.

Henry found me. Maybe it was three weeks later, maybe four. I didn't know because I didn't give a damn. I was sitting on a bench with a couple of other gentlemen.

"Go away. You're Henry. I remember you. Go away, Henry."

"Gus! Get up out of that! You're drunk! Come home with me, Gus."

One of the other gentlemen back-slid to the extent of taking some of Henry's money for helping Henry get me home. Once there, I slept the clock around.

Henry woke me, sponging my face with warm water. "Lost thirty pounds or more," he was muttering. "Filthy rags—ten-day beard—"

"You know what happened to me," I said, as if that excused and explained everything.

"Yes, I know what happened to you," he roared. "You lost your cotton-headed filly. And did you stand up and take it? No! You lay down and let yourself get kicked like the jelly-bellied no-good you are!"

"But she wouldn't—"

"I know, I know. She refused to see you any more. That's got nothing to do with it. You're wound up with her—finished. And you tried to run away. You tried to escape into filth and rotgut liquor. Don't you realize that you do nothing that way but burn up what's clean in you and leave all that's rotten, with the original wound festering in the middle of it?"

I turned my face to the wall, but I couldn't stop his voice. "Get up and bathe and shave and eat a decent meal! Try to act like a human being until you can give as good an imitation as you used to."

"No," I said thickly.

Suddenly he was on his knees by the bed, an arm across my shoulders. "Stop your blubbering," he said gently. "Gus—you're a grown man now." He sat back on his haunches, frowning and breathing too deeply. Suddenly he rolled me over on my back, began slapping my face with his right hand, back and front, back and front, over and over and over.

And then something snapped inside me and I reared up off the bed and sent a whistling roundhouse at him. He ducked under it and jarred me with a left to the temple. And then we went to work. I was big and emaciated, and he was little and inspired. It was quite a show. It ended with him stretched out on the carpet.

"Thanks, Gus," he grinned weakly.

"Why'd you get me so riled up? Why'd you make me hit you?"

"Applied psychology," he said, getting up groggily. I helped him.

I felt my swollen nose. "I thought psychology was brain stuff!"

"Listen, pal. You and I are going to straighten old Gus out for good. You've got something deep inside that hurts—right? What did you see in that white-headed babe, anyway?"

"She's . . . she's . . . I just can't get along without her."

"You got slushy. I think your taste is lousy." Henry's eyes were narrowed and he teetered on the balls of his feet. He knew when he was treading on thin ice, but he was going through with this. "What do you see in an anemic-looking wretch like that? Give me nice, firm, rosy girls with some blood in their veins. *Heh!* Her, with her white hair and white skin and two great big black holes for eyes. She looks like a ghost! She isn't worth—"

I roared and charged. He stepped nimbly out of the way. I charged right past him and into the bathroom. "Where's your razor?" I shouted. "Where's the soap?" And I dove into the shower.

When I came out of the bathroom and started climbing into some clothes, he demanded an explanation. "What did I say? What did I do?" He was hopping exultantly from one foot to the other.

"You said it a long while back," I said. "So did Beatrice Dix. Something about, 'He'll annoy you just as long as he finds the girl attractive.'" I laced the second shoe, demanded some money, and pounded out before I had the sentence well finished.

I rang somebody else's bell at the apartment house and when the buzzer burped at me I headed for the stairs. I rang Iola's bell and waited breathlessly. The knob turned and I crowded right in. She was drawing a negligee about her. Her eyes were red-rimmed.

"Gus!" She drew back, turned and ran to a lamp table. "Oh, you *fool!* Why do you have to make it harder for us?" She moved so fast I couldn't stop her. She had the gun in her hand.

"Hold on, you little dope!" I roared. "That may be a way out, but you're not going out alone. We're going together!"

"Gus—"

"And doing it together we're not doing it that way! Give me that thing!" I strode across the room, lifted it out of her hand. I opened the magazine, took the barrel in one hand and the butt in the other and twisted them apart, throwing the pieces at her feet. "Now get in there and get dressed. We've got things to do!" She hesitated, and I pushed her roughly toward the bedroom. "One of us is going to dress you," I said somberly.

She squeaked and moved. I tramped up and down the living room, gleefully kicking the broken gun on every trip. She was ready in about four minutes; she came out frightened and puzzled and radiant. I took her wrist and dragged her out of the apartment. As soon as we passed under the garlic on the door, my skin began to tingle, then to itch, and suddenly I felt that I was a mass of open, festering sores. And on top of this came the slime again. I gritted my teeth and sluiced down my pain with sheer exultation.

We piled into a taxi and I gave an address. When Iola asked questions I laughed happily. We pulled up at a curb and I paid off the driver. "Go in there," I said.

"A beauty parlor! But what—"

I pushed her in. A white-uniformed beautician came forward timidly. I took a strand of Iola's white hair and tossed it. "Dye this," I said. "Dye it black!"

"Gus!" gasped Iola. "You're mad! I don't *want* to be a brunette! I haven't the coloring for—"

"Coloring? You know what kind of coloring you have, with those big black holes of eyes and that white skin and hair? *You look like a ghost!* Don't you see? That's why he hounded you! That's why he loved you and was jealous of you!"

Her eyes got very bright. She looked in a mirror and said, "Gus—you remember that summer I told you about, when he first spoke to me? I was wearing a long white dress—white shoes—"

"Get in there and be a brunette," I growled. The operator took her.

I settled down into a big chair to wait. I was suffering a thousand different agonies, a hundred different kinds of torments. Pains and horrid creeping sensations flickered over my body the way colors shift on a color-organ. I sat there taking it, and taking it, and then I heard the operator's voice from the back of the studio. "There you are, ma'am. All done. Look in there—how do you like it?"

And deep within me I almost heard a sound like a snort of disgust, and then there was a feeling like an infinite lightening of pressure. And then my body was fresh and whole again, and the ghostly pains were gone.

Iola came out and flung her arms around my neck. As a brunette she was stunning.

Henry Gade was our best man.

The Bones

DONZEY CAME TO the door with a pair of side-cutting pliers in his hand and soldering flux smeared on the side of his jaw. "Oh—Farrel. Come in."

"Hi, Donzey." The town's police force ducked his head under the doorway and followed the mechanic through a littered living room into what had once been a pantry. It was set up as a workshop, complete with vises, a power lathe, a small drill press and row upon row of tools. It was a great deal neater than the living room. By the window was a small table on which was built an extraordinarily complicated radio set which featured a spherical antenna and more tubes and transformers and condensers than a small-town bicycle repairman can be expected to buy and still eat. Farrel added a stick of gum to his already oversize wad and stared at it.

"That it?" he asked.

"That's it," said Donzey proudly. He sat down beside the table and picked up an electric soldering iron. "She ought to work this time," he said, holding the iron close to his cheek to see if it were hot enough.

"And I used to think FM was the initials of a college," said Farrel.

"Not in radio," said Donzey. The lump of solder in his hand slumped into glittering fluidity, sealed a joint. "And this is a different kind of frequency modulation, too. This is the set that's going to make us some real money, Farrel."

"Yeah," said the sheriff without enthusiasm. He was thinking of the irrepressible Donzey's flotation motor, that was supposed to use the power developed by a chain of hollow balls floating to the top of a tank; of his ingenious plan for zoning highways by disappearing concrete walls between the lanes—a swell idea only somebody else had patented it. Also there was a little matter of a gun which could be set to fire thirty bullets at any interval between a fifth of a second to thirty minutes. Only nobody wanted it. Donzey was as unsuccessful as he was enthusiastic. He kept body and soul indifferently together only because he had infinite powers of persuasion. He could sell one of his ideas to the proverbial brass monkey—more; he could get a man like Farrel to invest capital in an idea like his directional FM transmitter. His basic principle was a signal beamed straight up, which would strike the Heaviside layer and bounce *almost* straight down, thus being receivable only in the receiver at which it was aimed. Donzey had got the idea over at the pool parlor. If you could aim an eight-ball at a six-ball, off the cushion, you ought to be able to aim a signal from the transmitter to the receiver, off the Heaviside layer. The thing would be handy as a wireless field telephone for military liaison.

Of course, Donzey knew little about radio. But he always worked on the theory that logic was as good or better than book-learning. His mind was as incredibly facile as his stubby fingers. What it lacked in exactitude it made up for in brilliance. Seeing the wiring on the set, an electrical engineer would have sighed and asked Donzey if he was going to put tomato sauce on all that spaghetti. Donzey would have called the engineer a hidebound conservative. Because of Donzey's pragmatic way of working, the world will never know the wiring diagram of that set. Donzey figured that if it worked he could build more like it. If it didn't, who cared how it was made?

Donzey laid the soldering iron on the bed it had charred out for itself on the workbench, brushed back his wiry black hair without effect, and announced that he was ready. "She may not work just yet," he said, plugging the set in and holding his breath for a moment in silent prayer until he was sure that the fuse was not going to blow. "But then again she might." When the tubes began to glow, he cut in the loudspeaker. It uttered a horrifying roar; he tuned it down to a hypnotic hum.

Farrel folded himself into a chair and stared glumly at the proceedings, wondering whether or not he would ever get his twenty-eight dollars and sixty cents out of this contraption. Donzey switched off the speaker and handed him a headset. "Put these on and see what you get."

Farrel clamped the phones over his ears and tried to look bored. Donzey went back to his knobs and dials.

"Anything yet?"

"Yeah." Farrel shifted his cud. "It howls like a houn' dawg."

Donzey grunted and put a finger on one phone connection and a thumb on the other. Farrel swore and snatched off the headset. "What you tryin' to do," he growled, rubbing a large, transparent ear, "make me deef?"

"Easy with the phones, son." Donzey was fifteen years younger than the sheriff, but he could say "son" and make it stick. "Phone condenser's shot. And that's the last .00035 I have. Got to rig up something. Wait a minute." He flew out of the room.

Farrel sighed and walked over to the window. Donzey was locally famous for the way he "rigged things up." He rigged up a super-charger for the municipal bandit-chaser which really worked, once you got used to its going backward in second gear. Farrel was not at all surprised to see Donzey out in the yard, busily rummaging through the garbage can.

He entered the room a moment later, unabashedly blowing the marrow out of a section of mutton bone. "Got a cigarette?" he said, wiping his mouth. Farrel dourly handed over a pack. Donzey ripped it open, spilling the smokes over the workbench. He stripped off the tinfoil, tore it in half, and after cleaning up the bone inside and out with Farrel's handkerchief, poked some of the foil into the bone and wrapped it carefully in the other piece. "Presto," he said. "A condenser."

"My handkerchief—" began Farrel.

"You'll be able to buy yourself a trainload of 'em when we put this on the market," said Donzey with superb confidence. He busily connected the outside layer of tinfoil to one phone plug and the inside wad to the other. "Now," he said, handing the earphones to the sher-iff, "that ought to do it. I'm sending from this key. There's no con-nection between transmitter and receiver. The signal's going straight up—I hope. It should come straight down."

"But I don't know that dit-dot stuff," said Farrel, putting on the headset nevertheless.

"Don't have to," said Donzey. "I'll play "Turkey in the Straw." You ought to recognize that."

They sat down and again Donzey switched on the juice. His fingers found the key as his eyes found Farrel's face; and then his fingers forgot about the key.

Farrel's heavy lids closed for a long second, while his lantern jaw slowly lit up. Then the eyes began to open, slowly. At just the halfway mark, they stopped and the man did something extraordinary with his nostrils. A long sigh escaped him, and his wide lips flapped resoundingly in the breeze. His head tilted slowly to one side.

"Mmmwaw," he said.

"Farrel!" snapped Donzey, horrified.

"M-m-ba-a-a—"

Before Donzey could reach him he reared up out of his chair, tossing his head back. By some miracle the earphones stayed in place. Farrel's hands hit the floor; he landed on one palm and one wrist, which grated audibly. His huge feet kicked out and his arms gave way. He landed on his face, the wire from the headset tightened and the table on which the radio stood began to lean out from the wall. Donzey squalled and put out his arms to catch his darling; and catch it he did. His hands gripped the chassis, perfectly grounded, and as he hugged the set to him to save it, the upper terminal of a 6D6 tube contacted his chin. He suddenly felt as if a French 75 had gone off in his face. He saw several very pretty colors. One of them, he recalled later, looked like the smell of a rose, and another looked like a loud noise. He hit the floor with a bump, number instinct acting just far enough to twist his body under the precious radio. Nothing broke but the power line; and as soon as that parted, Farrel scrambled most profanely to his feet.

"Get up, you hind-end of a foot," he roared, "so I can slap you down again!"

"Wh-wh-whooee!" said Donzey's lungs, trying to get the knack of breathing again.

"Go away," breathed the quivering mass under the radio. Donzey waited a few seconds, and when Farrel still continued to hang over him, he decided to go on waiting. He knew that the canny old sheriff would never plow through a cash investment to get to him. As long as the radio was perched on his chest he was safe.

"Who you fink you're pwayin' twickf on?" said the sheriff through a rapidly swelling lip.

"I wasn't pwaying any twickf," mimicked Donzey. "Sizzle down, bud. What happened?"

"I ftarted to go cwavy, vat's all. What kind of devil'f gadget iv vat, anyway?"

Sensing that the sheriff's anger was giving way to self-pity, Donzey took a chance on lifting the radio off himself. "My gosh, man— you're hurt!"

Farrel followed Donzey's eyes to his rapidly swelling wrist. "Yeah ... I— Hey! It hurts!" he said, surprised.

"It should," said Donzey. While Farrel grunted, he bound it against a piece of board, and then went for a couple of ice cubes for the now balloon-like lip. As soon as Farrel was comfortable, Donzey started asking questions.

"What happened when I switched on the set?"

Farrel shuddered. "It was awful. I seen pictures."

"Pictures? You mean—pictures, like television?" Donzey's gadgeteer's heart leaped at the ideas that thronged into his cluttered mind. Maybe his set, by some odd circuiting, could induce broadcast television signals directly on the mind! Maybe he had invented an instrument for facilitating telepathy. Maybe he had stumbled on something altogether new and unheard of. Any way you looked at it, there was millions in it. *Piker,* he told himself, *there's billions in it!*

"Nah," said Farrel. His face blanched; like many a bovine character before him he suddenly realized he had swallowed his cud.

"Don't worry about it," said the observant Donzey. "Chewing gum won't hurt you. Chew some more and forget it. Now, about those pictures—"

"Them ... they wasn't like television. They wasn't like nothin' I ever heard about before. They were colored pictures—"

"Moving pictures?"

"Oh, yeah. But they were all foggy. Things close to me, they were clear. Anything more'n thirty feet away was—fuzzy."

"Like a camera out of focus?"

"Um. But things 'way far away, they were clear as a bell."

"What did you see?"

"Hills—fields. I didn't recognize that part of the country. But it all looked different. The grass was green, but sort of gray, too. An' the sky was just—blank. It all seemed good. I dunno—you won't laugh at me, Donzey?" asked the sheriff suddenly.

"Good gosh no!"

"Well, I was—*eatin'* the grass!" Farrel peered timidly at the mechanic and then seemed reassured. "It was queer. I couldn't figure time at all. I don't know how long it went on—might 'a' been years. Seemed like it was raining sometimes. Sometimes it was cold, an' that didn't bother me. Sometimes it was hot, and boy, that did."

"Are you telling me you *felt* things in those pictures?"

Farrel nodded soberly. "Donzey, I was *in* those pictures."

Donzey thought, *What have I got here? Transmigration? Teleportation? Clairvoyance? Why, there's ten billion in it!*

"What got me," said Farrel thoughtfully, "was that everything seemed so good. Until the end. There was miles of alleys, like, and then a great big dark building. I was scared, but everyone else seemed to be going my way, so I went along. Then some feller with a ... a cleaver, he ... I tried to get away, but I couldn't. He hit me. I hollered."

"I'll say you did." They shuddered together for a moment.

"That's all," said Farrel. "He hit me twice, and I woke up on the floor with a busted wing and saw you all mixed up with the radio. Now you tell me—what happened?"

"You seemed to go into a kind of trance. You hollered, and then started thrashing around. You did a high-dive onto the deck an' dragged the radio off the table. I caught it an' my chin hit it where it was hot. It knocked me silly. The whole thing didn't last twenty seconds."

"Donzey," said the sheriff, standing up, "you can keep the money I put into this thing. I don't want no more of it." He went to the door. "Course, if you should make a little money, don't forget who helped you get a start."

Donzey laughed. "I'll keep in touch with you," he said. "Look— about that big building you went into. You said you were scared, but everybody else was going the same way, so you went along. What were the others like?"

Farrel looked at him searchingly. "Did I say 'everybody else'?" "You did."

"That's funny." Farrel scratched his head with his unbandaged arm. "All the rest of 'em was—sheep." And he went out.

For a long time after Farrel had gone, Donzey sat and stared at the radio. "Sheep," he muttered. He got up and set the transmitter carefully back on the table, rapidly checking over the wiring and tubes to see that all was safe and unbroken. "Sheep?" he asked himself. What had an FM radio to do with sheep? He put away his pliers and sal ammoniac and solder and flux; hung his friction tape on its peg; picked up the soldering iron by the point and was reminded that it was still plugged in. He looked down at his scorched palm. "Sheep!" he said absently.

It wasn't anything you could just figure out, like what made an automobile engine squeak when you ran it more than two hundred miles without any oil, or why most of the lift comes from the top surface of an airplane's wing. It was something you had to try out, like getting drunk or falling in love. Donzey switched on the radio, sat down and picked up the headset. As he adjusted the crownpiece back down to man-size, he was struck by an ugly thought. Farrel had been in a bad way when he was inside this headset. He was— dreaming, was it?—that some guy was striking him with a cleaver just as he lurched forward and cut the juice. Suppose he hadn't cut it—would he have died, like the ... the sheep he thought he was?

Donzey lay the earphones down and went into the bedroom for his alarm clock. Bolting it to the table, he wrapped a cord around the alarm key and led it to the radio switch. Then he set it carefully, so it would go off in one minute and turn off the set. He put on the headset, waited twenty-five seconds, and turned it on. Fifteen seconds to warm up, and then—

It happened for him, too, that gray grass and blank sky, the time-lessness, the rain, the cold, the heat, and the sheep. The—*other* sheep. He ate the grass and it was good. He was frightened and milled with the others through those alleyways. He saw the dark building. He—and the alarm shrilled, the set clicked off, and he sat there sweating, a-tremble. This was bad. Oh, but bad.

Any money in it? Would anybody pay for pictures you could live in? And die in?

He had a wholesome urge to take his little humdinger—a machinist's hammer—and ding the hum out of the set. He got the better of the urge. He did, however, solemnly swear never to eat another bite of lamb or mutton. That noise Farrel had made—

Mutton? Wasn't there some mutton involved in the radio? He looked at it—at the phone condenser. An innocent-looking little piece of bone, hollow, with the tinfoil inside and out. Giggling without mirth, he took a piece of wire and shorted the homemade condenser out of the circuit, set his time switch, and put on the phones. Nothing happened. He reached over, snatched the wire away. Immediately he was eating gray-green grass under a blank sky, and it was good—good—and now the cold—and then the alarm, and he was back in his chair, staring at the mutton-bone condenser.

"That bone," he whispered, "just ain't dead yet!"

He went and stood at the front door, thinking of the unutterable horror of that dark building, the milling sheep. Farrel's sprained wrist. The mutton bone. "Somewhere, somehow," he told himself, "there's a hundred billion in it!"

Ringing a doorbell with a hand burdened by a huge bundle of groceries while the other is in a sling, presents difficulties, but Sheriff Farrel managed it. Turning the knob was harder, but Farrel managed that, too, when there was no response to the bell. From the inside room came the most appalling series of sounds—a chuckling, hysterical gabbling which rose in pitch until it was cut off with a frightful gurgling. Farrel tossed his burden on a seedy divan and ran into the workshop.

Donzey was lolling in the chair by the radio with the earphones on. His face was pale and his eyes were closed, and he twitched. The radio, in the two weeks since Farrel had seen it, had undergone considerable change. It was now compactly boxed in a black enameled sheet-iron box, from which protruded the controls and a pair of adjustable steer clips, which held what looked like a small white stick. The old speaker, the globular antenna, and all of the external spaghetti was gone. Among the dials on the control panel was that of a clock with a sweep second-hand. This and Donzey's twitching were the only movements in the room.

Suddenly the set clicked and Donzey went limp. Farrel gazed with sad apprehension at the mechanic, thinking that being his pallbearer would be little trouble.

"Donzey—"

Donzey shook his head and sat up. He was thinner, and his eyes told the sheriff that he was in the throes of something or other. He leaped up and pumped Farrel's good hand. "Just the man I wanted to see. It works, Farrel—it works!"

"Yeah, we're rich," said Farrel dourly. "I heard all that before. Heck with it. Come out o' here." He dragged Donzey into the living room and indicated the bundle on the divan. "Start in on that."

Donzey investigated. "What's this for?"

"Eatin', dope. The whole town's talkin' about you starvin' yourself. If I hadn't given you that money, you wouldn't have built that radio."

"Well, you don't have to feed me," said Donzey warmly.

"I feed any stray dog that follers me home," said Farrel. "An' I ain't responsible for 'em bein' hungry. Eat, now."

"Who said I was hungry?"

"Goes without sayin'. A guy that goes scrabblin' around Tookey's butcher shop lookin' for bones twice a day just ain't gettin' enough Vitamin B."

Donzey laughed richly, looked at the sheriff and laughed again. "Oh—that! I wasn't hungry!"

"Don't start pullin' the wool over my eyes. You'll eat that stuff or I'll spread it on the floor and roll you in it." He took the bag and upended it over the couch.

Donzey, with awe, looked at the bread, the butter, the preserves, canned fruit, steak, potatoes, lard, vegetables— "Farrel, for gosh sakes! Black market. It must be, for all that—"

"It ain't," said the sheriff grimly. He herded Donzey into the kitchen, brushed a lead-crucible and a miniature steam engine off the stove and started to cook.

Donzey protested volubly until the steak started to sizzle, and then was stopped by an excess of salivary fluid. He was a little hungry, after all.

Farrel kept packing it in him until he couldn't move, and then sat down opposite and began to eye him coldly. "Now what's all this about?" he asked. "Why didn't you come to me for a handout?"

"I didn't need a handout," said Donzey, "and if I did I was too busy to notice it. Farrel, we've got the biggest thing of the century sitting in there!"

"It shoots a signal where you want it to, like you said?"

"Huh? What do you…. Oh, you mean the Heaviside beam thing? Nah," said Donzey with scorn. "Son, this is *big!*"

"Hm-m-m," said Farrel, looking at his sling. "But what good is it?"

"An entirely new school of thought will be built up around this thing," exulted Donzey. "It touches on philosophy, my boy, and metaphysics—the psychic sciences, even."

"What good is it?"

"Course, I can only guess on the whys and wherefores. When you came in, I was a chicken. I got my neck wrung. Sound silly? Well, it wouldn't to you … you *know.* But nobody else would believe me. I was a chicken—"

"What good is it?"

"—because between the clips I've built on the set I put a sliver of chicken bone. There was mutton on it when you tried it. I've been cattle and swine through that gadget, Farrel. I've been a sparrow and a bullfrog and an alley cat and a rock bass. I know how each one of them lived and died!"

"Swell," said Farrel. "But what good is it?"

"What good is it? How can you ask me such a question? Can't you think of anything but money?"

This sudden reversal caught Farrel right between the eyes. He rose with dignity, as if he were sitting on an elevator. "Donzey," he said, "you're a thief an' a robber, an' I don't want no more to do with you. Miz' Curtis was sayin' the other day that Donzey is a boy that's goin' places. I guess it's up to me to tell you where to go." He told him and stamped out.

Donzey laughed, reached for a toothpick and set about enjoying the last of that delicious steak. Farrel was a nice guy, but he lacked imagination.

Come to think of it, what good *was* the gadget?

Two hours later a small package was delivered. It contained a note and a splinter of bone. The note read:

> I know I'm bein a fool, but I can't forget the first time I met that FM thing of yours. Maybe for once in your life you can put one of your contraptions to work.
>
> Seems as how Bill Kelley just was in here wantin me to trace his wife Eula. They been havin fights—well, you know Bill, he always treated her like she was in third grade. I often wondered why she didn't take out a long time ago, the way he used to smack her around and all, and seems like she did.
>
> Bill allows she has run out with somebody, he don't know who. Anyway, right after he left a deputy comes in and says he has found Eula out on the highway in her car. Says she is all busted up. I drove out there and sure enough there she is. She is all by herself and she is dead. Car climbed a power pole on the wrong side of a cyclone fence. What I want you to find out is whether there was anyone with her. She had a compound fracture and it wasn't no trouble to get this sample. See what you can get.
>
> FARREL

Donzey realized that he still had the bone splinter in his hand. He laid it quickly on the table and stared at it as if he expected it to moan at him. He had known for some time that he would have to get a human bone to experiment with, but he would rather have had an anonymous one. He had known Eula Kelley for years. Farrel's clumsy note didn't begin to state the tragedy of her life since she married the town's rich man. She was a Kelley, and she had been a Walsh before that, and he wasn't surprised that she had finally decided to leave him. But it didn't make sense that she had left with another man. Not Eula.

Feeling a little sick, Donzey clipped the bone into his machine, set it for twenty seconds, put on the phones and threw the switch. He sat quite still until it clicked off, and then, white and shaken, adjusted the time switch for forty seconds. Once again he "listened," then made his final setting of fifty-two seconds—enough to take him right up to the mental image of Eula's death. More than that he dared not do. His great fear was that someday his psychic identification with the bone's individuality would be carried with it into death.

Farrel arrived and found him sitting on the steps, his jaw muscles knotting furiously, his sharp eyes full of puzzled anger. Farrel left a deputy in his car and went inside with Donzey.

"Get anything?" he asked.

"Plenty. Farrel, that Bill Kelley ought to be shot, and I'd like to do the shooting."

"Yeah. He's a louse. That ain't our affair. Was there anyone with her?"

"I—think there was. You better see for yourself."

Farrel shot him a quizzical glance and then sat down beside the machine. Donzey turned it on as the sheriff donned the headset, and then sat back, watching. He was sorry that he had to put Farrel through it, but he felt that the sheriff should know the story that splinter had to tell. His mind ran back over Eula's idea-patterns, the images they yielded. It was a story of incredible sordidness, and of a man's utter cruelty to a woman. It told of the things he had done, things he had said. Eula had borne it and borne it, and her ego had slowly been crushed under the weight of it. Then there was that last terrible incident, and she had run away from him. It didn't matter where she was running to, as long as it was away. And there was the flight of hope, the complete death of relief, when she realized, out there on the highway, that there was no escape. Bill Kelley's mark was on her; she couldn't leave him or her life with him. She knew exactly what she was doing when she threw the wheel hard over and closed her eyes against the beginning of that tearing crash.

The set clicked off. Farrel stared at Donzey, and drew a deep, shuddering breath.

"It don't seem right, Donzey, knowing things like that about a woman. I always knew Bill was a snake, but—"

"Yeah," said Donzey. "I know."

Farrel peeled off the headset and went to the door. "Harry," he called to his deputy, "go get Bill Kelley."

"What's that for?" asked Donzey when he returned.

"Strictly outside the law," said Farrel very quietly. "I'm goin' to give Bill Kelley somethin' he needs." He took off his badge and laid it on the bench.

Donzey suddenly remembered hearing that, years ago, Eula Walsh had married Bill Kelley when she was engaged to Farrel. He wondered if would have called Farrel in if he had remembered that before, and decided that he would have.

"Farrel," he said after a time, "about that other person in the car—"

Farrel's big head came up. "That's right—there was somebody— I got just the impression of it, just before the crash. I don't rightly remember—seems like it was someone I know, though."

"Me, too. I can't understand it, Farrel. She wasn't running away with anybody. She wasn't interested in anybody or anything except in getting away. I didn't get any intimation of her meeting anyone, or even being with anyone until that last few seconds."

"That's right. What did he look like?"

"Sort of ... well, medium-sized and ... damn if I remember. But I don't think I've seen him before."

"I haven't, either," said Farrel. "I don't know that it's really important. If she ran away with somebody, she rated it. I don't think she did, but ... heck, he was probably just a hitchhiker that she was too upset to think about," he finished lamely.

"A woman don't commit suicide with a stranger along," Donzey said.

"A woman's liable to do anything after she's been through what Eula went through." The doorbell pealed. "That'll be Kelley."

As Farrel went to the door, Donzey noticed that his palms were wet. Farrel opened the door and the deputy's voice drifted in: "I saw Kelley, sheriff. He wouldn't come."

"He wouldn't come? Why?"

Harry's voice was aggrieved. "Aw, he seemed to have a wild hair up his nose. Got real mad. Started foamin' at the mouth. Said by golly the police were public servants. Said he wasn't used to bein' ordered around like a criminal. Said if you want to see him you got to come to him, or prove he committed a crime. Sour-castic son-of-a-gun."

"That ain't all he is," said Farrel. "Forget it, Harry. Shove off. I'll walk into town when I'm through here." He banged the door. "Donzey, we're goin' to fix that feller."

Donzey didn't like to see a big, easy-going lug like Farrel wearing that icy grin. The huge hands that pinned the badge back in its place shook ever so little.

"Sure," said Donzey futilely, "sure—we'll get him."

Farrel spun on his heel as if Kelley's face were under it, and stalked out.

It was about three days later that one of Farrel's stooges at the county hospital sent up a bone specimen from an appendicitis death. Attached was a brief case history:

> Cause of death, appendicitis. Age, about forty; male. Appendix ruptured suddenly in Sessions Restaurant at 8:30 pm. Went on operating table about 9:15. Doctor in charge administered adrenalin by pericardial hypodermic. Patient roused sufficiently to allow operation. Removal of appendix and sponging of peritoneum successful. Death by post-operative hemorrhage, 9:28.

"We have," muttered Donzey as he clipped the bone into the machine, "a little scientist in our midst. Ol' Doc Grinniver up to his tricks again! A ruptured appendix and he tosses in a jolt of adrenalin to 'rouse' the patient, in the meantime making his heart pump poison all over his body, high-pressure." He picked up his earphones and glanced at the report again. " 'Post-operative hemorrhage' my blue eyeballs! That was peritonitis! Oh, well, I guess he would have died anyway, and I guess the old butcher couldn't get hold of a guinea pig with appendicitis." He sat down at the machine, adjusted the time switch, and his mind slipped into the bone emanations.

It was the usual life-and-death story, but with a difference. The man had been in the midst of a slimy little office intrigue which seemed to have taken command of most of his thoughts in the last few months; but the ragged stab of pain when his appendix burst drove all that out. Pain is like that, and Donzey had found that people handled it in two ways. They let it pile up on them until it suffocated them, or they floated up and up in it until it supported them; they lay in it like a bed. The second way, though, required a knack which took years to develop, and Donzey was glad he could learn it from other people's experience.

This particular case took it the first way, and it wasn't very nice. The agony grew and dimmed all his senses except the one that feels pain; and that grew. Pretty soon he couldn't even think. But when it got past that stage, it began to overwhelm his sensories, too, and the pain lessened. His eyes were open—had been, because he realized that his eyeballs were dry—but slowly he began to see again. Someone was bending over him. He was on the operating table. He had been to the movies, and he never remembered seeing anyone in dark clothes around an operating table before. And as his vision strengthened and the figure became clearer and clearer, he felt first curiosity, then awe, then the absolute, outside utmost in terror. Like a beam of negative energy, he felt it soaking up the heat of his body, his very life. It was a huge and monstrous thing. He had strength for just one thing; he closed his eyes just a tenth of a second before the dark one's face swam into focus; and then, in the same instant, the doctor's needle entered his heart. The warmth flowed back weakly, and when he dared to open his eyes again the dark one was gone.

And then the operation; and he felt every scrape and slice of it. When Donzey thought about it afterward, he felt his own appendix literally squirm in sympathy—not an experience measuring up to the highest standards of animal comfort. Soon enough it was over, and the set clicked off with a nice life margin of two minutes to go.

Donzey sat for a long time thinking this over. His was a mechanic's mind, and such a mind seldom rejects anything because it has never heard of it before, or because it has heard otherwise. This machine now—it proposed certain very important questions. Donzey spread the questions out on a blank spot in his brain and looked at them.

The machine showed what death felt like, just before it happened. That was the really valuable point—it *happened*, it wasn't a light going out. It was a force swinging into action, so strong that it could impress itself on the carefully constructed thought patterns mysteriously apparent in bones. All right—

What was this force called Death?

Donzey thought of that dark figure in the operating theater of the county hospital, and knew without a doubt that that question was answered. He was very happy that the late possessor of that piece of bone had had the consideration to close his eyes before he had taken a good look. Or was it the adrenalin that drove the dark thing out of sight? What had being in sight to do with death? Did looking on the Dark One—the capitalization was Donzey's—result in death? Could that be it? Were sickness and accidents merely phenomena that gave man the power to see death? And was that sight the thing that took their life force out of their now useless bodies? And—

Would seeing Death in the machine kill a man?

Donzey looked respectfully at the machine and thought, "I could easy enough try it and find out," without making the slightest move to do so.

Farrel arrived that evening, and for once the grim old man looked benignly happy. He clapped Donzey on the back, smiled, and sat down wordlessly.

"If I know you, Farrel," said Donzey, "all that showing of the teeth means that you are about to be real unkind to someone. It wouldn't be me, would it?"

"In a way," said the sheriff. "I'm goin' to bust up your place a little. You won't mind that, will you?"

"Nah," said Donzey, wondering what this was all about. "What are you going to bust up, what with, and why?"

"Answerin' your questions in order," said Farrel, grinning hugely, "Whatever gets in my way while I'm playing, a certain Mr. William Kelley, and you know as well as I do."

"Oh." Donzey rubbed his hands together. "So he's coming here? Or are you having him shipped by express?"

"He's coming of his own free will. He dropped into my office this morning and breezed up the place with a lot of noise about my not finding out who his wife ran away with. She's dead and he don't care about that. What makes him mad is that all these years he's been supportin' a woman who— You know Bill Kelley."

Donzey felt a little sick. "How can a man be so rock-bottom lousy?"

"Aw, he's been practicing for years. Anyhow, I calmed him down and told him I knew a feller ... that's you ... who had found out who was in the car with his wife. I told him to come over at eight-thirty and see you. You can shove along now or stay and see the fun. This is the one place in town where I know I can do what I want without being interrupted."

"Which is—"

"Just what happened to Eula. She was rushing along in her car; she turned over and got all smashed up. I'm goin' to turn him over and smash him up." Farrel's smile was positively childlike.

"I'll stick around and watch," said Donzey. "By the way—" He hesitated.

"What?"

"I do know who was in the car with Eula."

"Yeah? Who?"

Donzey told him. "You don't say," say Farrel. "Well, well. Skull an' a scythe, an' all that?"

"Nah," said Donzey. "That's just a picture somebody drew. Looks as much like Him as a political cartoon does of a presidential candidate." The doorbell rang. "Farrel," said Donzey quickly, "I want him to see Eula's bone picture. Of all people in the world, he ought to appreciate it the most. Please."

Farrel said thoughtfully, "That'll be O.K. Then I don't have to explain nothin'. When the machine's through, I'll start, and he'll know just why."

Donzey went to the door and let in a superbly tailored gray sports suit with a pin-checked topcoat which contained an overload of pig eyes, flabby jowls and a voice like a fingernail on a piece of slate. Bill Kelley stamped past Donzey as if he were a butler or even a photoelectric door opener. He had apparently started griping even before he rang the bell, because he entered in the middle of a sentence.

"—come to a hovel like this on a wild goose chase just because a fool of a sheriff can't get any information. I'm going to find out how much of my taxes goes to keep that fellow in office, and get an exemption. I'm the public, dammit, and I ought to be able to deal with a public servant. Hello, Farrel. What's all this nonsense, now?"

Farrel's voice cut through Kelley's because it was so deep and so very quiet. "That little man behind you is the guy I was tellin' you about. He's seen the man in Eu...Mrs. Kelley's car."

"Oh. Well? Well? Speak up, man. Who was it? If he's in business, I'll break him. If he's on relief, I'll have him taken off. If he's the kind of worthless tramp Eula would probably take up with, I'll hire some muscles I know to take care of him. Well? Well?"

"You can see him for yourself, *Mr.* Kelley," said Donzey evenly.

"I don't want to see him!" stormed Kelley. "Is he here?" He peered around.

Donzey had a flash of him grunting and wallowing in mud. "Not exactly. Sit down over there, and I'll show you a sort of moving picture."

Kelley opened his mouth to protest but found himself lifted off the floor, swung around and dropped into a chair. He squealed indignantly, saw Farrel's great horse face hovering close to his, turned a pinkish shade of gray and shut his mouth.

"Easy, Farrel," said Donzey gently, and put the earphones on Bill Kelley. Rummaging through his new filing cabinet, he clipped a specimen onto the machine and turned on the switch. Kelley's eyes closed.

They stood looking at their prisoner.

"Farrel—" said Donzey smoothly. The sheriff looked up. "What I was saying before he came… I've been wondering if it isn't the sight of Death that actually takes the…the soul out of a man."

Farrel grunted and turned back to Kelley. He was following the man's mind through that tragic maze of Eula's life. His jaw muscles kept knotting and slackening, beating like a heart.

Kelley suddenly stiffened. His eyes opened wide—so wide that the lids seemed about to fold back on themselves. The man's horrified gaze was directed at them, but they both sensed that he saw neither of them. For a full minute no one in the room moved.

"He's seen the show," muttered Farrel. "What's he doing—stalling?" Then he realized that Kelley's staring eyes weren't looking at anything any more.

Donzey nodded. "Yup," he said, "it's seeing Him does it."

"What's the matter with him?"

"Why," said Donzey, "I reckon he climbed into that car with Eula. You see, I didn't set the time switch."

"Oh," said Farrel. He went and lifted up Kelley's wrist. "*Tsk, tsk.* Whaddye know. This here guy's up an' died on us. Heh! In a automobile accident that happened more'n a week ago!"

The Hag Séleen

It was while we were fishing one afternoon, Patty and I, that we first met our friend the River Spider. Patty was my daughter and Anjy's. Tacitly, that is. Figuratively she had originated in some hot corner of hell and had left there with such incredible violence that she had taken half of heaven with her along her trajectory and brought it with her.

I was sprawled in the canoe with the nape of my neck on the conveniently curved cedar stern piece of the canoe, with a book of short stories in my hands and my fish pole tucked under my armpit. The only muscular energy required to fish that way is in moving the eyes from the page to the float and back again, and I'd have been magnificently annoyed if I'd had a bite. Patty was far more honest about it; she was fast asleep in the bilges. The gentlest of currents kept my mooring line just less than taut between the canoe and a half-sunken snag in the middle of the bayou. Louisiana heat and swampland mosquitoes tried casually to annoy me, and casually I ignored them both.

There was a sudden thump on the canoe and I sat upright just as a slimy black something rose out of the muddy depths. It came swiftly until the bow of the canoe rested on it, and then more slowly. My end of the slender craft sank and a small cascade of blood-warm water rushed on, and down, my neck. Patty raised her head with a whimper; if she moved suddenly I knew the canoe would roll over and dump us into the bayou. "Don't move!" I gasped.

She turned puzzled young eyes on me, astonished to find herself looking downward. "Why, daddy?" she asked, and sat up. So the canoe did roll over and it did dump us into the bayou.

I came up strangling, hysterical revulsion numbing my feet and legs where they had plunged into the soft ooze at the bottom. "Patty!" I screamed hoarsely.

She popped up beside me, trod water while she knuckled her eyes. "I thought we wasn't allowed to swim in the bayou, daddy," she said.

I cast about me. Both banks presented gnarled roots buried in rich green swamp growth, and I knew that the mud there was deep and sticky and soft. I knew that that kind of mud clutches and smothers. I knew that wherever we could find a handhold we could also find cottonmouth moccasins. So I knew that we had to get into our canoe again, but fast!

Turning, I saw it, one end sunken, the other high in the air, one thwart fouled in the black tentacles of the thing that had risen under us. It was black and knotted and it dripped slime down on us, and for one freezing second I thought it was alive. It bobbed ever so slowly, sluggishly, in the disturbed water. It was like breathing. But it made no further passes at us. I told Patty to stay where she was and swam over to what I could reach of the canoe and tugged. The spur that held it came away rottenly and the canoe splashed down, gunwale first, and slowly righted itself half full of water. I heard a shriek of insane laughter from somewhere in the swamp but paid no attention. I could attend to that later.

We clung to the gunwales while I tried to think of a way out. Patty kept looking up and down the bayou as if she thought she hadn't enough eyes. "What are you looking for, Patty?"

"Alligators," she said.

Yeah, I mused, that's a thought. We've got to get out of here! I felt as if I were being watched and looked quickly over my shoulder. Before my eyes could focus on it, something ducked behind a bush on the bank. The bush waved its fronds at me in the still air. I looked back at Patty—

"Patty! Look out!"

The twisted black thing that had upset us was coming down, moving faster as it came, and as I shrieked my warning its tangled mass came down on the child. She yelped and went under, fighting the slippery fingers.

I lunged toward her. "Patty!" I screamed. "Pat—"

The bayou bubbled where she had been. I dived, wrenching at

85

the filthy thing that had caught her. Later—it seemed like minutes later, but it couldn't have been more than five seconds—my frantic hand closed on her arm. I thrust the imprisoning filth back, hauled her free, and we broke surface. Patty, thank Heaven, remained perfectly still with her arms as far around me as they would go. Lord knows what might have happened if she had struggled.

We heard the roar of a bull alligator and that was about all we needed. We struck out for the bank, clawed at it. Fortunately Patty's hands fell on a root, and she scuttled up it like a little wet ape. I wasn't so lucky—it was fetid black mud that I floundered through. We lay gasping, at last on solid ground.

"Mother's gonna be mad," said Patty after a time.

"Mother's going to gnash her teeth and froth at the mouth," I said with a good deal more accuracy. We looked at each other and one of the child's eyes closed in an eloquent wink. "Oh, yeah," I said, "and how did we lose the canoe?"

Patty thought hard. "We were paddling along an' a big fella scared you with a gun and stoled our canoe."

"How you talk! I wouldn't be scared!"

"Oh, *yes* you would," she said with conviction.

I repressed an unpaternal impulse to throw her back into the bayou. "That won't do. Mother would be afraid to have a man with a gun stompin' around the bayou. Here it is. We saw some flowers and got out to pick them for mother. When we came back we found the canoe had drifted out into the bayou, and we knew she wouldn't want us to swim after it, so we walked home."

She entered into it with a will. "Silly of us, wasn't it?" she asked.

"Sure was," I said. "Now get those dungarees off so's I can wash the mud out of 'em."

A sun suit for Patty and bathing trunks for me were our household garb; when we went out for the afternoon we pulled on blue denim shirts and slacks over them to ward off the venomous mosquitoes. We stripped off the dungarees and I searched the bank and found a root broad enough for me to squat on while I rinsed off the worst of the filth we had picked up in our scramble up the bank. Patty made herself comfortable on a bed of dry Spanish moss that she tore out of the trees. As I worked, a movement in midstream caught my eye. A black tentacle poked up out of the water, and, steadily then, the slimy branches of the thing that had foundered us came sloshing into the mottled sunlight. It was a horrible sight, the horror of which was completely dispelled by the sight of the sleek green flank of the canoe which bobbed up beside it.

I ran back up my root, tossed the wet clothes on a convenient branch, broke a long stick off a dead tree and reached out over the water. I could just reach one end of the canoe. Slowly I maneuvered it away from its black captor and pulled it to me. I went into mud up to my knees in the process but managed to reach it; and then it was but the work of a moment to beach it, empty out the water and set it safely with its stern on the bank. Then I pegged out our clothes in a patch of hot sunlight and went back to Patty.

She was lying on her back with her hands on her eyes, shielding them from the light. Apparently she had not seen me rescue the canoe. I glanced at it and just then saw the slimy mass in mid-bayou start sinking again.

"Daddy," she said drowsily, "what was that awful thing that sinked us?"

"What they call a sawyer," I said. "It's the waterlogged butt of a cypress tree. The bottom is heavy and the top is light, and when the roots catch in something on the bottom the current pushes the top under. Then one of the branches rots and falls off, and the top end gets light again and floats up. Then the current will push it down again. It'll keep that up for weeks."

"Oh," she said. After a long, thoughtful pause she said, "Daddy—"

"What?"

"Cover me up." I grinned and tore down masses of moss with which I buried her. Her sleepy sigh sounded from under the pile. I lay down in the shade close by, switching lazily at mosquitoes.

I must have dozed for a while. I woke with a start, fumbling through my mind for the thing that had disturbed me. My first glance was at the pile of moss; all seemed well there. I turned my head. About eight inches from my face was a pair of feet.

I stared at them. They were bare and horny and incredibly scarred. Flat, too—splayed. The third toe of each foot was ever so much longer than any of the others. They were filthy. Attached to the feet was a scrawny pair of ankles; the rest was out of my range of vision. I debated sleepily whether or not I had seen enough, suddenly realized that there was something not quite right about this, and bounced to my feet.

I found myself staring into the blazing eye of the most disgusting old hag that ever surpassed imagination. She looked like a Cartier illustration. Her one good eye was jaundiced and mad; long, slanted—feline. It wasn't until long afterward that I realized that her pupil was not round but slitted—but not vertically like a cat's eyes, but horizontally. Her other eye looked like—well, I'd rather not say. It couldn't possibly have been of any use to her. Her nose would have been hooked if the tip were still on it. She was snaggle-toothed, and her fangs were orange. One shoulder was higher than the other, and the jagged lump on it spoke of a permanent dislocation. She had enough skin to adequately cover a sideshow fat lady, but she couldn't have weighed more than eighty pounds or so. I never saw great swinging wattles on a person's upper arms before. She was clad in a feathered jigsaw of bird and small animal skins. She was diseased and filthy and—and evil.

And she spoke to me in the most beautiful contralto voice I have ever heard.

"How you get away from River Spider?" she demanded.

"River Spider?"

She pointed, and I saw the sawyer rising slowly from the bayou. "Oh—that." I found that if I avoided that baleful eye I got my speech back. I controlled an impulse to yell at her, chase her away. If Patty woke up and saw that face—

"What's it to you?" I asked quietly, just managing to keep my voice steady.

"I send River Spider for you," she said in her Cajun accent.

"Why?" If I could mollify her—she was manifestly furious at something, and it seemed to be me—perhaps she'd go her way without waking the child.

"Because you mus' go!" she said. "This my countree. This swamp belong Séleen. Séleen belong this swamp. Wan man make *p'tit cabane* in bayou, Séleen *l'enchante.* Man die far away, smash."

"You mean you haunted the man who had my cabin built and he died?" I grinned. "Don't be silly."

"Man is dead, no?"

I nodded. "That don't cut ice with me, old lady. Now look—we aren't hurting your old swamp. We'll get out of it, sure; but we'll go when we're good and ready. You leave us alone and we'll sure as hell"—I shuddered, looking at her—"leave you alone."

"You weel go *now—ce jour!*" She screamed the last words, and the pile of moss behind me rustled suddenly.

"I won't go today or tomorrow or next week," I snapped. I stepped toward her threateningly. "Now beat it!"

She crouched like an animal, her long crooked hands half raised. From behind me the moss moved briskly, and Patty's voice said, "Daddy, what . . . oh. *Ohh!*"

That does it, I said to myself, and lunged at the old woman with some crazy idea of shoving her out of the clearing. She leaped aside like a jackrabbit and I tripped and fell on my two fists, which dug into my solar plexus agonizingly. I lay there mooing "uh! uh! u-u-uh!" trying to get some wind into my lungs, and finally managed to get an elbow down and heave myself over on my side. I looked, and saw Séleen crouched beside Patty. The kid sat there, white as a corpse, rigid with terror, while the old nightmare crooned to her in her lovely voice.

"Ah! *C'est une jolie jeune-fille, ça! Ah, ma petite, ma fleur douce, Séleen t'aime, trop, trop*—" and she put out her hand and stroked Patty's neck and shoulder.

When I saw the track of filth her hand left on the child's flesh, a white flame exploded in my head and dazzled me from inside. When I could see again I was standing beside Patty, the back of one hand aching and stinging; and Séleen was sprawled eight feet away, spitting out blood and yellow teeth and frightful curses.

"Go away." I whispered it because my throat was all choked up. "Get—out—of—here—before—I—kill you!"

She scrambled to her knees, her blazing eye filled with hate and terror, shook her fist and tottered swearing away into the heavy swamp growth.

When she had gone I slumped to the ground, drenched with sweat, cold outside, hot inside, weak as a newborn babe from reaction. Patty crawled to me, dropped her head in my lap, pressed the back of my hand to her face and sobbed so violently that I was afraid she would hurt herself. I lifted my hand and stroked her hair. "It's all right, now, Patty—don't be a little dope, now—come on," I said more firmly, lifting her face by its pointed chin and holding it until she opened her eyes. "Who's Yehudi?"

She gulped bravely. "Wh-who?" she gasped.

"The little man who turns on the light in the refrigerator when you open the door," I said. "Let's go find out what's for dinner."

"I ... I—" She puckered all up the way she used to do when she slept in a bassinet—what I used to call "baby's slow burn." And then she wailed the same way. "I don' want dinno-o-o!"

I thumped her on the back, picked her up and dropped her on top of her dungarees. "Put them pants on," I said, "and be a man." She did, but she cried quietly until I shook her and said gently, "Stop it now. I didn't carry on like that when I was a little girl." I got into my clothes and dumped her into the bow of the canoe and shoved off.

All the way back to the cabin I forced her to play one of our pet games. I would say something—anything—and she would try to say something that rhymed with it. Then it would be her turn. She had an extraordinary rhythmic sense, and an excellent ear.

I started off with "We'll go home and eat our dinners."

"An' Lord have mercy on us sinners," she cried. Then, "Let's see you find a rhyme for 'month'!"

"I bet I'll do it ... jutht thith onthe," I replied. "I guess I did it then, by cracky."

"Course you did, but then you're wacky. Top that, mister funny-lookin'!"

I pretended I couldn't, mainly because I couldn't, and she soundly kicked my shin as a penance. By the time we reached the cabin she was her usual self, and I found myself envying the resilience of youth. And she earned my undying respect by saying nothing to Anjy about the afternoon's events, even when Anjy looked us over and said, "Just look at you two filthy kids! What have you been doing—swimming in the bayou?"

"Daddy splashed me," said Patty promptly.

"And you had to splash him back. Why did he splash you?"

"'Cause I spit mud through my teeth at him to make him mad," said my outrageous child.

"Patty!"

"Mea culpa," I said, hanging my head. "'Twas I who spit the mud."

Anjy threw up her hands. "Heaven knows what sort of a woman Patty's going to grow up to be," she said, half angrily.

"A broad-minded and forgiving one like her lovely mother," I said quickly.

"Nice work, bud," said Patty.

Anjy laughed. "Outnumbered again. Come in and feed the face."

On my next trip into Minette I bought a sweet little S. & W. .38 and told Anjy it was for alligators. She was relieved.

I might have forgotten about the hag Séleen if it were not for the peculiar chain of incidents which had led to our being here. We had started with some vague idea of spending a couple of months in Natchez or New Orleans, but a gas station attendant had mentioned that there was a cabin in the swamps for rent very cheap down here. On investigation we found it not only unbelievably cheap, but deep in real taboo country. Not one of the natives, hardened swamp runners all, would go within a mile of it. It had been built on order for a very wealthy Northern gentleman who had never had a chance to use it, due to a swift argument he and his car had had one day when he turned out to pass a bridge. A drunken rice farmer told me that it was all the doing of the Witch of Minette, a semimythological local character who claimed possession of that corner of the country. I had my doubts, being a writer of voodoo stories and knowing therefore that witches and sech are nonsense.

After my encounter with Séleen I no longer doubted her authenticity as a horrid old nightmare responsible for the taboo. But she could rant, chant, and ha'nt from now till a week come Michaelmas—when *is* Michaelmas, anyway?—and never pry me loose from that cabin until I was ready to go. She'd have to fall back on enchantment to do it, too—of that I was quite, quite sure. I remembered her blazing eye as it had looked when I struck her, and I knew that she would never dare to come within my reach again. If she as much as came within my sight with her magics I had a little hocus-pocus of my own that I was sure was more powerful than anything she could dream up. I carried it strapped to my waist, in a holster, and while it couldn't call up any ghosts, it was pretty good at manufacturing 'em.

As for Patty, she bounced resiliently away from the episode. Séleen she dubbed the Witch of Endor, and used her in her long and involved games as an archvillain in place of Frankenstein's monster, Adolf Hitler, or Miss McCauley, her schoolteacher. Many an afternoon I watched her from the hammock on the porch, cooking up dark plots in the witch's behalf and then foiling them in her own coldbloodedly childish way. Once or twice I had to put a stop to it, like the time I caught her hanging the Witch of Endor in effigy, the effigy being a rag doll, its poor throat cut with benefit of much red paint. Aside from these games she never mentioned Séleen, and I respected her for it. I saw to it that she didn't stray alone into the swamp and relaxed placidly into my role of watchful skeptic. It's nice to feel oneself superior to a credulous child.

Foolish, too. I didn't suspect a thing when Patty crept up behind me and hacked off a lock of my hair with my hunting knife. She startled me and I tumbled out of the hammock onto my ear as she scuttled off. I muttered imprecations at the little demon as I got back into the hammock, and then comforted myself by the reflection that I was lucky to have an ear to fall on—that knife was sharp.

A few minutes later Anjy came out to the porch. Anjy got herself that name because she likes to wear dresses with masses of tiny pleats and things high on her throat, and great big picture hats. So *ingenue* just naturally became Anjy. She is a beautiful woman with infinite faith and infinite patience, the proof of which being that: a—she married me, and b—she stayed married to me.

"Jon, what sort of crazy game is your child playing?" She always said "your child" when she was referring to something about Patty she didn't like.

"S'matter?"

"Why, she just whipped out that hog-sticker of yours and made off with a hank of my hair."

"No! Son of a gun! What's she doing—taking up barbering? She just did the same thing to me. Thought she was trying to scalp me and miscalculated, but I must have been wrong—she wouldn't miss twice in a row."

"Well, I want you to take that knife away from her," said Anjy. "It's dangerous."

I got out of the hammock and stretched. "Got to catch her first. Which way'd she go?"

After a protracted hunt I found Patty engaged in some childish ritual of her own devising. She pushed something into a cleft at the foot of a tree, backed off a few feet, and spoke earnestly. Neither of us could hear a word she said. Then she backed still farther away and squatted down on her haunches, watching the hole at the foot of the tree carefully.

Anjy clasped her hands together nervously, opened her mouth. I put my hands over it. "Let me take care of it," I whispered, and went out.

"Whatcha doin', bud?" I called to Patty as I came up. She started violently and raised one finger to her lips. "Catchin' rabbits?" I asked as loudly as I could without shouting. She gestured me furiously away. I went and sat beside her.

"Please, daddy," she said. "I'm making a magic. It won't work if you stay here. Just this once—please!"

"Nuts," I said bluntly. "I chased all the magic away when I moved here."

She tried to be patient. "Will you *please* go away? Oh, daddy. Daddy, PLEASE!"

It was rough but I felt I had to do it. I lunged for her, swept her up, and carried her kicking and squalling back to the cabin. "Sorry, kiddo, but I don't like the sort of game you're playing. You ought to trust your dad."

I meant to leave her with Anjy while I went out to confiscate that bundle of hair. Not that I believe in such nonsense. But I'm the kind of unsuperstitious apple that won't walk under a ladder *just in case* there's something in the silly idea. But Patty really began to throw a whingding, and there was nothing for me to do but to stand by until it had run its course. Patty was such a good-natured child, and only good-natured children can work themselves up into that kind of froth. She screamed and she bit, and she accused us of spoiling everything and we didn't love her and she wished she was dead and why couldn't we leave her alone—"Let me alone," she shrieked, diving under the double bed and far beyond our reach. "Take your *hands* off me!" she sobbed when she was ten feet away from us and moving fast. And then her screams became wordless and agonized when we cornered her in the kitchen. We had to be rough to hold her, and her hysteria was agony to us. It took more than an hour for her fury to run its course and leave her weeping weak apologies and protestations of love into her mother's arms. Me, I was bruised outside and in, but inside it hurt the worst. I felt like a heel.

I went out then to the tree. I reached in the cleft for the hair but it was gone. My hand closed on something far larger, and I drew it out and stood up to look at it.

It was a toy canoe, perhaps nine inches long. It was an exquisite piece of work. It had apparently been carved painstakingly from a solid piece of cedar, so carefully that nowhere was the wood any more than an eighth of an inch thick. It was symmetrical and beautifully finished in brilliant colors. They looked to me like vegetable stains—dyes from the swamp plants that grew so riotously all around us. From stem to stern the gunwales were pierced, and three strips of brilliant bark had been laced and woven into the close-set holes. Inside the canoe were four wooden spurs projecting from the hull, the end of each having a hole drilled through it, apparently for the purpose of lashing something inside.

I puzzled over it for some minutes, turning it over and over in my hands, feeling its velvet smoothness, amazed by its metrical delicacy. Then I laid it carefully on the ground and regarded the mysterious tree.

Leafless branches told me it was dead. I got down on my knees and rummaged deep into the hole between the roots. I couldn't begin to touch the inside wall. I got up again, circled the tree. A low branch projected, growing sharply upward close to the trunk before it turned and spread outward. And around it were tiny scuff marks in the bark. I pulled myself up onto the branch, cast about for a handhold to go higher. There was none. Puzzled, I looked down—and there, completely hidden from the ground, was a gaping hole leading into the hollow trunk!

I thrust my head into it and then clutched the limb with both arms to keep from tottering out of the tree. For that hole reeked with the most sickly, noisome smell I had encountered since . . . since Patty and I—

Séleen!

I dropped to the ground and backed away from the tree. The whole world seemed in tune with my revulsion. What little breeze there had been had stopped, and the swampland was an impossible painting in which only I moved.

Never taking my eyes off the tree, I went back step by step, feeling behind me until my hand touched the wall of the cabin. My gaze still riveted to the dead bole of the tree, I felt along the wall until I came to the kitchen door. Reaching inside, I found my ax and raced back. The blade was keen and heavy, and the haft of it felt good to me. The wood was rotten, honeycombed, and the clean blade bit almost noiselessly into it. *Thunk!* How dare she, I thought. What does she mean by coming so near us! *Thunk!* I prayed that the frightful old hag would try to fight, to flee, so that I could cut her down with many strokes. It was my first experience with the killer instinct and I found it good.

The sunlight faded out of the still air and left it hotter.

At the uppermost range of my vision I could see the trunk trembling with each stroke of the ax. Soon, now—soon! I grinned and my lips cracked; every other inch of my body was soaking wet. She who would fill Patty's clean young heart with her filthy doings! Four more strokes would do it; and then I remembered that skinny hand reaching out, touching Patty's flesh; and I went cold all over. I raised the ax and heard it hiss through the thick air; and my four strokes were one. Almost without resistance that mighty stroke swished into and through the shattered trunk. The hurtling ax head swung me around as the severed tree settled onto its stump. It fell, crushing its weight into the moist earth, levering itself over on its projecting root; and the thick bole slid toward me, turned from it as I was, off balance. It caught me on the thigh, kicking out at me like a sentient, vicious thing. I turned over and over in the air and landed squashily at the edge of the bayou. But I landed with my eyes on the tree, ready to crawl, if need be, after whatever left it.

Nothing left it. Nothing. There had been nothing there, then, but the stink of her foul body. I lay there weakly, weeping with pain and reaction. And when I looked up again I saw Séleen again—or perhaps it was a crazed vision. She stood on a knoll far up the bayou, and as I watched she doubled up with silent laughter. Then she straightened and lifted her arm; and, dangling from her fingers, I saw the tiny bundle of hair. She laughed again though I heard not a sound. I knew then that she had seen every bit of it—had stood there grinning at my frantic destruction of her accursed tree. I lunged toward her, but she was far away, and across the water; and at my movement she vanished into the swamp.

I dragged myself to my feet and limped toward the cabin. I had to pass the tree, and as I did the little canoe caught my eye. I tucked it under my arm and crept back to the cabin. I tripped on the top step of the porch and fell sprawling, and I hadn't strength to rise. My leg was an agony, and my head spun and spun.

Then I was inside and Anjy was sponging off my head, and she laughed half hysterically when I opened my eyes. "Jon, Jon, beloved, what have you done? Who did this to you?"

"Who ... heh!" I said weakly. "A damn fool, sweetheart. Me!" I got up and stood rockily. "How's Pat?"

"Sleeping," said Anjy. "Jon, what on earth is happening?"

"I don't know," I said slowly, and looked out through the window at the fallen tree. "Anjy, the kid took that hair she swiped and probably some of her own and poked it all into that tree I just cut down. It—seems important for me to get it back. Dunno why. It ... anyway, I got out there as soon as we had Pat quieted, but the hair had disappeared in the meantime. All I found was this." I handed her the canoe.

She took it absently. "Pat told me her story. Of course it's just silly, but she says that for the past three days that tree has been talking to her. She says it sang to her and played with her. She's convinced it's a magic tree. She says it promised her a lovely present if she would poke three kinds of hair into a hole at the roots, but if she told anyone the magic wouldn't work." Anjy looked down at the little canoe and her forehead puckered. "Apparently it worked," she whispered.

I couldn't comment without saying something about Séleen, and I didn't want that on Anjy's mind, so I turned my back on her and stood looking out into the thick wet heat of the swamp.

Behind me I heard Patty stir, shriek with delight as she saw the canoe. "My present ... my pretty present! It was a *real* magic!" And Anjy gave it to her.

I pushed down an impulse to stop her. As long as Séleen had the hair the harm was done.

Funny, how suddenly I stopped being a skeptic.

The silence of the swamp was shattered by a great cloud of birds—birds of every imaginable hue and size, screaming and cawing and chuckling and whirring frantically. They startled me and I watched them for many minutes before it dawned on me that they were all flying one way. The air grew heavier after they had gone. Anjy came and stood beside me.

And then it started to rain.

I have never seen such rain, never dreamed of it. It thundered on the shingles, buckshotted the leaves of the trees, lashed the mirrored bayou and the ground alike, so that the swamp was but one vast brown stream of puckered mud.

Anjy clutched my arm. "Jon, I'm frightened!" I looked at her and knew that it wasn't the rain that had whitened her lips, lit the fires of terror in her great eyes. "Something out there—*hates* us," she said simply.

I shook her off, threw a poncho over me. "Jon—you're not—"

"I got to," I gritted. I went to the door, hesitated, turned back and pressed the revolver into her hand. "I'll be all right," I said, and flung out into the storm. Anjy didn't try to stop me.

I knew I'd find the hag Séleen. I knew I'd find her unharmed by the storm, for was it not a thing of her own devising? And I knew I must reach her—quickly, before she used that bundle of hair. Why, and how did I know? Ask away. I'm still asking myself, and I have yet to find an answer.

I stumbled and floundered, keeping to the high ground, guided, I think, by my hate. After a screaming eternity I reached a freakish rocky knoll that thrust itself out of the swamp. It was cloven and cracked, full of passages and potholes; and from an opening high on one side I saw the guttering glare of firelight. I crept up the rough slope and peered within.

She crouched over the flames, holding something to her withered breast and crooning to it. The rock walls gathered her lovely, hateful voice and threw it to me clear and strong—to me and to the turgid bayou that seethed past the cleft's lower edge.

She froze as my eyes fell upon her, sensing my presence; but like many another animal she hadn't wit enough to look upward. In a moment she visibly shrugged off the idea, and she turned and slid and shambled down toward the bayou. Above her, concealed by the split rock, I followed her until we were both at the water's edge with only a four-foot stone rampart between us. I could have reached her easily then, but I didn't dare attack until I knew where she had hidden that bundle of hair.

The wind moaned, rose an octave. The rain came in knives instead of sheets. I flattened myself against the rock while Séleen shrank back into the shelter of the crevice. I will never know how long we were there, Séleen and I, separated by a few boulders, hate a tangible thing between us. I remember only a shrieking hell of wind and rubble, and then the impact of something wet and writhing and whimpering against me. It had come rolling and tumbling down the rocky slope and it lodged against me. I was filled with horror until I realized that it sheltered me a little against the blast. I found the strength to turn and look at it finally. It was Patty.

I got her a little under me and stuck it out till the wind had done its work and was gone, and with it all the deafening noise—all but the rush of the bayou and Séleen's low chuckle.

"Daddy—" She was cut and battered. "I brought my little boat!" She held it up weakly.

"Yes, butch. Sure. That's dandy. Patty—what happened to mother?"

"She's back there," whimpered Patty. "The cabin sagged, like, an' began m-movin', an' then it just fell apart an' the bits all flew away. I couldn' find her so I came after you."

I lay still, not breathing. I think even my heart stopped for a little while.

Patty's whisper sounded almost happy. "Daddy—I—hurt—all—over—"

Anjy was gone then. I took my hatred instead, embraced it and let it warm me and give me life and hope and strength the way she used to. I crawled up the rock and looked over. I could barely see the hag, but she was there. Something out in the bayou was following the rhythmic movement of her arms. Something evil, tentacled, black. Her twisted claws clutched a tiny canoe like the one she had left in the tree for Patty. And she sang:

> River Spider, black and strong,
> Folks 'bout here have done me wrong.
> Here's a gif' I send to you,
> Got some work for you to do.
>
> If Anjy-woman miss the flood,
> River Spider, drink her blood.
> Little one was good to me,
> Drown her quick and let her be.
>
> River Spider, Jon you know,
> Kill that man, and—kill—him—slow!

99

And Séleen bent and set the canoe on the foaming brown water. Our hair was tied inside it.

Everything happened fast then. I dived from my hiding place behind and above her, and as I did so I sensed that Patty had crept up beside me, and that she had seen and heard it all. And some strange sense warned Séleen, for she looked over her crooked shoulder, saw me in midair, and leaped into the bayou. I had the terrified, malevolent gleam of her single eye full in my face, but I struck only hard rock, and for me even that baleful glow went out.

Patty sat cross-legged with my poor old head in her lap. It was such a gray morning that the wounds on her face and head looked black to me. I wasn't comfortable, because the dear child was rolling my head back and forth frantically in an effort to rouse me. The bones in my neck creaked as she did it and I knew they could hear it in Scranton, Pennsylvania. I transmitted a cautionary syllable but what she received was a regular houn'-dawg howl.

"Owoo! Pat—"

"Daddy! Oh, you're awake!" She mercifully stopped gyrating the world about my tattered ears.

"What happened?" I moaned, half sitting up. She was so delighted to see my head move that she scrambled out from under so that when the ache inside it pounded it back down, it landed stunningly on the rock.

"Daddy darling, I'm sorry. But you got to stop layin' around like that. It's time to get up!"

"Uh. How you know?"

"I'm hungry, that's how, so there."

I managed to sit up this time. I began to remember things and they hurt so much that the physical pain didn't matter any more. "Patty! We've got to get back to the cabin!"

She puckered up. I tried to grin at her and she tried to grin back, and there is no more tragedy left in the world for me after having seen that. I did a sort of upward totter and got what was left of my feet and legs under me. Both of us were a mess, but we could navigate.

We threaded our way back over a new, wrecked landscape. It was mostly climbing and crawling and once when Patty slipped and I reached for her I knocked the little canoe out of her hand. She actually broke and ran to pick it up. "Daddy! You got to be careful of this!"

I groaned. It was the last thing in the world I ever wanted to see. But then— Anjy had said that she should have it. And when she next dropped it I picked it up and handed it back to her. And then snatched it again.

"Patty! What's this?" I pointed to the little craft's cargo: a tiny bundle of hair.

"That's the little bag from the tree, silly."

"But how ... where ... I thought—"

"I made a magic," she said with finality. "Now please, daddy, don't stand here and talk. We have to get back to ... y-you know."

If you don't mind, I won't go into detail about how we dragged trees and rubbish away to find what was left of our cabin, and how we came upon the pathetic little heap of shingles and screening and furniture and how, wedged in the firm angle of two mortised two-by-fours, we found Anjy. What I felt when I when I lifted her limp body away from the rubble, when I kissed her pale lips—that is mine to remember. And what I felt when those lips returned my kiss—oh, so faintly and so tenderly—that, too, is mine.

We rested, the three of us, for five days. I found part of our store of canned goods and a fishing line, though I'm sorry now that we ate any of the fish, after what happened. And when the delirium was over, I got Patty's part of the story. I got it piecemeal, out of sequence, and only after the most profound cross-questioning. But the general drift was this:

She had indeed seen that strange performance in the rocky cleft by the bayou; but what is more, by her childish mysticism, she understood it. At least, her explanation is better than anything I could give. Patty was sure that the River Spider that had attacked us that time in the bayou was sent by Séleen, to whom she always referred as the Witch of Endor. "She did it before, daddy, I jus' betcha. But she didn't have anythin' strong enough for to put on the canoe." I have no idea what she did use—flies, perhaps, or frogs or crayfish.

"She hadda have some part of us to make the magic, an' she made me get it for her. She was goin' to put that li'l ol' hair ball in a canoe, an' if a River Spider caught it then the Spider would get us, too."

When I made that crazed leap for the old woman she had nowhere to go but into the bayou. Pat watched neither of us. She watched the canoe. She always claimed that she hooked it to shore with a stick, but I have a hunch that the little idiot plunged in after it. "They was one o' those big black sawyer things right there," she said, "an' it almos' catched the canoe. I had a lot of trouble." I'll bet she did.

"You know," she said pensively, "I was mad at that ol' Witch of Endor. That was a mean thing she tried to do to us. So I did the same thing to her. I catched the ugliest thing I could find—all crawly and nasty an' bad like the Witch of Endor. I found a nice horrid one, too, you betcha. An' I tied him into my canoe with your shoelaces, daddy. You di'n' say not to. An' I singed to it:

> Ol' Witch of Endor is your name,
> An' you an' Witchie is the same;
> Don't think it's a game.

She showed me later what sort of creature she had caught for her little voodoo boat. Some call it a mud puppy and some call it a hell-bender, but it is without doubt the homeliest thing ever created. It is a sort of aquatic salamander, anywhere from three inches to a foot and a half in length. It has a porous, tubercular skin with two lateral streamers of skin on each side; and these are always ragged and torn. The creature always looks as if it is badly hurt. It has almost infinitesimal fingered legs, and its black shoe-button eyes are smaller than the head of a hatpin. For the hag Séleen there could be no better substitute.

"Then," said Patty complacently, "I singed that song the way the Witch of Endor did:

> River Spider, black an' strong,
> Folks 'bout here have done me wrong.
> Here's a gif' I send to you,
> Got some work for you to do.

"The rest of the verse was silly," said Pat, "but I had to think real fast for a rhyme for 'Witch of Endor' an' I used the first thing that I could think of quicklike. It was somepin I read on your letters, daddy, an' it was silly."

And that's all she would say for the time being. But I do remember the time she called me quietly down to the bayou and pointed out a sawyer to me, because it was the day before Carson came in a power launch from Minette to see if we had survived the hurricane; and Carson came six days after the big blow. Patty made absolutely sure that her mother was out of hearing, and then drew me by the hand down to the water's edge. "Daddy," she said, "we got to keep this from mother on account of it would upset her," and she pointed.

Three or four black twisted branches showed on the water, and as I watched they began to rise. A huge sawyer, the biggest I'd ever seen, reared up and up—and tangled in its coils was a ... a *something*.

Séleen had not fared well, tangled in the whips of the River Spider under water for five days, in the company of all those little minnows and crawfish.

Patty regarded it critically while my stomach looped itself around violently and finally lodged between my spine and the skin of my back. "She ain't pretty a-*tall!*" said my darling daughter. "She's even homelier'n a mud puppy, I betcha."

As we walked back toward the lean-to we had built, she prattled on in this fashion: "Y'know, daddy, that was a real magic. I thought my verse was a silly one but I guess it worked out right after all. Will you laugh if I tell you what it was?"

I said I did not feel like laughing.

"Well," said Patty shyly, "I said:

> Spider, kill the Witch of Endor
> If five days lapse, return to sender.

That's my daughter.

Killdozer!

Before the race was the deluge, and before the deluge another race, whose nature it is not for mankind to understand. Not unearthly, not alien, for this was their earth and their home.

There was a war between this race, which was a great one, and another. The other was truly alien, a sentient cloudform, an intelligent grouping of tangible electrons. It was spawned in mighty machines by some accident of a science beyond our aboriginal conception of technology. And then the machines, servants of the people, became the people's masters, and great were the battles that followed. The electron-beings had the power to warp the delicate balances of atom-structure, and their life-medium was metal, which they permeated and used to their own ends. Each weapon the people developed was possessed and turned against them, until a time when the remnants of that vast civilization found a defense—

An insulator. The terminal product or by-product of all energy research—neutronium.

In its shelter they developed a weapon. What it was we shall never know, and our race will live—or we shall know, and our race will perish as theirs perished. Sent to destroy the enemy, it got out of hand and its measureless power destroyed them with it, and their cities, and their possessed machines. The very earth dissolved in flame, the crust writhed and shook and the oceans boiled. Nothing escaped it, nothing that we know as life, and nothing of the pseudo-life that had evolved within the mysterious force-fields of their incomprehensible machines, save one hardy mutant.

Mutant it was, and ironically this one alone could have been killed by the first simple measures used against its kind—but it was past time for simple expediences. It was an organized electron-field possessing intelligence and mobility and a will to destroy, and little else.

Stunned by the holocaust, it drifted over the grumbling globe, and in a lull in the violence of the forces gone wild on Earth, sank to the steaming ground in its half-conscious exhaustion. There it found shelter—shelter built by and for its dead enemies. An envelope of neutronium. It drifted in, and its consciousness at last fell to its lowest ebb. And there it lay while the neutronium, with its strange constant flux, its interminable striving for perfect balance, extended itself and closed the opening. And thereafter in the turbulent eons that followed, the envelope tossed like a gray bubble on the surface of the roiling sphere, for no substance on Earth would have it or combine with it.

The ages came and went, and chemical action and reaction did their mysterious work, and once again there was life and evolution. And a tribe found the mass of neutronium, which is not a substance but a static force, and were awed by its aura of indescribable chill, and they worshiped it and built a temple around it and made sacrifices to it. And ice and fire and the seas came and went, and the land rose and fell as the years went by, until the ruined temple was on a knoll, and the knoll was an island. Islanders came and went, lived and built and died, and races forgot. So now, somewhere in the Pacific to the west of the archipelago called Islas Revillagigeda, there was an uninhabited island. And one day—

CHUB HORTON AND Tom Jaeger stood watching the *Sprite* and her squat tow of three cargo lighters dwindle over the glassy sea. The big ocean-going towboat and her charges seemed to be moving out of focus rather than traveling away. Chub spat cleanly around the cigar that grew out of the corner of his mouth.

"That's that for three weeks. How's it feel to be a guinea pig?"

"We'll get it done." Tom had little crinkles all around the outer ends of his eyes. He was a head taller than Chub and rangy, and not so tough, and he was a real operator. Choosing him as a foreman for the experiment had been wise, for he was competent and he commanded respect. The theory of airfield construction that they were testing appealed vastly to him, for here were no officers-in-charge, no government inspectors, no time-keeping or reports. The government had allowed the company a temporary land grant, and the idea was to put production-line techniques into the layout and grading of the project. There were six operators and two mechanics and more than a million dollars' worth of the best equipment that money could buy. Government acceptance was to be on a partially completed basis, and contingent on government standards. The theory obviated both goldbricking and graft, and neatly sidestepped the man-power problem. "When that black-topping crew gets here, I reckon we'll be ready for 'em," said Tom.

He turned and scanned the island with an operator's vision and saw it as it was, and in all the stages it would pass through, and as it would look when they had finished, with five thousand feet of clean-draining runway, hard-packed shoulders, four acres of plane-park, the access road and the short taxiway. He saw the lay of each lift that the power shovel would cut as it brought down the marl bluff, and the ruins on top of it that would give them stone to haul down the salt-flat to the little swamp at the other end, there to be walked in by the dozers.

"We got time to run the shovel up there to the bluff before dark."

They walked down the beach toward the outcropping where the equipment stood surrounded by crates and drums of supplies. The three tractors were ticking over quietly, the two-cycle Diesel chuckling through their mufflers and the big D-7 whacking away its metronomic compression knock on every easy revolution. The Dumptors were lined up and silent, for they would not be ready to work until the shovel was ready to load them. They looked like a mechanical interpretation of Dr. Dolittle's "Pushme-pullyou," the fantastic animal with two front ends. They had two large driving wheels and two small steerable wheels. The motor and the driver's seat were side by side over the front—or smaller—wheels; but the driver faced the dump body between the big rear wheels, exactly the opposite of the way he would sit in a dump truck. Hence, in traveling from shovel to dumping-ground, the operator drove backwards, looking over his shoulder, and in dumping he backed the machine up but he himself traveled forward—quite a trick for fourteen hours a day! The shovel squatted in the midst of all the others, its great hulk looming over them, humped there with its boom low and its iron chin on the ground, like some great tired dinosaur.

Rivera, the Puerto Rican mechanic, looked up grinning as Tom and Chub approached, and stuck a bleeder wrench into the top pocket of his coveralls.

"She says 'Sigalo,'" he said, his white teeth flashlighting out of the smear of grease across his mouth. "She says she wan' to get dirt on dis paint." He kicked the blade of the Seven with his heel.

Tom sent the grin back—always a surprising thing in his grave face.

"That Seven'll do that, and she'll take a good deal off her bitin' edge along with the paint before we're through. Get in the saddle, Goony. Build a ramp off the rocks down to the flat there, and blade us off some humps from here to the bluff yonder. We're walking the dipper up there."

The Puerto Rican was in the seat before Tom had finished, and with a roar the Seven spun in its length and moved back along the outcropping to the inland edge. Rivera dropped his blade and the sandy marl curled and piled up in front of the dozer, loading the blade and running off in two even rolls at the ends. He shoved the load toward the rocky edge, the Seven revving down as it took the load, *blat blat blatting* and pulling like a supercharged ox as it fired slowly enough for them to count the revolutions.

"She's a hunk of machine," said Tom.

"A hunk of operator, too," gruffed Chub, and added, "for a mechanic."

"The boy's all right," said Kelly. He was standing there with them, watching the Puerto Rican operate the dozer, as if he had been there all along, which was the way Kelly always arrived places. He was tall, slim, with green eyes too long and an easy stretch to the way he moved, like an attenuated cat. He said, "Never thought I'd see the day when equipment was shipped set up ready to run like this. Guess no one ever thought of it before."

"There's times when heavy equipment has to be unloaded in a hurry these days," Tom said. "If they can do it with tanks, they can do it with construction equipment. We're doin' it to build something instead, is all. Kelly, crank up the shovel. It's oiled. We're walking it over to the bluff."

Kelly swung up into the cab of the big dipper-stick and, diddling the governor control, pulled up the starting handle. The Murphy Diesel snorted and settled down into a thudding idle. Kelly got into the saddle, set up the throttle a little, and began to boom up.

"I still can't get over it," said Chub. "Not more'n a year ago we'd a had two hundred men on a job like this."

Tom smiled. "Yeah, and the first thing we'd have done would be to build an office building, and then quarters. Me, I'll take this way. No timekeepers, no equipment-use reports, no progress and yardage summaries, no nothin' but eight men, a million bucks worth of equipment, an' three weeks. A shovel an' a mess of tool crates'll keep the rain off us, an' army field rations'll keep our bellies full. We'll get it done, we'll get out and we'll get paid."

Rivera finished the ramp, turned the Seven around and climbed it, walking the new fill down. At the top he dropped his blade, floated it, and backed down the ramp, smoothing out the rolls. At a wave from Tom he started out across the shore, angling up toward the bluff, beating out the humps and carrying fill into the hollows. As he worked, he sang, feeling the beat of the mighty motor, the micrometric obedience of that vast implacable machine.

"Why doesn't that monkey stick to his grease guns?"

Tom turned and took the chewed end of a match stick out of his mouth. He said nothing, because he had for some time been trying to make a habit of saying nothing to Joe Dennis. Dennis was an ex-accountant, drafted out of an office at the last gasp of a defunct project in the West Indies. He had become an operator because they needed operators badly. He had been released with alacrity from the office because of his propensity for small office politics. It was a game he still played, and completely aside from his boiled-looking red face and his slightly womanish walk, he was out of place in the field; for boot-licking and back-stabbing accomplish even less out on the field than they do in an office. Tom, trying so hard to keep his mind on his work, had to admit to himself that of all Dennis' annoying traits the worst was that he was as good a pan operator as could be found anywhere, and no one could deny it.

Dennis certainly didn't.

"I've seen the day when anyone catching one of those goonies so much as sitting on a machine during lunch would kick his fanny," Dennis groused. "Now they give 'em a man's work and a man's pay."

"*Doin'* a man's work, ain't he?" Tom said.

"He's a damn Puerto Rican!"

Tom turned and looked at him levelly. "Where was it you said you come from," he mused. "Oh yeah. Georgia."

"What do you mean by that?"

Tom was already striding away. "Tell you as soon as I have to," he flung back over his shoulder. Dennis went back to watching the Seven.

Tom glanced at the ramp and then waved Kelly on. Kelly set his housebrake so the shovel could not swing, put her into travel gear, and shoved the swing lever forward. With a crackling of drive chains and a massive scrunching of compacting coral sand, the shovel's great flat pads carried her over and down the ramp. As she tipped over the peak of the ramp the heavy manganese steel bucket-door gaped open and closed, like a hungry mouth, slamming up against the bucket until suddenly it latched shut and was quiet. The big Murphy Diesel crooned hollowly under compression as the machine ran downgrade and then the sensitive governor took hold and it took up its belly-beating thud.

Peebles was standing by one of the dozer-pan combines, sucking on his pipe and looking out to sea. He was grizzled and heavy, and from under the bushiest gray brows looked the calmest gray eyes Tom had ever seen. Peebles had never gotten angry at a machine—a rare trait in a born mechanic—and in fifty-odd years he had learned it was even less use getting angry at a man. Because no matter what, you could always fix what was wrong with a machine. He said around his pipestem:

"Hope you'll give me back my boy, there."

Tom's lips quirked in a little grin. There had been an understanding between old Peebles and himself ever since they had met. It was one of those things which exists unspoken—they knew little about each other because they had never found it necessary to make small talk to keep their friendship extant. It was enough to know that each could expect the best from the other, without persuasion.

"Rivera?" Tom asked. "I'll chase him back as soon as he finishes that service road for the dipper-stick. Why—got anything on?"

"Not much. Want to get that arc welder drained and flushed and set up a grounded table in case you guys tear anything up." He paused. "Besides, the kid's filling his head up with too many things at once. Mechanicing is one thing; operating is something else."

"Hasn't got in his way much so far, has it?"

"Nope. Don't aim t' let it, either. 'Less you need him."

Tom swung up on the pan tractor. "I don't need him that bad, Peeby. If you want some help in the meantime, get Dennis."

Peebles said nothing. He spat. He didn't say anything at all.

"What's the matter with Dennis?" Tom wanted to know.

"Look yonder," said Peebles, waving his pipestem. Out on the beach Dennis was talking to Chub, in Dennis' indefatigable style, standing beside Chub, one hand on Chub's shoulder. As they watched they saw Dennis call his side-kick, Al Knowles.

"Dennis talks too much," said Peebles. "That most generally don't amount to much, but that Dennis, he sometimes says too much. Ain't got what it takes to run a show, and knows it. Makes up for it by messin' in between folks."

"He's harmless," said Tom.

Still looking up the beech, Peebles said slowly:

"Is, so far."

Tom started to say something, then shrugged. "I'll send you Rivera," he said, and opened the throttle. Like a huge electric dynamo, the two-cycle motor whined to a crescendo. Tom lifted the dozer with a small lever by his right thigh and raised the pan with the long control sprouting out from behind his shoulder. He moved off, setting the rear gate of the scraper so that anything the blade bit would run off to the side instead of loading into the pan. He slapped the tractor into sixth gear and whined up to and around the crawling shovel, cutting neatly in under the boom and running on ahead with his scraper blade just touching the ground, dragging to a fine grade the service road Rivera had cut.

Dennis was saying, "It's that little Hitler stuff. Why should I take that kind of talk? 'You come from Georgia,' he says. What is he— a Yankee or something?"

"A crackah f'm Macon," chortled Al Knowles, who came from Georgia, too. He was tall and stringy and round-shouldered. All of his skill was in his hands and feet, brains being a commodity he had lived without all his life until he had met Dennis and used him as a reasonable facsimile thereof.

"Tom didn't mean nothing by it," said Chub.

"No, he didn't mean nothin'. Only that we do what he says the way he says it, specially if he finds a way we don't like it. *You* wouldn't do like that, Chub. Al, think Chub would carry on thataway?"

"Sure wouldn't," said Al, feeling it expected of him.

"Nuts," said Chub, pleased and uncomfortable, and thinking, what have I got against Tom?—not knowing, not liking Tom as well as he had. "Tom's the man here, Dennis. We got a job to do—let's skit and git. Man can take anything for a lousy six weeks."

"Oh, sho'," said Al.

"Man can take just so much," Dennis said. "What they put a man like that on top for, Chub? What's the matter with you? Don't you know grading and drainage as good as Tom? Can Tom stake out a side hill like you can?"

"Sure, sure, but what's the difference, long as we get a field built? An' anyhow, hell with bein' the boss-man. Who gets the blame if things don't run right, anyway?"

Dennis stepped back, taking his hand off Chub's shoulder, and stuck an elbow in Al's ribs.

"You see that, Al? Now there's a smart man. That's the thing Uncle Tom didn't bargain for. Chub, you can count on Al and me to do just that little thing."

"Do just what little thing?" asked Chub, genuinely puzzled.

"Like you said. If the job goes wrong, the boss gets blamed. So, if the boss don't behave, the job goes wrong."

"Uh-huh," agreed Al with the conviction of mental simplicity.

Chub double-took this extraordinary logical process and grasped wildly at anger as the conversation slid out from under him. "I didn't say any such thing! This job is goin' to get done, no matter what! There'll be no damn goldbrick badge on me or anybody else around here if I can help it."

"Tha's the ol' fight," feinted Dennis. "We'll show that guy what we think of his kind of slowdown."

"You talk too much," said Chub and escaped with the remnants of coherence. Every time he talked with Dennis he walked away feeling as if he had an unwanted membership card stuck in his pocket that he couldn't throw away with a clear conscience.

Rivera ran his road up under the bluff, swung the Seven around, punched out the master clutch and throttled down, idling. Tom was making his pass with the pan, and as he approached, Rivera slipped out of the seat and behind the tractor, laying a sensitive hand on the final drive casing and sprocket bushings, checking for overheating. Tom pulled alongside and beckoned him up on the pan tractor.

"*Que pase,* Goony? Anything wrong?"

Rivera shook his head and grinned. "Nothing wrong. She is perfect, that '*De Siete*.' She—"

"That what? 'Daisy Etta'?"

"*De siete.* In Spanish, D-7. It means something in English?"

"Got you wrong," smiled Tom. "But Daisy Etta is a girl's name in English, all the same."

He shifted the pan tractor into neutral and engaged the clutch, and jumped off the machine. Rivera followed. They climbed aboard the Seven, Tom at the controls.

Rivera said "Daisy Etta," and grinned so widely that a soft little clucking noise came from behind his back teeth. He reached out his hand, crooked his little finger around one of the tall steering clutch levers, and pulled it all the way back. Tom laughed outright.

"You got something there," he said. "The easiest runnin' cat ever built. Hydraulic steerin', clutches and brakes that'll bring you to a dead stop if you spit on 'em. Forward an' reverse lever so's you got all your speeds front and backwards. A little different from the old jobs. They had no booster springs, eight-ten years ago; took a sixty-pound pull to get a steerin' clutch back. Cuttin' a side-hill with an angle-dozer really was a job in them days. You try it sometime, dozin' with one hand, holdin' her nose out o' the bank with the other, ten hours a day. And what'd it get you? Eighty cents an hour an' "— Tom took his cigarette and butted the fiery end out against the horny palm of his hand—"these."

"Santa Maria!"

"Want to talk to you, Goony. Want to look over the bluff, too, at the stone up there. It'll take Kelly pret' near an hour to get this far and sumped in, anyhow."

They growled up the slope, Tom feeling the ground under the four-foot brush, taking her up in a zigzag course like a hairpin road on a mountainside. Though the Seven carried a muffler on the exhaust stack that stuck up out of the hood before them, the blat of the four big cylinders hauling fourteen tons of steel upgrade could outshout any man's conversation, so they sat without talking. Tom driving, Rivera watching his hands flick over the controls.

The bluff started in a low ridge running almost the length of the little island, like a lopsided backbone. Toward the center it rose abruptly, sent a wing out toward the rocky outcropping at the beach where their equipment had been unloaded, and then rose again to a small, almost square plateau area, half a mile across. It was humpy and rough until they could see all of it, when they realized how incredibly level it was, under the brush and ruins that covered it. In the center—and exactly in the center they realized suddenly—was a low, overgrown mound. Tom threw out the clutch and revved her down.

"Survey report said there was stone up here," Tom said, vaulting out of the seat. "Let's walk around some."

They walked toward the knoll, Tom's eyes casting about as he went. He stooped down into the heavy, short grass and scooped up a piece of stone, blue-gray, hard and brittle.

"Rivera—look at this. This is what the report was talking about. See—more of it. All in small pieces, though. We need big stuff for the bog if we can get it."

"Good stone?" asked Rivera.

"Yes, boy—but it don't belong here. Th' whole island's sand and marl and sandstone on the outcrop down yonder. This here's a bluestone, like a diamond clay. Harder'n blazes. I never saw this stuff on a marl hill before. Or near one. Anyhow, root around and see if there is any big stuff."

They walked on. Rivera suddenly dipped down and pulled grass aside.

"Tom—here's a beeg one."

Tom came over and looked down at the corner of stone sticking up out of the topsoil. "Yeh. Goony, get your girlfriend over here and we'll root it out."

Rivera sprinted back to the idling dozer and climbed aboard. He brought the machine over to where Tom waited, stopped, stood up and peered over the front of the machine to locate the stone, then sat down and shifted gears. Before he could move the machine Tom was on the fender beside him, checking him with a hand on his arm.

"No, boy—no. Not third. First. And half throttle. That's it. Don't try to bash a rock out of the ground. Go on up to it easy; set your blade against it, lift it out, don't boot it out. Take it with the middle of your blade, not the corner—get the load on both hydraulic cylinders. Who told you to do like that?"

"No one tol' me, Tom. I see a man do it, I do it."

"Yeah? Who was it?"

"Dennis, but—"

"Listen, Goony, if you want to learn anything from Dennis, watch him while he's on a pan. He dozes like he talks. That reminds me— what I wanted to talk to you about. You ever have any trouble with him?"

Rivera spread his hands. "How I have trouble when he never talk to me?"

"Well, that's all right then. You keep it that way. Dennis is O.K., I guess, but you better keep away from him."

He went on to tell the boy then about what Peebles had said concerning being an operator and a mechanic at the same time. Rivera's lean dark face fell, and his hand strayed to the blade control, touching

it lightly, feeling the composition grip and the machined locknuts
that held it. When Tom had quite finished he said:

"O.K., Tom—if you want, you break 'em, I feex 'em. But if you
wan' help some time, I run *Daisy Etta* for you, no?"

"Sure, kid, sure. But don't forget, no man can do everything."

"You can do everything," said the boy.

Tom leaped off the machine and Rivera shifted into first and crept
up to the stone, setting the blade gently against it. Taking the load,
the mighty engine audibly bunched its muscles; Rivera opened the
throttle a little and the machine set solidly against the stone, the
tracks slipping, digging into the ground, piling loose earth up behind.
Tom raised a fist, thumb up, and the boy began lifting his blade. The
Seven lowered her snout like an ox pulling through mud; the front
of the tracks buried themselves deeper and the blade slipped upward
an inch on the rock, as if it were on a ratchet. The stone shifted, and
suddenly heaved itself up out of the earth that covered it, bulging
the sod aside like a ship's slow bow-wave. And the blade lost its grip
and slipped over the stone. Rivera slapped out the master clutch
within an ace of letting the mass of it poke through his radiator core.
Reversing, he set the blade against it again and rolled it at last into
daylight.

Tom stood staring at it, scratching the back of his neck. Rivera
got off the machine and stood beside him. For a long time they said
nothing.

The stone was roughly rectangular, shaped like a brick with one
end cut at about a thirty-degree angle. And on the angled face was
a square-cut ridge, like the tongue on a piece of milled lumber. The
stone was 3 x 3 x 2 feet, and must have weighed six or seven hundred pounds.

"Now that," said Tom, bug-eyed, "didn't grow *here*, and if it did
it never grew that way."

"*Una piedra de una casa,*" said Rivera softly. "Tom, there was a
building here, no?"

Tom turned suddenly to look at the knoll.

"There is a building here—or what's left of it. Lord on'y knows
how old—"

They stood there in the slowly dwindling light, staring at the knoll; and there came upon them a feeling of oppression, as if there were no wind and no sound anywhere. And yet there was a wind, and behind them *Daisy Etta* whacked away with her muttering idle, and nothing had changed and—was that it? That nothing had changed? That nothing would change, or could, here?

Tom opened his mouth twice to speak, and couldn't, or didn't want to—he didn't know which. Rivera slumped down suddenly on his hunkers, back erect, and his eyes wide.

It grew very cold. "It's cold," Tom said, and his voice sounded harsh to him. And the wind blew warm on them, the earth was warm under Rivera's knees. The cold was not a lack of heat, but a lack of something else—warmth, but the specific warmth of life-force, perhaps. The feeling of oppression grew, as if their recognition of the strangeness of the place had started it, and their increasing sensitivity to it made it grow.

Rivera said something, quietly, in Spanish.

"What are you looking at?" asked Tom.

Rivera started violently, threw up an arm, as if to ward off the crash of Tom's voice.

"I . . . there is nothin' to see, Tom. I feel this way wance before. I dunno—" He shook his head, his eyes wide and blank. "An' after, there was being wan hell of a thunderstorm—" His voice petered out.

Tom took his shoulder and hauled him roughly to his feet. "Goony! You slap-happy?"

The boy smiled, almost gently. The down on his upper lip held little spheres of sweat. "I ain' nothin', Tom. I'm jus' scare like hell."

"You scare yourself right back up there on that cat and git to work," Tom roared. More quietly then, he said, "I know there's something—wrong—here, Goony, but that ain't goin' to get us a runway built. Anyway, I know what to do about a dawg 'at gits gun-shy. Ought to be able to do as much fer you. Git along to th' mound now and see if it ain't a cache o' big stone for us. We got a swamp down there to fill."

Rivera hesitated, started to speak, swallowed and then walked slowly over to Seven. Tom stood watching him, closing his mind to the impalpable pressure of something, somewhere near, making his guts cold.

The bulldozer nosed over to the mound, grunting, reminding Tom suddenly that the machine's Spanish slang name was *puerco*—pig, boar. Rivera angled into the edge of the mound with the cutting corner of the blade. Dirt and brush curled up, fell away from the mound and loaded from the bank side, out along the moldboard. The boy finished his pass along the mound, carried the load past it and wasted it out on the flat, turned around and started back again.

Ten minutes later Rivera struck stone, the manganese steel screaming along it, a puff of gray dust spouting from the cutting corner. Tom knelt and examined it after the machine had passed. It was the same kind of stone they had found out on the flat—and shaped the same way. But here it was a wall, the angled faces of the block ends obviously tongued and grooved together.

Cold, cold as—

Tom took one deep breath and wiped sweat out of his eyes.

"I don't care," he whispered, "I got to have that stone. I got to fill me a swamp." He stood back and motioned to Rivera to blade into a chipped crevice in the buried wall.

The Seven swung into the wall and stopped while Rivera shifted into first, throttled down and lowered his blade. Tom looked up into his face. The boy's lips were white. He eased in the master clutch, the blade dipped and the corner swung neatly into the crevice.

The dozer blatted protestingly and began to crab sideways, pivoting on the end of the blade. Tom jumped out of the way, ran around behind the machine, which was almost parallel with the wall now, and stood in the clear, one hand raised ready to signal, his eyes on the straining blade. And then everything happened at once.

With a toothy snap the block started and came free, pivoting outward from its square end, bringing with it its neighbor. The block above them dropped, and the whole mound seemed to settle. And *something* whooshed out of the black hole where the rocks had been. Something like a fog, but not a fog that could be seen, something huge that could not be measured. With it came a gust of that cold which was not cold, and the smell of ozone, and the prickling crackle of a mighty static discharge.

Tom was fifty feet from the wall before he knew he had moved. He stopped and saw the Seven suddenly buck like a wild stallion, once, and Rivera turning over twice in the air. Tom shouted some meaningless syllable and tore over to the boy, where he sprawled in the rough grass, lifted him in his arms, and ran. Only then did he realize that he was running from the machine.

It was like a mad thing. Its moldboard rose and fell. It curved away from the mound, howling governor gone wild, controls flailing. The blade dug repeatedly into the earth, gouging it up in great dips through which the tractor plunged, clanking and bellowing furiously. It raced away in a great irregular arc, turned and came snorting back to the mound, where it beat at the buried wall, slewed and scraped and roared.

Tom reached the edge of the plateau sobbing for breath, and kneeling, laid the boy gently down on the grass.

"Goony, boy ... hey—"

The long silken eyelashes fluttered, lifted. Something wrenched in Tom as he saw the eyes, rolled right back so that only the whites showed. Rivera drew a long quivering breath which caught suddenly. He coughed twice, threw his head from side to side so violently that Tom took it between his hands and steadied it.

"*Ay ...Maria madre ...que me pasado*, Tom—w'at has happen to me?"

"Fell off the Seven, stupid. You ...how you feel?"

Rivera scrabbled at the ground, got his elbows half under him, then sank back weakly. "Feel O.K. Headache like hell. W-w'at happen to my feets?"

"Feet? They hurt?"

"No hurt—" The young face went gray, the lips tightened with effort. "No nothin', Tom."

"You can't move 'em?"

Rivera shook his head, still trying. Tom stood up. "You take it easy. I'll go get Kelly. Be right back."

He walked very quickly and when Rivera called to him he did not turn around. Tom had seen a man with a broken back before.

At the edge of the little plateau Tom stopped, listening. In the deepening twilight he could see the bulldozer standing by the mound. The motor was running; she had not stalled herself. But what stopped Tom was that she wasn't idling, but revving up and down as if an impatient hand were on the throttle—*hroom hrooom,* running up and up far faster than even a broken governor should permit, then coasting down to near silence, broken by the explosive punctuation of sharp and irregular firing. Then it would run up and up again, almost screaming, sustaining a r.p.m. that threatened every moving part, shaking the great machine like some deadly ague.

Tom walked swiftly toward the Seven, a puzzled and grim frown on his weather-beaten face. Governors break down occasionally, and once in a while you will have a motor tear itself to pieces, revving up out of control. But it will either do that or it will rev down and quit. If an operator is fool enough to leave his machine with the master clutch engaged, the machine will take off and run the way the Seven had—but it will not turn unless the blade corner catches in something unresisting, and then the chances are very strong that it will stall. But in any case, it was past reason for any machine to act this way, revving up and down, running, turning, lifting and dropping the blade.

The motor slowed as he approached, and at last settled down into something like a steady and regular idle. Tom had the sudden crazy impression that it was watching him. He shrugged off the feeling, walked up and laid a hand on the fender.

The Seven reacted like a wild stallion. The big Diesel roared, and Tom distinctly saw the master clutch lever snap back over center. He leaped clear, expecting the machine to jolt forward, but apparently it was in a reverse gear, for it shot backwards, one track locked, and the near end of the blade swung in a swift vicious arc, breezing a bare fraction of an inch past his hip as he danced back out of the way.

And as if it had bounced off a wall, the tractor had shifted and was bearing down on him, the twelve-foot blade rising, the two big headlights looming over him on their bow-legged supports, looking like the protruding eyes of some mighty toad. Tom had no choice but to leap straight up and grasp the top of the blade in his two hands, leaning back hard to brace his feet against the curved moldboard. The blade dropped and sank into the soft topsoil, digging a deep little swale in the ground. The earth loading on the moldboard rose and churned around Tom's legs; he stepped wildly, keeping them clear of the rolling drag of it. Up came the blade then, leaving a four-foot pile at the edge of the pit; down and up the tractor raced as the tracks went into it; up and up as they climbed the pile of dirt. A quick balance and overbalance as the machine lurched up and over like a motorcycle taking a jump off a ramp, and then a spine-shaking crash as fourteen tons of metal smashed blade-first into the ground.

Part of the leather from Tom's tough palms stayed with the blade as he was flung off. He went head over heels backwards, but had his feet gathered and sprang as they touched the ground; for he knew that no machine could bury its blade like that and get out easily. He leaped to the top of the blade, got one hand on the radiator cap, vaulted. Perversely, the cap broke from its hinge and came away in his hand, in that split instant when only that hand rested on anything. Off balance, he landed on his shoulder with his legs flailing the air, his body sliding off the hood's smooth shoulder toward the track now churning the earth beneath. He made a wild grab at the air intake pipe, barely had it in his fingers when the dozer freed itself and shot backwards up and over the hump. Again that breathless fight pivoting over the top, and the clanking crash as the machine landed, this time almost flat on its tracks.

The jolt tore Tom's hand away, and as he slid back over the hood the crook of his elbow caught the exhaust stack, the dull red metal biting into his flesh. He grunted and clamped the arm around it. His momentum carried him around it, and his feet crashed into the steering clutch levers. Hooking one with his instep, he doubled his legs and whipped himself back, scrabbling at the smooth warm metal, crawling frantically backward until he finally fell heavily into the seat.

"Now," he gritted through the red wall of pain, "you're gonna git operated." And he kicked out the master clutch.

The motor wailed, with the load taken off so suddenly. Tom grasped the throttle, his thumb down on the ratchet release, and he shoved the lever forward to shut off the fuel.

It wouldn't shut off; it went down to a slow idle, but it would-n't shut off.

"There's one thing you can't do without," he muttered, "com-pression."

He stood up and leaned around the dash, reaching for the com-pression-release lever. As he came up out of the seat, the engine revved up again. He turned to the throttle, which had snapped back into the "open" position. As his hand touched it the master clutch lever snapped in and the howling machine lurched forward with a jerk that snapped his head on his shoulders and threw him heavily back into the seat. He snatched at the hydraulic blade control and threw it to "float" position; and then as the falling moldboard touched the ground, into "power down." The cutting edge bit into the ground and the engine began to labor. Holding the blade control, he pushed the throttle forward with his other hand. One of the steering clutch levers whipped back and struck him agonizingly on the kneecap. He involuntarily let go of the blade control and the moldboard began to rise. The engine began to turn faster and he realized that it was not responding to the throttle. Cursing, he leaped to his feet; the sud-denly flailing steering clutch levers struck him three times in the groin before he could get between them.

Blind with pain, Tom clung gasping to the dash. The oil-pressure gauge fell off the dash to his right, with a tinkling of broken glass, and from its broken quarter-inch line scalding oil drenched him. The shock of it snapped back his wavering consciousness. Ignoring the blows of the left steering clutch and the master clutch which had started the same mad punching, he bent over the left end of the dash and grasped the compression lever. The tractor rushed forward and spun sicken-ingly, and Tom knew he was thrown. But as he felt himself leave the decking his hand punched the compression lever down. The great valves at the cylinder heads opened and locked open; atomized fuel and superheated air chattered out, and as Tom's head and shoulders struck the ground the great wild machine rolled to a stop, stood silently except for the grumble of water boiling in the cooling system.

Minutes later Tom raised his head and groaned. He rolled over and sat up, his chin on his knees, washed by wave after wave of pain.

As they gradually subsided, he crawled to the machine and pulled himself to his feet, hand over hand on the track. And groggily he began to cripple the tractor, at least for the night.

He opened the cock under the fuel tank, left the warm yellow fluid gushing out on the ground. He opened the drain on the reservoir by the injection pump. He found a piece of wire in the crank box and with it tied down the compression release lever. He crawled up on the machine, wrenched the hood and ball jar off the air intake precleaner, pulled off his shirt and stuffed it down the pipe. He pushed the throttle all the way forward and locked it with the locking pin. And he shut off the fuel on the main line from the tank to the pump.

Then he climbed heavily to the ground and slogged back to the edge of the plateau where he had left Rivera.

They didn't know Tom was hurt until an hour and a half later— there had been too much to do—rigging a stretcher for the Puerto Rican, building him a shelter, an engine crate with an Army pup tent for a roof. They brought out the first-aid-kit and the medical books and did what they could—tied and splinted and dosed with an opiate. Tom was a mass of bruises, and his right arm, where it had hooked the exhaust stack, was a flayed mass. They fixed him up then, old Peebles handling the sulfa powder and bandages like a trained nurse. And only then was there talk.

"I've seen a man thrown off a pan," said Dennis, as they sat around the coffee urn munching C rations. "Sittin' up on the arm rest on a cat, looking backwards. Cat hit a rock and bucked. Threw him off on the track. Stretched him out ten feet long." He in-whistled some coffee to dilute the mouthful of food he had been talking around, and masticated noisily. "Man's a fool to set up there on the side of his butt even on a pan. Can't see why th' goony was doin' it on a dozer."

"He wasn't," said Tom.

Kelly rubbed his pointed jaw. "He set flat on th' seat an' was th'owed?"

"That's right."

After an unbelieving silence Dennis said, "What was he doin'— drivin' over sixty?"

Tom looked around the circle of faces lit up by the over-artificial brilliance of a pressure lantern, and wondered what the reaction would be if he told it all just as it was. He had to say something, and it didn't look as if it could be the truth.

"He was workin'," he said finally. "Bucking stone out of the wall of an old building up on the mesa there. One turned loose an' as it did the governor must've gone haywire. She bucked like a loco hoss and run off."

"Run off?"

Tom opened his mouth and closed it again, and just nodded.

Dennis said, "Well, reckon that's what happens when you put a mechanic to operatin'."

"That had nothin' to do with it," Tom snapped.

Peebles spoke up quickly. "Tom—what about the Seven? Broke up any?"

"Some," said Tom. "Better look at the steering clutches. An' she was hot."

"Head's cracked," said Harris, a burly young man with shoulders like a buffalo and a famous thirst.

"How do you know?"

"Saw it when Al and me went up with the stretcher to get the kid while you all were building the shelter. Hot water runnin' down the side of the block."

"You mean you walked all the way out to the mound to look at that tractor while the kid was lyin' there? I told you where he was!"

"Out to the mound!" Al Knowles' pop eyes teetered out of their sockets. "We found that cat stalled twenty feet away from where the kid was!"

"What!"

"That's right, Tom," said Harris. "What's eatin' you? Where'd you leave it?"

"I told you . . . by the mound . . . the ol' building we cut into."

"Leave the startin' motor runnin'?"

"Starting motor?" Tom's mind caught the picture of the small, two-cylinder gasoline engine bolted to the side of the big Diesel's crankcase, coupled through the Bendix gear and clutch to the flywheel of the Diesel to crank it. He remembered his last glance at the still machine, silent but for the sound of water boiling. "Hell no!"

Al and Harris exchanged a glance. "I guess you were sort of slap-happy at the time, Tom," Harris said, not unkindly. "When we were halfway up the hill we heard it, and you know you can't mistake that racket. Sounded like it was under a load."

Tom beat softly at his temples with his clenched fists. "I left that machine dead," he said quietly. "I got compression off her and tied down the lever. I even stuffed my shirt in the intake. I drained the tank. But—I didn't touch the starting motor."

Peebles wanted to know why he had gone to all that trouble. Tom just looked vaguely at him and shook his head. "I shoulda pulled the wires. I never thought about the starting motor," he whispered. Then, "Harris—you say you found the starting motor running when you got to the top?"

"No—she was stalled. And hot—awmighty hot. I'd say the startin' motor was seized up tight. That must be it, Tom. You left the startin' motor runnin' and somehow engaged the clutch an' Bendix." His voice lost conviction as he said it—it takes seventeen separate motions to start a tractor of this type. "Anyhow, she was in gear an' crawled along on the little motor."

"I done that once," said Chub. "Broke a con rod on a Eight, on a highway job. Walked her about three-quarters of a mile on the startin' motor that way. Only I had to stop every hundred yards and let her cool down some."

Not without sarcasm, Dennis said, "Seems to me like the Seven was out to get th' goony. Made one pass at him and then went back to finish the job."

Al Knowles haw-hawed extravagantly.

Tom stood up, shaking his head, and went off among the crates to the hospital they had jury-rigged for the kid.

A dim light was burning inside, and Rivera lay very still, with his eyes closed. Tom leaned in the doorway—the open end of the engine crate—and watched him for a moment. Behind him he could hear the murmur of the crew's voices; the night was otherwise windless and still. Rivera's face was the peculiar color that olive skin takes when drained of blood. Tom looked at his chest and for a panicky moment thought he could discern no movement there. He entered and put a hand over the boy's heart. Rivera shivered, his eyes flew open, and he drew a sudden breath which caught raggedly at the back of his throat. "Tom . . . Tom!" he cried weakly.

"O.K., Goony . . . *que pase?*"

"She comeen back . . . Tom!"

"Who?"

"*El de siete.*"

Daisy Etta—"She ain't comin" back, kiddo. You're off the mesa now. Keep your chin up, fella."

Rivera's dark, doped eyes stared up at him without expression. Tom moved back and the eyes continued to stare. They weren't seeing anything. "Go to sleep," he whispered. The eyes closed instantly.

Kelly was saying that nobody ever got hurt on a construction job unless somebody was dumb. "An' most times you don't realize how dumb what you're doin' is until somebody does get hurt."

"The dumb part was gettin' a kid, an' not even an operator at that, up on a machine," said Dennis in his smuggest voice.

"I heard you try to sing that song before," said old Peebles quietly. "I hate to have to point out anything like this to a man because it don't do any good to make comparisons. But I've worked with that fella Rivera for a long time now, an' I've seen 'em as good but doggone few better. As far as you're concerned, you're O.K. on a pan, but the kid could give you cards and spades and still make you look like a cost accountant on a dozer."

Dennis half rose and mouthed something filthy. He looked at Al Knowles for backing and got it. He looked around the circle and got none. Peebles lounged back, sucking on his pipe, watching from under those bristling brows. Dennis subsided, running now on another tack.

"So what does that prove? The better you say he is, the less reason he had to fall off a cat and get himself hurt."

"I haven't got the thing straight yet," said Chub, in a voice whose tone indicated "I hate to admit it, but—"

About this time Tom returned, like a sleepwalker, standing with the brilliant pressure lantern between him and Dennis. Dennis rambled right on, not knowing he was anywhere near: "That's something you never will find out. That Puerto Rican is a pretty husky kid. Could be Tom said something he didn't like an' he tried to put a knife in Tom's back. They all do, y'know. Tom didn't get all that bashin' around just stoppin' a machine. They must of went round an' round for a while an' the goony wound up with a busted back. Tom sets the dozer to walk him down while he lies there and comes on down here and tries to tell us—" His voice fluttered to a stop as Tom loomed over him.

Tom grabbed the pan operator up by the slack of his shirt front with his uninjured arm and shook him like an empty burlap bag.

"Skunk," he growled. "I oughta lower th' boom on you." He set Dennis on his feet and backhanded his face with the edge of his forearm. Dennis went down—cowered down, rather than fell. "Aw, Tom, I was just talkin'. Just a joke, Tom, I was just—"

"Yellow, too," snarled Tom, stepping forward, raising a solid Texan boot. Peebles barked "Tom!" and the foot came back to the ground.

"Out o' my sight," rumbled the foreman. "Git!"

Dennis got. Al Knowles said vaguely, "Naow, Tom, y'all cain't—"

"You, y'wall-eyed string-bean!" Tom raved, his voice harsh and strained. "Go 'long with your Siamese twin!"

"O.K., O.K.," said Al, white-faced, and disappeared into the dark with Dennis.

"Nuts to this," said Chub. "I'm turnin' in." He went to a crate and hauled out a mosquito-hooded sleeping bag and went off without another word. Harris and Kelly, who were both on their feet, sat down again. Old Peebles hadn't moved.

Tom stood staring out into the dark, his arms straight at his sides, his fists knotted.

"Sit down," said Peebles gently. Tom turned and stared at him.

"Sit down. I can't change that dressing 'less you do." He pointed at the bandage around Tom's elbow. It was red, a widening stain, the tattered tissues having parted as the big Georgian bunched his infuriated muscles. He sat down.

"Talkin' about dumbness," said Harris calmly, as Peebles went to work, "I was about to say that I got the record. I done the dumbest thing anybody ever did on a machine. You can't top it."

"I could," said Kelly. "Runnin' a crane dragline once. Put her in boom gear and started to boom her up. Had an eighty-five-foot stick on her. Machine was standing on wooden mats in the middle of a swamp. Heard the motor miss and got out of the saddle to look at the filter-glass. Messed around back there longer than I figured, and the boom went straight up in the air and fell backwards over the cab. Th' jolt tilted my mats an' she slid backwards slow and stately as you please, butt-first into the mud. Buried up to the eyeballs, she was." He laughed quietly. "Looked like a ditching machine!"

"I still say I done the dumbest thing ever, bar none," said Harris. "It was on a river job, widening a channel. I come back to work from a three-day binge, still rum-dumb. Got up on a dozer an' was workin' around on the edge of a twenty-foot cliff. Down at the foot of the cliff was a big hickory tree, an' growin' right along the edge was a great big limb. I got the dopey idea I should break it off. I put one track on the limb and the other on the cliff edge and run out away from the trunk. I was about halfway out, an' the branch saggin' some, before I thought what would happen if it broke. Just about then it did break. You know hickory—if it breaks at all it breaks altogether. So down we go into thirty feet of water—me an' the cat. I got out from under somehow. When all them bubbles stopped comin' up I swum around lookin' down at it. I was still paddlin' around when the superintendent came rushin' up. He wants to know what's up. I yell at him, 'Look down there, the way that water is movin' an' shiftin', looks like the cat is workin' down there.'" He pursed his lips and *tsk tsked.* "My, that man said some nasty things to me."

"Where'd you get your next job?" Kelly exploded.

"Oh, he didn't fire me," said Harris soberly. "Said he couldn't afford to fire a man as dumb as that. Said he wanted me around to look at whenever he felt bad."

Tom said, "Thanks, you guys. That's as good a way as any of sayin' that everybody makes mistakes." He stood up, examining the new dressing, turning his arm in front of his lantern. "You all can think what you please, but I don't recollect there was any dumbness went on that mesa this evenin'. That's finished with, anyway. Do I have to say that Dennis' idea about it is all wet?"

Harris said one foul word that completely disposed of Dennis and anything he might say.

Peebles said, "It'll be all right. Dennis an' his popeyed friend'll hang together, but they don't amount to anything. Chub'll do whatever he's argued into."

"So you got 'em all lined up, hey?" Tom shrugged. "In the meantime, are we going to get an airfield built?"

"We'll get it built," Peebles said. "Only—Tom, I got no right to give you any advice, but go easy on the rough stuff after this. It does a lot of harm."

"I will if I can," said Tom gruffly. They broke up and turned in.

Peebles was right. It did do harm. It made Dennis use the word "murder" when they found, in the morning, that Rivera had died during the night.

The work progressed in spite of everything that had happened. With equipment like that, it's hard to slow things down. Kelly bit two cubic yards out of the bluff with every swing of the big shovel, and Dumptors are the fastest short haul earth movers yet devised. Dennis kept the service road clean for them with his pan, and Tom and Chub spelled each other on the bulldozer they had detached from its pan to make up for the lack of the Seven, spending their alternate periods with transit and stakes. Peebles was rod-man for the surveys, and in between times worked on setting up his field shop, keeping the water cooler and battery chargers running, and lining up his forge and welding tables. The operators fueled and serviced their own equipment, and there was little delay. The rocks and marl that came out of the growing cavity in the side of the central mesa—a whole third of it had to come out—were spun down to the edge of the swamp, which lay across the lower end of the projected runway, in the hornet-howling dump-tractors, their big driving wheels churning up vast clouds of dust, and were dumped and spread and walked in by the whining two-cycle dozer. When muck began to pile up in front of the fill, it was blasted out of the way with carefully placed charges of sixty percent dynamite and the craters filled with rocks and stone from the ruins, and surfaced with easily compacting marl, run out of a clean deposit by the pan.

And when he had his shop set up, Peebles went up the hill to get the Seven. When he got it he just stood there for a moment scratching his head, and then, shaking his head, he ambled back down the hill and went for Tom.

"Been looking at the Seven," he said, when he had flagged the moaning two-cycle and Tom had climbed off.

"What'd you find?"

Peebles held out an arm. "A list as long as that." He shook his head. "Tom, what really happened up there?"

"Governor went haywire and she run away," Tom said promptly, deadpan.

"Yeah, but—" For a long moment he held Tom's eyes. Then he sighed. "O.K., Tom. Anyway, I can't do a thing up there. We'll have to bring her back and I'll have to have this tractor to tow her down. And first I have to have some help—the track idler adjustment bolt's busted and the right track is off the track rollers."

"Oh-h-h. So that's why she couldn't get to the kid, running on the starting motor. Track would hardly turn, hey?"

"It's a miracle she ran as far as she did. That track is really jammed up. Riding right up on the roller flanges. And that ain't the half of it. The head's gone, like Harris said, and Lord only knows what I'll find when I open her up."

"Why bother?"

"What?"

"We can get along without that dozer," said Tom suddenly. "Leave her where she is. There's lots more for you to do."

"But what for?"

"Well, there's no call to go to all that trouble."

Peebles scratched the side of his nose and said, "I got a new head, track master pins—even a spare starting motor. I got tools to make what I don't stock." He pointed at the long row of dumps left by the hurtling dump-tractors while they had been talking. "You got a pan tied up because you're using this machine to doze with, and you can't tell me you can't use another one. You're gonna have to shut down one or two o' those Dumptors if you go on like this."

"I had all that figured out as soon as I opened my mouth," Tom said sullenly. "Let's go."

They climbed on the tractor and took off, stopping for a moment at the beach outcropping to pick up a cable and some tools.

Daisy Etta sat at the edge of the mesa, glowering out of her stilted headlights at the soft sward which still bore the impression of a young body and the tramplings of the stretcher-bearers. Her general aspect was woebegone—there were scratches on her olive-drab paint and the bright metal of the scratches was already dulled red by the earliest powder-rust. And though the ground was level, she was not, for her right track was off its lower rollers, and she stood slightly canted, like a man who has had a broken hip. And whatever passed for consciousness within her mulled over that paradox of the bulldozer that every operator must go through while he is learning his own machine.

It is the most difficult thing of all for the beginner to understand, that paradox. A bulldozer is a crawling powerhouse, a behemoth of noise and toughness, the nearest thing to the famous irresistible force. The beginner, awed and with the pictures of unconquerable Army tanks printed on his mind from the newsreels, takes all in his stride and with a sense of limitless power treats all obstacles alike, not knowing the fragility of a cast-iron radiator core, the mortality of tempered manganese, the friability of over-heated babbitt, and most of all, the ease with which a tractor can bury itself in mud. Climbing off to stare at a machine which he has reduced in twenty seconds to a useless hulk, or which was running a half-minute before on ground where it now has its tracks out of sight, he has that sense of guilty disappointment which overcomes any man on having made an error in judgment.

So, as she stood, *Daisy Etta* was broken and useless. These soft persistent bipeds had built her, and if they were like any other race that built machines, they could care for them. The ability to reverse the tension of a spring, or twist a control rod, or reduce to zero the friction in a nut and lock-washer, was not enough to repair the crack in a cylinder head nor bearings welded to a crankshaft in an over-heated starting motor. There had been a lesson to learn. It had been learned. *Daisy Etta* would be repaired, and the next time—well, at least she would know her own weaknesses.

Tom swung the two-cycle machine and edged in next to the Seven, with the edge of his blade all but touching *Daisy Etta's* push-beam. They got off and Peebles bent over the drum-tight right track.

"Watch yourself," said Tom.

"Watch what?"

"Oh—nothin', I guess." He circled the machine, trained eyes probing over frame and fittings. He stepped forward suddenly and grasped the fuel-tank drain cock. It was closed. He opened it; golden oil gushed out. He shut it off, climbed up on the machine and opened the fuel cap on top of the tank. He pulled out the bayonet gauge, wiped it in the crook of his knee, dipped and withdrew it.

The tank was more than three quarters full.

"What's the matter?" asked Peebles, staring curiously at Tom's drawn face.

"Peeby, I opened the cock to drain this tank. I left it with oil runnin' out on the ground. She shut herself off."

"Now, Tom, you're lettin' this thing get you down. You just thought you did. I've seen a main-line valve shut itself off when it's worn bad, but only 'cause the fuel pump pulls it shut when the motor's runnin'. But not a gravity drain."

"Main-line valve?" Tom pulled the seat up and looked. One glance was enough to show him this one was open.

"She opened this one, too."

"O.K.—O.K. Don't look at me like that!" Peebles was as near to exasperation as he could possibly get. "What difference does it make?"

Tom did not answer. He was not the type of man who, when faced with something beyond his understanding, would begin to doubt his own sanity. His was a dogged insistence that what he saw and sensed was what had actually happened. In him was none of the fainting fear of madness that another, more sensitive, man might feel. He doubted neither himself nor his evidence, and so could free his mind for searching out the consuming "why" of a problem. He knew instinctively that to share "unbelievable" happenings with anyone else, even if they had really occurred, was to put even further obstacles in his way. So he kept his clamlike silence and stubbornly, watchfully, investigated.

The slipped track was so tightly drawn up on the roller flanges that there could be no question of pulling the master pin and opening the track up. It would have to be worked back in place—a very delicate operation, for a little force applied in the wrong direction would be enough to run the track off altogether. To complicate things, the blade of the Seven was down on the ground and would have to be lifted before the machine could be maneuvered, and its hydraulic hoist was useless without the motor.

Peebles unhooked twenty feet of half-inch cable from the rear of the smaller dozer, scratched a hole in the ground under the Seven's blade, and pushed the eye of the cable through. Climbing over the moldboard, he slipped the eye on the big towing hook bolted to the underside of the belly-guard. The other end of the cable he threw out on the ground in front of the machine. Tom mounted the other dozer and swung into place, ready to tow. Peebles hooked the cable onto Tom's drawbar, hopped up on the Seven. He put her in neutral, disengaged the master clutch, and put the blade control over into "float" position, then raised an arm.

Tom perched upon the arm rest of his machine, looking backwards, moved slowly, taking up the slack in the cable. It straightened and grew taut, and as it did it forced the Seven's blade upward. Peebles waved for slack and put the blade control into "hold." The cable bellied downward away from the blade.

"Hydraulic system's O.K., anyhow," called Peebles, as Tom throttled down. "Move over and take a strain to the right, sharp as you can without fouling the cable on the track. We'll see if we can walk this track back on."

Tom backed up, cut sharply right, and drew the cable out almost at right angles to the other machine. Peebles held the right track of the Seven with the brake and released both steering clutches. The left track now could turn free, the right not at all. Tom was running at a quarter throttle in his lowest gear, so that his machine barely crept along, taking the strain. The Seven shook gently and began to pivot on the taut right track, unbelievable foot-pounds of energy coming to bear on the front of the track where it rode high up on the idler wheel. Peebles released the right brake with his foot and applied it again in a series of skilled, deft jerks. The track would move a few inches and stop again, force being applied forward and sideward alternately, urging the track persuasively back in place. Then, a little jolt and she was in, riding true on the five truck rollers, the two track carrier rollers, the driving sprocket and the idler.

Peebles got off and stuck his head in between the sprocket and the rear carrier, squinting down and sideways to see if there were any broken flanges or roller bushes. Tom came over and pulled him out by the seat of his trousers. "Time enough for that when you get her in the shop," he said, masking his nervousness. "Reckon she'll roll?"

"She'll roll. I never saw a track in that condition come back that easy. By gosh, it's as if she was tryin' to help!"

"They'll do it sometimes," said Tom, stiffly. "You better take the two-tractor, Peeby. I'll stay with this'n."

"Anything you say."

And cautiously they took the steep slope down, Tom barely holding the brakes, giving the other machine a straight pull all the way. And so they brought *Daisy Etta* down to Peebles' outdoor shop, where they pulled her cylinder head off, took off her starting motor, pulled out a burned clutch facing, had her quite helpless—

And put her together again.

"I tell you it was outright, cold-blooded murder," said Dennis hotly. "An' here we are takin' orders from a guy like that. What are we goin' to do about it?" They were standing by the cooler—Dennis had run his machine there to waylay Chub.

Chub Horton's cigar went down and up like a semaphore with a short circuit. "We'll skip it. The blacktopping crew will be here in another two weeks or so, an' we can make a report. Besides, I don't know what happened up there any more than you do. In the meantime we got a runway to build."

"You don't know what happened up there? Chub, you're a smart man. Smart enough to run this job better than Tom Jaeger even if he wasn't crazy. And you're surely smart enough not to believe all that cock and bull about that tractor runnin' out from under that grease-monkey. Listen—" he leaned forward and tapped Chub's chest. "He said it was the governor. I saw that governor myself an' heard ol' Peebles say there wasn't a thing wrong with it. Th' throttle control rod had slipped off its yoke, yeah—but you know what a tractor will do when the throttle control goes out. It'll idle or stall. It won't run away, whatever."

"Well, maybe so, but—"

"But nothin'! A guy that'll commit murder ain't sane. If he did it once, he can do it again and I ain't fixin' to let that happen to me."

Two things crossed Chub's steady but not too bright mind at this. One was that Dennis, whom he did not like but could not shake, was trying to force him into something that he did not want to do. The other was that under all of his swift talk Dennis was scared spitless.

"What do you want to do—call up the sheriff?"

Dennis ha-ha-ed appreciatively—one of the reasons he was so hard to shake. "I'll tell you what we can do. As long as we have you here, he isn't the only man who knows the work. If we stop takin' orders from him, you can give 'em as good or better. An' there won't be anything he can do about it."

"Doggone it, Dennis," said Chub, with sudden exasperation. "What do you think you're doin'—handin' me over the keys to the kingdom or something? What do you want to see me bossin' around here for?" He stood up. "Suppose we did what you said? Would it get the field built any quicker? Would it get me any more money in my pay envelope? What do you think I want—glory? I passed up a chance to run for councilman once. You think I'd raise a finger to get a bunch of mugs to do what I say—when they do it anyway?"

"Aw, Chub—I wouldn't cause trouble just for the fun of it. That's not what I mean at all. But unless we do something about that guy we ain't safe. Can't you get that through your head?"

"Listen, windy. If a man keeps busy enough he can't get into trouble. That goes for Tom—you might keep that in mind. But it goes for you, too. Get back up on that rig an' get back to the marl pit." Dennis, completely taken by surprise, turned to his machine.

"It's a pity you can't move earth with your mouth," said Chub as he walked off. "They could have left you do this job singlehanded."

Chub walked slowly toward the outcropping, switching at beach pebbles with a grade stake and swearing to himself. He was essentially a simple man and believed in the simplest possible approach to everything. He liked a job where he could do everything required and where nothing turned up to complicate things. He had been in the grading business for a long time as an operator and survey party boss, and he was remarkable for one thing—he had always held aloof from the cliques and internecine politics that are the breath of life to most construction men. He was disturbed and troubled at the back-stabbing that went on around him on various jobs. If it was blunt, he was disgusted, and subtlety simply left him floundering and bewildered. He was stupid enough so that his basic honesty manifested itself in his speech and actions, and he had learned that complete honesty in dealing with men above and below him was almost invariably painful to all concerned, but he had not the wit to act otherwise, and did not try to. If he had a bad tooth, he had it pulled out as soon as he could. If he got a raw deal from a superintendent over him, that superintendent would get told exactly what the trouble was, and if he didn't like it, there were other jobs. And if the pulling and hauling of cliques got in his hair, he had always said so and left. Or he had sounded off and stayed; his completely selfish reaction to things that got in the way of his work had earned him a lot of regard from men he had worked under. And so, in this instance, he had no hesitation about choosing a course of action. Only—how did you go about asking a man if he was a murderer?

He found the foreman with an enormous wrench in his hand, tightening up the new track adjustment bolt they had installed in the Seven.

"Hey, Chub! Glad you turned up. Let's get a piece of pipe over the end of this thing and really bear down." Chub went for the pipe, and they fitted it over the handle of the four-foot wrench and hauled until the sweat ran down their backs, Tom checking the track clearance occasionally with a crowbar. He finally called it good enough and they stood there in the sun gasping for breath.

"Tom," panted Chub, "did you kill that Puerto Rican?"

Tom's head came up as if someone had burned the back of his neck with a cigarette.

"Because," said Chub, "if you did you can't go on runnin' this job."

Tom said, "That's a lousy thing to kid about."

"You know I ain't kiddin'. Well, did you?"

"No!" Tom sat down on a keg, wiped his face with a bandanna. "What's got into you?"

"I just wanted to know. Some of the boys are worried about it."

Tom's eyes narrowed. "Some of the boys, huh? I think I get it. Listen to me, Chub. Rivera was killed by that thing there." He thumbed over his shoulder at the Seven, which was standing ready now, awaiting only the building of a broken cutting corner on the blade. Peebles was winding up the welding machine as he spoke. "If you mean, did I put him up on the machine before he was thrown, the answer is yes. That much I killed him, and don't think I don't feel it. I had a hunch something was wrong up there, but I couldn't put my finger on it and I certainly didn't think anybody was going to get hurt."

"Well, what was wrong?"

"I still don't know." Tom stood up. "I'm tired of beatin' around the bush, Chub, and I don't much care any more what anybody thinks. There's somethin' wrong with that Seven, something that wasn't built into her. They don't make tractors better'n that one, but whatever it was happened up there on the mesa has queered this one. Now go ahead and think what you like, and dream up any story you want to tell the boys. In the meantime you can pass the word— nobody runs that machine but me, understand? Nobody!"

"Tom—"

Tom's patience broke. "That's all I'm going to say about it! If anybody else gets hurt, it's going to be me, understand? What more do you want?"

He strode off, boiling. Chub stared after him, and after a long moment reached up and took the cigar from his lips. Only then did he realize that he had bitten it in two; half the butt was still inside his mouth. He spat and stood there shaking his head.

"How's she going, Peeby?"

Peebles looked up from the welding machine. "Hi, Chub, have her ready for you in twenty minutes." He gauged the distance between the welding machine and the big tractor. "I should have forty feet of cable," he said, looking at the festoons of arc and ground cables that hung from the storage hooks in the back of the welder. "Don't want to get a tractor over here to move the thing, and don't feel like cranking up the Seven just to get it close enough." He separated the arc cable and threw it aside, walked to the tractor, paying the ground cable off his arms. He threw out the last of his slack and grasped the ground clamp when he was eight feet from the machine. Taking it in his left hand, he pulled hard, reaching out with his right to grasp the moldboard of the Seven, trying to get it far enough to clamp on to the machine.

Chub stood there watching him, chewing on his cigar, absent-mindedly diddling with the controls on the arc-welder. He pressed the starter-button, and the six-cylinder motor responded with a purr. He spun the work-selector dials idly, threw the arc generator switch—

A bolt of incredible energy, thin, searing, blue-white, left the rod-holder at his feet, stretched itself *fifty feet* across to Peebles, whose fingers had just touched the moldboard of the tractor. Peebles' head and shoulders were surrounded for a second by a violet nimbus, and then he folded over and dropped. A circuit breaker clacked behind the control board of the welder, but too late. The Seven rolled slowly backward, without firing, on level ground, until it brought up against the road-roller.

Chub's cigar was gone, and he didn't notice it. He had the knuckles of his right hand in his mouth, and his teeth sunk into the pudgy flesh. His eyes protruded; he crouched there and quivered, literally frightened out of his mind. For old Peebles was burned almost in two.

They buried him next to Rivera. There wasn't much talk afterwards; the old man had been a lot closer to all of them than they had realized until now. Harris, for once in his rum-dumb, lightheaded life, was quiet and serious, and Kelly's walk seemed to lose some of its litheness. Hour after hour Dennis' flabby mouth worked, and he bit at his lower lip until it was swollen and tender. Al Knowles seemed more or less unaffected, as was to be expected from a man who had something less than the brains of a chicken. Chub Horton had snapped out of it after a couple of hours and was very nearly himself again. And in Tom Jaeger swirled a black, furious anger at this unknowable curse that had struck the camp.

And they kept working. There was nothing else to do. The shovel kept up its rhythmic swing and dig, swing and dump, and the Dumptors screamed back and forth between it and the little that was left of the swamp. The upper end of the runway was grassed off; Chub and Tom set grade stakes and Dennis began the long job of cutting and filling the humpy surface with his pan. Harris manned the other and followed him, a cut behind. The shape of the runway emerged from the land, and then that of the paralleling taxiway; and three days went by. The horror of Peebles' death wore off enough so that they could talk about it, and very little of the talk helped anybody. Tom took his spells at everything, changing over with Kelly to give him a rest from the shovel, making a few rounds with a pan, putting in hours on a Dumptor. His arm was healing slowly but clean, and he worked grimly in spite of it, taking a perverse sort of pleasure from the pain of it. Every man on the job watched his machine with the solicitude of a mother with her first-born; a serious break-down would have been disastrous without a highly skilled mechanic.

The only concession that Tom allowed himself in regard to Peebles' death was to corner Kelly one afternoon and ask him about the welding machine. Part of Kelly's rather patchy past had been spent in a technical college, where he had studied electrical engineering and women. He had learned a little of the former and enough of the latter to get him thrown out on his ear. So, on the off-chance that he might know something about the freak arc, Tom put it to him.

Kelly pulled off his high-gauntlet gloves and batted sandflies with them. "What sort of an arc was that? Boy, you got me there. Did you ever hear of a welding machine doing like that before?"

"I did not. A welding machine just don't have that sort o' push. I saw a man get a full jolt from a 400-amp welder once, an' although it sat him down it didn't hurt him any."

"It's not amperage that kills people," said Kelly, "it's voltage. Voltage is the pressure behind a current, you know. Take an amount of water, call it amperage. If I throw it in your face, it won't hurt you. If I put it through a small hose you'll feel it. But if I pump it through them tiny holes on a Diesel injector nozzle at about twelve hundred pounds, it'll draw blood. But a welding arc generator just is not wound to build up that kind of voltage. I can't see where any short circuit anywhere through the armature or field windings could do such a thing."

"From what Chub said, he had been foolin' around with the work selector. I don't think anyone touched the dials after it happened. The selector dial was run all the way over to the low current application segment, and the current control was around the halfway mark. That's not enough juice to get you a good bead with a quarter-inch rod, let alone kill somebody—or roll a tractor back thirty feet on level ground."

"Or jump fifty feet," said Kelly. "It would take thousands of volts to generate an arc like that."

"Is it possible that something in the Seven could have pulled that arc? I mean, suppose the arc wasn't driven over, but was drawn over? I tell you, she was hot for four hours after that."

Kelly shook his head. "Never heard of any such thing. Look, just to have something to call them, we call direct current terminals positive and negative, and just because it works in theory we say that current flows from negative to positive. There couldn't be any more positive attraction in one electrode than there is negative drive in the other; see what I mean?"

"There couldn't be some freak condition that would cause a sort of oversize positive field? I mean one that would suck out the negative flow all in a heap, make it smash through under a lot of pressure like the water you were talking about through an injector nozzle?"

"No, Tom. It just don't work that way, far as anyone knows. I dunno, though—there are some things about static electricity that nobody understands. All I can say is that what happened couldn't happen and if it did it couldn't have killed Peebles. And you know the answer to that."

Tom glanced away at the upper end of the runway, where the two graves were. There was bitterness and turbulent anger naked there for a moment, and he turned and walked away without another word. And when he went back to have another look at the welding machine, *Daisy Etta* was gone.

Al Knowles and Harris squatted together near the water cooler.

"Bad," said Harris.

"Nevah saw anythin' like it," said Al. "Ol' Tom come back f'm the shop theah just raisin' Cain. 'Weah's 'at Seven gone? Weah's 'at Seven?' I never heered sech cah'ins on."

"Dennis did take it, huh?"

"Sho' did."

Harris said. "He came spoutin' around to me a while back, Dennis did. Chub'd told him Tom said for everybody to stay off that machine. Dennis was mad as a wet hen. Said Tom was carryin' that kind o' business too far. Said there was probably somethin' about the Seven Tom didn't want us to find out. Might incriminate him. Dennis is ready to say Tom killed the kid."

"Reckon he did, Harris?"

Harris shook his head. "I've known Tom too long to think that. If he won't tell us what really happened up on the mesa, he has a reason for it. How'd Dennis come to take the dozer?"

"Blew a front tire on his pan. Came back heah to git anothah rig—maybe a Dumptor. Saw th' Seven standin' theah ready to go. Stood theah lookin' at it and cussin' Tom. Said he was tired of bashin' his kidneys t'pieces on them othah rigs an' bedamned if he wouldn't take suthin' that rode good fo' a change. I tol' him ol' Tom'd raise th' roof when he found him on it. He had a couple mo' things t'say 'bout Tom then."

"I didn't think he had the guts to take the rig."

"Aw, he talked hisself blind mad."

They looked up as Chub Horton trotted up, panting. "Hey, you guys, come on. We better get up there to Dennis."

"What's wrong?" asked Harris, climbing to his feet.

"Tom passed me a minute ago lookin' like the wrath o' God and hightailin' it for the swamp fill. I asked him what was the matter and he hollered that Dennis had taken the Seven. Said he was always talkin' about murder and he'd get his fill of it foolin' around that machine." Chub went wall-eyed, licked his lips beside his cigar.

"Oh-oh," said Harris quietly. "That's the wrong kind o' talk for just now."

"You don't suppose he—"

"*Come on!*"

They saw Tom before they were halfway there. He was walking slowly, with his head down. Harris shouted. Tom raised his face, stopped, stood there waiting with a peculiarly slumped stance.

"Where's Dennis?" barked Chub.

Tom waited until they were almost up to him and then weakly raised an arm and thumbed over his shoulder. His face was green.

"Tom—is he—"

Tom nodded, and swayed a little. His granite jaw was slack.

"Al, stay with him. He's sick. Harris, let's go."

Tom was sick, then and there. Very. Al stood gaping at him, fascinated.

Chub and Harris found Dennis. All of twelve square feet of him, ground and churned and rolled out into a torn-up patch of earth. *Daisy Etta* was gone.

Back at the outcropping, they sat with Tom while Al Knowles took a Dumptor and roared away to get Kelly.

"You saw him?" he said dully after a time.

Harris said, "Yeh."

The screaming Dumptor and a mountainous cloud of dust arrived,

Kelly driving, Al holding on with a death-grip to the dump-bed guards. Kelly flung himself off, ran to Tom. "Tom—what is all this? Dennis dead? And you . . .you—"

Tom's head came up slowly, the slackness going out of his long face, a light suddenly coming into his eyes. Until this moment it had not crossed his mind what these men might think.

"I—what?"

"Al says you killed him."

Tom's eyes flicked at Al Knowles, and Al winced as if the glance had been a quirt.

Harris said, "What about it, Tom?"

"Nothing about it. He was killed by that Seven. You saw that for yourself."

"I stuck with you all along," said Harris slowly. "I took everything you said and believed it."

"This is too strong for you?" Tom asked.

Harris nodded. "Too strong, Tom."

Tom looked at the grim circle of faces and laughed suddenly. He stood up, put his back against a tall crate. "What do you plan to do about it?"

There was a silence. "You think I went up there and knocked that windbag off the machine and ran over him?" More silence. "Listen. I went up there and saw what you saw. He was dead before I got there. That's not good enough either?" He paused and licked his lips. "So after I killed him I got up on the tractor and drove it far enough away so you couldn't see or hear it when you got there. And then I sprouted wings and flew back so's I was halfway here when you met me—*ten minutes* after I spoke to Chub on my way up!"

Kelly said vaguely, "Tractor?"

"Well," said Tom harshly to Harris, "was the tractor there when you and Chub went up and saw Dennis?"

"No—"

Chub smacked his thigh suddenly. "You could of drove it into the swamp, Tom."

Tom said angrily, "I'm wastin' my time. You guys got it all figured out. Why ask me anything at all?"

142

"Aw, take it easy," said Kelly. "We just want the facts. Just what did happen? You met Chub and told him that Dennis would get all the murderin' he could take if he messed around that machine. That right?"

"That's right."

"Then what?"

"Then the machine murdered him."

Chub, with remarkable patience, asked, "What did you mean the day Peebles was killed when you said that something had queered the Seven up there on the mesa?"

Tom said furiously, "I meant what I said. You guys are set to crucify me for this and I can't stop you. Well, listen. Something's got into that Seven. I don't know what it is and I don't think I ever will know. I thought that after she smashed herself up that it was finished with. I had an idea that when we had her torn down and helpless we should have left her that way. I was dead right but it's too late now. She's killed Rivera and she's killed Dennis and she sure had something to do with killing Peebles. And my idea is that she won't stop as long as there's a human being alive on this island."

"Whaddaya know!" said Chub.

"Sure, Tom sure," said Kelly quietly. "That tractor is out to get us. But don't worry; we'll catch it and tear it down. Just don't you worry about it any more; it'll be all right."

"That's right, Tom," said Harris. "You just take it easy around camp for a couple of days till you feel better. Chub and the rest of us will handle things for you. You had too much sun."

"You're a swell bunch of fellows," gritted Tom, with the deepest sarcasm. "You want to live," he shouted, "git out there and throw that maverick bulldozer!"

"That maverick bulldozer is at the bottom of the swamp where you put it," growled Chub. His head lowered and he started to move in. "Sure we want to live. The best way to do that is to put you where you can't kill anybody else. Get him!"

He leaped. Tom straightened him with his left and crossed with his right. Chub went down, tripping Harris. Al Knowles scuttled to a toolbox and dipped out a fourteen-inch crescent wrench. He circled around, keeping out of trouble, trying to look useful. Tom loosened a haymaker at Kelly, whose head seemed to withdraw like a turtle's; it whistled over, throwing Tom badly off balance. Harris, still on his knees, tackled Tom's legs; Chub hit him in the small of the back with a meaty shoulder, and Tom went flat on his face. Al Knowles, holding the wrench in both hands, swept it up and back like a baseball bat; at the top of its swing Kelly reached over, snatched it out of his hands and tapped Tom delicately behind the ear with it. Tom went limp.

It was late, but nobody seemed to feel like sleeping. They sat around the pressure lantern, talking idly. Chub and Kelly played an inconsequential game of casino, forgetting to pick up their points; Harris paced up and down like a man in a cell, and Al Knowles was squinched up close to the light, his eyes wide and watching, watching—

"I need a drink," said Harris.

"Tens," said one of the casino players.

Al Knowles said, "We shoulda killed him. We oughta kill him now."

"There's been too much killin' already," said Chub. "Shut up, you." And to Kelly, "With big casino," sweeping up cards.

Kelly caught his wrist and grinned. "Big casino's ten of diamonds, not the ten of hearts. Remember?"

"Oh."

"How long before the blacktopping crew will be here?" quavered Al Knowles.

"Twelve days," said Harris. "And they better bring some likker."

"Hey, you guys."

They fell silent.

"Hey!"

"It's Tom," said Kelly. "Building sixes, Chub."

"I'm gonna go kick his ribs in," said Knowles, not moving.

"I heard that," said the voice from the darkness. "If I wasn't hogtied—"

"We know what you'd do," said Chub. "How much proof do you think we need?"

"Chub, you don't have to do any more to him!" It was Kelly, flinging his cards down and getting up. "Tom, you want water?"

"Yes."

"Siddown, siddown," said Chub.

"Let him lay there and bleed," Al Knowles said.

"Nuts!" Kelly went and filled a cup and brought it to Tom. The big Georgian was tied thoroughly, wrists together, taut rope between elbow and elbow behind his back, so that his hands were immovable over his solar plexus. His knees and ankles were bound as well, although Knowles' little idea of a short rope between ankles and throat hadn't been used.

"Thanks, Kelly." Tom drank greedily, Kelly holding his head. "Goes good." He drank more. "What hit me?"

"One of the boys. 'Bout the time you said the cat was haunted."

"Oh, yeah." Tom rolled his head and blinked with pain.

"Any sense asking you if you blame us?"

"Kelly, does somebody else have to get killed before you guys wake up?"

"None of us figure there will be any more killin'—now."

The rest of the men drifted up. "He willing to talk sense?" Chub wanted to know.

Al Knowles laughed, "Hyuk! hyuk! Don't he look dangerous now."

Harris said suddenly, "Al, I'm gonna hafta tape your mouth with the skin off your neck."

"Am I the kind of guy that makes up ghost stories?"

"Never have that I know of, Tom." Harris kneeled down beside him. "Never killed anyone before, either."

"Oh, get away from me. Get away," said Tom tiredly.

"Get up and make us," jeered Al.

Harris got up and backhanded him across the mouth. Al squeaked, took three steps backward and tripped over a drum of grease. "I told you," said Harris almost plaintively. "I *told* you, Al."

Tom stopped the bumble of comment. "Shut up!" he hissed. "SHUT UP!" he roared.

They shut.

"Chub," said Tom, rapidly, evenly. "What did you say I did with that Seven?"

"Buried it in the swamp."

"Yeh. Listen."

"Listen at what?"

"Be quiet and listen!"

So they listened. It was another still, windless night, with a thin crescent of moon showing nothing true in the black and muffled silver landscape. The smallest whisper of surf drifted up from the beach, and from far off to the right, where the swamp was, a scandalized frog croaked protest at the manhandling of his mudhole. But the sound that crept down, freezing their bones, came from the bluff behind their camp.

It was the unmistakable staccato of a starting engine.

"The Seven!"

" 'At's right, Chub," said Tom.

'Wh-who's crankin' her up?"

"Are we all here?"

"All but Peebles and Dennis and Rivera," said Tom.

"It's Dennis' ghost," moaned Al.

Chub snapped, "Shut up, lamebrain."

"She's shifted to Diesel," said Kelly, listening.

"She'll be here in a minute," said Tom. "Y'know, fellas, we can't all be crazy, but you're about to have a time convincin' yourself of it."

"You like this, doncha?"

"Some ways. Rivera used to call that machine *Daisy Etta,* 'cause she's *de siete* in Spig. *Daisy Etta,* she wants her a man."

"Tom," said Harris. "I wish you'd stop that chatterin'. You make me nervous."

"I got to do somethin'. I can't run," Tom drawled.

"We're going to have a look," said Chub. "If there's nobody on that cat, we'll turn you loose."

"Mighty white of you. Reckon you'll get back before she does?"

"We'll get back. Harris, come with me. We'll get one of the pan tractors. They can outrun a Seven. Kelly, take Al and get the other one."

"Dennis' machine has a flat tire on the pan," said Al's quivering voice.

"Pull the pin and cut the cables, then! Git!" Kelly and Al Knowles ran off.

"Good huntin', Chub."

Chub went to him, bent over. "I think I'm goin' to have to apologize to you, Tom."

"No you ain't. I'd a done the same. Get along now, if you think you got to. But hurry back,"

"I got to. An' I'll hurry back."

Harris said, "Don't go 'way, boy." Tom returned the grin, and they were gone. But they didn't hurry back. They didn't come back at all.

It was Kelly who came pounding back, with Al Knowles on his heels, a half hour later. "Al—gimme your knife."

He went to work on the ropes. His face was drawn.

"I could see some of it," whispered Tom. "Chub and Harris?"

Kelly nodded. "There wasn't nobody on the Seven like you said." He said it as if there was nothing else in his mind, as if the most rigid self-control was keeping him from saying it over and over.

"I could see the lights," said Tom. "A tractor angling up the hill. Pretty soon another, crossing it, lighting up the whole slope."

"We heard it idling up there somewhere," Kelly said. "Olive-drab paint—couldn't see it."

"I saw the pan tractor turn over—oh, four, five times down the hill. It stopped, lights still burning. Then something hit it and rolled it again. That sure blacked it out. What turned it over first?"

"The Seven. Hanging up there just at the brow of the bluff. Waited until Chub and Harris were about to pass, sixty, seventy feet below. Tipped over the edge and rolled down on them with her clutches on. Must've been going thirty miles an hour when she hit. Broadside. They never had a chance. Followed the pan as it rolled down the hill and when it stopped booted it again."

"Want me to rub yo' ankles?" asked Al.

"You! Get outa my sight!"

"Aw, Tom—" whimpered Al.

"Skip it, Tom," said Kelly. "There ain't enough of us left to carry on that way. Al, you mind your manners from here on out, hear?"

"Ah jes' wanted to tell y'all. I knew you weren't lyin' 'bout Dennis, Tom, if only I'd stopped to think. I recollect when Dennis said he'd take that tractuh out . . . 'membah, Kelly? . . . He went an' got the crank and walked around to th' side of th' machine and stuck it in th' hole. It was barely in theah befo' the startin' engine kicked off. "Whadda ya know!" he says t'me. "She started by herse'f! I nevah pulled that handle!" And I said, "She sho' rarin' to go!'"

"You pick a fine time to 'recollec' something," gritted Tom. "C'mon—let's get out of here."

"Where to?"

"What do you know that a Seven can't move or get up on?"

"That's a large order. A big rock, maybe."

"Ain't nothing that big around here," said Tom.

Kelly thought a minute, then snapped his fingers. "Up on the top of my last cut with the shovel," he said. "It's fourteen feet if it's an inch. I was pullin' out small rock an' topsoil, and Chub told me to drop back and dip out marl from a pocket there. I sumped in back of the original cut and took out a whole mess o' marl. That left a big neck of earth sticking thirty feet or so out of the cliff. The narrowest part is only about four feet wide. If *Daisy Etta* tries to get us from the top, she'll straddle the neck and hang herself. If she tries to get us from below, she can't get traction to climb; it's too loose and too steep."

"And what happens if she builds herself a ramp?"

"We'll be gone from there."

"Let's go."

Al agitated for the choice of a Dumptor because of its speed, but was howled down. Tom wanted something that could not get a flat tire and that would need something really powerful to turn it over. They took the two-cycle pan tractor with the bulldozer blade that had been Dennis' machine and crept out into the darkness.

It was nearly six hours later that *Daisy Etta* came and woke them up. Night was receding before a paleness in the east, and a fresh ocean breeze had sprung up. Kelly had taken the first lookout and Al the second, letting Tom rest the night out. And Tom was far too tired to argue the arrangement. Al had immediately fallen asleep on his watch, but fear had such a sure, cold hold on his vitals that the first faint growl of the big Diesel engine snapped him erect. He tottered on the edge of the tall neck of earth that they slept on and squeaked as he scrabbled to get his balance.

"What's giving?" asked Kelly, instantly wide awake.

"It's coming," blubbered Al. "Oh my, oh my—"

Kelly stood up and stared into the fresh, dark dawn. The motor boomed hollowly, in a peculiar way heard twice at the same time as it was thrown to them and echoed back by the bluffs under and around them.

"It's coming and what are we goin' to do?" chanted Al. "What is going to happen?"

"My head is going to fall off," said Tom sleepily. He rolled to a sitting position, holding the brutalized member between his hands. "If that egg behind my ear hatches, it'll come out a full-sized jackhammer." He looked at Kelly. "Where is she?"

"Don't rightly know," said Kelly. "Somewhere down around the camp."

"Probably pickin' up our scent."

"Figure it can do that?"

"I figure it can do anything," said Tom. "Al, stop your moanin'."

The sun slipped its scarlet edge into the thin slot between sea and sky, and rosy light gave each rock and tree a shape and a shadow. Kelly's gaze swept back and forth, back and forth, until, minutes later, he saw movement.

"There she is!"

"Where?"

"Down by the grease rack."

Tom rose and stared. "What's she doin'?"

After an interval Kelly said, "She's workin'. Diggin' a swale in front of the fuel drums."

"You don't say. Don't tell me she's goin' to give herself a grease job."

"She don't need it. She was completely greased and new oil put in the crankcase after we set her up. But she might need fuel."

"Not more'n half a tank."

"Well, maybe she figures she's got a lot of work to do today." As Kelly said this Al began to blubber. They ignored him.

The fuel drums were piled in a pyramid at the edge of the camp, in forty-four-gallon drums piled on their sides. The Seven was moving back and forth in front of them, close up, making pass after pass, gouging earth up and wasting it out past the pile. She soon had a huge pit scooped out, about fourteen feet wide, six feet deep and thirty feet long, right at the very edge of the pile of drums.

"What you reckon she's playin' at?"

"Search me. She seems to want fuel, but I don't . . . look at that! She stopped in the hole; . . . turnin' . . . smashing the top corner of the moldboard into one of the drums on the bottom!'

Tom scraped the stubble on his jaw with his nails. "An' you wonder how much that critter can do! Why, she's got the whole thing figured out. She knows if she tried to punch a hole in a fuel drum that she'd only kick it around. If she did knock a hole in it, how's she going to lift it? She's not equipped to handle hose, so . . . see? Look at her now! She just get herself lower than the bottom drum on the pile, and punches a hole. She can do that then, with the whole weight of the pile holding it down. Then she backs her tank under the stream of fuel runnin' out!"

"How'd she get the cap off?"

Tom snorted and told them how the radiator cap had come off its hinges as he vaulted over the hood the day Rivera was hurt.

"You know," he said after a moment's thought, "if she knew as much then as she does now, I'd be snoozin' beside Rivera and Peebles. She just didn't know her way around then. She run herself like she'd never run before. She's learned plenty since."

"She has," said Kelly, "and here's where she uses it on us. She's headed this way."

She was. Straight out across the roughed-out runway she came, grinding along over the dew-sprinkled earth, yesterday's dust swirling up from under her tracks. Crossing the shoulder line, she took the tougher ground skillfully, angling up over the occasional swags in the earth, by-passing stones, riding free and fast and easily. It was the first time Tom had actually seen her clearly running without an operator, and his flesh crept as he watched. The machine was unnatural, her outline somehow unreal and dreamlike purely through the lack of the small silhouette of a man in the saddle. She looked hulked, compact, dangerous.

"What are we gonna do?" wailed Al Knowles.

"We're gonna sit and wait," said Kelly, "and you're gonna shut your trap. We won't know for five minutes yet whether she's going to go after us from down below or from up here."

"If you want to leave," said Tom gently, "go right ahead." Al sat down.

Kelly looked ruminatively down at his beloved power shovel, sitting squat and unlovely in the cut below them and away to their right. "How do you reckon she'd stand up against the dipper stick?"

"If it ever came to a rough-and-tumble," said Tom, "I'd say it would be just too bad for *Daisy Etta*. But she wouldn't fight. There's no way you could get the shovel within punchin' range; *Daisy*'d just stand there and laugh at you."

"I can't see her now," whined Al.

Tom looked. "She's taken the bluff. She's going to try it from up here. I move we sit tight and see if she's foolish enough to try to walk out here over that narrow neck. If she does, she'll drop on her belly with one truck on each side. Probably turn herself over trying to dig out."

The wait then was interminable. Back over the hill they could hear the laboring motor; twice they heard the machine stop momentarily to shift gears. Once they looked at each other hopefully as the sound rose to a series of bellowing roars, as if she were backing and filling; then they realized that she was trying to take some particularly steep part of the bank and having trouble getting traction. But she made it; the motor revved up as she made the brow of the hill, and she shifted into fourth gear and came lumbering out into the open. She lurched up to the edge of the cut, stopped, throttled down, dropped her blade on the ground and stood there idling. Al Knowles backed away to the very edge of the tongue of earth they stood on, his eyes practically on stalks.

"O.K.—put up or shut up," Kelly called across harshly.

"She's looking the situation over," said Tom. "That narrow pathway don't fool her a bit."

Daisy Etta's blade began to rise, and stopped just clear of the ground. She shifted without clashing her gears, began to back slowly, still at little more than an idle.

"She's gonna jump!" screamed Al. "I'm gettin' out of here!"

"Stay here, you fool," shouted Kelly. "She can't get us as long as we're up here! If you go down, she'll hunt you down like a rabbit."

The blast of the Seven's motor was the last straw for Al. He squeaked and hopped over the edge, scrambling and sliding down the almost sheer face of the cut. He hit the bottom running.

Daisy Etta lowered her blade and raised her snout and growled forward, the blade loading. Six, seven, seven and a half cubic yards of dirt piled up in front of her as she neared the edge. The loaded blade bit into the narrow pathway that led out to their perch. It was almost all soft, white, crumbly marl, and the great machine sank nose down into it, the monstrous overload of topsoil spilling down on each side.

"She's going to bury herself!" shouted Kelly.

"No—wait." Tom caught his arm. "She's trying to turn—she made it! She made it! She's ramping herself down to the flat!"

"She is—and she's cut us off from the bluff!"

The bulldozer, blade raised as high as it could possibly go, the hydraulic rod gleaming clean in the early light, freed herself of her tremendous load, spun around and headed back upward, sinking her blade again. She made one more pass between them and the bluff, making a cut now far too wide for them to jump, particularly to the crumbly footing at the bluff's edge. Once down again, she turned to face their haven, now an isolated pillar of marl, and revved down, waiting.

"I never thought of this," said Kelly guiltily. "I knew we'd be safe from her ramping up, and I never thought she'd try it the other way!"

"Skip it. In the meantime, here we sit. What happens—do we wait up here until she idles out of fuel, or do we starve to death?"

"Oh, this won't be a siege, Tom. That thing's too much of a killer.

Where's Al? I wonder if he's got guts enough to make a pass near here with our tractor and draw her off?"

"He had just guts enough to take our tractor and head out," said Tom. "Didn't you know?"

"He took our—*what?*" Kelly looked out toward where they had left their machine the night before. It was gone. "Why the dirty little yellow rat!"

"No sense cussin'," said Tom steadily, interrupting what he knew was the beginning of some really flowery language. "What else could you expect?"

Daisy Etta decided, apparently, how to go about removing their splendid isolation. She uttered the snort of too-quick throttle, and moved into their peak with a corner of her blade, cutting out a huge swipe, undercutting the material over it so that it fell on her side and track as she passed. Eight inches disappeared from that side of their little plateau.

"Oh-oh. That won't do a-tall," said Tom.

"Fixin' to dig us down," said Kelly grimly. "Take her about twenty minutes. Tom, I say leave."

"It won't be healthy. You just got no idea how fast that thing can move now. Don't forget, she's a good deal more than she was when she had a man runnin' her. She can shift from high to reverse to fifth speed forward like that"—he snapped his fingers—"and she can pivot faster'n you can blink and throw that blade just where she wants it."

The tractor passed under them, bellowing, and their little table was suddenly a foot shorter.

"Awright," said Kelly. "So what do you want to do? Stay here and let her dig the ground out from under our feet?"

"I'm just warning you," said Tom. "Now listen. We'll wait until she's taking a load. It'll take her a second to get rid of it when she knows we're gone. We'll split—she can't get both of us. You head out in the open, try to circle the curve of the bluff and get where you can climb it. Then come back over here to the cut. A man can scramble off a fourteen-foot cut faster'n any tractor ever built. I'll cut in close to the cut, down at the bottom. If she takes after you, I'll get clear all right. If she takes after me, I'll try to make the shovel and at least give her a run for her money. I can play hide an' seek in an' around and under that dipper-stick all day if she wants to play."

"Why me out in the open?"

"Don't you think those long laigs o' yours can outrun her in that distance?"

"Reckon they got to," grinned Kelly. "O.K., Tom."

They waited tensely. *Daisy Etta* backed close by, started another pass. As the motor blatted under the load, Tom said, "Now!" and they jumped. Kelly, catlike as always, landed on his feet. Tom, whose knees and ankles were black and blue with rope bruises, took two staggering steps and fell. Kelly scooped him to his feet as the dozer's steel prow came around the bank. Instantly she was in fifth gear and howling down at them. Kelly flung himself to the left and Tom to the right, and they pounded away, Kelly out toward the runway, Tom straight for the shovel. *Daisy Etta* let them diverge for a moment, keeping her course, trying to pursue both; then she evidently sized Tom up as the slower, for she swung toward him. The instant's hesitation was all Tom needed to get the little lead necessary. He tore up to the shovel, his legs going like pistons, and dived down between the shovel's tracks.

As he hit the ground, the big manganese-steel moldboard hit the right track of the shovel, and the impact set all forty-seven tons of the great machine quivering. But Tom did not stop. He scrabbled his way under the rig, stood up behind it, leaped and caught the sill of the rear window, clapped his other hand on it, drew himself up and tumbled inside. Here he was safe for the moment; the huge tracks themselves were higher than the Seven's blade could rise, and the floor of the cab was a good sixteen inches higher than the top of the track. Tom went to the cab door and peeped outside. The tractor had drawn off and was idling.

"Study away," gritted Tom, and went to the big Murphy Diesel. He unhurriedly checked the oil with the bayonet gauge, replaced it, took the governor cut-out rod from its rack and inserted it in the governor casing. He set the master throttle at the halfway mark, pulled up the starter-handle, twitched the cut-out. The motor spat a wad of blue smoke out of its hooded exhaust and caught. Tom put the rod back, studied the fuel-flow glass and pressure gauges, and then went to the door and looked out again. The Seven had not moved, but it was revving up and down in the uneven fashion it had shown up on the mesa. Tom had the extraordinary idea that it was gathering itself to spring. He slipped into the saddle, threw the master clutch. The big gears that half-filled the cab obediently began to turn. He kicked the brake-locks loose with his heels, let his feet rest lightly on the pedals as they rose.

Then he reached over his head and snapped back the throttle. As the Murphy picked up he grasped both hoist and swing levers and pulled them back. The engine howled; the two-yard bucket came up off the ground with a sudden jolt as the cold friction grabbed it. The big machine swung hard to the right; Tom snapped his hoist lever forward and checked the bucket's rise with his foot on the brake. He shoved the crowd lever forward; the bucket ran out to the end of its reach, and the heel of the bucket wiped across the Seven's hood, taking with it the exhaust stack, muffler and all, and the pre-cleaner on the air intake. Tom cursed. He had figured on the machine's leaping backward. If it had, he would have smashed the cast-iron radiator core. But she had stood still, making a split-second decision.

Now she moved, though, and quickly. With that incredibly fast shifting, she leaped backwards and pivoted out of range before Tom could check the shovel's mad swing. The heavy swing-friction blocks smoked acridly as the machine slowed, stopped and swung back. Tom checked her as he was facing the Seven, hoisted his bucket a few feet, and rehauled, bringing it about halfway back, ready for anything. The four great dipper-teeth gleamed in the sun. Tom ran a practiced eye over cables, boom and dipper-stick, liking the black polish of crater compound on the sliding parts, the easy tension of well-greased cables and links. The huge machine stood strong, ready and profoundly subservient for all its brute power.

Tom looked searchingly at the Seven's ruined engine hood. The gaping end of the broken air-intake pipe stared back at him. "Aha!" he said. "A few cupfuls of nice dry marl down there'll give you something to chew on."

Keeping a wary eye on the tractor, he swung into the bank, dropped his bucket and plunged it into the marl. He crowded it deep, and the Murphy yelled for help but kept on pushing. At the peak of the load a terrific jar rocked him in the saddle. He looked back over his shoulder through the door and saw the Seven backing off again. She had run up and delivered a terrific punch to the counterweight at the back of the cab. Tom grinned tightly. She'd have to do better than that. There was nothing back there but eight or ten tons of solid steel. And he didn't much care at the moment whether or not she scratched his paint.

He swung back again, white marl running away on both sides of the heaped bucket. The shovel rode perfectly now, for a shovel is counterweighted to balance true when standing level with the bucket loaded. The hoist and swing frictions and the brake linings had heated and dried themselves of the night's condensation moisture, and she answered the controls in a way that delighted the operator in him. He handled the swing lever lightly, back to swing to the right, forward to swing to the left, following the slow dance the Seven had started to do, stepping warily back and forth like a fighter looking for an opening. Tom kept the bucket between himself and the tractor, knowing that she could not hurt a tool that was built to smash hard rock for twenty hours a day and like it.

Daisy Etta bellowed and rushed in. Tom snapped the hoist lever back hard, and the bucket rose, letting the tractor run underneath. Tom punched the bucket trip, and the great steel jaw opened, cascading marl down on the broken hood. The tractor's fan blew it back in a huge billowing cloud. The instant that it took Tom to check and dump was enough, however, for the tractor to dance back out of the way, for when he tried to drop it on the machine to smash the coiled injector tubes on top of the engine block, she was gone.

The dust cleared away, and the tractor moved in again, feinted to the left, then swung her blade at the bucket, which was just clear of the ground. Tom swung to meet her, her feint having gotten her in a little closer than he liked, and bucket met blade with a shower of sparks and a clank that could be heard for half a mile. She had come in with her blade high, and Tom let out a wordless shout as he saw that the A-frame brace behind the blade had caught between two of his dipper-teeth. He snatched at his hoist lever and the bucket came up, lifting with it the whole front end of the bulldozer.

Daisy Etta plunged up and down and her tracks dug violently into the earth as she raised and lowered her blade, trying to shake herself free. Tom rehauled, trying to bring the tractor in closer, for the boom was set too low to attempt to lift such a dead weight. As it was, the shovel's off track was trying its best to get off the ground. But the crowd and rehaul frictions could not handle her alone; they began to heat and slip.

Tom hoisted a little; the shovel's off track came up a foot off the ground. Tom cursed and let the bucket drop, and in an instant the dozer was free and running clear. Tom swung wildly at her, missed. The dozer came in on a long curve; Tom swung to meet her again, took a vicious swipe at her which she took on her blade. But this time she did not withdraw after being hit, but bored right in, carrying the bucket before her. Before Tom realized what she was doing his bucket was around in front of the tracks and between them, on the ground. It was as swift and skillful a maneuver as could be imagined, and it left the shovel without the ability to swing as long as *Daisy Etta* could hold the bucket trapped between the tracks.

Tom crowded furiously, but that succeeded only in lifting the boom higher in the air since there is nothing to hold a boom down but its own weight. Hoisting did nothing but make his frictions smoke and rev the engine down dangerously close to the stalling point.

Tom swore again and reached down to the cluster of small levers at his left. These were the gears. On this type of shovel, the swing lever controls everything except crowd and hoist. With the swing lever, the operator, having selected his gear, controls the travel—that is, power to the tracks—in forward and reverse; booming up and booming down; and swinging. The machine can do only one of these things at a time. If she is in travel gear, she cannot swing. If she is in swing gear, she cannot boom up or down. Not once in years of operating would this inability bother an operator; now, however, nothing was normal.

Tom pushed the swing gear control down and pulled up on the travel. The clutches involved were jaw clutches, not frictions, so that he had to throttle down to an idle before he could make the castellations mesh. As the Murphy revved down, *Daisy Etta* took it as a signal that something could be done about it, and she shoved furiously into the bucket. But Tom had all controls in neutral and all she succeeded in doing was to dig herself in, her sharp new cleats spinning deep into the dirt.

Tom set his throttle up again and shoved the swing lever forward. There was a vast crackling of drive chains; and the big tracks started to turn.

Daisy Etta had sharp cleats; her pads were twenty inches wide and her tracks were fourteen feet long, and there were fourteen tons of steel on them. The shovel's big flat pads were three feet wide and twenty feet long, and forty-seven tons aboard. There was simply no comparison. The Murphy bellowed the fact that the work was hard, but gave no indications of stalling. *Daisy Etta* performed the incredible feat of shifting into forward gear while she was moving backwards, but it did her no good. Round and round her tracks went, trying to drive her forward, gouging deep; and slowly and surely she was forced backward toward the cut wall by the shovel.

Tom heard a sound that was not part of a straining machine; he looked out and saw Kelly on top of the cut, smoking, swinging his feet over the edge, making punching motions with his hands as if he had a ringside seat at a big fight—which he certainly had.

Tom now offered the dozer little choice. If she did not turn aside before him, she would be borne back against the bank and her fuel tank crushed. There was every possibility that, having her pinned there, Tom would have time to raise his bucket over her and smash her to pieces. And if she turned before she was forced against the bank, she would have to free Tom's bucket. This she had to do.

The Murphy gave him warning, but not enough. It crooned as the load came off, and Tom knew that the dozer was shifting into a reverse gear. He whipped the hoist lever back, and the bucket rose as the dozer backed away from him. He crowded it out and let it come smashing down—and missed. For the tractor danced aside—

and while he was in travel gear he could not swing to follow it. *Daisy Etta* charged then, put one track on the bank and went over almost on her beam-ends, throwing one end of her blade high in the air. So totally unexpected was it that Tom was quite unprepared. The tractor flung itself on the bucket, and the cutting edge of the blade dropped between the dipper teeth. This time there was the whole weight of the tractor to hold it there. There would be no way for her to free herself—but at the same time she had trapped the bucket so far out from the center pin of the shovel that Tom couldn't hoist without overbalancing and turning the monster over.

Daisy Etta ground away in reverse, dragging the bucket out until it was checked by the bumper-blocks. Then she began to crab sideways, up against the bank and when Tom tried tentatively to rehaul, she shifted and came right with him, burying one whole end of her blade deep into the bank.

Stalemate. She had hung herself up on the bucket, and she had immobilized it. Tom tried to rehaul, but the tractor's anchorage in the bank was too solid. He tried to swing, to hoist. All the overworked frictions could possibly give out was smoke. Tom grunted and throttled to an idle, leaned out the window. *Daisy Etta* was idling too, loudly without her muffler, the stackless exhaust giving out an ugly flat sound. But after the roar of the two great motors the partial silence was deafening.

Kelly called down, "Double knockout, hey?"

"Looks like it. What say we see if we can't get close enough to her to quiet her down some?"

Kelly shrugged. "I dunno. If she's really stopped herself, it's the first time. I respect that rig, Tom. She wouldn't have got herself into that spot if she didn't have an ace up her sleeve."

"Look at her, man! Suppose she was a civilized bulldozer and you had to get her out of there. She can't raise her blade high enough to free it from those dipper-teeth, y'know. Think you'd be able to do it?"

"It might take several seconds," Kelly drawled. "She's sure high and dry."

"O.K., let's spike her guns."

"Like what?"

"Like taking a bar and prying out her tubing." He referred to the coiled brass tubing that carried the fuel, under pressure, from the pump to the injectors. There were many feet of it, running from the pump reservoir, stacked in expansion coils over the cylinder head.

As he spoke *Daisy Etta's* idle burst into that maniac revving up and down characteristic of her.

"What do you know!" Tom called above the racket. "Eavesdropping!"

Kelly slid down the cut, stood up on the track of the shovel and poked his head in the window. "Well, you want to get a bar and try?"

"Let's go!"

Tom went to the toolbox and pulled out a pinch bar that Kelly used to replace cables on his machine, and swung to the ground. They approached the tractor warily. She revved up as they came near, began to shudder. The front end rose and dropped and the tracks began to turn as she tried to twist out of the vise her blade had dropped into.

"Take it easy, sister," said Tom. "You'll just bury yourself. Set still and take it, now, like a good girl. You got it comin'."

"Be careful," said Kelly. Tom hefted the bar and laid a hand on the fender.

The tractor literally shivered, and from the rubber hose connection at the top of the radiator, a blinding steam of hot water shot out. It fanned and caught them both full in the face. They staggered back, cursing.

"You O.K., Tom?" Kelly gasped a moment later. He had got most of it across the mouth and cheek. Tom was on his knees, his shirt tail out, blotting his face.

"My eyes...oh, my eyes—"

"Let's see!" Kelly dropped down beside him and took him by the wrists, gently removing Tom's hands from his face. He whistled. "Come on," he gritted. He helped Tom up and led him away a few feet. "Stay here," he said hoarsely. He turned, walked back toward the dozer, picking up the pinch-bar. "You dirty—!" he yelled, and flung it like a javelin at the tube coils. It was a little high. It struck the ruined hood, made a deep dent in the metal. The dent promptly inverted with a loud *thung-g-g!* and flung the bar back at him. He ducked; it whistled over his head and caught Tom in the calves of his legs. He went down like a poled ox, but staggered to his feet again.

"Come on!" Kelly snarled, and taking Tom's arm, hustled him around the turn of the cut. "Sit down! I'll be right back."

"Where are you going? Kelly—be careful!"

"Careful and how!"

Kelly's long legs ate up the distance back to the shovel. He swung into the cab, reached back over the motor and set up the master throttle all the way. Stepping up behind the saddle, he opened the running throttle and the Murphy howled. Then he hauled back on the hoist lever until it knuckled in, turned and leaped off the machine in one supple motion.

The hoist drum turned and took up slack; the cable straightened as it took the strain. The bucket stirred under the dead weight of the bulldozer that rested on it; and slowly, then, the great flat tracks began to lift their rear ends off the ground. The great obedient mass of machinery teetered forward on the tips of her tracks, the Murphy revved down and under the incredible load, but it kept the strain. A strand of the two-part hoist cable broke and whipped around, singing; and then she was balanced—over-balanced—

And the shovel had hauled herself right over and had fallen with an earth-shaking crash. The boom, eight tons of solid steel, clanged down onto the blade of the bulldozer, and lay there, crushing it down tightly onto the imprisoning row of dipper-teeth.

Daisy Etta sat there, not trying to move now, racing her motor impotently. Kelly strutted past her, thumbing his nose, and went back to Tom.

"Kelly! I thought you were never coming back! What happened?"

"Shovel pulled herself over on her nose."

"Good boy! Fall on the tractor?"

"Nup. But the boom's laying across the top of her blade. Caught like a rat in a trap."

"Better watch out the rat don't chew its leg off to get out," said Tom, dryly. "Still runnin', is she?"

"Yep. But we'll fix that in a hurry."

"Sure. Sure. How?"

"How? I dunno. Dynamite, maybe. How's the optics?"

Tom opened one a trifle and grunted. "Rough. I can see a little, though. My eyelids are parboiled, mostly. Dynamite, you say? Well, let's think first. Think."

Tom sat back against the bank and stretched out his legs. "I tell you, Kelly, I been too blessed busy these last few hours to think much, but there's one thing that keeps comin' back to me—somethin' I was mullin' over long before the rest of you guys knew anything was up at all, except that Rivera had got hurt in some way I wouldn't tell you all about. But I don't reckon you'll call me crazy if I open my mouth now and let it all run out?"

"From now on," Kelly said fervently, "nobody's crazy. After this I'll believe anything." He sat down.

"O.K. Well, about that tractor. What do you suppose has got into her?"

"Search me. I dunno."

"No—don't say that. I just got an idea we can't stop at 'I dunno.' We got to figure all the angles on this thing before we know just what to do about it. Let's just get this thing lined up. When did it start? On the mesa. How? Rivera was opening an old building with the Seven. This thing came out of there. Now here's what I'm getting at. We can dope these things out about it: It's intelligent. It can only get into a machine and not into a man. It—"

"What about that? How do you know it can't?"

"Because it had the chance to and didn't. I was standing right by the opening when it kited out. Rivera was up on the machine at the time. It didn't directly harm either of us. It got into the tractor, and the tractor did. By the same token, it can't hurt a man when it's out of a machine, but that's all it wants to do when it's in one. O.K.?

"To get on: once it's in the machine it can't get out again. We know that because it had plenty of chances and didn't take them. That scuffle with the dipper-stick, f'r instance. My face woulda been plenty red if it had taken over the shovel—and you can bet it would have if it could."

"I got you so far. But what are we going to do about it?"

"That's the thing. You see, I don't think it's enough to wreck the tractor. We might burn it, blast it, and still not hurt whatever it was that got into it up on the mesa."

"That makes sense. But I don't see what else we can do than just break up the dozer. We haven't got a line on actually what the thing is."

"I think we have. Remember I asked you all those screwy questions about the arc that killed Peebles. Well, when that happened, I recollected a flock of other things. One—when it got out of that hole up there, I smelled that smell that you notice when you're welding; sometimes when lightning strikes real close."

"Ozone," said Kelly.

"Yeah—ozone. Then, it likes metal, not flesh. But most of all, there was that arc. Now, that was absolutely screwy. You know as well as I do—better—that an arc generator simply don't have the push to do a thing like that. It can't kill a man, and it can't throw an arc no fifty feet. But it did. An' that's why I asked you if there could be something—a field, or some such—that could *suck* current out of a generator, all at once, faster than it could flow. Because this thing's electrical; it fits all around."

"Electronic," said Kelly doubtfully, thoughtfully.

"I wouldn't know. Now then. When Peebles was killed, a funny thing happened. Remember what Chub said? The Seven moved back—straight back, about thirty feet, until it bumped into a roadroller that was standing behind it. It did that with no fuel in the starting engine—without even using the starting engine, for that matter—and with the compression valves locked open!

"Kelly, that thing in the dozer can't do much, when you come right down to it. It couldn't fix itself up after that joyride on the mesa. It can't make the machine do too much more than the machine can do ordinarily. What it actually can do, seems to me, is to make a spring push instead of pull, like the control levers, and make a fitting slip when it's supposed to hold, like the ratchet on the throttle lever. It can turn a shaft, like the way it cranks its own starting motor.

But if it was so all-fired high-powered, it wouldn't have to use the starting motor! The absolute biggest job it's done so far, seems to me, was when it walked back from that welding machine when Peebles got his. Now, why did it do that just then?"

"Reckon it didn't like the brimstone smell, like it says in the Good Book," said Kelly sourly.

"That's pretty close, seems to me. Look, Kelly—this thing *feels* things. I mean, it can get sore. If it couldn't it never woulda kept driving in at the shovel like that. It can think. But if it can do all those things, then it can be *scared!*"

"Scared? Why should it be scared?"

"Listen. Something went on in that thing when the arc hit it. What's that I read in a magazine once about heat—something about molecules runnin' around with their heads cut off when they got hot?"

"Molecules do. They go into rapid motion when heat is applied. But—"

"But nothin'. That machine was hot for four hours after that. But she was hot in a funny way. Not just around the place where the arc hit, like as if it was a welding arc. But hot all over—from the moldboard to the fuel-tank cap. Hot everywhere. And just as hot behind the final drive housings as she was at the top of the blade where the poor guy put his hand.

"And look at this." Tom was getting excited, as his words crystallized his ideas. "She was scared—scared enough to back off from that welder, putting everything she could into it, to get back from that welding machine. And after that, she was sick. I say that because in the whole time she's had that what-ever-ya-call-it in her, she's never been near men without trying to kill them, except for those two days after the arc hit her. She had juice enough to start herself when Dennis came around with the crank, but she still needed someone to run her till she got her strength back."

"But why didn't she turn and smash up the welder when Dennis took her?"

"One of two things. She didn't have the strength, or she didn't have the guts. She was scared, maybe, and wanted out of there, away from that thing."

"But she had all night to go back for it!"

"Still scared. Or . . . oh, *that's* it! She had other things to do first. Her main idea is to kill men—there's no other way you can figure it. It's what she was built to do. Not the tractor—they don't build 'em sweeter'n that machine; but the thing that's runnin' it."

"What *is* that thing?" Kelly mused. "Coming out of that old building—temple—what have you—how old is it? How long was it there? What kept it in there?"

"What kept it in there was some funny gray stuff that lined the inside of the buildin'," said Tom. "It was like rock, an' it was like smoke.

"It was a color that scared you to look at it, and it gave Rivera and me the creeps when we got near it. Don't ask me what it was. I went up there to look at it, and it's gone. Gone from the building, anyhow. There was a little lump of it on the ground. I don't know whether that was a hunk of it, or all of it rolled up into a ball. I get the creeps again thinkin' about it."

Kelly stood up. "Well, the heck with it. We been beatin' our gums up here too long anyhow. There's just enough sense in what you say to make me want to try something nonsensical, if you see what I mean. If that welder can sweat the Ol' Nick out of that tractor, I'm on. Especially from fifty feet away. There should be a Dumptor around here somewhere; let's move from here. Can you navigate now?"

"Reckon so, a little." Tom rose and together they followed the cut until they came on the Dumptor. They climbed on, cranked it up and headed toward camp.

About half way there Kelly looked back, gasped, and putting his mouth close to Tom's ear, bellowed against the scream of the motor. "Tom! 'Member what you said about the rat in the trap biting off a leg?"

"Well, *Daisy* did too! She's left her blade an' pushbeams an' she's followin' us in!"

They howled into the camp, gasping against the dust that followed when they pulled up by the welder.

Kelly, said, "You cast around and see if you can find a drawpin to hook that rig up to the Dumptor with. I'm goin' after some water an' chow!"

Tom grinned. Imagine old Kelly forgetting that a Dumptor had no drawbar! He groped around to a toolbox, peering out of the narrow slit beneath swollen lids, felt behind it and located a shackle. He climbed up on the Dumptor, turned it around and backed up to the welding machine. He passed the shackle through the ring at the end of the steering tongue of the welder, screwed in the pin and dropped the shackle over the front towing hook of the Dumptor. A Dumptor being what it is, having no real front and no real rear, and direct reversing gears in all speeds, it was no trouble to drive it "backwards" for a change.

Kelly came pounding back, out of breath. "Fix it? Good. Shackle? No drawbar! *Daisy's* closin' up fast; I say let's take the beach. We'll be concealed until we have a good lead out o' this pocket, and the going's pretty fair, long as we don't bury this jalopy in the sand."

"Good," said Tom as they climbed on and he accepted an open tin of K. "Only go easy; bump around too much and the welder'll slip off the hook. An' I somehow don't want to lose it just now."

They took off, zooming up the beach. A quarter of a mile up, they sighted the Seven across the flat. It immediately turned and took a course that would intercept them.

"Here she comes," shouted Kelly, and stepped down hard on the accelerator. Tom leaned over the back of the seat, keeping his eye on their tow. "Hey! Take it easy! Watch it!

"Hey!"

But it was too late. The tongue of the welding machine responded to that one bump too many. The shackle jumped up off the hook, the welder lurched wildly, slewed hard to the left. The tongue dropped to the sand and dug in; the machine rolled up on it and snapped it off, finally stopped, leaning crazily askew. By a miracle it did not quite turn over.

Kelly tramped on the brakes and both their heads did their utmost to snap off their shoulders. They leaped off and ran back to the welder. It was intact, but towing it was now out of the question. "If there's going to be a showdown, it's gotta be here."

The beach here was about thirty yards wide, the sand almost level, and undercut banks of sawgrass forming the landward edge in a series of little hummocks and headlands. While Tom stayed with the machine, testing starter and generator contacts, Kelly walked up one of the little mounds, stood up on it and scanned the beach back the way he had come. Suddenly he began to shout and wave his arms.

"What's got into you?"

"It's Al!" Kelly called back. "With the pan tractor!"

Tom dropped what he was doing, and came to stand beside Kelly. "Where's the Seven? I can't see."

"Turned on the beach and followin' our track. Al! Al! You little skunk, c'mere!"

Tom could now dimly make out the pan tractor cutting across directly toward them and the beach.

"He don't see *Daisy Etta,*" remarked Kelly disgustedly, "or he'd sure be headin' the other way."

Fifty yards away Al pulled up and throttled down. Kelly shouted and waved to him. Al stood up on the machine, cupped his hands around his mouth. "Where's the Seven?"

"Never mind that! Come here with that tractor!"

Al stayed where he was. Kelly cursed and started out after him. "You stay away from me," he said when Kelly was closer.

"I ain't got time for you now," said Kelly. "Bring that tractor down to the beach."

"Where's that *Daisy Etta?*" Al's voice was oddly strained.

"Right behind us." Kelly tossed a thumb over his shoulder. "On the beach."

Al's pop eyes clicked wide almost audibly. He turned on his heel and jumped off the machine and started to run. Kelly uttered a wordless syllable that was somehow more obscene than anything else he had ever uttered, and vaulted into the seat of the machine. "Hey!" he bellowed after Al's rapidly diminishing figure. "You're runnin' right into her." Al appeared not to hear, but went pelting down the beach.

Kelly put her into fifth gear and poured on the throttle. As the tractor began to move he whacked out the master clutch, snatched the overdrive lever back to put her into sixth, rammed the clutch in again, all so fast that she did not have time to stop rolling. Bucking and jumping over the rough ground the fast machine whined for the beach.

Tom was fumbling back to the welder, his ears telling him better than his eyes how close the Seven was—for she was certainly no nightingale, particularly without her exhaust stack. Kelly reached the machine as he did.

"Get behind it," snapped Tom. "I'll jamb the tierod with the shackle, and you see if you can't bunt her up into that pocket between those two hummocks. Only take it easy—you don't want to tear up that generator. Where's Al?"

"Don't ask me. He run down the beach to meet *Daisy*."

"He *what?*"

The whine of the two-cycle drowned out Kelly's answer, if any. He got behind the welder and set his blade against it. Then in a low gear, slipping his clutch in a little, he slowly nudged the machine toward the place Tom indicated. It was a little hollow in between two projecting banks. The surf and the high-tide mark dipped inland here to match it; the water was only a few feet away.

Tom raised his arm and Kelly stopped. From the other side of the projecting shelf, out of their sight now, came the flat roar of the Seven's exhaust. Kelly sprang off the tractor and went to help Tom, who was furiously throwing out coils of cable from the rack of the welder. "What's the game?"

"We got to ground that Seven some way," panted Tom. He threw the last bit of cable out to clear it of kinks and turned to the panel.

"How was it—about sixty volts and the amperage on 'special application'?" He spun the dials, pressed the starter button. The motor responded instantly. Kelly scooped up ground clamp and rod holder and tapped them together. The solenoid governor picked up the load and the motor hummed as a good live spark took the jump.

"Good," said Tom, switching off the generator. "Come on, Lieutenant General Electric, figure me out a way to ground that maverick."

Kelly tightened his lips, shook his head. "I dunno—unless somebody actually claps this thing on her."

"No, boy, can't do that. If one of us gets killed—"

Kelly tossed the ground clamp idly, his lithe body taut. "Don't give me that, Tom. You know I'm elected because you can't see good enough yet to handle it. You know you'd do it if you could. You—"

He stopped short, for the steadily increasing roar of the approaching Seven had stopped, was blatting away now in that extraordinary irregular throttling that *Daisy Etta* affected.

"Now, what's got into her?"

Kelly broke away and scrambled up the bank. "Tom!" he gasped. "Tom—come up here!"

Tom followed, and they lay side by side, peering out over the top of the escarpment at the remarkable tableau.

Daisy Etta was standing on the beach, near the water, not moving. Before her, twenty or thirty feet away, stood Al Knowles, his arms out in front of him, talking a blue streak. *Daisy* made far too much racket for them to hear what he was saying.

"Do you reckon he's got guts enough to stall her off for us?" said Tom.

"If he has, it's the queerest thing that's happened yet on this old island," Kelly breathed, "an' that's saying something."

The Seven revved up till she shook, and then throttled back. She ran down so low then that they thought she had shut herself down, but she caught on the last two revolutions and began to idle quietly. And then they could hear.

Al's voice was high, hysterical. "—I come t' he'p you, I come t' he'p you, don' kill me, I'll he'p you—" He took a step forward; the dozer snorted and he fell to his knees. "I'll wash you an' grease you and change yo' ile," he said in a high singsong.

"The guy's not human," said Kelly wonderingly.

"He ain't housebroke either," Tom chuckled.

"—lemme he'p you. I'll fix you when you break down. I'll he'p you kill those other guys—"

"She don't need any help!" said Tom.

"The louse," growled Kelly. "The rotten little double-crossing polecat!" He stood up. "Hey, you Al! Come out o' that. I mean now! If she don't get you I will, if you don't move."

Al was crying now. "Shut up!" he screamed. "I know who's bawss hereabouts, an' so do you!" He pointed at the tractor. "She'll kill us all iff'n we don't do what she wants!" He turned back to the machine. "I'll k-kill 'em fo' you. I'll wash you and shine you up and f-fix yo' hood. I'll put yo' blade back on. . . ."

Tom reached out and caught Kelly's legs as the tall man started out, blind mad. "Git back here," he barked. "What you want to do—get killed for the privilege of pinnin' his ears back?"

Kelly subsided and came back, threw himself down beside Tom, put his face in his hands. He was quivering with rage.

"Don't take on so," Tom said. "The man's plumb loco. You can't argue with him any more'n you can with *Daisy*, there. If he's got to get his, *Daisy'll* give it to him."

"Aw, Tom, it ain't that. I know he ain't worth it, but I can't sit up here and watch him get himself killed. I can't, Tom."

Tom thumped him on the shoulder, because there were simply no words to be said. Suddenly he stiffened, snapped his fingers.

"There's our ground," he said urgently, pointing seaward. "The water—the wet beach where the surf runs. If we can get our ground clamp out there and her somewhere near it—"

"Ground the pan tractor. Run it out into the water. It ought to reach—partway, anyhow."

"That's it—c'mon."

They slid down the bank, snatched up the ground clamp, attached it to the frame on the pan tractor.

"I'll take it," said Tom, and as Kelly opened his mouth, Tom shoved him back against the welding machine. "No time to argue," he snapped, swung on to the machine, slapped her in gear and was off. Kelly took a step toward the tractor, and then his quick eyes saw a bight of the ground cable about to foul a wheel of the welder. He stopped and threw it off, spread out the rest of it so it would pay off clear. Tom, with the incredible single-mindedness of the trained operator, watched only the black line of the trailing cable on the sand behind him. When it straightened he stopped. The front of the tracks were sloshing in the gentle surf. He climbed off the side away from the Seven and tried to see. There was movement, and the growl of her motor now running at a bit more than idle, but he could not distinguish much.

Kelly picked up the rod holder and went to peer around the head of the protruding bank. Al was on his feet, still crooning hysterically, sidling over toward *Daisy Etta*. Kelly ducked back, threw the switch on the arc generator, climbed the bank and crawled along through the sawgrass paralleling the beach until the holder in his hand tugged and he knew he had reached the end of the cable. He looked out at the beach; measured carefully with his eye the arc he would travel if he left his position and, keeping the cable taut, went out on the beach. At no point would he come within seventy feet of the possessed machine, let alone fifty. She had to be drawn in closer. And she had to be maneuvered out to the wet sand, or in the water—

Al Knowles, encouraged by the machine's apparent decision not to move, approached, though warily, and still running off at the mouth. "—we'll kill 'em off an' then we'll keep it a secret and th' bahges'll come an' take us offen th' island and we'll go to anothah job an' kill us lots mo' ... an' when yo' tracks git dry an' squeak we'll wet 'em with blood, and you'll be rightly king o' the hill ... look yondah, look yondah, *Daisy Etta*, see them theah, by the otheh tractuh, theah they are, kill 'em, *Daisy*, kill 'em, *Daisy*, an' lemme he'p ... heah me. *Daisy*, heah me, say you heah me—" and the motor roared in response. Al laid a timid hand on the radiator guard, leaning far over to do it, and the tractor still stood there grumbling but not moving. Al stepped back, motioned with his arm, began to walk off slowly toward the pan tractor, looking backwards as he did so like a man training a dog. "C'mon, c'mon, theah's one theah, le's *kill'm, kill'm, kill'm* ..."

And with a snort the tractor revved up and followed.

Kelly licked his lips without effect because his tongue was dry, too. The madman passed him, walking straight up the center of the beach, and the tractor, now no longer a bulldozer, followed him; and there the sand was bone dry, sun-dried, dried to powder. As the tractor passed him, Kelly got up on all fours, went over the edge of the bank onto the beach, crouched there.

Al crooned, "I love ya, honey, I love ya, 'deed I do—"

Kelly ran crouching, like a man under machine-gun fire, making himself as small as possible and feeling as big as a barn door. The torn-up sand where the tractor had passed was under his feet now; he stopped, afraid to get too much closer, afraid that a weakened, badly grounded arc might leap from the holder in his hand and serve only to alarm and infuriate the thing in the tractor. And just then Al saw him.

"There!" he screamed; and the tractor pulled up short. "Behind you! Get'm, *Daisy! Kill'm, kill'm, kill'm.*"

Kelly stood up almost wearily, fury and frustration too much to be borne. "In the water," he yelled, because it was what his whole being wanted. "Get'er in the water! Wet her tracks, Al!"

"Kill'm, kill'm—"

As the tractor started to turn, there was a commotion over by the pan tractor. It was Tom, jumping, shouting, waving his arms, swearing. He ran out from behind his machine, straight at the Seven. *Daisy Etta*'s motor roared and she swung to meet him, Al barely dancing back out of the way. Tom cut sharply, sand spouting under his pumping feet, and ran straight into the water. He went out to about waist deep, suddenly disappeared. He surfaced, spluttering, still trying to shout. Kelly took a better grip on his rod holder and rushed.

Daisy Etta, in following Tom's crazy rush, had swung in beside the pan tractor, not fifteen feet away; and she, too, was now in the surf. Kelly closed up the distance as fast as his long legs would let him; and as he approached to within that crucial fifty feet, Al Knowles hit him.

Al was frothing at the mouth, gibbering. The two men hit full tilt; Al's head caught Kelly in the midriff as he missed a straightarm, and the breath went out of him in one great *whoosh!* Kelly went down like tall timber, the whole world turned to one swirling red-gray haze. Al flung himself on the bigger man, clawing, smacking, too berserk to ball his fists.

"Ah'm go' to kill you," he gurgled. "She'll git one, I'll git t'other, an' then she'll know—"

Kelly covered his face with his arms, and as some wind was sucked at last into his laboring lungs, he flung them upward and sat up in one mighty surge. Al was hurled upward and to one side, and as he hit the ground Kelly reached out a long arm, and twisted his fingers into the man's coarse hair, raised him up, and came across with his other fist in a punch that would have killed him had it landed square. But Al managed to jerk to one side enough so that it only amputated a cheek. He fell and lay still. Kelly scrambled madly around in the sand for his welding-rod holder, found it and began to run again. He couldn't see Tom at all now, and the Seven was standing in the surf, moving slowly from side to side, backing out, ravening. Kelly held the rod-clamp and its trailing cable blindly before him and ran straight at the machine. And then it came — that thin, soundless bolt of energy. But this time it had its full force, for poor old Peebles' body had not been the ground that this swirling water offered. *Daisy Etta* literally leaped backwards toward him, and the water around her tracks spouted upward in hot steam. The sound of her engine ran up and up, broke, took on the rhythmic, uneven beat of a swing drummer. She threw herself from side to side like a cat with a bag over its head. Kelly stepped a little closer, hoping for another bolt to come from the clamp in his hand, but there was none, for—

"The circuit breaker!" cried Kelly.

He threw the holder up on the deck plate of the Seven in front of the seat, and ran across the little beach to the welder. He reached behind the switchboard, got his thumb on the contact hinge and jammed it down.

Daisy Etta leaped again, and then again, and suddenly her motor stopped. Heat in turbulent waves blurred the air over her. The little gas tank for the starting motor went out with a cannon's roar, and the big fuel tank, still holding thirty-odd gallons of Diesel oil, fol-lowed. It puffed itself open rather than exploded, and threw a great curtain of flame over the ground behind the machine. Motor or no motor, then, Kelly distinctly saw the tractor shudder convulsively. There was a crawling movement of the whole frame, a slight wave of motion away from the fuel tank, approaching the front of the machine, and moving upward from the tracks. It culminated in the crown of the radiator core, just in front of the radiator cap; and suddenly an area of six or seven square inches literally *blurred* around the edges. For a second, then, it was normal, and finally it slumped molten, and liquid metal ran down the sides, throwing out little sparks as it encountered what was left of the charred paint. And only then was Kelly conscious of agony in his left hand. He looked down. The welding machine's generator had stopped, though the motor was still turning, having smashed the friable coupling on its drive shaft. Smoke poured from the generator, which had become little more than a heap of slag. Kelly did not scream, though, until he looked and saw what had happened to his hand—

When he could see straight again, he called for Tom, and there was no answer. At last he saw something out in the water, and plunged in after it. The splash of cold salt water on his left hand he hardly felt, for the numbness of shock had set in. He grabbed at Tom's shirt with his good hand, and then the ground seemed to pull itself out from under his feet. That was it, then—a deep hole right off the beach. The Seven had run right to the edge of it, had kept Tom there out of his depth and—

He flailed wildly, struck out for the beach, so near and so hard to get to. He gulped a stinging lungful of brine, and only the lovely shock of his knee striking solid beach kept him from giving up to the luxury of choking to death. Sobbing with effort, he dragged Tom's dead weight inshore and clear of the surf. It was then that he became conscious of a child's shrill weeping; for a mad moment he thought it was he himself, and then he looked and saw that it was Al Knowles. He left Tom and went over to the broken creature.

"Get up, you," he snarled. The weeping only got louder. Kelly rolled him over on his back—he was quite unresisting—and belted him back and forth across the mouth until Al began to choke. Then he hauled him to his feet and led him over to Tom.

"Kneel down, scum. Put one of your knees between his knees." Al stood still. Kelly hit him again and he did as he was told.

"Put your hands on his lower ribs. There. O.K. Lean, you rat. Now sit back." He sat down, holding his left wrist in his right hand, letting the blood drop from the ruined hand. "Lean. Hold it—sit back. Lean. Sit. Lean. Sit."

Soon Tom sighed and began to vomit weakly, and after that he was all right.

This is the story of *Daisy Etta*, the bulldozer that went mad and had a life of its own, and not the story of the missile test that they don't talk about except to refer to it as the missile test that they don't talk about. But you may have heard about it for all that—rumors, anyway. The rumor has it that an early IRBM tested out a radically new controls system by proving conclusively that it did not work. It was a big bird and contained much juice, and flew far, far afield. Rumor goes on to assert that a) it alighted somewhere in the unmapped rain forests of South America and that b) there were no casualties. What they *really* don't talk about is the closely guarded report asserting that both a) and b) are false. There are only two people (aside from yourself, now) who know for sure that though a) is certainly false, b) is strangely true, and there were indeed no casualties.

Al Knowles may well know too, but he doesn't count.

It happened two days after the death of *Daisy Etta*, as Tom and Kelly sat in (of all places) the coolth of the ruined temple. They were poring over paper and pencil, trying to complete the impossible task of making a written statement of what had happened on the island, and why they and their company had failed to complete their contract. They had found Chub and Harris, and had buried them next to the other three. Al Knowles was back in the shadows, tied up, because they had heard him raving in his sleep, and it seemed he could not believe *Daisy* was dead and he still wanted to go around killing operators for her. They knew that there must be an investigation, and they knew just how far their story would go; and having escaped a monster like *Daisy Etta*, they found life too sweet to want any part of it spent under observation or in jail.

The warhead of the missile struck near the edge of their camp, just between the pyramid of fuel drums and the dynamite stores. The second stage alighted a moment later two miles away, in the vicinity of the five graves. Kelly and Tom stumbled out to the rim of the mesa, and for a long while watched the jetsam fall and the flotsam rise. It was Kelly who guessed what must have happened, and "Bless their clumsy little hearts," he said happily. And he took the scribbled papers from Tom and tore them across.

But Tom shook his head, and thumbed back at the mound. "He'll talk."

"Him?" said Kelly, with such profound eloquence in his tone that he clearly evoked the image of Al Knowles, with his mumbling voice and his drooling mouth and his wide glazed eyes. "Let him," Kelly said, and tore the papers again.

So they let him.

Abreaction

I SAT AT the controls of the big D-8 bulldozer, and I tried to remember. The airfield shoulder, built on a saltflat, stretched around me. Off to the west was a clump of buildings—the gas station and grease rack. Near it was the skeletal silhouette of a temporary weather observation post with its spinning velocimeter and vane and windsock. Everything seemed normal, but there was something *else.* . . .

I could remember people, beautiful people in shining, floating garments. I remembered them as if I had seen them just a minute ago, and yet at a distance; but the memories were of faces close—close. One face—a golden girl; eyes and skin and hair three different shades of gold.

I shook my head so violently that it hurt. I was a bulldozer operator. I was—what was I supposed to be doing? I looked around me, saw the gravel spread behind me, the bare earth ahead; knew, then, that I was spreading gravel with the machine. But I seemed to—to—Look, without the physical fact of the half-done job around me, I wouldn't have known why I was there at all!

I knew where I had seen that girl, those people. I thought I knew . . . but the thought was just where I couldn't reach it. My mind put out searching tendrils for that knowledge of place, that was so certainly there, and the knowledge receded so that the tendrils stretched out thin and cracked with the effort, and my head ached from it.

A big trailer-type bottom-dump truck came hurtling and howling over the shoulder toward me, the huge fenderless driving wheels throwing clots of mud high in the air. The driver was a Puerto Rican, a hefty middle-aged fellow. I knew him well. Well—didn't I? He threw out one arm, palm up, signaling "Where do you want it?" I pointed vaguely to the right, to the advancing edge of the spread gravel. He spun his steering wheel with one hand, put the other on the trip-lever on his steering column, keeping his eyes on my face. As he struck the edge of the gravel fill with his wheels I dropped my hand; he punched the lever and the bottom of the trailer opened up, streaming gravel out in a windrow thirty feet long and a foot deep—twelve cubic yards of it, delivered at full speed. The driver waved and headed off, the straight-gut exhaust of his high-speed Diesel snorting and snarling as the rough ground bounced the man's foot on the accelerator.

I waved back at the Puerto Rican—what was his name? I knew him, didn't I? He knew me, the way he waved as he left. His name—was it Paco? Cruz? Eulalio? Damn it, no, and I knew it as well as I knew my own—

But I didn't know my own name!

Oh hell, oh hell, I'm crazy. I'm scared. I'm scared crazy. What had happened to my head?... Everything whirled around me and without effort I remembered about the people in the shining clothes and as my mind closed on it, it evaporated again and there was nothing there.

Once when I was a kid in school I fell off the parallel bars and knocked myself out, and when I came to it was like this. I could see everything and feel and smell and taste anything, but I couldn't remember anything. Not for a minute. I would ask what had happened, and they would tell me, and five minutes later I'd ask again. They asked me my address so they could take me home, and I couldn't remember it. They got the address from the school files and took me home, and my feet found the way in and up four flights of stairs to our apartment—I didn't remember which way to go, but my feet did. I went in and tried to tell my mother what was the matter with me and I couldn't remember, and she put me to bed and I woke four hours later perfectly all right again.

In a minute, there on the bulldozer, I didn't get over being scared but I began to get used to it, so I could think a little. I tried to remember everything at first, but that was too hard, so I tried to find something I could remember. I sat there and let my mind go quite blank. Right away there was something about a bottom-dump truck and some gravel. It was there, clear enough, but I didn't know where it fit nor how far back. I looked around me and there was the windrow of gravel waiting to be spread. Then that was what the truck was for; and—had it just been there, or had I been sitting there for long, for ever so long, waiting to remember that I must spread it?

Then I saw that I could remember ideas, but not events. Events were there, yes, but not in order. No continuity. A year ago—a second ago—same thing. Nothing clear, nothing very real, all mixed up. Ideas were there whatever, and continuity didn't matter. That I could remember an idea, that I could know that a windrow of gravel meant that gravel must be spread: *that* was an idea, a condition of things which I could recognize. The truck's coming and going and dumping, that was an event. I knew it had happened because the gravel was there, but didn't know when, or if anything had happened in between.

I looked at the controls and frowned. Could I remember what to do with them? This lever and that pedal—what did they mean to me? Nothing, and nothing again. . . .

I mustn't think about that. I don't have to think about that. I must think about *what* I must do and not how I must do it. I've got to spread the stone. Here there is spread stone and there there is none, and at the edge of the spread stone is the windrow of gravel. So, watching it, seeing how it lay, I let my hands and feet remember about the levers and pedals. They throttled up, raised the blade off the ground, shifted into third gear, swung the three-ton moldboard and its twelve-foot cutting edge into the windrow. The blade loaded and gravel ran off the ends in two even rolls, and my right hand flicked to and away from me on the blade control, knowing how to raise it enough to let the gravel run out evenly underneath the cutting edge, not too high so that it would make a bobble in the fill for the tracks to teeter on when they reached it—for a bulldozer builds the road it walks on, and if the road is rough the machine see-saws forward and the blade cuts and fills to make waves which, when the tracks reach them, makes the machine see-saw and cut waves, which, when the tracks reach them . . . anyway, my hands knew what to do, and my feet; and they did it all the time when I could only see what was to be done, and could not understand the events of doing it.

This won't do, I thought desperately. I'm all right, I guess, because I can do my work. It's all laid out in front of me and I know what has to be done and my hands and feet know how to do it; but suppose somebody comes and speaks to me or tells me to go somewhere else, I who can't even remember my own name. My hands and my feet have more sense than my head.

So I thought that I had to inventory everything I could trust, everything I knew positively. What were the things I knew?

The machine was there and true, and the gravel, and the bottom-dump that brought it. My being there was a real thing. You have to start everything with the belief that you yourself exist.

The job, the work, they were true things.

Where was I?

I must be where I should be, where I belonged, for the bottom-dump driver knew me, knew I was there, knew I was waiting for stone to spread. The airfield was there, and the fact that it was unfinished. "Airfield" was like a corollary to me, with the runway and the windsock its supporting axioms, and I had no need to think further. The people in the shining garments, and the girl—

But there was nothing about them here. Nothing at all.

To spread stone was a thing I had to do. But was that all? It wasn't just spreading stone. I had to spread it to—to—

Not to help finish the airfield. It wasn't that. It was something else, something—

Oh. Oh! I had to spread stone to *get* somewhere.

I didn't want to get anywhere, except maybe to a place where I could think again, where I could know what was happening to me, where I could reach out with my mind and grasp those important things, like my name, and the name of the bottom-dump driver, Paco, or Cruz, or Eulalio or maybe Emanualo von Hachmann de la Vega, or whatever. But being able to think straight again and know all these important things was arriving at a *state* of consciousness, not at a *place.* I knew, I knew, somehow I knew truly, that to arrive at that state I had to arrive at a point.

Suddenly, overwhelmingly, I had a flash of knowledge about the point—not what it was, but how it was, and I screamed and hurt my throat and fell blindly back in the seat of the tractor trying to push away *how* it was.

My abdomen kneaded itself with the horror of it. I put my hands on my face and my hands and face were wet with sweat and tears. Afraid? Have you ever been afraid to die, seeing Death looking right at you; closer than that; have you seen Death turn away from you because He knows you must follow Him? Have you seen that, and been afraid?

Well, this was worse. For this I'd hug Death to me, for He alone could spare me what would happen to me when I reached the place I was going to.

So I wouldn't spread stone.

I wouldn't do anything that would bring me closer to reaching the place where that thing would happen to me. *Had happened* to me.... I wouldn't do it. That was an important thing.

There was one other important thing. I must not go on like this, not knowing my name, and what the name of the bottom-dump driver was, and where this airfield and this base were, and all those things.

These two things were the most important things in the world. In *this* world.... THIS world....

This world, this world—*other* world....

There was a desert all around me.

Ha! So the airfield wasn't real, and the bottom-dump wasn't real, and the anemometer and the grease racks weren't real. Ha! (Why worry about the driver's name if he wasn't real?)

The bulldozer was real, though. I was sitting on it. The six big cylinders were ticking over, and the master-clutch lever was twitching rhythmically as if its lower end were buried in something that breathed. Otherwise—just desert, and some hills over there, and a sun which was too orange.

Think, now, think. This desert means something important. I wasn't surprised at being in the desert. That was important. This place in the desert was near something, near an awful something that would hurt me.

I looked all around me. I couldn't see it, but it was there, the something that would hurt so. I wouldn't go through that again—

Again.

Again—that was an important thing. I wouldn't spread stone and reach that place. I wouldn't go through that which had happened to me even if I stayed crazy like I was for the rest of eternity. Let them put me away and tie me up and shake their heads over me and walk away and leave me, and put bars on the window to slice the light of the crooked moon into black and silver bars on the floor of my cell. I didn't care about all that. I could face the ache of wanting to know about my name and the name of the driver of the bottom-dump (he was a Puerto Rican so his name must be Villamil or Roberto, not Bucyrus-Erie or Caterpillar Thirteen Thousand) and the people in the shining clothes; I *was* facing all that, and I knew how it hurt, but I would not go through that place again and be hurt so much more. Not again. Not again.

Again. Again again again. What is the again-ness of everything? Everything I am doing I am doing again. I could remember that feeling from before—years ago it used to happen to me every once in a while. You've never been to a certain village before, we'll say, and you come up over the crown of the hill on your bicycle and see the way the church is and the houses, and the turn of that crooked cobblestoned street, the shape and tone of the very flower stems. You know that if you were asked, you could say how many pickets were in the white gate in the blue-and-white fence in the little house third from the corner. All the scientists nod and smile and say you did see it for the second time—a twentieth of a second after the first glimpse; and that the impact of familiarity was built up in the next twentieth of a second. And you nod and smile too and say well, whaddaye know. But you know, you *know* you've seen that place before, no matter what they say.

That's the way I knew it, sitting there on my machine in the desert and not surprised, and having that feeling of again-ness; because I was remembering the last time the bottom-dump came to me there on the airfield shoulder, trailing a plume of blue smoke from the exhaust stack, bouncing and barking as it hurtled toward me. It meant nothing at first, remembering, that it came, nor that it was the same driver, the Puerto Rican; and of course he was carrying the same-sized load of the same material. All trips of the bottom-dump were pretty much the same. But there was one thing I remembered— *now* I remembered—

There was a grade-stake driven into the fill, to guide the depth of the gravel, and *it was no nearer to me than it had ever been.* So that hadn't been the same bottom-dump, back another time. It was the *same time,* all over again! The last time was wiped out. I was on a kind of escalator and it carried me up until I reached the place where I realized about what I had to go through, and screamed. And then I was snatched back and put on the bottom again, at the place where the Puerto Rican driver Señor What's-his-name dumped the gravel and went away again.

And this desert, now. This desert was a sort of landing at the side of escalator, where I might fall sometimes instead of going all the way to the bottom where the truck came. I had been here before, and I was here again. I had been at the unfinished air base again and again. And there was the other place, with the shining people, and the girl with all those kinds of gold. That was the same place with the crooked moon.

I covered my eyes with my hands and tried to think. The clacking Diesel annoyed me, suddenly, and I got up and reached under the hood and pulled the compression release. Gases chattered out of the ports, and a bubble of silence formed around me, swelling, the last little sounds scampering away from me in all directions, leaving me quiet.

There was a soft thump in the sand beside the machine. It was one of the shining people, the old one, whose forehead was so broad and whose hair was fine, fine like a cobweb. I knew him. I knew his name, too, though I couldn't think of it at the moment.

He dismounted from his flying-chair and came to me.

"Hello," I said. I took my shirt from the seat beside me and hung it on my shoulder. "Come on up."

He smiled and put up his hand. I took it and helped him climb up over the cat. His hands were very strong. He stepped over me and sat down.

"How do you feel?" Sometimes he spoke aloud, and sometimes he didn't, but I always understood him.

"I feel—mixed up."

"Yes, of course," he said kindly. "Go on. Ask me about it."

I looked at him. "Do I—*always* ask you about it?"

"Every time."

"Oh." I looked all around, at the desert, at the hills, at the dozer, at the sun which was too orange. "Where am I?"

"On Earth," he said; only the word he used for Earth meant Earth only to him. It meant *his* earth.

"I know that," I said. "I mean, where am I really? Am I on that air base, or am I here?"

"Oh, you are here," he said.

Somehow I was vastly relieved to hear it. "Maybe you'd better tell me all about it again."

"You said 'again'," he said, and put his hand on my arm. "You're beginning to realize . . . good, lad. Good. All right. I'll tell you once more.

"You came here a long time ago. You followed a road with your big noisy machine, and came roaring down out of the desert to the city. The people had never seen a noisy machine before, and they clustered around the gate to see you come. They stood aside to let you pass, and wondered, and you swung the machine and crushed six of them against the gate-posts."

"I *did?*" I cried. Then I said, "I did. Oh, I did."

He smiled at me again. "Shh. Don't. It was a long time ago. Shall I go on?

"We couldn't stop you. We have no weapons. We could do nothing in the face of that monster you were driving. You ranged up and down the streets, smashing the fronts of buildings, running people down, and laughing. We had to wait until you got off the machine, and then we overpowered you. You were totally mad. It was," he added thoughtfully, "a very interesting study."

"Why did I do it?" I whispered. "How could I do such things to—*you?*"

"You had been hurt. Dreadfully hurt. You had come here, arriving somewhere near this spot. You were crazed by what you had endured. Later, we followed the tracks of your machine back. We found where you had driven it aimlessly over the desert, and where, once, you had left the machine and lived in a cave, probably for weeks. You ate desert grasses and the eight-legged crabs. You killed everything you could, through some strange, warped revenge motivation.

"You were crazed with thirst and revenge, and you were very thin, and your face was covered with hair, of all extraordinary things, though analysis showed that you had a constant desire for a hairless face. After treatment you became almost rational. But your time-sense was almost totally destroyed. And you had two almost unbreakable psychological blocks—your memory of how you came here, and your sense of identity.

"We did what we could for you, but you were unhappy. The moons had an odd effect on you. We have two, one well inside the other in its orbit, but both with the same period. Without instruments they appear to be an eclipse when they are full. The sight of what you called that crooked moon undid a lot of our work. And then you would get attacks of an overwhelming emotion you term 'remorse,' which appeared to be something like cruelty and something like love and included a partial negation of the will to survive ... and you could not understand why we would not punish you. Punish you—when you were sick!"

"Yes," I said. "I—remember most of it now. You gave me everything I could want. You even gave me—gave me—"

"Oh—that. Yes. You had some deep-seated convictions about love, and marriage. We felt you would be happier—"

"I was, and then I wasn't. I—I wanted—"

"I know. I know," he said soothingly. "You wanted your name again, and somehow you wanted your own earth."

I clenched my fists until my forearms hurt. "I should be satisfied," I cried. "I should be. You are all so kind, and she—and she—she's been—" I shook my head angrily. "I must be crazy."

"You generally ask me," he said smiling, "at this point, how you came here."

"I do?"

"You do. I'll repeat it. You see, there are irregularities in the fabric of space. No—not space, exactly. We have a word for it—" (he spoke it) "—which means, literally, 'space which is time which is psyche.' It is a condition of space which by its nature creates time and thought and matter. Your world, relative to ours, is in the infinitely great, or in the infinitely small, or perhaps in the infinitely distant, either in space or in time—it does not matter, for they are all the same thing in their ultimate extensions ... but to go on:

"While you were at your work, you ran your machine into a point of tension in this fabric—a freak, completely improbable position in—" (he spoke the word again) "—in which your universe and ours were tangential. You—went through."

I tensed as he said it.

"Yes, that was the thing. It caused you inconceivable agony. It drove you mad. It filled you full of vengeance and fear. Well, we—cured you of everything but the single fear of going through that agony again, and the peculiar melancholy involving the loss of your ego—your desire to know your own name. Since we failed there—" he shrugged "—we have been doing the only thing left to us. We are trying to send you back."

"Why? Why bother?"

"You are not content here. Our whole social system, our entire philosophy, is based on the contentment of the individual. So we must do what we can ... in addition, you have given us a tremendous amount of research material in psychology and in theoretical cosmogony. We are grateful. We want you to have what you want.

Your fear is great. Your desire is greater. And to help you achieve your desire, we have put you on this course of abreaction."

"Abreaction?"

He nodded. "The psychological re-enactment, or retracing, of everything you have done since you came here, in an effort to return you to the entrance-point in exactly the same frame of mind as that in which you came through it. We cannot find that point. It has something to do with your particular psychic matrix. But if the point is still here, and if, by hypnosis, we can cause you to do exactly what you did when you first came through—why, then, you'll go back."

"Will it be—dangerous?"

"Yes," he said, unhesitatingly. "Even if the point of tangency is still here, where you emerged, it may not be at the same point on your earth. Don't forget—you have been here for eleven of your years.... And then there's the agony—bad enough if you do go through, infinitely worse if you do not, for you may drift in— in *somewhere* forever, quite conscious, and with no possibility of release.

"You know all this, and yet you still want us to try.... " He sighed. "We admire you deeply, and wonder too; for you are the bravest man we have ever known. We wonder most particularly at your culture, which can produce such an incredible regard for the ego.... Shall we try again?"

I looked at the sun which was too orange, and at the hills, and at his broad, quiet, beautiful face. If I could have spoken my name then, I think I should have stayed. If I could have seen *her* just at that moment, I think I should have waited a little longer, at least.

"Yes," I said. "Let's try it again."

I was so afraid that I couldn't remember my name or the name of Gracias de Nada, or something, the fellow who drove the bottom-dump. I couldn't remember how to run the machine; but my hands remembered, and my feet.

Now I sat and looked at the windrow; and then I pulled back the throttle and raised the blade. I swung into the windrow, and the gravel loaded clean onto the blade and cleanly ran off in two even rolls at the sides. When I sensed that the gravel was all off the blade, I stopped, shifted into high reverse, pulled the left steering clutch to me, let in the master clutch, stamped the left brake. . . .

That was the thing, then. Back-blading that roll out—the long small windrow of gravel that had run off the ends of my blade. As I backed over it, the machine straddling it, I dropped the blade on it and floated it so that it smoothed out the roll. Then it was that I looked back—force of habit, for a bulldozer that size can do real damage backing into powerpoles or buildings—and I saw the muzzy bit of fill.

It was a patch of spread gravel that seemed whirling, blurred at the edges. Look into the sun and then suddenly at the floor. There will be a muzzy patch there, whirling and swirling like that. I thought something funny had happened to my eyes. But I didn't stop the machine, and then suddenly I was in it.

Again.

It built up slowly, the agony. It built up in a way that promised more and then carefully fulfilled the promise, and made of the peak of pain a further promise. There was no sense of strain, for everything was poised and counterbalanced and nothing would break. All of the inner force was as strong as all the outer forces, and all of me was the point of equilibrium.

Don't try to think about it. Don't try to imagine for a second. A second of that, unbalanced, would crush you to cosmic dust. There were years of it for me; years and years. . . . I was in an unused stockpile of years, somewhere in a hyperspace, and the weight of them all was on me and in me, consecutively, concurrently.

I woke up very slowly. I hurt all over, and that was an excruciating pleasure, because the pain was only physical.

I began to forget right away.

A company doctor came in and peeped at me. I said, "Hi."

"Well, well," he said, beaming. "So the flying catskinner is with us again."

"What flying catskinner? What happened? Where am I?"

"You're in the dispensary. You, my boy, were working your

bulldozer out on the fill and all of a sudden took it into your head to be a flying kay-det at the same time. That's what they say, anyhow. I do know that there wasn't a mark around the machine where it lay—not for sixty feet. You sure didn't drive it over there."

"What are you talking about?"

"That, son, I wouldn't know. But I went and looked myself. There lay the Cat, all broken up, and you beside it with your lungs all full of your own ribs. Deadest looking man I ever saw get better."

"I don't get it. Did anybody see this happen? Are you trying to—"

"Only one claims to have seen it was a Puerto Rican bottom-dump driver. Doesn't speak any English, but he swears on every saint in the calendar that he looked back after dumping a load and saw you and twenty tons of bulldozer *forty feet in the air,* and then it was coming down!"

I stared. "Who was the man?"

"Heavy-set fellow. About forty-five. Strong as a rhino and seemed sane."

"I know him," I said. "A good man." Suddenly, then, happily: "Doc—you know what his name is?"

"No. Didn't ask. Some flowery Spanish moniker, I guess."

"No, it isn't," I said. "His name is Kirkpatrick. Alonzo Padin de Kirkpatrick."

He laughed. "The Irish are a wonderful people. Go to sleep. You've been unconscious for nearly three weeks."

"I've been unconscious for eleven years," I said, and felt foolish as hell because I hadn't meant to say anything like that and couldn't imagine what put it into my head.

Poor Yorick

IF YOU DON'T want to read an unpleasant story, we are even. Because I didn't want to write it either.

It can be told because it's doubtful whether June will ever get hold of it because she doesn't read the way you do. She is one of those who flatter themselves that they are too busy to waste time reading. She talks a great deal instead, and is only one-third of a person, the other two-thirds being entertainment-receptors for the radio and the movies respectively.

But she is inordinately pretty. She is very very blond and her lips are full and red, and her eyes are the color of grape juice, but bright. Her skin has indirect lighting and the lobes of her ears are always pink. She has a fiance, as she calls him in two syllables, in the South Pacific. He is a nice fellow and entirely suited to her. He and her kid brother had been inducted together and managed to stay together, and were buddies the way they always had been. She called him her kid brother because she was three-eighths of an inch taller than he, although he was older. So it was all nice and cosy, with them to watch over each other and with her to stay at home and be proud of them both. The fiance, whose name was Hal, wrote all the time, and her kid brother never wrote, which was all right too, as long as one of them did.

There was a lot of hard work and rough stuff out there but Hal found time to wrap up and send a present for her, and by hook or by crook it got to her. She opened it with two oh's and an ooh, in the presence of both of her elderly and very gentle parents, and as the last of the wrapping fell away her mouth tried to "Eeek!" while she swallowed her gum, and her father spun on his heel and started to walk out but had to come right back to fix up her mother, who had silently fainted. The present was a Japanese skull.

After her mother was quiet and comfortable June went back into the front parlor—not a living-room, a parlor—and she and the skull stared at each other for quite a while. All the courage she had concentrated in the gingerly tip of one index finger which went out and touched it and jumped back as if the thing were hot. But it wasn't hot. It wasn't cold either. It was just smooth, and quite as clean-looking as anything could be. It was as clean as a kitchen sink. She touched it again, and gradually she saw that it was just ugly, that was all. She put out both hands and put one on each side of the skull and lifted it. She almost dropped it then because it was so light and she wasn't prepared for that. But she held it and she had it and it was of value because Hal had sent it. And war was like that anyway, and it is good to have us at home care a little less about how we used to think about such things. All this she thought while she held the skull and it grinned quietly at her. After all, we all got one like it behind our face, she thought. She carried it upstairs and put it in her kid brother's room, because that was the only place where no one would have to sleep with it, and after all they all ate in the parlor.

It was in the house for two days. The rest of that first day she kept it to herself but after that it was too good to keep, so the parade of her young contemporaries was called up and filed in awed and low-toned morbidity past the skull. Each of them was shocked and in a few minutes began to get raucous and crack wise to cover it up, and it made June feel good to see how scared they all were. It belonged to her and she wasn't scared—any more.

One of them put her kid brother's new top-hat, that he had gotten for a present with his tuxedo three months before he was drafted, on the skull, and that seemed to take the curse off it because it sure looked comical. It wasn't a bad fit either because her brother was a little bit of a fellow too.

After a while there wasn't anybody new to call up and show off the skull to. June racked her brains and suddenly thought of Doc Winninger. Doc Winninger was the dentist and he was the only man she knew of that had a skull. It perched up on top of his chiffonnier-thing in his office, that held all the drills and picks and things, high up, right up where you could see it when he was working on you.

Only hardly anybody ever noticed it. She called up Doc Winninger and he promised to come around because she made it so urgent although she didn't tell him what for; she wanted to surprise him.

When he came she took his hat and coat and led him right upstairs. She got him lined up just right in front of her kid brother's room and said, "Here's the Jap that Hal sent me," and threw the door open. Doc Winninger took two steps into the room and then saw the skull and stopped and said, "Good God!" And the shocked expression on his broad red face with the heavy jowls and the brilliant oval spectacles was all that she could have wished. "Isn't he a beaut?" she said. The skull was wearing her kid brother's topper and sure was a scream.

"Hal sent you that?"

"He sure did. Isn't he the one, though? The big crazy."

Doc turned his back on the skull and faced her. She didn't know why his face looked the way it did, but whatever it was it made her stop smiling. "A fine trophy," he said.

He made her defensive. "That little yellow rat is prettier now than he ever was when he was alive. That's what Hal calls a good Jap!"

"Those Burma nurses ... are we fighting that kind of war now? Is that what this means?" he said, thumbing over his shoulder at the skull.

"Do you mean is Hal shooting little kids? Gee, Doc, you know better than that."

"Oh. Well—I have to go." He started out but June blocked him. She felt somehow cheated. "Wait. You didn't even take a good look."

"I saw enough, Junie." He sounded as if he was sorry for her or something. As if she was sick.

"Aw, now wait. There is something you'd want to look at. That Jap's had teeth filled. Don't you want to see if the Japs do as good a job as you do?"

She had hit him where he felt it. He turned back into the room and picked up the skull. He glanced at the two fillings in the upper lateral incisors, suddenly stared. June had the feeling that he stopped breathing. When he turned around his old face was working. "June—

this is— is . . ." He stopped and swallowed and then sort of grinned at her. "June, could I take this along and keep it for a couple of days? There's something very interesting that I— I want to show to somebody."

June was annoyed with him but she could see he was so excited about it that she couldn't refuse him. She laughed. "I knew I'd get you going! Sure, go ahead. But be careful of it. It means a lot to me."

"I can see it would." He walked out the door and down the stairs, carrying the skull, and making small talk over his shoulder. "What do you hear from Hal?"

"Him! He's well and fighting mad. Him and my kid brother got separated a while back on little mopping-up patrols, but we'll hear about the kid when Hal joins up with him again. That little monkey never writes."

June's parents were glad to see the skull go out of the house although they didn't say anything about it. But they were just as mad as June when Doc Winninger called up two days later and said he was sorry but he had left the skull in a taxi and when he located the taxi the skull was gone. They were so mad about it that they got another dentist and never went to him again. Even if he had been their dentist since before the kids were born.

Which was all right with Doc Winninger. He knew the family too well. He knew every filling in their mouths. He didn't lose the skull, he took it right to the middle of the bridge and threw it into the river. He didn't take it to a doctor to find out for sure if it was an oriental skull or not. He didn't want to know. He liked to think the whole thing about the fillings was a coincidence, even if June's kid brother was such a tiny little fellow.

Crossfire

DEAR ——

Before me is a bottle of cognac ... half full. I have drunk half the bottle. It is young. It burns. It is good. I sit now in a large kitchen, the most important room of this particular farm house, and look out to a yard that is quite active, in a natural sort of way ... i.e., a boar is presently servicing a sow, and I find it most diverting, or, to say the least ... distracting. It is now a question of will ... mind over country matters, in order for me to take advantage of the last moments of light to type a word or two to you. I am disappointed in the lazy performance of this boar whose seed will turn to sucklings, and many of them, no doubt. How unjust. My wildest efforts amount to nothing!—that is, nothing but a transitory sense of satisfaction. I must interrupt this biological scribendi to partake of more cognac. That pig depresses me. I must have a drink. He's unmindful of 88's bursting seeds of death about his cycle of natural functions ... but I'm not. I, alone and feeling a neuter entity whilst this boar exercises his male root, must have done with this nonsense....

A short while ago I prevailed upon the owner of this farm to fix me up with a bucket of hot water ... so I could take what the boys call, "A whore's bath." Such a bath is, perhaps, more commonly known as a "sponge bath" ... but that latter denomination lacks oomph. You, in your 16-room house, probably have a shower-bath and proper tub with the best of plumbing. A bath is commonplace to you. Aha! ... but you don't have pigs to pork shop over!

I sent to London for some water colors and sketch pads. There are pastel colors in the brick and slate of the farm buildings that are exciting to me for I have seen nothing like them except at art exhibitions and in *Vogue* and *Harper's Bazaar.* I can believe Toulouse-Lautrec and

194

others pastel-minded. They seem no more out of harmony during these last rounds of sun than the red of a rose to the green of its leaf. It's French to the very soil; it's beautifully real, for the visual sensation tells me so. I have no talent for painting; all I have is the urge to try and daub a bit here and there. There is noise and destruction about me and the lazy, peaceful business of brush and pencil seems the right thing to do. Were it quiet and peaceful I'd probably like to wage waste and the noisy business of destruction. (the cognac is good)

Did I tell you about my first day in this hellzapoppin' place? I had quite an unforgettable experience . You've probably read about the abundance of snipers during the initial stages of this European operation. I had personal contact with one when I was on shore about one hour. At first I felt there was something unreal about my being on shore . . . like being on a movie set. The houses didn't look real. The first civilians I saw looked like extra players milling about for some De Mille production. The houses, shell-torn and strangely colored, looked more like prop buildings on the back lot at MGM. The sound and effects department was doing one helluva good job with shell bursts and smoke. Then it dawned on me that this was no Hollywood scene. People lying dead in the road more like wax effigies were really very dead people who a short while ago were very much alive. The smells attested to the truth of it all . . . smells of powder, burnt wood, scorched flesh, and strange new odors that told me here was something all too real. I was alone at first. Don't ask me why. I wouldn't know. I was alone until I got to a large farm some distance away from the beach, and there I met a couple of enlisted men that I had seen a few times before. Because of wild firing we kept low in a squat-walk. I knew I had to cross the large yard of this farm because 88's (or something like 'em) were trained on the road. A bullet sang past my face . . . so I did the easy thing. Ha. I ducked. I tho't it politic to crawl a little more and keep all ten of my eyes glued to the side quadrants and toward the sky. Another bullet zizzed by me too goddamned close, so I bellied it over to a farm wagon for cover. Yet another bullet came my way from the house and then one of the boys swore he saw a female firing from an open window on the ground floor. I turned and edged my way to the sight end of the wagon when I heard and felt my heel get clipped. It didn't frighten me. It made me mad as hell. I released the safety on my .45 and sent a slug at a movement in the curtain from whence all this lethal nonsense was coming. The boys hurled hand grenades in the upstairs windows and then we all made a rush to the main house. I soon found myself in the kitchen, where, sure enough, there was a female lying on the floor. From the door she looked young and slim. The rifle was a few feet away from her … so there was little danger from that gadget. Closer inspection showed her to be about twenty years old and too darned pretty for this kind of monkey business. She was conscious and able to talk despite a wicked hole through her shoulder (there's no doubt that a .45 makes a mean hole. I've seen what they do to jack rabbits when I was at Fort Bliss, Texas.) She spoke to me in French, tho' she could have been from almost anywhere. I doubt that she was French, tho'. She asked me why I shot her. Huh! I pointed at the rifle lying beside her and asked her why she shot at me. I got no answer for that. Fact is, I was in no mood to hang around since this spot was getting a little too hot for comfort. Anyway, she won't be shooting Yanks any more. It's a helluva mess, isn't it? I won't forget that as long as I live. On that same day we accounted for several other snipers. One was in a tree; another was in a church tower; and another was firing from the top floor of a barn. They were men, tho'.

I'll have a few tid-bits for you another time. Right now I am of a mind to make my daily pilgrimage to the local curate's brick outhouse where I can function with a modicum of security from German artillery. A couple of days ago this ancient outhouse, with me in it, seemed the target … for a shell went through the garden wall and burst close enough that my hind cheeks felt the hot breath and blast. I tho't my favorite part(s) would be missing and, had this been a less sturdily built house of contemplation and human passage, I have no doubt but that I would now be a cipher in masculine dress, a nullity fit for some ladies' bath house as an attendant, or something equally frustrating.

Write soon, my favorite people, and tell me all about life on Euclid Park Drive.

Love,

Noon Gun

JOE LOOKED DOWN at Mousie, walking so sedately beside him, and he thought, you're a second-rater, and so am I. Her name wasn't Mousie, but Sara Nell. He always called her Sara Nell except when he thought about her, and then she was Mousie. It was her hair, maybe, or the nose that was so very well shaped only one and a half sizes too large for her face. She had a little pointed face. Anyway it was Mousie, and it wasn't affectionate.

"What's the matter, Joe?" Her voice was lovely, though. And her eyes. She always seemed to be interested in what she was saying, and her eyes widened all the time she talked. In between times they never seemed to narrow, but got longer.

"Nothin'. Thinking."

Thinking about the kind of girls you saw so often in taxis, so seldom on the bus. So often on TV or in the movies, never in a store or bowling or anyplace around. On TV and the movies you can watch big good-looking guys soften 'em up, push 'em over. The big good-looking guys talk fast and they always have the right answer, and they just mow them down. You never saw a movie about a guy didn't have enough chin, who never had the right words at the right time and who had none at all when he was mad, or afraid, or when he really meant what he was saying. What kind of a chick would look the second time at a guy like that? If that's what you are, you wind up walking along the street with Mousie because you can't do better.

She was watching him, not looking where she was going, holding his arm very tight and close the way she always did. He liked that, but he never could figure it with the way she turned away when he tried to kiss her. He said, "I was thinking about the picture we saw, the second one."

197

"Oh. Didn't you like it?"

"Sure I did. Sure. It was swell. It didn't seem too phony either. I mean, the way he wiped out those two machine-gun nests, it could happen that way, I guess. And when he helped move all those wounded, and then dropped, and you realized he had a bullet in him all that time, that really sat me up. Only—"

"Only what, Joe?"

"Oh—nothing. Nothing much, just that I don't see him making all those wisecracks to that army nurse when he was hurt. Did you ever know anybody like that, Sara Nell? Are there guys like that, that don't ever get scared, and grin when they fight, and like say something funny when they get hurt?"

"I imagine so. I've seen—well, anyway, they wouldn't pay any attention to *me.*"

Oh, Joe thought. But I do. I do, but one of those guys wouldn't. You take the next best thing. He took his arm from her suddenly, so quickly that she opened up her long eyes and stared at him. They walked on, a little apart.

"I'm sorry, Joe."

"For what?"

"I don't know," she said very softly. "I just suddenly felt sorry."

Mousie! he thought furiously. You make me mad. You watch me all the time. You never say what you see. Why did I have to meet up with you? What good are you doing me? You're just as bad as I am. Why don't you tell me to go jump in the drink? . . . But heck, she didn't mean anything. She was just trying to be— "Let's go in here and have a drink before we go home."

She looked up into the neon glare above the entrance. "They ask how old you are."

"Not here they don't."

"All right, Joe." All right, Joe. All the time, all right, Joe.

They went into the place. It split the difference between a twist 'n' fizz joint and a real bar. It was mobbed. There were tables and booths and imitation morocco and all kinds of noise. "There's some seats," said Sara Nell as Joe hesitated.

"But there's a girl—"

"Nonsense," said Sara Nell. "One girl in a booth that is s'posed to be for four. Come on."

Joe thought he ought to be the one to find the seats, but why make anything of it? They slid side by side into the booth. Joe slung his hat up and out and for once it landed on a hook. Sara Nell laughed and patted his shoulder and the girl opposite smiled.

"Order me what you're having," Sara Nell said. She burrowed into her black handbag and came up with a compact. "I'll be right back."

When she was gone Joe fixed his mind and the base of his tongue on a Cuba libre and let his eyes wander over the room. The girl opposite was watching him; he sensed it rather than saw it. It made him acutely uncomfortable. He tried hard not to look at her and very nearly succeeded. She was blonde and bigger than Mousie; that he could see out of the corner of his eye. . . . But if he was with Mousie he didn't feel that he should— But heck, he could look at her, couldn't he? She wouldn't think he was crawling up her leg if she'd seen him come in with another girl. He obeyed his usual reflex when he felt confused, and took out his cigarettes.

"Please—"

The voice was husky, throaty. He looked across the table, right straight at her.

She was incredible. Her hair was long and thick, golden with firelights. He thought her eyes were green. Her face was round, the skin very white and flawless, and the lobes of her ears were altogether pink. She was dangling an unlit cigarette in her fingers, and was looking at his battered lighter.

"Oh, excuse me," Joe said, and dropped his own lit cigarette into his lap. He flapped and plucked and got it, and corralled it in the ash tray, fumbled up his lighter, and spun the wheel. It caught with its usual bonfire effect.

The girl yelped, recoiled, then laughed and leaned forward. She watched him as she lit up, instead of the flame. He saw that her eyes weren't green at all. They were blue, with a little crooked golden ring around each pupil. In the light of the booth's little table lamp, the movement of her mouth on the cigarette showed up a fine line of down on her upper lip. He had an impulse to touch it.

He snapped the lighter shut and displayed it. "Swedish," he announced. "I got it off a guy on a ship. You can't get 'em here. It's sort of beat up now. It dropped out of my pocket one day and I ran a bulldozer over it."

"A bulldozer? You run a bulldozer?"

He nodded eagerly. "You ever watch one work?"

"Oh yes," she said. "I rode on one once, for a couple minutes. They're the biggest, strongest—"

"I know." He nodded. He knew, too. He thought she had run out of words. Couldn't find words for the blatting of those mighty engines, the unspeakable power of twenty-one tons of steel and racket and brute force, the whole thing obedient as cadets on parade. He looked across at her, at the miracle that had happened to her face to make it interested in his work, and in him. In *him*—and she with that calendar face, that TV Hollywood face.

"My girl fr— the girl I'm with, she never saw a bulldozer," he said.

"Well, I have. Is it hard to run one of those things?"

So Joe talked about it. Something inside him filled up and burst warmly, and spilled out in words. He had never been able to talk to a girl like this before. There was a time in high school, a girl called Peggy, and he suddenly found himself talking about her, because this blonde miracle understood about him and the bulldozer.

"You remind me of a girl called Peggy, when I was a kid," he told her. "Once I had a class with her, she sat right next to me, well I never could bring myself to say a word to her. You know how it is with kids. Well she passed and I flunked and after that I never saw her but on Wednesdays. On Wednesdays she would carry the flag in assembly. I used to live from one Wednesday to the next, just waiting for her. Just to watch. I never did speak a word to her. Well that went on for three years until the senior prom and she came with a friend of mine. And me stag. And he came over and said, 'Hi, Joe, you know Peggy.' I just nodded my head yes and she smiled at me. Know what I did? I left the dance," he said in recalled wonderment, "I left and went straight on home." He looked up from his kneading fingers to see the blonde girl's eyes fixed on his face. He blushed. "I guess I was a dope. As a kid."

"I think that was cute," said the blonde warmly. "Did you say your name was Joe? Mine's Bette."

"Oh," said Joe. "Pleased t' meecha. Mine's Joc, all right. Betty."

"Bette, with an E, not Betty. Betty's such a common name, don't you think?"

Joe, by now too far away from bulldozing and feeling lost, didn't know what he thought, and didn't have to, for he suddenly became conscious of two square hands with stubby fingers and an oversized signet ring on the table beside him. He looked up and saw that they terminated thick arms which in turn supported a pair of wide shoulders wearing an overpadded sports jacket. From a pink-cheeked baby face, a mean little pair of eyes leered viciously at him. One side of the mouth opened and said harshly, "Hiya, Bette. Who's yer friend?"

"Oh! Gordon. Gordon, meet Joe. Joe's just waiting for his girl. She's powdering her nose." There was an urgency in her deep sweet voice, and, looking up at the man's little eyes, Joe felt a miserable cold lump form in his stomach.

"Yeh?" Gordon slid in next to Bette and said heavily, "Let's jest sit here and help him wait for her."

"He doesn't believe it!" said Bette, and laughed with her mouth. "Gordon, where you been? I been waiting for you thirty minutes."

"Hadda stop an' paste a guy said he was going to make time with you, hon," said Gordon, winking at Joe. Joe smiled weakly. There was something wrong about all this, and he wished suddenly that Sara Nell would hurry up.

"He's a bulldozer operator," said Bette, nodding at Joe, who nodded back like a marionette. And for just a fraction of a second the arrogance slipped off Gordon's face, leaving it bland, years younger. Then he caught it again: "*He* is? Well—long as he din't bring his bulldozer."

Joe said, "Ha. Ha," and was appalled at how hollow it sounded.

Sara Nell had slid in beside him before he fully realized she was back. She was saying something about she hoped she hadn't been too long.

You have been, Joe thought. He said, "Sara Nell, this's uh, Bette and Gordon." Sara Nell bobbed her head as each name was mentioned. Bette said "Hello!" and smiled.

Gordon glanced briefly at Sara Nell's face, intently at the front of her dress, shrugged his shoulders and turned in his seat to face Bette more directly. He said not a word.

Joe sat silent and miserable. A waitress scuffed up. "Cuba libre," Joe said. Sara Nell shook her head. "I don't want anything now."

"Coke," said Bette. Surprise slanted into Joe's mind. She should have said "Champagne cocktail," or something. Didn't they always?

"I'll have a drink with you," Gordon said pointedly to Bette, "when you and him are finished." The waitress shuffled off again.

"Aw, Gordon, don't be like that. Joe didn't mean anything, did you, Joe? Does he look like a wolf or something?"

Gordon flicked a glance, not at Joe, but at Sara Nell. He said, "Hell no."

"Well, he isn't," said Bette complacently. "I know. He was telling me just before you came—"

Oh no, Joe thought, holy smoke, don't tell him *that*! I didn't tell you that about Peggy so you would—

But she was. In her own way, which wasn't like what he had told her. She made it different. She made it as if he was still the same kind of a cube he was when he was a kid. She made it sound as if it had happened just yesterday, instead of three whole years ago, nearly four. He opened his mouth to say something, and nothing would come. He felt Sara Nell's hand on his arm and realized he was half out of his seat, hanging there clumsily. He dropped back and closed his eyes and let the silly little anecdote come pouring over him like hot oil from a busted hydraulic line.

When Bette was quite finished, finished also with an expansion of how *very* cute she thought it all was, Gordon said,

"Shee—*yit*."

It made Joe jump. Bette apparently noticed nothing. Joe didn't have to look at Sara Nell.

Joe said, "Aw, Bette, you shouldn't've told about that."

"Why not?" Gordon grated. "She can say what she wants. It's a free country, ain't it?"

"Sure, but—"

"But nothin', who do you think you are, Nicky Khruschev or something?"

"Gordon," said Bette, "will you leave the kid alone?"

"Aw, it's all right," said Joe.

Sara Nell said suddenly, "Joe, will you take me home? I have an awful headache."

Joe looked at her in amazement. He had never heard her voice be shrill before. "You got a headache?"

"Sure she has," said Gordon. "Name's Joe." He brought his thick hand down on the table and guffawed.

"Very f—" Joe began, but something choked him. He had to swallow before he could say, "Very funny." To Sara Nell he said desperately, "I ordered a *drink*."

"Please Joe ... " she said. The face she had now, this was new to him too. "Please. Now. I feel sick."

Joe opened his mouth, but before he could say anything Sara Nell was up and walking away. He rose, tried a smile and a shrug that somehow didn't quite come off, reached for his hat and started off after her.

"Hey. *You*!"

He stopped. Gordon said, "Who's supposed to pay for the drinks, deadbeat? Me?"

Infuriatingly, Sara Nell came back to him, accompanied him to the table. He said to her, "If it wasn't for you—" He got his wallet out. Gordon was sitting back making his little eyes even smaller. Joe took out a bill and tossed it to him. "Here. When she comes. With the drinks. We got to. Go."

Bette said goodbye, but Joe couldn't answer. He took Sara Nell's arm and hurried her out. "Joe! Your change!"

"Skip it. I got plenty of money."

Outside it was red and dark, red and dark with the neon, and the cool air took the hot fuzziness that filled him and compressed it into a fiery ball. "*You*!" he gritted. "What'd you want to rush me out like that for? You want that guy to think I was afraid of him?"

Sara Nell made a strange little sound and snatched her arm away from him. They stopped walking. Joe said, "One more crack outta him and I'd'a had to paste him one."

"Joe!" she cried as if she had been stabbed, "don't talk out of the side of your mouth!"

"What's the matter with you?"

She placed her hands carefully together and looked down at them. Her bag swung from her left wrist, and from its wide gilded clasp. The neon letter B, reversed, appeared and disappeared. B for Bar. B for Backwards. B for Bette. She spoke to him carefully, and at last in her own full voice again. "Joe . . . I don't want you to be mad at me. I have no claim on you, and you can do what you want. But—"

"What are you talking about?"

"Please don't throw your money away. You work too hard for it."

"For God's sake, I told you. I got plenty."

"All right, Joe. But . . . ten dollars is a lot for a drink you didn't even have."

"Ten—did I put ten dollars on that table?"

"That's what you took out of your wallet."

Joe whipped out his wallet and fanned through it. "Holy smoke." he looked up at the pulsing glare, and back at his wallet.

Sara Nell said, probably to herself, "Those awful people . . ."

"Aw, they're okay," Joe said. He put away his wallet. "He just talks too much for his own good, that's all. . . . Well," he demanded suddenly, "we just going to stand here?"

She just stood there.

"Come on," he growled.

"All right, Joe," she said. They walked away from the bar. After a while she said, "Let's walk all the way."

"I got enough mon—"

"I want to," she said.

They walked in too much silence after it had been normally dark for a time, and he lashed out, "All right, so you didn't like them! So they're not your type, that's all. So forget them!"

"All right, Joe."

All the time, all right Joe. And watching him. She had always been watching him, ever since he met her. She watched him eat. She watched him walk. Did she ... did she *think* while she watched? She never said. He had such an abrupt vision of the crooked golden ring on blue pupils that he blinked; the vision jagged along with him, fading no faster than the afterimage of a flash bulb. Oh God, no matter what, this Mousie would never do that to him, or anything like it.

He found, after a while, that she had his arm again. He had not been aware of her taking it. She said, "Joe. Did I ever tell you about my brother Jackie and the noon gun?"

"What about it?"

"We used to live near the fort. Every time they shot that cannon at noon Jackie would start to cry, even when he was a baby. Everybody knew about it. Everybody used to laugh at him, to kid him out of it. They used to look at their watches and hang around him waiting. And sure enough when the gun went off he'd jump and start to cry.

"Well, one summer when he was about thirteen, my uncle John and Aunt Helen were visiting, and Jackie cried like that, and Uncle John gave me two dollars but he said to Jackie he was ashamed they had the same name. I—I guess he was only trying to help. But anyway, at night Jackie told me he would never cry at the noon gun again. The way he said it, Joe, he scared me. I was so worried, the way he acted, I kept my eye on him all the next morning.

"Well, about eleven-thirty he sort of slid out of the yard without saying anything and I waited a second and went after him. He took the hill road and went right up to the fort, and jumped over the road wall at the top and went on around the side of the building and sat down on the grass with his back to the wall. And there right over his head was that cannon." She was quiet for so long that he nudged her.

"What'd he do?"

"Nothing. He just sat there looking out at the sea. At five minutes to twelve he could hear the voices of the gun crew. I could too, where I was hiding. Then he sort of squinched up his face and dug his fingers into the dirt. And he started to cry. He didn't try to wipe his face. He kept his hands in the dirt. It must have been to keep him from putting his fingers in his ears. Finally the gun went off—*blam!*—and he jumped like a jack-in-the-box. Afterwards, he sat there for a minute until he stopped crying, and he wiped off his face with his handkerchief and wiped his hands on his pants.

"What'd you say to him?"

"Oh—nothing. I ran home. He never did know I saw him."

"Now why did he want to do a thing like that?"

Sara Nell looked up at him. "He was a funny kid. You know, he never did cry at that noon gun any more. For a couple of weeks he'd sort of tighten up when it went off, but after a while he stopped doing that even. And then he'd just grin."

They reached her gate. Joe said, "That's the craziest story I ever heard."

She reached behind her, opened the gate, slid through and closed it between them. "Well ... goodnight, Joe. Thanks for the show and all." She turned and went up the steps. At the top she looked back and saw him still standing there. She said good night again and when he didn't answer she went into the house.

At the click of the door Joe started, took a step toward the gate. There was something so very final about the click; it left him alone, and it told him what he hadn't known until then—that he didn't want to be alone. He stared at the lighted windows for a moment, and finally shrugged. "That dame," he said out of the corner of his mouth. He turned and started downtown.

"I guess I shoulda pasted that guy one," he muttered. He put his hands in his pockets and hunched his shoulders. In the back of his mind, a most intimate possession of his, a sort of private movie projector, began reeling off a new feature, in technicolor. He saw himself in the bar, striding up to the table, a thin smile on his merciless lips. Gordon looked up and turned pale. "Well, wise guy?" said Joe out of the corner of his mouth. Gordon said, "Now, looka, a joke's a joke, huh?" Joe slowly extended his hand. Gordon said, "Okay, okay," and put the change from Joe's ten into it. Joe put the money in his pocket and stood there rocking on the balls of his feet, - staring Gordon down. "Punk!" he spat. Bette rose and ran to him and threw her arms around him. "Don't hit him, Joe!" Joe gently disengaged her and shoved her carelessly aside.

Fadeout.

Joe took his hands out of his pockets and walked a little faster.

Another reel. Joe and Gordon standing toe to toe, slugging it out. Bette shouting, "Come on, Joey!" A right, a left, another right, and Gordon was down, blood streaming from his nose and mouth. "Oh, Joe, my Joe ... " and as he turned to face her and the hot promise of her parted lips, he saw too late that the coward on the floor had a gun. *Blam!* But with the explosion, Bette's tear-filled face was blanked out by the superimposed picture of a kid sitting in a swirl of smoke under the muzzle of a cannon, digging his hands into the dirt and crying.

Joe shook his head in annoyance. He tried to get a close-up of Bette, whose dress was torn somehow, saying, "You've killed him, you rat! You've killed my Joe!"—flinging herself down beside him as he gasped his life out; but it couldn't jell.

Gordon, he thought bitterly. Gordon is the guy who grins when he fights. A tough guy. Smack him one in the nose. He grins. When the noon gun goes off, he grins. Pump him full of lead, and he cracks wise with the Army nurse. The blonde Army nurse.

I'll get him out on the fill where I'm working, Joe thought. I'll be up on my dozer, and I'll run him down. I'll slap her in sixth gear. Just a touch on the steering clutches. He can't dodge *me*. I got twenty-one tons at my fingertips. Blade him under. Lock a track and spin him into the dirt and spread him out and backblade him into nothing but a stain in the mud. In technicolor again, he pictured himself up on the machine, approaching the bar. He dropped his blade and swung into the front of the building. *Blam!* But instead of people running and screaming, instead of chrome-pipe chairs bouncing and scattering off the blade, instead of a sweaty Gordon crying, "He brought his bulldozer!" there was just the kid under the gun again, crying without trying to wipe his face.

"I got to do it," Joe said suddenly in a strained voice. He thought, what right have I to horn in on them? and replied instantly, I can just ask for my change.

Ahead of him the lurid neon over the bar made the street and housefronts alternately blood and black, blood and black. He crossed over toward it and stumbled on the curbstone. His heart was pounding so hard that he had to catch his breath in between beats. He went in.

There were not many people left. He thought suddenly, maybe they've gone. He craned his neck toward the booths and instantly saw Bette's beacon of hair.

He wiped his palms on the sides of his trousers. The waitress was behind the bar. Maybe she'd have the change. Maybe he wouldn't have to ask Gordon at all. He went over to her. She looked tireder than she had before.

"I gave you ten dollars for a Cuba libre and a Coke a while back," he said. "I was sitting over there. Have you got the change?"

"Oh—you're the feller ordered and then went out. Was that your ten? I give the change to your friend there. Ask him about it."

"Thanks." Joe swallowed. "I—I guess I will." He looked at the waitress. She was numbly mopping the bar with a grey towel. "I'll go ask him about it right now." It didn't seem to make any difference to her; she just went on mopping. "Yes," said Joe. "Well, thanks."

He walked away from the bar. Maybe he ought to have a little drink first. As the thought occurred to him it was canceled by a reaction against any more stalling that jolted him to his ankles. He was trembling ever so slightly, all over, when he walked back to the booths.

I'll just say "Hi," easy-like, he told himself. But when he got there he couldn't say anything at all. He put his hands down on the table and leaned on them. He looked at Gordon and wished that little muscle in his cheek would stop twitching.

"Well, will you look what crept in!" said Gordon. "What do *you* want?"

"My money," whispered Joe. He cleared his throat. "My money," he said.

"You lose some money?" Gordon nudged Bette. "He lost his money."

"Better forget it, kid," said Bette.

Joe said, "I left ten dollars here to pay for drinks."

"That's your hard luck," said Gordon. "I don't know nothing about it. Why'n't you save yourself some bad trouble and beat it?

"Give it to me."

"Look, son—ain't it worth ten bucks to you to keep me from feeding you your teeth? How're you gonna prove anything?"

Joe was suddenly certain that his mouth would form just one more statement before it dried up altogether. He said the only thing that would come into his mind. "Give it to me."

Gordon carefully and ostentatiously adjusted his heavy signet ring. Joe became fearfully aware of what that big ring could do. "I guess I gotta give it to him," said Gordon. He got up and stepped so close to Joe that Joe could smell the liquor on his breath. "Now get outta here," rasped Gordon. He put his open palm against Joe's face and shoved.

Joe stepped backwards, his arms flailing for balance, until his knees brought up against a chair, and he fell over it backwards and crashed to the floor on his head and shoulders. He rolled over and tried to get up. Gordon stepped over and kicked him in the stomach, and when he put his hands down, kicked him in the head.

It made a noise inside his head like nothing he had ever heard. Just *blam!* and then the whole world was full of roiling smoke. It began to clear, and he became conscious of a bleating noise—the waitress. He raised his head and looked past the thick columns of Gordon's legs, and saw Bette's face. She was not saying, "Oh, Joe, my Joe ..." She was smiling, with her mouth half open. He could see almost all her upper teeth. She was smiling at Gordon.

Gordon stepped back as he got to his knees and then to his feet. "You kicked me," he said inanely, and then rushed.

He felt his hands close around Gordon's forearms. They felt almost squashy in his grip. He forgot all about dream-fights, movie and TV fights, the one-two, the feint and duck and right cross. He bent Gordon's arms until the square hands were fluttering under the baby chin, and he bore down with all the power that ten hours a day pulling steering clutches can give. Gordon went to his knees. "Money," said Joe. He pulled Gordon back on his feet, released his arms, grabbed a handful of hair and hauled Gordon's head back until he could see the skin on the pink throat stretching. Holding him like that, he swung at Gordon's jaw, cheek, nose, eye, mouth, jaw. He kept swinging until Bette screamed. Then he let go, and Gordon came down and over and around his feet like something dumped out of a truck.

The waitress was saying, "Stop it! Stop it!" Joe said, to his own astonishment, "You stop it. You're making all the racket," and went over to Bette. "I want my money," he said.

"I got it," she said. "Gosh, Joe, we were only having fun with you." She opened her pocketbook and took out a ten, the whole ten, and put it on the table. Joe picked it up and slid it into his wallet, and took out a dollar and gave it to the waitress. "Throw some water on him," he said.

Bette looked at the feebly stirring figure on the floor. "You didn't need to get mad like that," she said. "Now when he comes to he's going to take it out on me. I'm gettin' out of here." She walked off.

Joe found his hat, picked it up, dusted it off, put it on. Bette was waiting for him outside on the sidewalk. The blinking neon did strange things to the color of her hair.

"Are you going my way?" she asked him, holding his arm.

"What's your way?"

She pointed. He shook his head. She said, "I could go the other way."

He took her hand off his arm. "I got a date," he said.

His head hurt.

He went straight to Sara Nell's house, thinking about what he should say when he saw her. He thought up plenty, but when he stood in the light of her opened door, he forgot it all and said only, "I got the money. They had it, all right."

"Joe! You're hurt!"

"I feel fine." How she got into his arms he couldn't imagine. He held her close and stroked her hair. She didn't turn her face away. His eyes were hot. He said, "You're so *little!* You're no bigger'n a little old mouse. I oughta call you Mousie."

She said, "All right, Joe."

He held her close, but he was careful, because his arms were so strong he didn't want to hurt her.

Bulldozer Is a Noun

IN SPITE OF the resilient walls and acoustabsorbing floors, Jay Scanlon's startled *"What?"* carried through four different offices, causing three typing errors, one inadvertent subtotal and two cases of mild profanity. The erg-per-worker meter on his desk, wired to every business machine in the place, chalked up eighteen man-minutes lost time, divided that by the number of office employees, and advanced the quitting-time gong relays by two-tenths of a second.

"I'm sorry, Jay," said Pellit. He unfolded out of his chair and helped himself to a cigarette, which he struck on his thumbnail. "We've got to have the guy, and on his terms. There isn't any other way out."

Jay's contorted features relaxed into their usual expression of undershot wistfulness. "It's not right. It's—sacreligious, practically. The man's an iconoclast. This is a technological culture and has been for the past three thousand years. I'll admit the necessity for going back to techniques that were in use practically in the dawn of time, but I don't see where we can't get along without a crackpot who says right out loud that he'd rather live in the past."

"Yeah, he talks too much. But he's a topnotch researcher. Universal Synthetics has come a long way by its policy of buying, making, and hiring the best. And he's the best there is."

Jay snorted. He pointed at his unlovely but appealing head and said, "See that face? That's the best I've got too. For the same reason. Sure he's the best. There's no other human on the three planets who is crazy enough to have wasted his whole life in digging up useless information. It's—it's—" he searched for the strongest word he could find, lowered his voice to be sure the stenos couldn't hear him, and said, "It's *inefficient!*"

Pellit started. "Please, Jay. It doesn't call for foul language. The trend of events has proved that his work is of some use, or we wouldn't be seeing him this afternoon."

Jay sighed. "I know. I know. But he couldn't have known of that. Not thirty years ago when he started burrowing in the Archives. It's *unplanned,* don't you see? It's *sinful!* What's funny?"

Pellit turned loose the smile that had been puckering his cheeks. "I can't help it, Jay. The beautiful paradox! The complete stasis of progress! Onward and Upward—that's what we've been fed since we were children, and ninety generations before us. We've lived by it and worked by it, and we have progressed. We're moving onward and upward all right, but at such a uniform rate that we're completely hidebound. As a unit we progress; within the unit we're in complete and utter stasis. By going backward to the Metal Age techniques in this thing, our social unit takes a big jump upward, but within it violates all our conventions, and we throw up our hands in holy horror like a pack of Monday-school teachers finding a steam-engine on the Altar at Willow Run Sanctuary."

"It isn't funny. And you're almost as bad as Mauritius the Drip ... why does he call himself that, anyway?"

"Oh, some idea of his that he feels identifies him with his work. 'Drip' was a widely used term back there somewhere in the umpteenth century, so he says; a widely used descriptive term of a typical period in which he considers himself an expert. Ask him about it."

"What'd it describe?"

"He claims that all the great men of the pre- Fourth and Last era were called drips at one time or another—the peace-making statesmen, the theoretical scientists, the advanced artists, and so on. So he figures he's a drip too."

"The guy should have a number," Jay said glumly. "All right; send him in."

The Anson dilator in the wall opposite opened, adding a cubicle of the waiting compartment to Jay's office. Mauritius the Drip was not sitting in the luxurious chair provided but was on the floor with his feet on the seat and his back to the wall. "In protest," he explained, indicating his pose, "as I must protest all of the artificialities of this effeminate culture."

Jay stared open-mouthed at the lanky apparition, with its rough beard-stubble, its anachronistic clothes, its long bony face on which was mounted an antediluvian pair of eye-lenses in thick mottled-amber frames. "What," said Jay with something like horror in his voice, "is that?"

"Mauritius the Drip," said Pellit. "This is Jay Scanlon."

"No, no," said Jay. "I mean all that—on his face."

Mauritius ran the edge of a thumbnail raspingly down his cheek. "That," he said hollowly, "is a beer. Every normal male would have one were it not for the effect of your ridiculous Rites of pubertescence, where the skin of the face is irradiated in the name of efficiency."

"Oh yes," said Pellit suddenly. "I seem to have heard of a legend to that effect. In the pre- Fourth and Last era that facial pilosity was cultivated by scratching with a sharp blade, wasn't it? they called it 'raising with a shaver,' didn't they?"

"You have been studious," said Mauritius loftily, "but careless. Your sources were at fault. It wasn't 'raising with a shaver,' but 'shaving with a razor.' A razor was the instrument used, and must have been the object meant by repeated references in the contemporary press to 'a check for a short beer.'"

"An expert was what I asked for," mourned Jay, "and an expert was what I got. Is there any possibility that we can get down to business?"

"Yes," said the Drip. "What is it that caused you irreverent progressives to summon me?"

"Irreverent," wailed Jay. The customary pathos in his face dissolved into a grieved sort of numbness. "Irreverent! And who's talking?"

Mauritius the Drip uncoiled and stood up, startlingly tall. "Yes, irreverent!" he said, stalking across to Jay's desk. "Look at me! What am I, besides the greatest antiquarian on the three planets?" He flung out a bony forefinger. "A true representative of a race, and faithful to it—all of it. What are you? A piddling example of a passing phase. Who, presented to an impartial interstellar being, would be the truest example of our genus—you, who glance lightly at today and concentrate forever on tomorrow and tomorrow—or I—" (every time the Drip used the nominative pronoun he got a quarter of an inch taller) "who live and think and work in everything humanity is and has been in seven thousand years? You, who base your faith on logic—does this logic tell you you have seven thousand years of *future* to back up your faith?"

"You spit when you talk," said Jay.

Pellit raised his fists to his temples and pounded softly. "Business, for heaven's sake, business. . . . Jay, whittle that stuff away and let's get down to it."

Mauritius the Drip turned to Pellit. "That," he said, "is a very interesting phrase. Would you like to know its origin?"

"No."

"It is derived from the name of the man who first developed jet propulsion for aircraft, a Captain George Whittle; the colloquial phrase referred to 'whittling down distances' because of the vast increase in speed that was then possible. Date, about nineteen sixty, toward the close of the Second War. The phrase, like everything else, has been corrupted since those noble days."

"Fascinating," mourned Jay Scanlon. "I find this whole conversation unproductive, to say the very least. I am sorry to say that we need your services. Would you care to have me say something further about it?"

"Jay," said Pellit frantically, reading the signs, "Don't throw him out!"

"I can't," moaned Jay, his eyes fixed on the erg-per-worker meter as if it were some sort of triptych. "Mauritius, we need your advices on a matter concerning which you just might be able to help us."

"That is self-evident, or I wouldn't be here. You're wasting time," said the Drip.

"Your fault," said Jay. "I never saw anything like it. You radiate procrastination." He drew a deep breath, and, rocking sideways in his chair, sat on his hands. Pellit grinned at him sympathetically.

"We are building a ship," said Jay, his sad voice quivering with enforced gentleness. "Interstellar, but big. The biggest thing that man has ever built. The keel is being laid in mile-long sections in Chicago

Center and is being floated out into Lake Michigan as each deadrise bilge-plate is fitted. Floating it saves us thousands of cradling operations. The superstructures are being added to the floating section. Except for electrical, electronic, and magnetronic installations, the ship will be entirely built of synthetics."

"The first successful synthetics, or plastics, as they were then known," said the Drip didactically, "were bakelite (so called because as a thermosetting plastic it was baked, and it was light) and celluloid. They were inv—"

"THE REASON WE—" shouted Jay over this local interference, "—called you in is that we have run into a logistic problem. We can synthesize any element—most in commercial quantities—and with them we can compound any synthetic. But almost without exception, our transmutatory processes are exothermic. Theoretically we can absorb a good part of this excess heat in compounding and treating our thermosetting materials; but even under ideal conditions—are you listening?"

"No," said the Drip. "I was, but I can't see the bearing of all this on my work. If you'll excuse me, and give me another appointment, I'll come back when you've gotten to the point."

Jay puckered up slowly and completely like a two-year-old just realizing that mother meant it when she said no dessert. "Pellit," he whispered, "why does he *do* that?"

"That," beamed the Drip, "is rudeness. It was the basic tone of the entire pre- Fourth and Last age. Men were men in those days. Friction between ego and ego, between nation and nation—that was a holy tradition. In those golden days, 'the common weal' could not be presented as an unanswerable argument to the desired action of man or state, as it is among you pantywaists. The man who earned the respect of the people was the man who forcibly bent the public mind to his own will. I will not freely co-operate with the internal stasis of this effeminately harmonious culture. I must be bludgeoned and forced into it against my will. I *will* uphold my position as a social misfit. I am the most offensive man in the known universe, and I hold my offensiveness as a sacred trust." He leaned over and smashed his fist down on the yielding synthetic of Jay's desktop.

"What your forebears had during their glorious history, the one constant in the ebb and flow of their social evolution was the 'underdog.' The underdog was the minority group, the constant author of change through strife, the source of the magnificently gruesome virility of the age. I am the underdog. I *will* be exploited. I *will* be oppressed, whether you like it or not. See?"

"This," said Jay Scanlon faintly, "is not reasonable."

"A strong term to use," said Pellit. "Remember, 'That which exists is reasonable.' Second Book, G.E. Schenectady."

"Thank you, Pellit. The Scriptures help."

"G.E. Schenectady," said the Drip gratuitously, "was, it may surprise you to learn, merely a pseudonym for the pamphleteer who composed your precious Edicts of Efficiency. The name originally applied to a corporation organized for private profit, circa—"

"*Stop it!*" Jay screamed. "I will not have another word of your iconoclastic semanticism in my office!"

"The Basic Tenet," said Mauritius suavely. "'Freedom of utterance in gatherings of three or more.'"

"I yield," said Jay, with the traditional conditioned reflex. "I ask that you restate and contin—"

"No, No!" cried the Drip eagerly. "Don't retract! Stop that uncerebrated mouthing! Don't you see that at last you are oppressing me? I'm persecuted. I'm ground under your heel. What was it you were saying about heat?"

Feeling that the enemy had encircled him only to reinforce his lines of supply, Jay sat and gaped. Pellit grabbed the opportunity.

"What Jay was getting at," he said, "was that although it is perfectly possible for us to transmute and synthesize all of our raw materials for this project, most of the processes involved are exothermic. What are we going to do with all the excess heat we can't use? We could circulate lake water, up to a point; but what to do when the lake warms up? In this one job alone we will release enough heat to raise *all* of the Great Lakes over 90°C—let alone just Lake Michigan."

"You'll kill all the fish."

"Fish? That's the least of it! Have you any idea of how long it would take for those bodies of water to cool? Fifty-eight trillion cubic meters of water at 90°? Over ten years. I think we could hypothesize an annual average loss of a possible 6.5°. It would be anyway twelve, possibly fifteen years. That's pasteurization with a vengeance! The lakes would be completely sterile. All of the bacteria of decomposition, all of the algae necessary to the carbon-oxygen cycle would perish. Can you imagine the windstorms, the rain, over those millions of square kilometers of hot area?" He shook his head. "And I'm just fooling with theory. All that would be true if we could distribute the heat evenly all over all of the lakes simultaneously. We can't. We couldn't hope to construct circulators which would do more than concentrate our surplus heat over more than the southern half of Lake Michigan. And then what would we have? In two months, a steaming swamp around Chicago Center, with a constant holocaust going on two hundred miles north as the cold water rushed in to compensate for our vaporization loss. Where is our advantage then, of floating the hull? What of the men who will have to work on it?"

"Why don't you use the ocean?"

"For the same reason. Too much heat locally distributed. You know our synthetics. Strong, but very light. That hull, big as it will be, won't displace much. Can you imagine the winds we'd generate offshore in the sea? Can you imagine what the windage stresses on a hull of that size would be? At least, in Lake Michigan, we can train repulsors from the hull to the shore on both sides at all times and in all stages of construction. And we won't have ocean storms to fight."

"Very fine," said the Drip. "So your precious efficient technology has fallen down!" He leered delightedly. "That, my friend, is the price of technical skill when it advances out of proportion to its milieu. As long as a machine civilization accomplishes nothing which could not be duplicated by muscle-power, however inefficiently, then it cannot start anything it is impossible to finish."

"All right," said Pellit resignedly. "We've substituted skill for strength to such a degree that when we need material in volume, we find that our techniques have outpaced themselves. How did a business discussion get turned into this 'you rub my nose in it and I'll rub yours,' anyway?"

"We need carbon," said Jay desperately, recovering from his own speechlessness, as Pellit relapsed exasperatedly into his. "We need it in bulk. And silicon. And boron. Of all the elements, those are the three which are easiest to compound into synthetic molecules. As I have said, we can synthesize what we need from lake water, air, and the surrounding earth, but it is impracticable. The alternative is to locate large deposits of specifically what we need, and extract it in bulk from the earth."

"That's mining," said the Drip. "There is a twenty-third century legend that youth was conscripted to work in mines. Anyhow, all young people were known as miners at one period."

"Mining? All right; call it that. And what we want from you is an idea of the equipment and techniques used when mass extraction of natural resources was an industry."

Mauritius the Drip pulled at his lower lip and looked at the ceiling. "That might be hard to get. My sources in the Archives are mixed, incomplete, and hopelessly jumbled by fools who, through the ages, have superimposed one filing system after another on the material. But I think I know. . ." He snapped his fingers suddenly and sat upright. "Bulldozer!" he roared. "Bulldozer!"

Jay's breath caught with such violence that he inhaled two cc of saliva and fell back choking. Pellit blanched and stood up. "Mauritius! You forget where you are! A roomful of stenos right through that open door, work to be—" He leaned over and looked at the meter. "Forty-three minutes lost time. Oh Lord—four 'show cause' requests and two resignations. Why can't you keep your offensiveness inside this office?"

Jay, red-eyed and gasping, said thinly, "He couldn't," with the two-tenths of a voice that was left him. "I fell against the general annunciator control. That w-word of his went all over this section."

Mauritius grinned jovially. "Ah, the power of semantics! Isn't it wonderful? Jay Scanlon, I sincerely wish I had meant to do that, but I didn't. So help me, that was the name of the machine they used; and a remarkable machine it was. I can see its ideological impact on the times, and its legendary quality through the Thousand-Year Dark. From a mechanical quintessence of primal brute power, the word became associated with any basic force, or driving urge. And then it became particularized. So nowadays bad children write it on fences.

Dear dear." He rose. "I'm going to the Archives now and see what I can dig up on it. By the way. I just thought of another way to be offensive. I am a historical purist. I refuse to have anything to do with your project unless you agree to use the proper names of the machines involved. That means every requisition, every shop order, every transcription, every job schedule." He laughed. His bony face was startlingly presentable when he did that. "And if you don't you bulldozers can go bulldoze yourselves." He strode through the Anson dilator, which blinked shut behind him.

"Oh ... " said Jay Scanlon; and it probably the most eloquent syllable he had ever uttered. He looked sadly at Pellit and shook his head. "Pellit, *can't* we get somebody else?"

Pellit shook his head too. "Can't do it, Jay. He's the only one. He lives in the Archives, you know. He's the only man alive who knows anything about them. He's willfully broken a two-thousand-year old tradition by his work. You know that. You know that after the Fourth and Last humanity slipped into the Thousand-Year Dark and went static. What few men that were left had enormous resources; there was no further cause for the age-old frictions that had culminated in the Fourth and Last. Their heritage was blood and force and death, and they turned their backs on it. All we are taught about that desperate period of human history has come to us through legend— and through the rare efforts of Mauritius and his few predecessors."

"And Segundo Revenir."

"Ah—Segundo was different. What an extraordinary man he must have been! Can you imagine yourself doing what he did? Can you imagine him, musing about his tragic and suicidal culture, fired with such a driving, burning faith in humanity and its future? It was his belief in the future that has become the basic philosophy of modern society. that is Onward and Upward. It was his lifetime of labor that built the Vaults of Constructive Culture, and the Call."

"Just what was the nature of the Call, Pellit? I don't think I ever thought much about it, except as one those things you learn about when you are very young and accept for life."

"Can't tell you precisely; it's out of my technology. But as I understand it, it was a gravitonic torsion-field set up over the Vaults, which as you know were buried in the center of the South American continent. The field varied regularly in intensity, enough to set up a signal detectable anywhere on Earth—*when* humans had shaken off enough of their stasis to build a machine which would detect it. The genius of the man! For a thousand lost years, mankind lived its useless, scavenging life in the great automatic cities—lived on the stored resources of the billions who died in the Fourth and Last—and around them beat ceaselessly the undetected Call. Only when Mickle and Bruder, two thousand years ago, discovered—or rediscovered—the principles of magnetronics and detected it, only then did men know that the Call existed. It was Svoboda who build the direction-finders which located the Vaults, and discovered Segundo Revenir's work.

"Segundo! Could mankind produce such a man again? We work and build for the future, on Segundo's precept that all our history is in tomorrow, and the morrow of tomorrow; but is there a man alive who could do what he did? He *knew* his tomorrows. He predicted the Third, and the Fourth and Last and the Thousand-Year Dark; and when he had reasoned it out he began to build the Vaults. He knew that only a handful would survive, and that for centuries they would have resources, and that while they had they would not progress. So in his Vaults he put basic examples of all mankind's Constructive Technology; not the fumbling, imperfect commercial applications, but careful and concise demonstrations of the principles involved in each science, clear and simple graphs and models of the three nuclear theories—gravitic, electronic, magnetic—and an indication of the few possible lines of research beyond which even he could not go at the time. He gave us a universal language so that we could understand what he had done."

"This is doing me good," said Jay, figuratively smoothing the feathers Mauritius had ruffled. "How on earth did you get the story as detailed as that?"

"I like it. Anybody can get it; few do, because it's traditional, basic, and—well, right. I—studied for the priesthood, you know."

"No, I didn't know. Then you're—"

"A misfit? Yes, Jay. Don't look so shocked! It happens, you know. Of course, I'm not like Mauritius. He's an extreme and probably hopeless case. I simply developed, belatedly, a bent for research too powerful to exist in the carefully balanced priestly mind. So my training was changed to public relations research, to the greater glory of the Wholly Efficient."

"I'm sorry. I'm not used to unusual things—who is? Go on about Segundo."

"Segundo... He was obviously a superb technologist; but his greatest brilliance was in his prophetic ability. All of his stupendous work was predicated on the belief that when the bulk of humanity killed itself off, the tiny remainder would at last learn what it had refused to learn in all its previous history: the fear of mankind. And he was right. Only man's fear of mankind, and the infinite resources available, checked the ancient cycle of race suicide. The design of the Call was part of this. What magnificent reasoning! If any social unit survived, it would exist on the principles of sharing, and it would unite in an attitude of shame and horror of the past. As long as it could live on the stored resources of the dead, it would not progress. The one danger-point would be when the end of the resources was in sight; then man's brutal acquisitiveness might assert itself. But Segundo's faith in humanity told him that when that happened someone would take the technological step necessary to develop magnetronics, the key technique of transmutation. Mickle and Bruder did it—and the Vaults were found. Can you see it? If humanity were to die, Segundo was ready to let it die in ignorance. If it wanted to live, it would help itself and when it helped itself, Segundo's great gift would fall at its feet, and humanity need never want for anything again."

"And what of Segundo himself? Is it really true that nothing is known of the man?"

"Quite true. Whether Segundo Revenir was a man or a group of men is something we shall never know. Certainly one man alone could not have built and filled the vaults. And it's very unlikely, though possible, that any one man could have had such a detailed grasp of all the sciences. In any case, Segundo's effacement of himself was only part of his faith. He had culled the best of his culture, and the worst was dead. But he obviously felt that he himself was a part of the worst, since he had lived in that tragic time. He did not do his work to perpetuate himself, but purely to immortalize what was constructive in humanity. So when he had finished his work, after he had designed the Call mechanism—a mechanism technologically centuries ahead of his contemporary science—he activated it, closed the vaults and went off into the jungle to die. He must have been very old, and he probably went unarmed. Did he return to civilization, to watch the frightful fulfillment of his prophecies? Probably not; I don't think he would trust his secret even to himself should he grow into a cackling and incautious senility. We know only that his secret was kept, and I think we can assume that he simply gave himself up to the jungle, for what value the jungle could get out of such an infinitesimal and unimportant package of tainted hydrocarbons."

Jay stared thoughtfully at the erg-per-worker meter. "And he never knew whether he succeeded."

"Nonsense!" snapped Pellit. "He was a prophet. He knew."

Jay flashed him an understanding glance. "And that's why, in his only message, he expressly forbade us to worship a man, and instead reverence the ideals of Efficiency and the History of the Future."

"That's right. Mankind's achievements outside of what was in the Vaults were hardly representative of anything that could be worshipped."

"What about the Inconsistencies?"

"I wish something could be done about that name! They weren't inconsistencies, by any means, those two precepts. Segundo asked that we retain the old calendar, at the same time he asked us to turn our backs on our history. Can't you see why? The date—any day's date—is a written phrase with a semantic impact. No human being ever disregards the date for very long. Therefore, if only subconsciously, we realize when we read or write or speak the date that human history is a little over two thousand years older than we, with our stability and progress, care to remember with pride. It's a reminder as constant and directional as the Call itself, and it helps to keep alive the one thing of value we learned from the Fourth and Last— man's fear of mankind. It reminds us that our origins were in horror and pain and shame, and it says a dozen times a day to millions of human beings, '*don't* let it happen again.' The other so-called inconsistency is the thing that started this discussion—good grief, it's getting late—I'm sorry, Jay."

"I can't think this is lost time. Go ahead."

"The existence of the Archives. Segundo warned against past human history in the strongest possible terms, in everything he did, including the way he died. He made it logically possible to ignore the past, by the gateways of achievement he opened for the future. And then he gave the location of the Archives, asked that they be opened and that free access to them be permitted. It does seem inconsistent, doesn't it?

"Well, it isn't. For those with strong stomachs, there is proof there galore that Segundo was right in every way. That's unimportant. The primary thing is that Segundo knew that someday someone—a sociologist, a technologist—anybody—would perhaps doubt the validity of Segundo's precepts, or get the idea that Segundo's researches had not been inclusive. In the Archives the doubter can find out how wrong he is. That's why I say that the important thing isn't *what* the proof might be, but the fact that it's there. Segundo has always been right. A visit to the Archives will convince anybody that nothing in there is applicable to the Wholly Efficient." He shuddered. "I was there once. A horrible place. Piles and bales and racks of scattered, fragmentary and now useless information—recordings on brittle acetate and clumsily magnetized wire, great chunks of wood-pulp rolled flat and printed and bound together at one edge so that you have to turn the sheets as you read. All of it opinionated, inaccurate, emotional. There is no system there. I asked Mauritius about it, and he said that most of it was deposited there by some forgotten idealist, probably during the Third War, as a feeble attempt to do the same thing that Segundo did perfectly, so much later. The stuff is shovelled in there—tons of it—apparently to await an editing and filing that was never done. Much of it was destroyed during the Third. What is left is a potpourri of opinionated trash, historical rationalization, prejudicial texts of what should be exact sciences, instruction pamphlets on machine operation and manufacturing techniques based on inefficient—beg pardon, Jay—principles; anything and everything. But there is nothing there of benefit to us, who have progressed so far. Even their art-forms are puny and puerile—and by the way, did it ever occur to you that Segundo's complete lack of art-form demonstrations in the Vaults was a studied oversight?"

"I always assumed that he ignored artistic accomplishment because he was a scientist—and that perhaps he thought art forms were not necessary to a functional culture."

"My eyeball! He knew that like religion, art is a self-perpetuating thing; that while sociology and technology can slip into the doldrums, art *will* go on, if it's no more than a new way a man finds of humming to himself. And he knew also that his researches were based on unchanging, natural laws. It was those laws and their application that he wanted to leave for us. But any and all art-forms he chose to leave for us would be chosen by his personal opinion and that of his group. Segundo left personalities out. Our art is necessary to us, as it must be to any culture, and he saw to it that it was *our* art, not his. And they talk about inconsistencies!"

"He seems to have thought of everything," mused Jay. "I—I wonder if he thought of Mauritius?"

"The Drip *is* different. Just how, I don't know—yes I do. The hunger for research is a strange and wonderful thing. Part of it is ingrained in our culture and condition—namely, the part that diverts research to the good of the Wholly works. But there is a part of the research psychosis that is self-energizing—the desire to do research for research's own sweet sake. That seems to be what Mauritius has to the exclusion of everything else. It is probably the basis of his social imbalance. I doubt that Segundo overlooked the possibility of a warping of that sort, but I think he probably trusted the inertia of a stable society to dissipate any harmful effect it might have."

"There's plenty about that guy that needs dissipating," growled Jay. "Unimportant or not, though, he doesn't fit into my conception of Segundo's idea that everything has its constructive social function, if that function can only be found."

Pellit spread his hands. "We need him now, don't we?" He laughed suddenly.

"Now what?"

"I was just thinking of the circular you're going to have to write," Pellit said. "Mauritius won't back down about the use of the word bul— ah, that word. I know him. It'll require a semantic defense. The situation will have to be explained to the personnel, and your circular will have to follow the 46-C program. There isn't any other way."

"You mean it has to be flashed on the public-address teletype every five minutes? Included in office correspondence? Used by the office force as a greeting?"

"All that."

"We'll be the laughingstock of the entire Wholly Union!"

"That's right. And you'd better do some laughing yourself first, or you'll never put over a 46-C."

OFFICE CIRCULAR

TO: All Personnel, Universal Synthetics, and all subcontractors on Star Ship project, Chicago Center
FROM: Jay Scanlon, Executive Director
SUBJECT: Use of term BULLDOZER

1. Circumstances force this office to unearth ancient techniques for moving raw material in bulk. In connection with this work, it is necessary to study, design or redesign, manufacture and operate several of the machines known to the ancients as BULLDOZER.

2. This word will of necessity occur repeatedly in connection with its preparation and work, in all departments. In the interest of the Wholly Efficient, its modern connections must be suppressed and, as far as possible, forgotten.

3. This end will be accomplished best if all personnel make a determined effort to remove its present undesirable effect, to lessen the semantic impact of its current definition.

4. It is therefore directed that all personnel make every effort toward a truly casual use of this term. BULLDOZER is a noun. BULLDOZE

and TO BE BULLDOZED are its active and passive verb-forms. There are innumerable ways in which it may be employed. To begin this effort, it is directed that all personnel greet each other as follows:

"Good morning, Bulldozer."

5. The subject matter of this circular is not to be construed as carte blanche in the use of bad language in these offices.

August Sixth 1945

(THERE IS MUSIC; it is sibelius and bach, it is richness and exactitude, a rushing bass and a wrenching treble, the bass aimed for the belly and the treble for the tear ducts . . .

there is a man asleep. he walks and moves and builds but he is asleep. his eyes are closed because he is asleep. he does not know how big he is because he is asleep. he is made of scar tissue.

there are voices. they are all his voice. the places where the voices are heard are all here where he is.)

Magazine Store:

who buys this crap?

that kind of thing is ridiculous. just to settle it for once and for all, where would they get the power?

(the echo begins. it whispers "power power power" until the whisper is a sheet, a screen, a thing all one color getting brighter. it never stops again. it gets behind the music and brings the music forward.)

School:
i am trying to be reasonable about this, children. i must make you understand that it harms you to escape into such tripe. confine yourselves to the books i give you. you must not clutter up your minds with such impossible nonsense.

Home:
pulp magazines again! must you read stories
about rockets
about space flight

about time travel
about space warps
about new sociologies
silly! where would they get the power?
(the echo deepens)

Cemetery:

...to finally prove the impossibility of the railroad's replacing the canal. how can you expect the smooth wheels of a locomotive resting with only the locomotive's weight on a smooth track—only one point for each wheel, gentlemen—to yield traction enough to move a train? who wants a means of transportation which would prohibit a man's using his own carriage as he now may use his own canal boat?

...these dreamers who want to build flying machines heavier than the air that supports them have not faced the issue. what would be the status of shipping today if ships depended upon their engines, not only to drive them, but to keep them afloat?

(from somewhere, the fingers of Langley, Lilienthal, Stephenson, Fulton touch the man's sealed eyelids. he rubs them, and rubs again, and finds that scars have not covered his eyes. he is afraid and keeps them closed.)

News Stand:

who writes this crap?

Places with Typewriters:

i wrote a story about decentralization, because cities could not dare exist when each city had bombs that ...
i wrote a story about a meteor detector that worked controls when it received the reflection of a radio signal ...
i wrote a story about a reaction engine ...
i wrote a story about a rocket projectile ...
i wrote a story about a robot flying bomb ...

Subway:

the heck with that stuff. i druther read stories about real life. i druther read something that has to do with me.

A Place with a Typewriter:
   i am afraid. i tell you that deep down inside i have a cold lump
   about this thing. i know we must be doing something about it
   because although it is old stuff to us we have been asked not to
   mention it in our stories for security reasons. it is too big for
   us. it can be good—it can give us power so cheap it would be
   free. it can give us a four-day work week, five hours a day. it
   can give us riches. but we are not old enough for it yet. i pray
   god that it will be discovered and used before this war is finished, so that everyone will know how big it is, how good, how
   horrible ... atomic power
(the "atomic" finds its place in the echo, in the interstices between
   "power power power" and gives a staccato tone to the sheet of
   sound. the man's eyes open a crack and now he sees, but he sees
   death, because death came to stand before him when his eyes
   opened. he is afraid and tries to close them but a whisper, a
   transparent whisper, creeps between his eyelids and holds them
   open.)

Whisper:
   on december seventh, nineteen forty four, the newspaper said
   there was no bombing activity over japan. somewhere else the
   newspaper said there was a small b-29 reconnaissance flight off
   the japanese coast, just where the japan deep is. the japanese
   islands sit on the edge of the japan deep like houses on the edge
   of a cliff. somewhere else the newspaper said there was a hell
   of an earthquake that day. that day was december the seventh,
   december the seventh, remember?

   (the whisper slips away to the figure of death, and the man who
   can see now realizes that death is transparent like the whisper,
   and through death he can see how big he is. he stretches his body
   and feels how strong he is. he opens his eyes a little more.)

Radio:
   the president says that the bomb that struck hiroshima on august
   the sixth nineteen forty five was atomic. the president does not
   call it atomic explosive. the president calls it atomic power.

(the echo is greater than the music now; greater than anything else but the man now.)

Places with Typewriters:

    we are writing stories about the future

    about machines that can think creatively

    about interstellar flight

    about the psychological fulfillment of mankind

    about mutations caused by hard radiation from atomic bombs

    about empathy, second-order space. contra-terrene matter, levitation, astral separation, telepathy, the intuitive mutation, universal synthesis, time-travel, silicon life, and the evolution of intelligence in rats.

Street Corner:

    why do you read that crap?

(but the man with the open eyes does not hear that. he is looking at himself, on the other side of death. he knows— he learned on august the sixth nineteen forty five that he alone is big enough to kill himself, or to live forever.)

The Chromium Helmet

"DADDY," SAID THE Widget.

"Yes, dear," I said, without detaching my eyes or my mind from the magazine I was reading.

"When was the time I had a great big doll, bigger'n me, and she suddenly laughed at me and gave me a handful of jellybeans?"

"Yes, dear," I said.

"Well, when was it?"

"When was what?"

The Widget clucked her tongue in disapproval. "I said, when was it I had a doll bigger'n me, that could laugh and talk and give me jelly beans?"

"Doll?" I said vaguely. "You never had a doll like that. You had one two years ago that said not only 'Mama' but 'Papa'."

"I stinkly remember about the jelly beans."

I sighed, feeling that this conversation was a little unproductive. "Why do you talk all the time?" I asked. It was a rhetorical question, but she cocked her head on one side and considered it carefully.

"I think it's 'cause I don't know any big words, like you and Mummy," she said, just in time to pull me out of my magazine again, "so I have to use lots and lots of little ones."

I grinned at her, and she nodded to herself, acknowledging her success in getting between me and what I was reading. She removed the conquest from the abstract by running and jumping up on one knee, sitting on the magazine. "Now tell me about the doll with the jelly beans."

"Widget, you never had a doll like that."

"Oh yes I did."

"Oh no—" I checked myself. That could go on for hours. "Tell me about it. Maybe I'll remember."

"She was a big doll. I put her to bed in Susie's crib." Susie was the Widget's Number One toy, a horrible pale-blue monolith of an earless rabbit. "The doll was so big her feet stuck out. I singed her to sleep and all of a sudden she threw up her hands and threw all the covers off, and she laughed at me and said I had a funny nose. I jumped up and started to ran away, but she called me. She said, 'Here's a pres-net for you.' And she reached into her pocket and gave me the presnet. It was jelly beans. She had on a red giggum pifanore."

"She had on a red gingham pinafore, and she gave you some jelly beans. What do you know. And I sup—oh!" In the time it took me to get that "oh" enunciated, I had seen my wife standing just inside the living-room door, with flour on her hands and on the tip of her nose, her bright head cocked to one side, listening; I had met her eye and caught her signal to go on talking to the Widget. I grinned; Carole was always poking and prying into what the Widget said, and coming up with starling conclusions culled from Freud and Jung and Watson. "And I suppose," I went on, "that the doll told you her name?"

"I didn't ask her."

"Darling, you always have names for your dolls," said Carole.

"Wh— Oh, hello, Mummy. No, this doll was differ-net. She wasn't *my* doll so much. It was like I was *her* doll."

Carole looked at me, puzzled. "Widget, you really remember about this?"

"Oh, yes."

"You're just pretending."

"No, Mummy, it isn't a pretend. I really and *truly* remember. Only I can't remember just when." She sounded very patient. "So that's why I asked Daddy."

I started to speak, but Carole checked me. "Was it a long time ago?"

"The doll?" The Widget's round little face wrinkled in concentration. "I don't know."

"Widget. Listen. You say you put her to bed in Susie's crib."

"Yes, in Susie's crib, an' she was so big her feet stuck out."

I suddenly realized the line Carole was taking. The Widget had gotten the crib for her birthday, nine months ago. "What were you wearing?" Carole asked.

The Widget closed her eyes. "It ... was ... mmm. Oh yes; it was my Aunt Marie dress, the one with the pink squirl."

"Marie sent that about four months ago, didn't she?" I asked. Carole nodded, and asked, "When did you first remember about the doll?"

"Oh, 'safternoon," said the Widget, without hesitation. "When I was having my hair dried under the cormium hemlet."

"Translate that," I said.

"Chromium helmet," said Carole. "I took her to the beauty parlor and had her shampooed while I finished the shopping. She loved it. And she went fast asleep under the drier. I was interested in all this because, for once in her young life, she hasn't said ten consecutive words all afternoon until now."

"Oh, heck, she obviously dreamed the whole thing."

"Oh heck, I obverlously did not," said the Widget with composure. "Dreams is all fuzzy. But I stinkly *remember* about that doll."

"Drop it, Godfrey," Carole said swiftly as I came up out my chair. I don't like to be flatly contradicted by anybody, even my infant daughter. "Widget, run on outside. Don't go away from the house. And don't contradict your father."

The Widget skipped across the room. "Yes Mummy. I'm sorry, Daddy." She opened the door, letting her body walk out while she kept her head inside. "But he contra-dicted me first," she said, and was gone.

"Parthian shot," I laughed. "Also, *touché*. Carole, why all the third degree?"

"Oh ... I dunno, Godfrey. It isn't like her to make up tall tales."

"Nonsense! Every kid does it."

"Every kid doesn't, only most kids. The Widget never has."

"O.K. So she's started. It's perfectly normal. Darling," I said, going to her, "wipe off that troubled look! You women amaze me. You really do. Fond as I am of my own kid, I've never been able to understand how a woman can study a baby's face literally by the hour, and always seem to find something new and different in it.

You've always done that, and now you're doing it with her mind. What's wrong in a child's being imaginative?"

She shook her head. "All right. Maybe I'm silly. But there's a difference between imagination and an actual remembrance of something which couldn't have happened."

"Don't be fooled because the Widget can't express herself any better than she does. I don't—"

Carole jumped up. "My cake!" and ran into the kitchen.

It began just as simply as that.

It was only a couple of days later that I got to the lab to find Henry straddling a chair, with the back holding his chin up, staring out of the window. I spoke to him twice before he heard me at all. Henry is a regular guy. Not only that, but he's married to my one and only sister.

"What's the matter, sadpan?" I asked.

"Nothin'."

I looked at him carefully. There's generally only one cause for such a beat-up expression. "Honeymoon over?" I asked.

"That's a lousy thing to say," Henry snapped. And it was. He and Marie had only been married four months or so. I shrugged. "Don't let me horn in," I said. "Only—I've known youse guys for a long time."

He got up out of the chair and kicked it. "Godfrey, did Marie ever have anything to do with Wickersham?"

"Wickersham!" I said in astonishment. "Good gosh no! You know better than that!" Wickersham was the man we worked for. He wasn't famous for anything because he didn't want to be. He was remarkable in many ways. His firm manufactured psychological and psychiatric precision equipment—reflex timers, hypnotic mirrors, encephalographs, and the like. Wickersham kept himself to himself; we hardly ever saw him at all. Once every few days he would circulate around the shops and labs, his wide shoulders hunched, his black eyes everywhere. I always had the impression that his eyes were camera lenses, and that he would develop all he had seen later, spread the proofs out in front of him on his desk and study them. Few of us had been in his office—there was no need. If we wanted to see him we pressed a button—there was one in each lab, office and shop in the building. He had an annunciator, and he would show up eventually, in his own time. And Lord help the button-pusher if Wickersham didn't think the problem in hand required a consultation! But as far as Marie was concerned—as far as any woman was concerned—that was nonsense. The woman didn't live who could move an icicle like that. "Henry—don't be dopey. They never even met."

"Yes they did," said Henry glumly. "Don't you remember the union banquet?"

"Oh—that. Yeah, but he . . . I mean, he wasn't there for any high jinks. He wanted to see how many of his men were in the union, that's all. Not that he cares. He pays way above the union scale. But what's this about Marie?"

Henry shook his head. "Somebody's nuts. Me, maybe. Marie comes drifting in about an hour after I got home last night. She's walking on air. She is plenty affectionate always, but—" he ran his finger around his collar— *"whew!* Not like that. She was all over me. Says she guessed she never appreciated me before. Says it was so brave of me to . . . to punch hell out of Wickersham, and spoil that Rock of Gibraltar face of his." His voice went vague. "Took me about five minutes to get all that on a slow double-take. I finally asked her to start from the beginning. I got it piecemeal, but the pitch is that Wickersham was down on one knee pouring his heart out to her, reciting Keats—"

"*Wickersham* was?"

He nodded dismally. "And I came in, hauled him to his feet, spun him around with the old one-two, and pitched him out on his ear."

"And where did all this happen?"

He looked up at me dazedly. "In a private room at Altair House."

"Altair House? You mean that gold-plated eatery on Sixty-fourth Street?"

"Yeh. And that's the craziest part of it all, because—I was never there in my life."

"Was she?"

"I asked her. She said sure she was—that one time; and didn't I remember?"

"She's kidding you, Henry."

"Nuts. You know your sister better than that. She kids around some, but not in that way. No; she—well, she *says* she remembers about it. I asked her when it happened—before or after we were married. That stopped her. *She didn't know!* She chewed on that for a while and then apparently decided I was kidding *her.* She said, 'All right, darling, if you don't want to talk about it,' and dropped the subject. Godfrey, what's happening to her?"

"She never came out with anything like that before," I said. "Marie's a pretty cool-headed gal. Always was, anyway. Maybe she dreamed it."

Henry snorted. "Dreamed it? Godfrey, there's a heck of a difference between a good healthy dream and an actual remembrance of something which couldn't happen."

And where had I heard something like that recently?

That was the same day that I looked up from my bench and saw Wickersham. The late afternoon sun streaming through the laboratory windows high-lighted his huge, strange face, making velvet hollows of his eyes. There was a nervous ripple along his slab-sided jaw; otherwise he was as always, carven, unnaturally still. Henry's wild story that same morning returned to me with shocking clarity, as I pictured my little, good-natured puppy of a brother-in-law smashing a fist into that great dark unreadable face.

"Oh!" I said. "I didn't see you."

I was standing in front of my work, but he seemed to look down through me and examine it lying there on the bench. "That's the Hardin contract?" he said.

"Yes. The tone generators with the secondary amplifier for building up the supersonic beat."

He moved his hand slowly up, pulled his lower lip, slowly put his hand down again, and I remember thinking that that was the first time I had ever seen him make anything approaching a nervous gesture. Then, "Hardin can wait," he said. "I want to put you on another job."

I blinked. This wasn't Wickersham's style at all. He did good work for his customers—the best. But once a job was started, it was kept in production until it was finished, no matter who came along with a rush order. His reputation was such that he could tell anyone to go fly it if they didn't like it. "What's the job?" I asked.

He looked at me. He had black eyes, and they seemed to be all pupil. He seemed to be daring me to look surprised. "It's a burglar alarm," he said.

"But we don't manufac . . . I mean," I said, "What kind of a burglar alarm?"

"An alarm with a psychological appeal," he said. "One that will not only announce that there is or has been an intruder, but will lead that intruder into being caught."

"You mean take his picture?"

"I mean, take *him*."

"What sort of an installation? I mean, will it cover a room, or a house, or what?"

"A large room, about forty by thirty, with two outside walls. Four windows, one outside door, two inside. Run up any kind of cost you like, but get it done and get it done fast. Use any man or machine in the shop; you have absolute priority. I'll bring you a floor plan in an hour. I want your preliminary layouts by then. Can you stay here tonight?"

That last was like asking a jailed convict to stick around for a while. Wickersham had other ways besides his customary double time for overtime to persuade his staff to do what he wanted. Oh well, I could use the money. "I'll have to call my wife," I said.

Wickersham apparently took that for acquiescence, for he turned and stalked off without another word. I watched him go. He walked as if he were keeping time with slow music; as if he were holding himself back from breaking into a run.

Henry's jeweler's lathe whined to a stop and he came over.

"D' you hear that?" I asked.

"Most of it," he said. "What's eatin' him?"

"You noticed it too?" I shook my head. "He looks like a dope addict. Only I can't say just how. Henry, I've known him and worked close to him for nearly six years now, and I don't know the first thing about him. What makes him tick anyway?"

"Search me," said Henry. "I don't know how he does it. Old

George, the night watchman, told me once that the Wick comes in before the sun is up, more often than not, and doesn't leave until midnight. Sometimes he's here, day and night, for three days at a stretch. He doesn't seem to talk to anybody but us, ever, and that's only occasionally, about the work. A guy just interested in making money don't carry on like that."

"He's making money all right," I said. "He knows more about applied psychology than most of his clients, and they're all tops in the field. Most times he gets his orders by clapping together a new gadget for controlled hypnosis or something, and calling in the doctors who'd be most interested. He don't wait for their orders. They come when he calls them, and glad to." I began to clear a space on my bench. "Maybe he is cracking; I dunno. I wouldn't be surprised; only—Henry, I just don't see a guy like that cracking."

"Maybe he's human, after all," said Henry, unhappily, and I knew he was thinking of Marie's wild tale. "Let's get to this alarm thing. What'd he say about the building?"

So we got to work on it. At five I called Carole. She wasn't happy about it, but you'd have to know her as well as I do to guess it. I marry the nicest people.

The alarm we doped out was a nice set-up, and I pitied the burglar who would come up against it—though I couldn't know how much I would pity him later. The come-on that the Wick wanted was an iron window-grating kept ajar over an unlocked window. The window was free to slide up only six inches, where it was stopped by a chrome-plated and highly visible catch. The catch was so stiff that it would require both hands to release it. The burglar would have to squeeze up close to the wall, put both arms into the half-open window, and reach up with his arms bent to get to the catch. As soon as he swiveled the catch—*bang!*—the sash came down on his biceps. No bells would ring, nor lights; the alarm was turned in at a remote station and the police could come and get their pigeon at their leisure. The whole layout was put on the ready by a black-light installation; that is, the building was surrounded on its two accessible sides by a lawn and a high stone wall, without a gate. The wall was topped by the beams; another two crossed the gateless doorway in the wall in an invisible X. When anyone approached the building with honest intentions, as for instance, the cop on the beat on his way to try the door, he would be timed by relays. If he went in and stayed inside the wall longer than three minutes, the grating over the side window would unlock and swing ajar. If he tried the door and came right back, the side window would stay locked, and would not tempt investigation. And if anyone climbed over the wall when it was so easy to walk in, then, of course, the trick grating would do its stuff immediately.

Wickersham came in to watch Henry and me about nine o'clock that night, and I handed him the sketch of the installation I had superimposed on his plan of the building. He glanced at it and tossed it on the bench, saying nothing, which was his way of dealing out a compliment. He stayed about half an hour, and we didn't hear a sound out of him except when Henry stopped working, wiped the sweat out of his eyes, and lit a cigarette. Then Wickersham heaved a sigh, a sigh which was ten times worse than if he had barked at Henry to get back to work. Henry hunched his shoulders and did.

At about half-past one in the morning I finished the window catch and got it mounted on a conventional flush fitting. I went over to Henry's bench; he was adjusting the focus on the last of the little UV projectors.

"That about all?"

"Yep," he said. "Buzz the Wick." He yawned. "And me for bed."

I pushed Wickersham's call-button, and we heard his office door crash open. "Jee-hosaphat!" said Henry. "He must've been in a racing crouch!"

"Finished?" said Wickersham as he came in. He might have added, "Good!" but it wouldn't occur to him. "Give me a hand with the parts, down to my car."

Henry said, "You want us to help with the installation?"

The Wick shook his head impatiently. "That's taken care of."

We gathered up everything the plans called for and a bunch of spare cable and fittings besides, and carried them down. As soon as the stuff was loaded, Wickersham swung in behind the wheel and roared off like a P-38.

"Funny business," I said, watching the car pull into a screaming turn at the first corner.

"Everything he does is funny business," said Henry, and yawned again. "Take me home and put me to bed."

I dropped Henry off and went home. The bedroom light went on as I wheeled into the drive, and the kitchen light was on as I locked the garage doors. There was never a time, early or late, when Carole wasn't up to see that I had something to nosh on when I came home. Which is the way a guy gets spoiled.

"Hi, Muscles," I said, slinging my hat at her. She caught it deftly, only to throw it over her shoulder and come and kiss me. "How's the Widget?"

"Talkative," said Carole, heading for the stove, where water was already heating the coffee. "Still going on about the talking doll in the giggum pinafore."

"Carole!" I went to her, put my face in the back of her shining hair. "You're *worried* about it!" I sniffed. "Mm. You smell good."

"Wave set," she said. "Don't muss me, darling. Yes I am a little worried." She was quiet a moment, her hands deftly cutting and spreading bread, her mind far from them. "Marie came today."

"Oh?"

"Henry tell you anything?"

"Yes. He—"

Carole began to cry.

"Darling! Carole, what the ... stop it, and tell me what's wrong!"

She didn't stop it. Carole doesn't cry very well. I don't think she really knows how. "I've been too happy, I guess, Godfrey. I feel ... I don't know, darling. Ashamed. I gloated at Marie."

"Too happy? A heck of a thing to cry about." I squeezed her. "Don't cry all over the liverwurst, honey."

"It isn't being too happy. I ... I don't really know what it is." She put down the knife, turned in my arms, and hid her face in my coat. "I'm frightened, Godfrey, I'm *frightened!*"

"But what are you afraid of?"

"I don't know," she whispered. She trembled suddenly, violently, and then was still. "I'm afraid of something, and I don't know what that something is. That's part of it. And part of it is that I'm frightened *because* I don't know what it is. There's a difference, do you see?"

"Sure I see." Suddenly I felt about her the way I do about the Widget. She seemed so tiny; there was so much she couldn't understand yet, somehow. I talked to her as if she were a child. I said, "What kind of a something is it, darling? Is it something that can hurt you?"

She nodded.

"How can it hurt you?" She was still so long that I thought she hadn't heard. "How can it hurt, darling? Can it jump out at you and knock you down? Is it that kind of a something?"

She shook her head promptly.

"Can it hurt—us?"

She nodded. I said, "How, Carole? How can it do something to us? Can it take something away from us?"

"It did take something away."

"What?"

"I don't know. I don't know. I don't know. I don't know," she mumbled.

I held her and stroked her shoulder, and I felt lost. After a while I went and sat at the table and she finished making sandwiches for me.

It didn't stop there. In three days I was in the shape Henry had been in when Marie first came out with that fantasy of hers—and in three days Henry was worse. Working, we did little more than to interrupt each other with accounts of the strange goings-on of our wives, and it wasn't fun.

"She won't forget it," said Henry, staring blindly at his bench. His production was way off—the little guy was a worker, but this thing had got between him and his work. "If I'd only known how serious it would be to her, I'd have grinned and said, 'yes, yes, go on.' But I couldn't then, and it's no use trying now. I've done my best to persuade her the thing between her and the Wick never happened, but it's no use. The more I persuade, the more upset she gets. If she believes me, she begins to doubt her own sanity. If she doesn't believe me, she can't figure out what motive I might have for lying about slugging the man." He spread his hands, his eyebrows coming up sorrowfully. He looked more than ever like a little lost puppy. "Dead end. What can you do?"

"You're lucky. At least Marie can put a name to what's worrying her. Carole can't. She's afraid, because she doesn't know what she's afraid of. She feels she's lost something, something important, and she is frightened because she doesn't know what it is. Where Marie's worried and—shall I say jealous, maybe?—and generally upset, Carole's scared silly. I've seen Marie worried before. I've never seen Carole scared."

Henry gave up his pretense of working and came around to my bench. "Carole is the coolest head I think I've ever run across," he said thoughtfully. "Maybe I am lucky. I . . . don't feel lucky though— Godfrey, let's quit griping about the effects and try to figure out causes. Do the two of them have the same trouble, or is it a coincidence?"

"Coincidence? Of course, Henry. The symptoms, if you want to call them that, are totally different."

"Oh, are they?"

"Well, what have they in common?" I said.

"Yeah," said Henry doubtfully. "Um—Nothing, I guess. Except— they've both lost something and it worries them."

"Lost something? Carole has, but what has Marie—oh. Oh, I think I see what you mean. Marie has a memory of an event which is itself lost, as far as placing it in her life is concerned. Like the Widget's doll with the giggum pinafore."

"Like what?"

I told him about it. "I have a feeling that's what sent Carole off the deep end, when you come to think about it," I said. "She worried about . . . hey! the Widget's trouble is the same as Marie's when you break it down. She had a vivid memory of something that never happened, too. And she frets because she thinks she's lost it." I stared at him.

"For that matter, you and I both have the same trouble," said Henry suddenly. "We've certainly lost something."

I knew what he meant—particularly for himself. There is a certain something about being newly married that shouldn't be spoiled.

His was being spoiled suddenly, which was so much worse. "No, Henry, I don't know why, but I think that's a side issue. Marie, the Widget, Carole. They have something. It's because they have something that we're in the state we're in." I suddenly noticed the remarkable fact that Henry wasn't even pretending to work. "Henry—we've got a deadline to meet on this job. Wickersham—"

Henry uttered one brief syllable that adequately disposed of Wickersham and the deadline. "All right—who had it first?"

"Why . . . Ma . . . no. Not Marie. The Widget and her doll. Then Marie and her melodrama. Then Carole and her . . . then Carole."

"The Widget, huh?"

"What are you driving at?" I snapped, seeing the vitreous sheen of stubbornness slip over Henry's eyes.

"Marie's always going over to your place, isn't she?"

"Henry, you're crazy! Contagion, for a . . . mental disorder?"

"She had it first, didn't she?"

"She's just a kid!"

Henry looked at me levelly. "Just a kid. Would you say that if the three of them came down with scarlet fever and she was the first to have it, and the three of them had been together so much?"

"Now look," I said, trying to keep my voice down. "I hope I'm wrong about what you're driving at. But there's nothing wrong with my kid, see?"

"You fellows lose something?" said Wickersham.

We literally jumped, used as we were to the Wick's cat-footing techniques. Henry stared at the big man, and his feet carried him back to his bench by pure reflex.

Wickersham stood there, teetering a bit on the balls of his feet, his big hands behind him. Suddenly his great still face broke, and his white, even teeth showed in a grin. Then he turned and walked out.

"To him," muttered Henry, "something is funny."

I said, "Sometimes I'm sorry he pays the kind of money he does."

We worked, then. If the Wick had tried, he couldn't have picked a sweeter moment to interrupt us. I was just on the point of achieving a thorough-going burn at Henry, with his goofy insinuations about the kid. Henry's glum and steady concentration at his bench kept me just under the blow-off point until it really began to hurt. Not another word passed between us, although I did drive him home as usual. But his words stuck.

"Widget," I said after dinner, "you're being very silly about this doll."

"Hm-m-m?" she said innocently.

"You know what I mean. Mummy says you've been talking her ears off about it."

"I want my doll again, that's all. Mrs. Wilton told Mummy that whenever she wanted anything from her old man, she just talked and talked about it until he gave it to her to shut her up."

"Widget! You shouldn't listen to that kind of thing!"

"Listen? Did you ever hear Mrs. Wilton talk, daddy?"

I laughed in spite of myself. Mrs. Wilton whispered at about a hundred and thirty-five decibels. "Widget, don't change the subject. If I could get you a doll like that, I would. Don't you know that?"

"You did, though. I had the doll."

"Darling, you didn't have the doll. Truly you didn't. I would certainly remember about it, but I *don't.*"

She opened her mouth to speak, and I braced myself for the blast of denial. I knew the symptoms. But instead her eyes filled with tears, and she ran out of the room to the kitchen, where Carole was doing the dishes.

I sat there feeling frustrated, feeling angry at myself and at the child. I tried to piece together the murmur of voices from the kitchen—the Widget's high and broken, Carole's soft and comforting—but I couldn't. The temptation to march in there and defend myself was powerful, but I knew that Carole was more than competent to handle the situation.

After what seemed like months, Carole appeared at the living-room door. "Stay out there and eat it all up, darling. There'll be more if you want it," she called back, her voice infinitely tender. Then she swung on me with sparks flashing out of her eyes.

"Godfrey, how can you be so *stupid?*" she said scathingly.

"What's the matter?"

"Oh, you idiot," she said, sinking tiredly into a chair. "It wasn't bad enough to have the child in the grip of a dangerous fantasy; you had to make it worse."

"I don't see that it's particularly dangerous, and I don't see how I made it worse," I said warmly. "Otherwise you may be right."

"Don't be sardonic," she said. "It doesn't suit your silly face. Oh darling, can't you see what's happened?" She leaned forward and spoke to me gently. "The Widget hasn't been unhappy about this thing. She's been bothered, and she's bothered me, but that's nothing I can't take."

"And what did I do?"

"You presented her with a new aspect to her problem. At first the doll was the important thing, but it wasn't overly important. But you have loaded her up with an insoluble abstract."

"What, sweetheart, are you driving at?"

"What, sweetheart," she mimicked, "do you think the child was crying about just now?"

"Search me. Disappointed about the final realization that her doll was a figment, I suppose."

"Nothing of the kind. She was crying because she had lost something more important than the doll. You see, beloved, strangely enough she trusts you. She believes you. She believes you now; but then if what you so solemnly told her is the truth, she is wrong about the doll."

"That was what I was after."

"But she *knows* she is right about the doll!"

"The doll idea is nonsense!"

"That doesn't matter. It's real enough to her. As far as she is concerned, the doll conception is the evidence of her senses. That's a tangible thing. The only evidence she has against it is your word. That's an abstract. She wants to believe it, but to do so she would have to deny a concrete realization. It isn't in human nature—normal human nature, that is—to choose, through faith, a fact when its alternative is supported by direct evidence."

"Oh ... oh. I begin to see what you mean. So she's lost—"

"Both. Both her doll and the completeness of her belief in you." Her lower lip suddenly seemed a little fuller. "The way Marie and ... and—"

I looked at her and thought of cat-footed Wickersham and his amused "Lost something?" and about then was when the thing began to get me mad.

All morning there was a coolness between Henry and me. I kept my nose pointed at my bench, and so did he. His suggestion that my Widget had in some way infected Carole and then Marie still griped me, and obviously his resentment of Marie's condition was aimed at the Widget through me. It wasn't cozy.

He broke the ice. At a little after noon he came over and nudged my elbow. "Let's go eat."

"I've got my lunch here. You know that."

He hesitated, then went back to his locker. I suddenly felt like a heel. "Wait up, Henry." We usually ate in the shop, but when we wanted some beer with it, we dropped around to O'Duff's, around the corner. I shut off my soldering iron and oscilloscope and joined him at the door.

After we were settled in the grill, munching sandwiches, Henry came out with it. "Look," he said, "I'm willing to drop what I said— *if* you can suggest an alternative. You ought to be able to. The whole thing's so crazy anyhow. It might be anything."

I grinned at him. "Heck, Henry, I know why you picked on that contagion angle. It was the only common denominator. Now, instead of jumping to conclusions, suppose we figure out a solider one."

"Suits me," he said, and then, "Godfrey, I hate to stay mad at anyone!"

"I know, I know," I smiled. "You're a good apple, Henry, in spite of your looks. Now let's get to it. When did our women-folks get this affliction, and how? What was it—time of day, environment, or what?"

"Hm-m-m. I dunno. Seems as if they got it outside somewhere. Marie walked into my house with it. I think you said the kid had it when you got home that evening?"

"Yeah, and Carole had been out. Hm-m-m, Widget in the afternoon, Carole in the evening—what about Marie?"

"She was late home that first night, the night she climbed all over me congratulating me for the Humphrey Bogart act."

"Where had she been?"

"Uh? I dunno. Shopping or something, I guess."

"Call her up and ask her."

"O.K.—wait. No, Godfrey, I don't want to remind her of it."

"I see your point. Uh—maybe we don't have to." I thought hard. One of the Widget's odd little mispronunciations was running around in my head. "Giggum pinafore," I said vaguely.

"*What?*" snapped Henry, startled.

I grinned. "Hold on— Uh ... oh. Got it! I got it, Henry! The cormium hemlet!"

"And I've got athlete's foot. What are you gibbering about?"

I grabbed his arm excitedly and spilled his beer. "Carole took the kid into the beauty shop for a shampoo. The Widget told me herself that she first remembered her talking doll under the cormium hemlet—chromium helmet. She fell fast asleep under the hair drier. And ... that's it, Henry! ... That night Carole first acted up, I started to mug around—I said she smelled good. She drew back a little and said, 'Wave set. Don't muss me.' Now, when Marie came in late that night, hallucination and all, could she have just come from—"

"The beauty shop!" said Henry. "Of course!" He pondered, while the beer ran over the table and dripped onto his trousers. Suddenly he leaped to his feet, turning over my beer. "Well, gee! What are we waiting for?"

I dropped a bill on the table, and hurtled after him, collaring him at the door. "Hey, cut it, Jackson," I puffed. "Wait for all the facts, f'evven's sakes. Unless I'm mistaken the place in question is the one known as Francy's—"

"Yeah, on Beverly Street. Let's go!" He was jittering with anxiety. Only then did I realize the pressures he had built up over this thing. But of course—Marie never did have the tact that Carole had. She must have pounded his ear by the hour. "But Henry—the place is closed. Out of business. *Kaput!*"

"It is? How do you know?"

"Carole told me last week. It's handy to both our houses—that's why Marie and Carole used it. But they didn't like it. Management changing all the time, and stuff."

"Godfrey—what are we gonna *do?*"

I shrugged. "Get back to work, that's all. Get on the phone there and stay on it until we find out who owns that place, and if we can get in to look it over."

"But gosh—suppose they've shipped all the equipment out?"

"Suppose they haven't. It only closed a couple of days ago. Anyhow—got any other ideas?"

"Me?" said Henry sadly, and began to slouch back toward the lab.

The Widget met me at the door when I got home that night. She put a finger on her lips and waved me back. I stopped, and she slipped out and closed the door.

"Daddy, we've got to do something about Mummy."

My stomach ran cold. "What's happened?"

She took one of my hands in both of hers and gave Carole's smile. "Oh, Daddy, I didn't mean to frighten you. Nothing's happened, on'y"—she puckered a little. "She cries alla time—or almost."

"Yes, monkey, I know. Has she said anything?"

The Widget shook her head solemnly. "She won't. She sits lookin' out th' windy, and when I come near she grabs me and runs tears down my neck."

"She hasn't been feeling very well, darling. But she'll be all right soon."

"Yeah," said the Widget. She gave a strange, up-and-sidewise glance that brought back what Carole had said about the child's loss. "Widget!" I snapped: and then, seeing how startled she was, I went down on one knee and took her shoulders. "Widget—don't you trust me?"

"Sure, Daddy," she said soothingly. I once heard a doctor say to a patient, "Sure you're Alexander the Great," in just that tone of voice. "So Mummy will be all right soon."

"That doesn't make you any happier."

Her clear gaze was searching. "You said she would be all right," she said carefully. "You didn't say *you* would make her all right."

"Oh," I said. "Oh." I stood up. "Turn off the heat, Widget, and stick around."

I found Carole in the kitchen, moving briskly. I could see right away the unusual fact that the chow she was rassling up was of the short-order variety. She probably hadn't started on it until I wheeled into the drive, which just wasn't normal.

She smiled at me with the front of her face and missed my hat when I tossed it.

"'Smatter, cookie?"

"Nothing," she said, and put her arms around me and began to cry.

I put my face in her bright hair. "That I can't take," I said softly. "What is it, darling? Still the thing that's gone?"

She nodded, her face pressed deep into my shoulder. It was some time before she could speak, and then she said, "It gets worse and worse, Godfrey."

"Just exactly what has changed, Carole?"

She shook her head in a tortured way, her eyes squinched shut, and twisted away from me. She stood with her back to me and her fists on her cheeks, and said, "Everything has changed, Godfrey. You, and I, and the Widget, and the house, and the way people talk. Once it was all perfect, lovely and perfect, and now it isn't. I don't know how, but it isn't. And I want it back the way it was!" The last words were a wail, the broken voice of a youngster who has lost his jackknife and was convinced until then that he was too old to cry.

"Come out here," I said gently, leading her into the living room. We sat on the couch together and I put my arms around her. "Darling, listen. I think Henry and I are on the track of this thing. No . . . no; don't. Pay attention." I told her all about how Henry and I seemed to have the thing pinned down to the beauty shop. "So this afternoon we got on the phone to find out who owned the place. We called general agents and the Chamber of Commerce and three guys named Smith. All blanks. We may or may not have a lead; to wit, four phone numbers that did not answer and one that was busy. Point is, we think that this goofy business isn't as mysterious as it pretends to be, and we think we can crack it."

She looked at me with all the world in her eyes, and poked my nose gently with her forefinger. "You're so sweet, Godfrey. You're so darned sweet," she said, and without the slightest change from the shape of her smile, she was crying again. "Whatever you do, you can't bring back the lost thing—mine, and the Widget's doll with the g-giggum pinafore, and Marie's Henry-the-Hero. They're gone."

"You'll forget that."

She shook her head. "The farther away, the more it's lost. It's like that; don't you see?"

I leaned back a bit from her and looked at her. Her cheeks were a little hollow. I had only known her to be sick once in all these years, and her cheeks got like that then. I tried to look ahead, to see what would happen; and the way she had changed in these few days was frightening; so what would happen to her if this went on?

Almost roughly I put her by and got up. "I can't take any more of this," I said. "I can't." I went to the telephone and dialed.

"Henry?"

"Is Henry there?" came Marie's voice tautly.

"Oh . . . hello, sis. No, he isn't."

"Godfrey, where's he gone?"

"Dunno. What's up?"

"Godfrey," she said, not answering. "Did he really hit Wickersham?"

Cautiously, I said, "If you say so."

"I don't know what to do," she said desolately. "I saw him do it. But I can't understand why he is still working for Wickersham. I can't understand why Wickersham would have him, or how he can work for the man after what happened."

"Now look. You haven't been trying to get him to quit?"

"Well, I—"

I saw Henry's domestic economy going down in swift spirals. "Hands off, kiddo. I'm telling you, sit tight, and don't push that kid around. Hear? He's got enough on his mind as it is." It was the old big-brother rough-stuff. I knew she needed it and I knew Henry couldn't do it.

"But where *is* he?" She sounded petulant but quelled.

"Probably on his way over here," I said on a wild guess. "I'll look out for him, don't worry; and I'll keep you informed. You curl up and unlax."

"All right, Godfrey. Thanks, honey."

Carole looked at me quizzically. "I'm hungry," I said. She gave me a wan smile, and a mockery of the mock salaam she used to tease me with. "Yes, master," she said and went out into the kitchen.

I was suddenly conscious of the Widget's level gaze. She stood by the hall door with her hands behind her, teetering a bit on her toes the way I used to before I realized she had picked it up.

"Are you just mad," she inquired, " or are you going to do something?"

"Is there always a difference?" I asked icily.

She annoyed me by hesitating. "Mostly—not," she said reflectively. Suddenly she was tiny and soft and helpless. "Daddy, you *got* to fix this!"

"Don't worry, bratlet. Mummy'll be happy again. Just you see."

"Yes," she said slowly. "Mummy'll be happy again." She looked extremely wistful as she spoke, and I suddenly got what she was driving at. "Aha! What, young lady, do you expect to get out of this?"

"Me?"

I laughed and held out my arms, and she ran into them. "Sweetheart, I will make you a promise about that doll. I won't get it for you unless I can get it for keeps. Understand? There'll be no more of this having-not-having, any more, ever."

And for once in her life, she kissed me instead of saying anything.

We sat down to a snack of toasted cheese and cocoa just as a violent knocking sound preceded Henry into the room.

"I—" he began between breaths.

Carole said clearly, "Beat it, Widget, darling. Take your plate; I'll take your cup. We'll fix you a party in your room."

Henry sent her a grateful look as she and the child left the room, and then burst out, "Godfrey, it's worse—much worse. Another single day of this and Marie and I won't have anything left. Godfrey, she won't leave it alone. She doesn't think about anything else but that crazy Wickersham deal. I've got to bust this thing open—or I'll bust."

I brought him a slug of rum. "That won't do any good," he said, and drank it down as if he were washing down aspirins. He'd never done that in his life before. "Godfrey, I've got to *do* something. Can't we go down and case that shop, anyway?"

"That's the first solid thing I've heard in a week," I said. "Let's go."

Carole came downstairs just then. "Call Marie, will you, honey?" I said half over my shoulder. "Tell her Henry is O.K. and he and I have gone to a wedding, or to get drunk, or something clever, will you?"

She nodded, and when we got the door she said, "And where *are* you going?"

I blew her a kiss, and she caught it and put it in her pocket, the way she always did. As long as I live I shall never forget her standing there in the light, worried, and loving, and beautiful.

Out in the garage, we swung into the jalopy and I kicked the starter. As the motor roared, Henry leaned forward and shut off the ignition. "Has it occurred to you that we just might get into that place?" he asked. "Just in case, don't you think it would be smart to take a tool or two?"

"What do you know!" I said admiringly. "And I thought I was the brains of this combo!" We climbed out and raced back to my bench. My toolbox, a couple of wrenches, a flashlight, and a battery-operated trouble lamp with an extension cord. The little power supply gave me an idea; I pulled a small black case out of the rack.

"Inductance bridge," I said. "Might be nice to have along. If that hair drier is what's caused this thing, it'll use power. It must be something new and it would be nice to know what's in it and where it's coming from."

"Good. Take your multi-tester, too. And here's a little slice bar."

Arms full, we staggered back to the car, loaded the gear into the back seat, and at last ground out of the garage.

We pulled up a block from the beauty shop, parked, and strolled up to have a look at it. The shop was on a side street. It was a sleazy-looking brick wart stuck on the off-corner of what looked like a block-long warehouse. There was a yard around its two open sides, and a brick wall with a silly-looking archway of wrought iron over the gate, forming the word "FRANCY'S" in tortured letters.

"Snazzy," said Henry disgustedly.

We paused outside the gateway. The side street was comfortingly dark except for a street lamp which was planted exactly in line with the gateway and the front door of the shop, throwing a path of brilliance up the cinder walk.

"That won't do," I said.

"It'll have to." He gave a quick look up the street. There were only two pedestrians in sight and both of those were walking away from us.

I hesitated. "I don't—" There was something niggling at the back of my mind, but I couldn't place it. Something about a wall. Heck with it. "Come on."

We walked up to the door as if our intentions were honorable. A sign there said "Closed until further notice."

"That ties it," said Henry. "There is definitely something ungood about this thing."

"Why?"

"Ever see a rented place close up without some information as to who to call for purchase or rental or emergency or something?"

"Hm-m-m. Not till now."

The door was locked. It was a great big solid door. "The window?" Henry breathed. We went down the couple of steps that led up to the door. There was so much light from the street lamp outside the wall that when we turned off the path, the darkness was like tar and seemed almost as hard to move through. We felt along the wall, blinking, until we came to a window."

"Barred," said Henry, and swore. "Godfrey—can you stand by while I get some tools? No sense in both of us marching in and out of this place as if it were a gentlemen's lounge."

"O.K. A pinch bar, screwdriver, and ... oh. Get the jack out from under the front seat, in case the window's clinched. The flashlights, the battery case, and the bridge."

"Holy smoke," said Henry. "You're a real second-story character."

"I'm a boy scout gone wrong, that's all."

He disappeared into the gloom. I lost him, then saw him silhouetted against the bright light from the open gateway. He went swiftly to the gateway, peered out to each side, and went through it. Behind me, in the dark, I heard the unmistakable sound of a relay.

If it had been a hand on my shoulder it couldn't have startled me more. I felt my way to the window, pushed my hand through the bars. There seemed nothing out of the ordinary about it. Feeling carefully along the lower sash, I touched three countersunk nail heads. I listened carefully, but could hear nothing else.

Henry got back in a couple of minutes, loaded to the ears with assorted equipment. I realized that the little guy just had to be doing something, whether it was useful or not. He came puffing and blowing through the darkness toward me.

"This way, Henry," I called softly. He bumped the side of the building with something of a clatter, and edged along until I said whoa. "Sweet Sue," he gasped. "Ain't I the eager beaver?"

"Why didn't you just drive in with the lights on and the horn blowing?" I griped. "You'd've had more fun with less effort. The blasted window's locked behind these bars, and nailed down to boot."

"Give me a flashlight," he said to himself, as he got from under his load.

"Oh; you don't believe me?" I asked again, and just then the relay clicked again. Henry grunted, found the light, hooded it with his fingers and aimed it at the window. "Did I hear a relay?"

"You did. I heard it a couple minutes ago."

"Just fine," said Henry. "Any second now this place will be all bells and lights and cops. That was a burglar alarm you heard."

I clapped a hand to my head. "Burglar alarm! How could I be such a dope?"

"Godfrey; what are we gonna do?"

"Just say 'Open Sesame'," I grinned. "Watch." He swung the light on me and I made a magician's pass at the window. Nothing happened.

"Well?" he said impatiently, and then the sash slid quietly up, there was a click, and the whole section of bars swung out from the wall.

"Cut off my shorts and call me leggy!" gaped Henry, a phrase reserved for really special occasions. "*Our* burglar alarm!"

"Things begin to shape up," I said slowly. "Not in any way I like."

Henry's mind was evidently racing off on another tangent. "Wickersham installed this himself after we built it," he said. "He must know who owns the place. Hey—let's call him up and get the score!"

"No!" I said violently. You had to be violent with Henry when he went off half-cocked. Harder to stop than any man I ever saw. "Figure it out for yourself. He wouldn't let us know where this installation was going when he put it in. So I don't think he'd let us know now."

"Why not?"

"That's what I'm trying to figure out. Henry, he ties into all this business some way. Marie's hallucination is about him. The 'chromium helmet' hair drier smells very much like one of his psychosomatic snivvies; and here we find a device built in his shop and installed by him, guarding that hair drier—"

"—or where that hair drier was. I see what you mean. The crumb!" Henry clutched at my arm suddenly. "Godfrey! Remember the day he seemed to think it was so funny when he overheard us talking about the girls?"

"I should forget that. I don't think there's any doubt about his knowing something about whatever's wrong with them."

"The trouble we had trying to figure out who own this joint," said Henry reminiscently. "I'd like to corner that guy and find out what makes."

"Tempting," I said. "But I think it would be smarter to find out everything we can before we do that. We've got to crack our own safe, here."

"You were psychic when you thought of bringing the jack," Henry said. "We can stick it under the sash and run it up. Something's got to give, and whatever it is it'll let us in."

"Yep; bust the window frame and swing a piece of it in front of the black-light beam inside, huh?"

"I forgot about that. Let's see; why hasn't the alarm gone off yet, anyhow?"

"Don't you remember, dopey? It isn't designed to ring an alarm until that sash comes down—preferably on someone's lunch hooks."

"Oh, yes. And the beam behind is in case someone thinks to cut out the pane instead of forcing the catch. What happens if it's broken?"

"Conventional alarm; bell, lights, and so on. Hard to say how he's hooked it up. The window comes down anyway; maybe in time to catch some part of Joe Burglar. We also don't know exactly where in the window the inside beam is placed. It might be horizontal, vertical, diagonal, or any combinations of 'em. Fortunately, there's only one projector."

"No wires on the glass, huh?" said Henry, throwing a thin beam up to the window. "Hm-m-m. You wouldn't have a glass cutter in your bag of tricks?"

"No, but I have something just as good." I rummaged in the tool kit and came up with a small three-cornered file. I broke it in two, cutting my thumb in the process. "We now have six glass cutters. Henry, see if you can find me a hacksaw."

He fumbled for a while and finally found it. I began to work cautiously on the bottom sash, cutting upward through the wood on each side until I heard it nick the glass, and being careful to keep the saw well outside, so that it would not move in across the black-light beam. Then I took a piece of the file, and starting from one saw cut in the sash, scribed up, across and down to the other cut.

"Bright boy," murmured Henry. "Now you break loose the cut-out piece of the sash, and most of the pane comes with it."

"In one piece, if I'm lucky," I said. "We'll have all kinds of fun if any of it falls inside. Window glass'll stop UV like crazy." I held my breath and tugged gently at the lower part of the sash, trying to keep the pressure even on each side. The little molding that was left came away with a gentle crackling; and then, with a very satisfactory single *crick!* the pane gave. It was quite cool that night, but as I put it gently down I wiped sweat out of my eyes. "That's my boy did that," Henry said.

"Now for that beam," I said. Wrapped in black cloth in the top tray of my tool kit was a glass tube containing several wires coated with fluorescin, which I used to test UV projectors. I took one out, a small one about eighteen gauge, and holding it by the extreme end, thrust it into the gaping window. "The wire shouldn't block enough of the beam to activate the alarm," I said. "And we just might be able to find out which is the projector side, and which the receiver."

I moved it slowly, keeping my hand well back; and suddenly the tip of the wire glowed greenish white, and I heard Henry's breath whoosh out. I circled the wire carefully, spotting the beam from edge to edge. It was, I decided, diagonal across the window; the beam had a rectangular cross section, and by watching the fluorescence of the coated wire very carefully, located the projector end of the beam. It was at the top.

"Made to order," I said. "Did you bring the . . . yes, you did. Good heavens, Henry; did you leave anything in the car?"

"Did you leave anything in your shop?" he countered, grinning. "Now, is there any way we can skin past that beam?"

"Nope. It's too wide. We'll have to cancel it."

"Easy to say."

"Easy to do." I had been plugging in wires to the battery case. "What is that . . . a little UV projector?"

"It is."

"Oh. You're going to aim it at the cell. But—the intensity won't be the same."

"Doesn't matter. This gizmo doesn't measure intensity. It's strictly an on-off proposition." I switched on the projector, tested it with the fluorescent wire, and then aimed it carefully down the place where the alarm's black-light beam should be. I took a flashlight in the other hand, and craning over the sill, saw the photocell built in down near the floor of the room. I put my projector up against it, stood aside, and said "Come on in."

Henry, chuckling, hopped up on the sill and dropped inside. I handed up all of the junk we had brought, and then followed him.

"Let's find out where to shut this thing off," whispered Henry, casting his light around.

"No you don't," I said. "Shutting it off might actuate something too. Let the silly thing sit there and watch for intruders like it was told to." I carefully slipped my projector aside; keeping the beam on the cell until it was clear of the other projector, up over the window.

"Now let's have a look at this place." Henry swept his light around, keeping it low.

It was a small beauty parlor, rather lavishly fixed up for its size. There were several curtained booths, very tiny, all open, each with its chair and mirrored cubby-hole table. A half-partition separated the front part, which proved to be an office, from the rear; otherwise the place was one big room. Against the back wall had been wheeled an array of permanent-wave machines, two manicure racks, and a hose and spray gadget for shampooing.

"And there's the dewjaw that's caused all this trouble," I said, pointing my light at a lone electric hair drier.

We pounced on it. The headpiece was simply an aluminum shell with an open throat inside; this led down through a pipe to a casing in the base, in which, supposedly were heating elements and a blower. "Turn it on," I said grimly, and went back to the window for some gear. Henry hunted over the drier until he found the switch. The quiet room filled with a low, rising whine which settled into a steady hum. "Better not stay too near it," I cautioned. I examined it from a distance. There was a chair under the headpiece; I tried to shove it aside with my foot, but it was bolted to the floor. "That's funny."

"That's the kind of thing we have to look out for," I said. "It wasn't done for nothing." I paused. "And another thing. Seems to me that even though this is a small place, it ought to have more than one drier. Does that mean that the one we're looking for has been moved out? Or is the one we're looking for one they couldn't move easily?"

"By gosh, it's bolted to the deck like the chair," said Henry.

"Let's do a job on it." We switched it off, got out some tools, and began to take the drier down. Off came the headpiece, the pipe, the support rod. I got the bolts off the casing and lifted the cover. Perfectly conventional blower and a half a dozen heavy nichrome elements. The switch gear was, it seemed to me, a little heavier than it had to be, and so was the power line; but the Underwriters would never kick about that. The power cable looked ordinary enough, but something prompted me to nick it with my knife. I was surprised to find that under the flexible rubber insulation, it was web-shielded.

I followed it to the wall; it was plugged into a standard socket, but there was a four-place receptacle next to it on the wall with two sockets unused. Why a special outlet for the drier?

Henry sat down in the chair and mopped his face. "Looks like a false alarm to me," he said, leaning back.

"I dunno. There's a couple of things—not too wrong, but—" I went back to the motor and blower assembly. It was still hooked up. I switched it on. It revved up, louder without the cover, a bit faster without the curved tube to resist the air flow. I stood up and walked around it. "Nothing wrong with it that I can see," I said. Henry didn't answer.

"Henry!"

No answer. I turned my light on him. He was sprawled back in the chair, fast asleep.

"Well, I'll be flayed and flustered. Get up out of there, you lazy ape!" I went and shook his shoulder. His head rolled limply, and sudden panic crawled under my belt. "*Henry!*" I pulled him out of the chair. His legs half took his weight, and then buckled, and he fell with a thump to his knees. Instantly his head snapped up. He blinked foolishly into the flashlight beam. "Wh... what goes on? Hey?"

"Are you all right?"

He climbed slowly to his feet, passed his hand over his eyes. "Must've dozed off. Hm-m-m! Sorry, Godfrey." He yawned. "My knees hurt."

"Henry, what happened to you?"

"Hm-m-m? I'm all right. Tired, I guess. Look, let's go home. The pursuit of knowledge is all very jolly, but there's no sense us getting jailed for it."

"Pursuit of knowledge? What are you gibbering about? Here we're on the track of the thing that's possesses our wives and my kid, to say nothing of Wickersham—"

"Aw, why be vengeful about it? *Nil nisi,* and stuff like that there. Let's go home."

"*Nil nisi* ... 'speak well of the' ... Henry, I don't get you!"

"Well, gee; Wickersham dead, and the girls all right again—what are we hanging around here for?"

"*What?*"

He sighed with an exaggeration of patience. "Wickersham is dead and Marie and Carole and the Widget are all right again. So why bother?"

"Wicker . . . wait a minute. How do you know? Who told you?"

"Why it was— He kicked off— Well, what do you know! I can't remember. He's dead, that's all. And the girls are all right."

"Are they though? And what was wrong with them?"

"*I* don't know. Something they ate, no doubt. Why the third degree?"

"Henry, it just isn't so. If it is, you couldn't possibly have found out about it."

"Are you trying to make a liar out of me?"

"Here . . . here, Shorter-than-me; don't get your back hair up."

"Well, I don't have to stand here and listen to you tell me that something I know isn't so."

"You *dreamed* it!"

"I did no such thing!" he said hotly. "I know when I know something!"

I stared at him, and gradually I realized what had happened, though I hadn't the faintest idea how. The thing Henry had wanted most in the world had come true—for him. And it was infinitely important that he keep the memory, even if it could be proved that it never happened. Like the Widget's doll. Like Marie's wish-fulfillment that the little guy take a poke at someone bigger and stronger than himself, someone who awed him. Like Carole's . . . what *was* Carole's wish-fulfilling memory?

The chromium helmet.

I looked at the pieces of it, scattered over the floor and then at the chair. A perfectly ordinary airplane-tubing chair, bolted to the floor—why?

"I'm going home," said Henry sullenly.

"Henry old horse, stick around a little. I'm sorry, boy; really, I was talking nonsense; you're right and I'm wrong. Please stay and give me a hand. There's something I've just *got* to find out. Will you, kiddo?"

"Well—" he said, a little mollified. "Gosh, Godfrey, you never disbelieved me before. What got into you?"

"Oh, I guess I'm excited, that's all. I *am* sorry, Jackson. Will you stick around?"

"You know I will. I guess I got a little hot, too."

"Good boy." Inside me, growing every microsecond, was a hot, ugly hatred of Wickersham. I didn't know the "whys" of all this, but I grimly determined to go on learning the "hows" until I could figure the man's motives. And it better be an accident that our women-folks were affected.

I looked at the chair again. There wasn't a single electrical connection to it that I could see. I was tempted to run out the bolts, but the super-caution that was growing almost as fast as the hatred, made me stop and think. I turned to my little inductance-bridge instead. I'd rigged it up to spot pipes and wiring in the wall between my house and the garage, where my workshop was, for I sometimes did some rather delicate electronic work there, and didn't care much for stray AC and magnetic fields that I couldn't get rid of or locate exactly so I could compensate for them. It was a dual-purpose rig— the bridge itself, for detecting metallic masses, and a matched-choke circuit for finding wild AC.

I asked Henry to find me a broomstick, and fitted together the T-shaped probe, setting it on the stick. I plugged in earphones and the leads to an illuminated meter which I had fixed to strap on my wrist. I hooked the whole Rube Goldberg up to the battery pack and switched it on.

"Henry," I said, "that power line is shielded. Rip the receptacle out of the wall, bearing in mind that it's hot. You'll probably find a conduit in the wall that's grounded to one side of the power line. Cast it adrift for me."

I went over the chair carefully, looking for any induced AC. There were a few strays—not enough to amount to anything.

Why was that chair bolted down?

To stay in one place, of course. Why?

I switched on the blower, and went over it again. Nothing, until I had the probe over the headrest on the back of the chair. And the hum in my earphones suddenly faded. I moved the probe; it got louder. Which was just silly. The gadget was built so that when AC was encountered, the sound would intensify. I moved it toward the chair, and found a spot six inches over the headrest where my signal utterly disappeared!

"There's something here, Henry," I called. "Just what I don't quite know. It acts like a very intense multi-phase AC; but I mean multi-phase. Some high harmonic of the sixty-cycle, phasing away like mad. It kills my detector signal completely."

"Your department, son," said Henry. "Don't double-talk me back to sleep. Tell it to Wickersham's ghost. You were right about this grounding here. What on earth's that for?"

I didn't bother to try to answer. I was puzzling myself by moving the probe in and out of that dead spot. It didn't make any sense at all. The chair gave no sign of carrying a thing. I gave it up, put the probe over my shoulder to get it out of the way, and went around the chair toward Henry.

The phones faded and came in again as I moved.

I stopped dead and flashed my light up, moving backward until it happened again. The probe was eight feet in the air this time, and what I found was a weak place in the signal. I waved it around, walking back and forth, repeating the process I had used with the fluorescent wire when we were working on the window. I found the field—for apparently that's what it was—tightest at the spot over the chair, diffusing outward and upward toward the corner of the ceiling.

"What are you doing—catching butterflies?"

"Catching something. Henry, the chair, which isn't connected to anything, has a field hanging over it which is beaming up into the air!"

"Wouldn't it be the other way around?"

"What do you mean?"

"Suppose the field over the chair is a focal spot?"

"It diffuses outward ... oh: I see what you mean. Hyperbolic reflector." I went around to the other side of the chair, and put the probe low. "You amaze me, my child! You're right! It diffuses downward on this side!"

I beamed my light upward to the corner of the room. It was no more remarkable than the other corners. The ceiling was decorated in bright gold stripes on dark cream paint. The moldings had been quarter-round plastered to get rid of the 90° angle of the walls to the ceiling, which gave the corners the inner surface of a quarter of a sphere. These were decorated with a series of close, fine gold lines— all that is, except the one that seemed to be radiating the haywire AC.

It was made of fine copper mesh.

"By all that's putrid," Henry gasped. "A focusing radiator!"

"And unless I'm mistaken, the inductance bridge here'll locate a pipe from that exclusive little receptacle in the wall, smack up to it," I said excitedly. I went over there so fast I jerked the cable out of the battery pack and dropped my flashlight. Henry had left his on the floor over by the receptacle; we were plunged in total blackness, floundering and swearing. I heard Henry say "Here it is!" and the *click-clicking* of the hex head on the flashlight as he fumbled it and it rolled on the floor.

"Don't light it!" I said. "I see something. Wait!"

Silence as thick as the darkness settled over us. Vaguely, then, as our eyes became accustomed to the dark, we saw a purple glow down low, near the floor.

"UV again," Henry said, "with a cheap filter-lens." He clicked on his light. The place where we had seen the glow was at the base of the dim outline of a walled-up door into the warehouse to which the beauty shop was semidetached.

"Now, that's silly," I said. I went over and confirmed my first glance; there was a small projector and an eye, the whole making a beam just long enough to cross the walled-up door. "Who's going to be walking through walled-up doorways?"

"Skip it for now, Godfrey. Check that beam radiator."

I went to the wall and began sweeping it with the inductance bridge. Sure enough; the volume-changes in my phones told me exactly the place where a conduit had been laid, from the receptacle to the ceiling, and along under the quarter-round fillet to the corner and the wire-mesh snivvy.

"I begin to get it," Henry said. "The switch was in the drier. Start that up, and you activate the beam, which focuses on the head of whoever's in the chair. Wickersham was a cute character."

"He sure is ... was, I mean."

"Hey—was that thing on when I went to sleep in the chair?" I thought fast. "Why no, Henry. Of course not."

"A good thing. I thought maybe it was. I'd hate to get a post-mortem kick from old granite-puss."

I changed the subject quickly. "Now, where's this rig powered from?" I got busy with the probe again, sweeping round and round the outlet. "The rectangular AC conduit is too near ... no ... I got it. Hm-m-m." Slowly I traced the field-interruption of the conduit along the wall, where it suddenly disappeared. "It's gone, right here," I said, pointing to the wall.

"That's right over the black-light ray—the walled-up door!"

I pulled off the phones and began to unstrap the wrist meter. "Henry, I'd say that if that electronic watchdog is there, that door opens. If that power line goes in there, we want to open it."

He nodded, and went for my little black-light lamp. We set it up to fool the photocell the way we had on the window, and then went to work on the nearly invisible door. We felt over every inch of it. There was a floor board in the front of the sill with a comparatively wide crack between it and its neighbor; ordinarily it would have been in the black light for its entire length. I rested one hand on this board as I felt the door; the plank shifted a little under my hand, and without a sound the door swung inward.

"Give me your gun," I said clearly, and pounced on Henry and put my hand over his mouth before he could say "What gun?" "There could be someone in there," I whispered.

He gave me the four-o with his fingers and thumb, and then aimed his light into the open door. Slowly we entered. I plucked Henry's sleeve, held up a halting palm, and trotted back to get the pinch bar, with which I jammed the door so it could not swing closed. "I've seen too many Karloff pictures," I muttered to him.

But the room was unoccupied. It was tiny—little more than a large closet. "*Wheee—ooo!*" Henry whistled. "Will you look at the *stuff!*"

It was a sight to gladden the heart of an electronics man. An oscilloscope with an eight-inch screen. A vacuum-tube voltmeter. The biggest, fanciest multimeter I have ever seen. An electronic power-supply control. Rolls and skeins of hook-up wire and shielding of all kinds, colors and sizes. Blank panel plates; knobs, dials; racks and racks of tubes ranging from peanuts to doorknobs. An elaborate transceiver. A bakelite-surfaced work table with power outlets spaced all around it, marked for every standard voltage, AC and DC, that I ever heard of anyone using and some I hadn't thought about yet. A vast color-indexed file of resistors and capacitances. A big commercial tube-tester. Floor to ceiling, it was packed with electronic treasure.

"I love my wife," said I archaically, "but oh you workshop!"

When we had gotten our breath back, Henry asked, "That drier rig still running?"

"Yep."

"Then would that be the transmitter of that beam?" He pointed to a small chassis with a cluster of tubes which glowed, and a huge transformer that hummed softly. "Will you look at that spaghetti," I breathed. "All spot-welded; not a soldered joint in sight!"

"This must be it," said Henry, poking a device on the bench; a handle with two tiny gray electrodes, one detachable. "Oh, what I wouldn't give for—"

"I know it's tough," I said, grinning, "but leave us keep our mind on our business. Let's look this thing over."

To go into detail the tests we made of that rig would not only be tedious; it might be dangerous. The principle, when we finally isolated it—and only with that splendid equipment could we have done it—was startlingly simple. I'd hate to have the job of making that hyperbolic web transmitting antenna, but like Columbus' egg trick, it wouldn't be too hard to duplicate once you got the idea. As for the beam itself, it was transmitted at such and such a fixed frequency, with harmonics, and with ninety and one hundred eighty degree beats to the fundamental *and* to certain of the harmonics, at such and such a wattage, with a so-and-so field tension at the focal point. The output stages had a wave-form like the first act of Disney's *Fantasia* run off in forty seconds.

I tell you; I feel about this thing the way I did when I was in war work, and some of the bright boys came up with gizmos for mass production that had been regarded as impossibilities in all the best people's books. Once in a while, in those days, you'd bump up against another electronics engineer whom you knew would be absolutely fascinated with the work you were doing. And because of military security, you had to keep your lips buttoned. But the pressure behind the button was something fantastic. That's the way I feel now. But I ardently wish I didn't know about it, or that I would quickly forget it; because that wave-form, at that power, at the point of focus, is the most utterly horrible thing I can conceive of.

After hours of concentrated work—and the effort it took to keep away from entrancing sidelines was no small part of the concentration—we got the final output wave-form on the 'scope. "That's it," I said.

"And it's all yours, Ameche my boy," said Henry, watching the complex thing writhe and shimmer on the screen. "All I want to do is put tomato sauce on it and eat it. Now we've got it—what do we do with it?"

I stared at the thing on screen. It was hypnotic, with that self-inverting three-dimensional effect that a cathode image has. "Only thing I can think of is to throw it around one hundred eighty degrees out of phase and re-radiate, focusing at the same point as the beam out there until it cancels out. Or until it overcompensates and undoes all the harm it has accomplished. But we've got to ... to try it out on someone."

Henry's eyes glinted. "Maybe we could snatch a body?"

"We've got to do something."

"Why bother? You've had your education. The girls are O.K. and the Wick is dead. And I'm hungry and sleepy and I got to work in the ... work in the—" His voice faltered. "Godfrey, I must be tuckered out. I can't seem to remember who we work for, now that Wickersham is—"

"Don't worry about it, " I said gently. "We have a little more to do here. We've got to knock together an inverter."

He spread his hands. "But why?"

"Please, Henry. For me. This once," I pleaded with him. "Holy smoke; we've come so far on the thing. Let's round it off."

"Oh all right. Jee-hoshaphat; you're worse than Wick used to be." He pulled out his watch and gaped at it. "Quarter to—" His eyes bugged. "Godfrey! It's quarter to *six!* In the morning! The girls—they'll be half nuts!"

He scrambled to the bench. There was a dial phone there. He snatched it off the cradle and jammed it to his ear, waiting for a dial tone. I saw him go white, and suddenly his eyes rolled up and he slumped to the floor, the telephone falling on the bench on a tangle of rubber-insulated wire. I stooped and half-lifted him, looking wildly around to find somewhere to put him. There was nowhere, so I straightened him out on the floor, and picked up the phone.

"—and a gross of 6SJ7's," said the phone. "And have you made up my silvering solutions?"

"Yes, *sir,*" said another voice.

"All right. I expect that shipment before eleven o'clock." The line clicked and went dead. Carefully I hung up the phone.

Wickersham's voice! It was obviously a bridge phone to the office; and Henry, listening for a mere hum on the phone, had heard it—heard the voice of a man whom he thought dead. And it was infinitely important to Henry that he believe Wickersham dead. It was about the most important thing there was.

I knelt beside him, pitying him more than I can find words to describe. Poor little, cheerful, chubby Henry! The guy just didn't deserve this kind of thing, wasn't equipped to handle it.

I chafed his hands, and suddenly he tossed his head restlessly and batted his eyelids. "Go to sleep," I said softly. "Go on."

Perhaps he was tuckered out physically and emotionally, or perhaps he was hyper-subject to hypnosis because of what the beam had done to him; but he began to relax almost immediately. I put a roll of rubberfoam cushioning under his head and he sank into it. Once he opened his eyes very wide and said, "He's just *got* to be dead!" I said quietly, "Sure. Sure. Sure." And he went to sleep.

Then I went back to the bench and got to work.

My eyes had begun to blur, but I tried to ignore it. When it got too bad I went out into the beauty shop and walked up and down, fast, turning circuit diagrams over in my mind; and then I would rush back in and go on. My feet hurt and my back hurt, and I was hungry.

But I finished the rig, and hooked it up, and hung the 'scope on it, and it worked. The strange wave-form of the beam transmitter dwindled under the matched out-of-phase signal of the inverter; subsided, receded; and it looked as if I had it whipped. I had everything else I needed but a guinea pig.

I had begun, by then, to fully understand the function of the beam. It took the ego's most heartfelt wish, and made it an accomplished fact; a thing which, to that ego, had actually happened. But because it was such a wanted—such a *needed* thing—the inevitable reaction was a tearing sense of loss. When contradictory evidence piled up, when the same senses that had, subjectively, told that ego that the needed thing was true and then that it was not true, the struggle between then was more than a human mind could cope with. There was only one surcease—another treatment under the beam. And then another. And never in human history has a more torturous instrument been devised. It was worse than any drug; for the drugs killed logic, but this thing *used* it, in opposite directions at the same time in the same mind; and the stronger of the two was that which was refuted by the most evidence.

What could I do? Whom could I use the thing on, when I knew as a technician that I had the antidote, but did not know as a physician or psychiatrist what the result would be? There was Marie. And Carole—and what strange battle was she fighting? And the Widget. And Henry.

I looked down at him, curled up on the floor, confined and shrouded with the utter sleep of the exhausted. I could expose myself to the beam; but how did I know what my deepest desire was—what the direction would be of my wishful thinking? Did anybody really know that? Exposure to the beam had turned Henry against any further research; apparently he had wanted the reasons for that research removed more than anything else in the universe. There was only one alternative to doing the work, and that was to believe it done, which was the course his mind took. And as he lay there sleeping, he still believed it, and would if I woke him and asked him to handle the controls while I tested it on myself. He'd refuse. I might be able to argue him into it; and if I did, how could I tell what would happen to me? Would I forget my discoveries in this devilish field, and condemn us all to the madness of some concreted dream?

No; I held too much responsibility. I couldn't try it on myself. Carole, then. A wave of sheer horror nearly stopped my heart at the thought. Marie—my sister.

Oh, you just don't do those things! No human being should be faced with such a choice.

The Widget.

Grave and clear-eyed, and sometimes so surprisingly adult, and all the while such a kid, such a baby, so little.

Why not the Widget? The thought came strongly—why not any of them? Didn't the oscilloscope say that I could negate the beam? I could start with the gain away down out of sight, and increase it slowly, micrometrically, with a vernier. Weren't the chances in my favor?

I was filled then with self-disgust. I didn't *know* enough. Surely I could have learned enough about the physiology of the mind to be able to judge what would happen, have some small guide—even increase the odds in my favor, large as they were.

This was silly. Of course they'd be all right, no matter which one I treated first. But—failure. Any failure. Carole with dementia praecox. The Widget a cretin. Marie a paranoid. Henry, drooling and having to be fed.

Henry. He never did look his age, and asleep he looked like a nine-year-old—a chubby nine-year-old with a two-day beard.

The decision came smoothly and without effort. I just suddenly knew it would be Henry.

"Come on, boy. C'mon, old hawss." I got him under the armpits and heaved him up. He lolled against me, got his feet under him and walked blearily as I led him. I took him out into the beauty parlor and said "Siddown, you," and grinned as I shoved his chest, and sat him in the chair. That's when he really woke up.

"What'sa big idea? In the chair—hey! Godfrey! What are you doing? You dope, the beam's going to—"

He began to struggle. He said, "You've gone crazy, just the way we're all going to go. Wickersham's dead, you fool; you don't have to do this." After that he didn't talk. He fought. Once he got out of the chair. I didn't hit him until I had him back in it, although he kicked me. When I had him in the chair again I brought up the heel of my hand and caught him under the chin with it. It closed his mouth with an astonishingly loud snap, as his teeth clicked together. His head went so far back against the rest that I thought I had broken his neck. I hit him very hard. I backed off from him, sobbing for breath, and when I had some air, I went back and straightened him out. He moved his head a little and moaned, and blood came from his mouth, so I knew he was all right although he must have bitten his tongue.

I limped back into the shop and threw the master switch on the projector. The silly little hair drier motor began to whine like wind around eaves.

I watched the 'scope, and when the wave form of the beam was fully formed, I switched in the plate voltage of the inverter, and started to crank up the gain. It was a feather-touch, a very little at a time. I had my hand braced solidly on the bench top, with my thumb and forefinger just touching the knob; and I brought up the gain only until the first effects got noticeable on the shimmering screen. Then I cut the master switch and ran out to Henry.

He seemed to be asleep, quite normally asleep, and very happy. His smile was all there more cherubic because his lower lip had started to swell, and blood ran freely out of the corner of his mouth. I shook him, and he awakened instantly, opened his eyes, grinned and then winced.

"Godfrey ... what hap—" He put his hand to his mouth and stared at the blood on his fingers, and then at me, and fright grew in his eyes. He leaped to his feet and stared around him. "Godfrey! Where are we? What are we doing here? What's happened to me? Is this a hospit— No; it couldn't be. Is it morning?"

He shuddered, and I had to guide him back into the chair as his legs started to tremble with weakness. He went back into the chair without the slightest recognition of its being anything but a chair.

The blood on his chin looked very red as the weakness bleached his face. I found a handkerchief and wiped it. It didn't do much good.

"What's the last thing you remember? I'll tell you everything I can from then on."

"Remember? I can't.... I was—" He leaned forward and put his forehead on his hands. He spat, and grunted. "I was walking down the back road, going to your place. Was I hit by a car?"

"What had happened before you left your house? Do you remember?"

"Yes," he said slowly. "Marie ... wouldn't stop talking about the ... time at the Altair when I hit ... when she thinks I—"

"Yes boy. I gotcha. I can tell you everything. One more question. Where's Wickersham?"

"Hm-m-m? Search me. The skunk. Down at the lab, most likely. Why?"

I realized I had been holding my breath, and let it out gratefully.

I had succeeded, and I had failed. My out-of-phase component wiped out the beam effect. It had also wiped out everything else— but completely. Like a refinement on the electric-shock treatment. Sweat ran down behind my ears as I thought of what might have happened if I had not used such a feather-touch on the gain of the inverter. How, without experimentation, could you judge the relative resistance of various minds? Would a woman's mind resist less, or more? If less, the danger was too great; the effective increase might be geometric, or exponential. If more, how judge the increase? My choice was, if anything, worse than it had been before. And yet— what could be worse than a loved one slowly going mad before your eyes? It would take so long.

I sat down on the floor, and Henry slumped in the chair, occasionally touching his swollen lip tenderly, and I told him everything that had happened. It was an astonishing thing for him, and for me too, to see his amazement at our burglarization of the premises, and my account of his violent contention that Wickersham was dead.

When I had quite finished, Henry said, "Well, we'll have to try it again."

"On whom?"

"Me, of course. Who else?"

"Henry, you're crazy! I can't do that to you any more!"

"Why not? You had reasons for choosing me in the first place; they still apply."

"The most important one doesn't—you weren't responsible enough to control the experiment, because of your fixation that the Wick was dead, and that therefore the experiment was unnecessary."

"Godfrey," said Henry, grinning with the part of his mouth he could still move, "you big lug, how am I going to handle you if you get as violent as I did?"

"That's right," I said.

I didn't decide, though, for all the time that we spent in the shop, going over circuit diagrams, our tired minds refused to help us out much.

"We've got to hit it from another angle," signed Henry after a particularly circular argument involving current versus impedance versus capacitance. "If we only knew something about the mind, something that would give us a hint as to what frequency does what to which part of the brain, to yield a clear, undistorted hallucination like what we're faced with."

"And then we'd know what we could do to distort it. Yeah." "Distort it," I said again.

Suddenly I was on my feet and a banshee yell was ricocheting off the walls. "For Heaven's sake, Godfrey," Henry said startled. "Don't *do* that! Remember the neighbors!"

"That's it!" I chortled. "That's it! Distortion. Distortion, you idiot!"

"Now wait. I think I— Distortion?"

"Of *course!*" I grabbed his arm and hurried him over to the bench, and started hauling out coils and sockets and resistors from the racks. "Distortion's much easier to handle than output! I can blend in any aberration to that wave form—from this to that, from now till then! That's our cure: it's got to be. Don't you see? The hallucination is induced by a wave—and its result is a picture with no distortion whatsoever. Not even facts can distort it. While it lasts, it is clean, consistent, flawless. It's perfection—something we're not geared to take. Hence the sense of loss when it's gone, and the violent subconscious drive to rationalize it or to get it back. Distort the wave ever so slightly, and it's no longer perfect. It becomes more real, but you can live with it."

"Well, I will be ... but how will you know how to distort it? I mean, what part of the wave should you distort?"

"It doesn't matter, don't you see? The very nature of perfection dictates that. It doesn't matter where it's spoiled—it's still spoiled!"

Henry's eyes glowed. "And if you distort just a little more, it'll get fuzzy around the edges. Out of focus. It will be a ... a—"

"A dream! Of course, and can be disposed of as such. Let's go, muscles; I think we've got it!"

I rigged up a simple oscillator circuit and hooked it to the oscilloscope. I got a spot on the screen and, carefully working the horizontal and vertical deflectors, got a nearly perfect ring.

"Now watch," I said. I turned up the gain. The ring expanded. I turned it up more—a little more—suddenly the edge of the ring quivered, zigzagged, and spread out, throwing out a little mutating finger of fluorescence. "There she broke." I checked with the vacuum-tube voltmeter, and noted the reading. "That's about the effect we want, on the overall wave structure of that blasted beam."

"Can do?"

"Can do," I said, " and a darned sight easier than the inversion."

In a very short while, with the aid of the little spot welder, we had the rig set up and ready to roll. "It's safer," I said. "Bound to be. There's so much less to be done to get the effect."

"Here I go," said Henry, and started toward the chair.

"Now wait. You know I've got to give you a shot of the original beam first." "Why sure. How else you going to cure me if I don't sicken first?"

He went out and sat down. "Shoot the sherbet to me, Herbert," he said languidly.

I went to the door of the little shop. "Henry, I can't."

He reared up and peered around at me. "You doubtful about whether I should do this?"

"Yes!"

"Well, I'm not. You're of two minds; one says I shouldn't, one says I should. I got one only, says I should. You're outnumbered two to one." He turned his back again, put his head against the rest, and closed his eyes.

I swore violently. But what can you do with a guy like that? Finding it a little difficult to see, I flipped on the master switch. The drier motor began to moan. It annoyed me more than I like to admit. I had meant to short it out half a dozen times, but never got around to it.

Henry didn't move and when I got out to him he was asleep. I went back and opened the switch. I dawdled. I was frankly afraid of what might happen to him. When I got out again he hadn't moved. He was sitting with his eyes open, smiling happily at the far wall. When he saw me he jumped up and took my hand warmly. "Well, you did it!"

"Did what?" I asked stupidly.

"I'm cured! I feel fine! It worked, didn't it?"

I opened my mouth to tell him exactly what stage he was in, but decided not to. "I have to give you the 'clincher' shot," I said instead.

"What's that?"

"Why the first one cures you; the second makes it stick," I explained, hoping earnestly that he wouldn't start to think about it.

"Oh," he said, leaned back in the chair and closed his eyes.

I nosed into the 'scope and threw up my circle. I figured that was easier to watch than that burbled-up beam wave. I threw in the beam projector, and after it was well warm, started to move in with the distortion. I didn't dare put in too much. Maybe the brain would be insensitive to an over-distorted wave: and then again maybe Henry'd spend the rest of his life with Lobblies following him. When the upper edge of the circle began to flatten a little, I stopped and sweated a while, and gradually eased it in until the ring broke. Then I cut everything, and, frantic with worry, ran to Henry.

He lay very still. I called him softly and he didn't move. I tentatively touched his shoulder. To my infinite relief his eyes opened and he grinned thickly at me through his swollen lips.

"Well, did it work?"

"What?" I asked tentatively.

"The cure."

"What do you think?"

"I don't know," he said, and yawned and stretched. "I had a dream about ... Godfrey, what was my fixation that time?"

"I think you're cured," I said happily. "What was your dream?"

"Well, a fuzzy sort of something about being cured. But of course, if I was going to dream at all, that would be the logical thing to dream about."

"Why?"

"Because it was uppermost in my mind. The most important thing."

"That was your fixation—that you were cured. The logical thing to have a fixation about. I had to lie to you to make you take the cure. You believed you were cured as soon as you were 'sick'!"

And then I phoned.

I made sure the phone was clear, and then hurriedly dialed. The phone barely had a chance to ring before Carole answered.

"Carole, darling!"

"Oh Godfrey—are you all right, sweetheart?"

"Hungry and sleepy and tired. I love you. We've whipped it! We've fixed it! You'll be all right, dear. Listen. I have to get off this phone but quick. Collect Marie and the Widget and get down to Francy's fast like crazy."

"Oh, darling—all right. Right away, soon's I can get a cab. Marie's here. She's been wanting to get the police all night. I wouldn't let her."

"Bless you! 'Bye!" I hung up. Henry was practically jumping up and down in his impatience to get on the phone and talk to Marie, but I put it behind me. "No you don't. You'd get to billing and cooing over the phone and Wickersham would ring in on you. We've got to get them taken care of first."

We gathered up our tools and I took them out to the car: I was no Mr. America, but Henry looked like a meat-scrap. I took the precaution to go in and out through the window after nullifying the U.V. I wasn't going to issue any invitation to Brother Wickersham, if he didn't already know we were here, which was doubtful.

But when the girls arrived, I felt I could forget about that. They came running up the path from a taxi, the Widget winning by seven lengths. I caught her up and hugged her till she grunted, and then slung her over one shoulder while I hugged Carole. I didn't look to see what passed between Marie and Henry, but it must have been something similar.

We trooped into the beauty shop. "Marie first," I said. "You've earned it, Henry."

"Aha!" grinned Henry. "It's a privilege now!"

"I'm sure of my stuff now. Come along, Carole, Widge!" I led them into the little laboratory. They both watched with some fascination as I switched on the heaters.

"O.K., Godfrey," Henry's voice floated in. I switched on.

"Watch the ring," I said to Carole. "When it breaks a little at the edge, Marie will forget that that thing happened. I mean, she'll remember it didn't happen. I mean—"

"I know, dear." She sighed.

"Hm-m-m! Why the sigh?"

"I was just thinking—she has a real something to lose. So has the Widget. Oh, I'm sorry, darling. I didn't mean to—"

"Skip it. You'll get a treatment. I have the littlest hunch why you reacted the way you did to this thing ... oh, I can't explain it all now, beloved, but I will. In a roundabout and rather agonizing way, I've been paid a wonderful compliment."

"I don't understand."

"You will."

"Daddy, where's the cormium hemlet?"

"Busted, finished, and fixed for good," I said. "Hey you. Your Daddy did something about it. That suit you?"

She looked me over. "S'about time."

"*Widget!*" said Carole.

"Mummy, every time you take to cryin' around the place, I'm

gonna be mad at him. Mostly I don't know why, but I knew men cause womenses tears alla time."

"Are you precocious, my darling daughter, or are you quoting Mrs. Wilton?"

"Mrs. Wilton," said the Widget. She considered for a moment, and then said, "Maybe I'm precocious, too."

Just then the nictating ring on the oscilloscope's screen wobbled and frayed at one edge. I cut the master switch. "Cut!" I called.

There wasn't a sound from the beauty shop. I ran out there, did a quick pivot and came back. "Marie and Henry," I said around the tongue in my cheek, "seem to appreciate each other again." Carole smiled. It seemed I had been waiting a long time for that smile. I kissed her. "Go on out there now. Do what Henry tells you. When you come back here, I dare you tell me you're frightened of anything."

Completely trusting, she went out. I held on to the child when she tried to follow.

"O.K.!" called Henry after a minute.

"What's Mummy doing?"

"She's taking a two-minute nap where the helmet used to be," I said as I threw the switches.

"Kin I?"

"Are you good?"

"Well . . . I dunno. I busted your shaving mug."

"Oh-oh."

"But then I took care of Mummy when you stayed out all night."

"What did you do?"

"I told her you was wonderful."

"You did? Bless your little heart!"

"Shucks. It's no more than you tell her yourself."

"Think we have her fooled, Widget?" I asked, laughing.

"We wouldn't if she thought how bad we were instead of how good we are."

"Now there you have something."

"Cut it," Henry called.

"Now you beat it. G'wan; scat, now!"

"Aw. Just 'cause you and Mummy's going to get mushy."

And we did. One look at those unclouded eyes, and I knew that she was all right again.

"A dream, darling," she murmured when I let her. "A silly dream. And I can't even remember what it was about. It was a dream that was—just like all of us, you, and me, and the Widget. I can't think why it was so bad."

"I know, now," I whispered. "Tell you later."

I went to work on the Widget's treatment, and when I got Henry's all clear, I went out there with Carole. The child was fast asleep, smiling. Carole leaned over and kissed her.

"Moh-mee?" she said with her eyes closed, the way she used to when she was half her age.

"Hello, Widge," I said.

"Hi." She knuckled her eyes.

"Have any dreams, sleepyhead?"

"Mmm-hm," she said with a rising inflection. She looked at me with eyes suddenly wide-awake and cautious.

"Go on, kiddo. The lid is off," I said. "You can talk about it now."

"You know everything, don't you, I bet. I dreamed about that ol' doll."

"Was it a dream?"

"Yes. It was a dream. But I'm going to pretend she was real. I wish she *was* real, that's what I wish."

Carole and I exchanged a startled glance.

"*And* I wish Mickey Mouse was real too. Mummy!"

"Yes, darling."

"I din't have enough breakfuss."

The Widget was all right.

"What's going on here!" roared a resonant baritone.

We all froze. "Wickersham," Henry whispered.

"Who's in there?" bellowed the voice.

"Your man Godfrey," I called. "Come on in."

He came striding in, tall and wide and black. The Widget scuttled close to her mother. Nobody else moved. Wickersham was halfway across the room when he saw Henry. The blood on Henry's clothes diverted him a little; he broke stride. He seemed a little less tall, then, as he stopped and swung around, looking at Marie, and Carole, and at the Widget, who twitched, and then at me.

"Company," I said. An idea crawled out of the back of my mind and out my mouth. "They're cured," I said quietly.

Wickersham's mouth sagged. His eyes darted to the women and back to me. I saw Henry go white.

Henry said, "You knew, then. You did it to them."

"Yes," Wickersham said. He said it to me.

Henry stepped up to Wickersham, who towered over him. Henry had the most extraordinary ripple running on the side of his jaw. "Put your hands up," he said, his voice half a plea, half a caress.

Marie said "Henry." Carole took Marie's arm and shook her head at her.

Wickersham glowered suddenly, reached out one long arm and put, rather than shoved, Henry behind him.

"The cure was his idea," I said, indicating Henry.

Wickersham turned and looked at Henry as if he had never seen him before. "You? *I* couldn't do it!" he rasped.

Then Henry hit him. Just once. Very fine.

After that, Wickersham was easy to talk to. He slumped on the edge of one of the sinks, with his chin sunk low, and he talked. I couldn't look at him. I didn't know him like this. It hurt, in a way. I think I felt, then, a thousandth part of the loss all the others had felt over their solidified dreams.

"I didn't mean it to come out this way," said Wickersham. "The wish-fulfillment synapses are what I was after, it's true. I wanted the brain, under that beam, to become a perfectly efficient machine. I wanted to visualize a goal, and then under the beam, to see the whole thing completed, with all of the intermediate steps obvious. I didn't know it would do what it did—and it only had to do that once. I didn't know it would drag something up out of the subconscious, make it real, make it so desirable to return to and so difficult to get along without. I hated to permit myself to go back to it again, and I couldn't bear to be away—I missed it so much."

"What made you subject these women to it?"

"Because of you," he said. "You two are the best team I have. I didn't feel I could persuade or drive you to the cure I needed. I didn't feel you would drive yourselves to the needed extent unless you had a personal reason for doing it."

"That may be true, Henry," I said.

"It isn't," said Henry clearly. "He couldn't bring himself to admit to us that he was under the influence of a hellish thing like this. Isn't that more like it, Wickersham?"

Wickersham didn't answer.

"What about that fantastically childish business with the burglar alarm and all the U.V.?"

"It had to be difficult for you all the way, or you wouldn't have had the push to go all the way."

"Nonsense," said Henry. I looked at him in amazement. I'd never seen Henry like this. He said, his voice challenging, "You tried to do it and failed. You like to think of us as lesser men than yourself. If you couldn't do it at all, you didn't want us to do it easily. Right?"

"I—didn't think it out that way."

Henry nodded. "And you want the cure."

"Yes," Wickersham whispered. "Yes—please."

I felt ill. "Do you own this place?"

"I bought it when I saw your wives going there."

Henry's jaw twitched again. "The secret," he said evenly, "is to feed your beam signal back a hundred and eighty degrees out of phase. About fifteen percent reverse feedback. For about fifteen minutes. Le's go, chillun."

They moved away from him, all but huddled in a group, toward the door. I stood where I was. Wickersham didn't move. I looked and saw Carole lingering at the door. When I turned back, Wickersham was looking out the door—not after anybody; not at anything. He was just looking. His great stony face was full of hollows in the wrong places and the shadows were no longer impressive, and distinguished, and strong. The eyes were red-rimmed, pale and yellowed.

"What was your dream, Wickersham, that you couldn't control?"

He made a movement with his head, a very slight one; but it pointed at Carole and answered my question. I took a step forward, furious, but he said, "No. Not her. Just—what you have."

And I couldn't pity him—he was so broken.

So I left him there, looking as if there were nothing alive but his eyes, and they were tied to the dead rest of him. I caught up with Carole at the path, and we walked quickly until we joined Henry and Marie. She was walking in a new way for her, not looking ahead, but holding her husband and watching his face, because she had seen her dream come true and was permitted to believe it. I put my hand on his shoulder. He stopped as if he had been waiting. Carole took Marie's arm, for she always understood these things without being told about them, and walked ahead.

"Henry," I said, "You just killed a man."

"He won't die."

"You know what that out-of-phase will do to him."

"You told me what a microfraction did to me."

"And he'll get fifteen minutes. There won't be anything left."

"What's he got now?" asked Henry.

"Very little," I admitted.

"He'll be better off after the treatment," he said steadily.

"Henry, I—"

"You could have told him the other treatment," he lashed out. "What would he have then?"

I thought of the Wickersham we worked for; silent, morose, efficient, and certainly not much use to himself. "I don't know why you did it, Henry, or why I let you. I think it's right, though." I also thought that for Henry, this was fighting; it was reprisal, and he would have to fight for everything after this. I could tell by the way he walked, by the way Marie walked with him.

We got in the car and took Henry and Marie home; and then at last we were alone—with the exception, of course, of the Widget, who was doing nip-ups in the back seat.

"Godfrey—what was the matter with me?"

I grinned. "Nothing."

"Nothing? Darling, you needn't try to hide anything."

"I'm not, Carole. Really I'm not. There's only one answer to the way you reacted to the opportunity to know your innermost desire."

"Well?"

"You just didn't react. You had everything you wanted. You were completely happy with what you had. You are a very rare creature, m'love."

"But I don't see why that should have made me so sickeningly sad—and frightened."

"The sadness wasn't much of it. You had your happiness brought to perfection, which is an unnatural state. But your memory of that perfection was so close to reality that you couldn't tell the difference. It was a very slight difference. It was every wall in the house without a fingermark on it. It was being able to close the oven door without the danger of getting your skirt caught in it, ever. In your particular fugue, only the little, unnoticeable details changed. It was perfection itself you thought you had known, and the lack of it that gave you the sense of loss. And when you felt you had lost something, and couldn't identify it, you were afraid."

"Oh—I see," she said thoughtfully. "Why couldn't you tell me before?"

"Didn't want to rub Henry's nose in it. You see, like the Widget, who wanted a doll, Marie wanted an aggressive husband. Marie and the Widget were both mourning the loss of the thing they wanted. You didn't lose anything; you were just afraid. Your not losing anything is the compliment I mentioned a while back. But darling, compliment me in a less roundabout way next time!"

"I love you," she said, with her eyes too.

"That's what I meant," I said, and began to drive with one arm.

There was a snort from the back seat. "What—again?" said the Widget.

Memorial

The Pit, in AD 5000, had changed little over the centuries. Still it was an angry memorial to the misuse of great power; and because of it, organized warfare was a forgotten thing. Because of it, the world was free of the wasteful smoke and dirt of industry. The scream and crash of bombs and the soporific beat of marching feet were never heard, and at long last the earth was at peace.

To go near The Pit was slow, certain death, and it was respected and feared, and would be for centuries more. It winked and blinked redly at night, and was surrounded by a bald and broken tract stretching out and away over the horizon; and around it flickered a ghostly blue glow. Nothing lived there. Nothing could.

With such a war memorial, there could only be peace. The earth could never forget the horror that could be loosed by war.

That was Grenfell's dream.

GRENFELL HANDED THE typewritten sheet back. "That's it, Jack. My idea, and—I wish I could express it like that." He leaned back against the littered workbench, his strangely asymmetrical face quizzical. "Why is it that it takes a useless person adequately to express an abstract?"

Jack Roway grinned as he took back the paper and tucked it into his breast pocket. "Interestin' question, Grenfell, because this *is* your expression, the words *are* yours. Practically verbatim. I left out the 'er's' and 'Ah's' that you play conversational hopscotch with, and strung together all the effects you mentioned without mentioning any of the technological causes. Net result: you think I did it, when you did. You think it's good writing, and I don't."

"You don't?"

Jack spread his bony length out on the hard little cot. His relaxation was a noticeable act, like the unbuttoning of a shirt collar. He laughed.

"Of course I don't. Much too emotional for my taste. I'm just a fumbling aesthete—useless, did you say? Mm-m-m yeah. I suppose so." He paused reflectively. "You see, you cold-blooded characters, you scientists, are the true visionaries. Seems to me the essential difference between a scientist and an artist is that the scientist mixes his hopes with patience.

"The scientist visualizes his ultimate goal, but pays little attention to it. He is all caught up with the achievement of the next step upward. The artist looks so far ahead that more often than not he can't see what's under his feet; so he falls flat on his face and gets called useless by scientists. But if you strip all of the intermediate steps away from the scientist's thinking, you have an artistic concept to which the scientist responds distantly and with surprise, giving some artist credit for deep perspicacity purely because the artist repeated something the scientist said."

"You amaze me," Grenfell said candidly. "You wouldn't be what you are if you weren't lazy and superficial. And yet you come out with things like that. I don't know that I understand what you just said. I'll have to think—but I do believe that you show all the signs of clear thinking. With a mind like yours, I can't understand why you don't use it to build something instead of wasting it in these casual interpretations of yours."

Jack Roway stretched luxuriously. "What's the use? There's more waste involved in the destruction of something which is already built than in dispersing the energy it would take to help build something. Anyway, the world is filled with builders—and destroyers. I'd just as soon sit by and watch, and feel things. I like my environment, Grenfell. I want to feel all I can of it, while it lasts. It won't last much longer. I want to touch all of it I can reach, taste of it, hear it, while there's time. What is around me, here and now, is what is important to me. The acceleration of human progress, and the increase of its mass—to use your own terms—are taking humanity straight to Limbo. You, with your work, think you are fighting humanity's inertia. Well, you are. But it's the kind of inertia called momentum. You command no force great enough to stop it, or even to change its course appreciably."

"I have atomic power."

Roway shook his head, smiling. "That's not enough. No power is enough. It's just too late."

"That kind of pessimism does not affect me," said Grenfell. "You can gnaw all you like at my foundations, Jack, and achieve nothing more than the loss of your front teeth. I think you know that."

"Certainly I know that. I'm not trying to. I have nothing to sell, no one to change. I am even more impotent than you and your atomic power; and you are completely helpless. Uh—I quarrel with your use of the term 'pessimist', though. I am nothing of the kind. Since I have resolved for myself the fact that humanity, as we know it, is finished, I'm quite resigned to it. Pessimism from me, under the circumstances, would be the pessimism of a photophobiac predicting that the sun would rise tomorrow."

Grenfell grinned. 'I'll have to think about that, too. You're such a mass of paradoxes that turn out to be chains of reasoning. Apparently you live in a world in which scientists are poets and the grasshopper has it all over the ant."

"I always did think that ant was a stinker."

"Why do you keep coming here, Jack? What do you get out of it? Don't you realize I'm a criminal?"

Roway's eyes narrowed. "Sometimes I think you wish you were a criminal. The law says you are, and the chances are very strong that you'll be caught and treated accordingly. Ethically, you know you're not. It sort of takes the spice out of being one of the hunted."

"Maybe you're right," Grenfell said thoughtfully. He sighed. "It's so completely silly. During the war years, the skills I had were snatched up and the government flogged me into the Manhattan Project, expecting, and getting, miracles. I have never stopped working along the same lines. And now the government has changed the laws, and pulled legality from under me."

"Hardly surprising. The government deals rather severely with soldiers who go on killing other soldiers after the war is over." He held up a hand to quell Grenfell's interruption. "I know you're not killing anyone, and are working for the opposite result. I was only pointing out that it's the same switcheroo. We the people," he said didactically, "have, in our sovereign might, determined that no atomic research be done except in government laboratories. We have then permitted our politicians to allow so little for maintenance of those laboratories—unlike our overseas friends—that no really exhaustive research can be done in them. We have further made it a major offense to operate such a bootleg lab as yours." He shrugged. "Comes the end of mankind. We'll get walloped first. If we put more money and effort into nuclear research than any other country, some other country would get walloped first. If we last another hundred years— which seems doubtful—some poor, spavined, underpaid government researcher will stumble on the aluminum-isotope space-heating system you have already perfected."

"That was a little rough," said Grenfell bitterly. "Driving me underground just in time to make it impossible for me to announce it. What a waste of time and energy it is to heat homes and buildings the way they do now! Space heating—the biggest single use for heat-energy—and I have the answer to it over there." He nodded toward a compact cube of lead-alloys in the corner of the shop. "Build it into a foundation, and you have controllable heat for the life of the building, with not a cent for additional fuel and practically nothing for maintenance." His jaw knotted. "Well, I'm glad it happened that way."

"Because it got you started on your war memorial—The Pit? Yeah. Well, all I can say is, I hope you're right. It hasn't been possible to scare humanity yet. The invention of gunpowder was going to stop war, and didn't. Likewise the submarine, the torpedo, the airplane, and that two-by-four bomb they pitched at Hiroshima."

"None of that applies to The Pit," said Grenfell. "You're right; humanity hasn't been scared off war yet; but the Hiroshima bomb rocked 'em back on their heels. My little memorial is the real stuff. I'm not depending on a fission effect, you know, with a release of one-tenth of one percent of the energy of the atom. I'm going to disrupt it completely, and get all the energy there is in it. And it'll be *more* than a thousand times as powerful as the Hiroshima bomb, because I'm going to use twelve times as much explosive; and it's going off on the ground, not fifteen hundred feet above it." Grenfell's brow, over suddenly hot eyes, began to shine with sweat. "And then—The Pit," he said softly. "The war memorial to end war, and all other war memorials. A vast pit, alive with bubbling lava, radiating death for ten thousand years. A living reminder of the devastation mankind has prepared for itself. Out here on the desert, where there are no cities, where the land has always been useless, will be the scene of the most useful thing in the history of the race—a never-ending sermon, a warning, an example of the dreadful antithesis of peace." His voice shook to a whisper, and faded.

"Sometimes," said Roway, "You frighten me, Grenfell. It occurs to me that I am such a studied sensualist, tasting everything I can, because I am afraid to feel any one thing that much." He shook himself, or shuddered. "You're a fanatic, Grenfell. Hyperemotional. A monomaniac. I hope you can do it."

"I can do it," said Grenfell.

Two months passed, and in those two months Grenfell's absorption in his work had been forced aside by the increasing pressure of current events. Watching a band of vigilantes riding over the waste to the south of his little buildings one afternoon, he thought grimly of what Roway had said. "Sometimes I think you wish you were a criminal." Roway, the sensualist, would say that. Roway would appreciate the taste of danger, in the same way that he appreciated all the other emotions. As it intensified, he would wait to savor it, no matter how bad it got.

Twice Grenfell shut off the instigating power of the carbon-aluminum pile he had built, as he saw government helicopters hovering on the craggy skyline. He knew of hard-radiation detectors; he had developed two different types of them during the war; and he wanted no questions asked. His utter frustration at being unable to announce the success of his space-heating device, for fear that he would be punished as a criminal and his device impounded and forgotten—that frustration had been indescribable. It had canalized his mind, and intensified the devoted effort he had put forth for the things he believed in during the war. Every case of neural shock he encountered in men who had been hurt by war and despised it, made him work harder on his monument—on The Pit. For if humans could be frightened by war, humanity could be frightened by The Pit.

And those he met who had been hurt by war and who still hated the late enemy—those who would have been happy to go back and kill some more, reckoning vital risk well worth it—those he considered mad, and forgot them.

So he could not stand another frustration. He was the center of his own universe, and he realized it dreadfully, and he had to justify his position there. He was a humanitarian, a philanthropist in the world's truest sense. He was probably as mad as any man who has, through his own efforts, moved the world.

For the first time, then, he was grateful when Jack Roway arrived in his battered old convertible, although he was deliriously frightened at the roar of the motor outside his laboratory window. His usual reaction to Jack's advent was a mixture of annoyance and gratification, for it was a great deal of trouble to get out to his place. His annoyance was not because of the interruption, for Jack was certainly no trouble to have around. Grenfell suspected that Jack came out to see him partly to get the taste of the city out of his mouth, and partly to be able to feel superior to somebody he considered of worth.

But the increasing fear of discovery, and his race to complete his work before it was taken from him by a hysterical public, had had the unusual effect of making him lonely. For such a man as Grenfell to be lonely bordered on the extraordinary; for in his daily life there were simply too many things to be done. There had never been enough hours in a day nor days in a week to suit him, and he deeply resented the encroachments of sleep, which he considered a criminal waste.

"Roway!" he blurted, as he flung the door open, his tone so warm that Roway's eyebrows went up in surprise. "What dragged you out here?"

"Nothing in particular," said the writer, as they shook hands. "Nothing more than usual, which is a great deal. How goes it?"

"I'm about finished." They went inside, and as the door closed,

Grenfell turned to face Jack. "I've been finished for so long I'm ashamed of myself," he said intently.

"Ha! Ardent confession so early in the day! What are you talking about?"

"Oh, there have been things to do," said Grenfell restlessly. "But I could go ahead with the ... with the big thing at almost any time."

"You hate to be finished. You've never visualized what it would be like to have the job done." His teeth flashed. "You know, I've never heard a word from you as to what your plans are after the big noise. You going into hiding?"

"I ... haven't thought much about it. I used to have a vague idea of broadcasting a warning and an explanation before I let go with the disruptive explosion. I've decided against it, though. In the first place, I'd be stopped within minutes, no matter how cautious I was with the transmitter. In the second place ... well, this is going to be so big that it won't need any explanation."

"No one will know who did it, or why it was done."

"Is that necessary?" asked Grenfell quietly.

Jack's mobile face stilled as he visualized The Pit, spewing its ten-thousand-year hell. "Perhaps not," he said. "Isn't it necessary, though, to you?"

"To me?" asked Grenfell, surprised. "You mean, do I care if the world knows I did this thing, or not? No; of course I don't. A chain of circumstance is occurring, and it has been working through me. It goes directly to The Pit; The Pit will do all that is necessary from then on. I will no longer have any part in it."

Jack moved, clinking and splashing, around the sink in the corner of the laboratory. "Where's all your coffee? Oh—here. Uh ... I have been curious about how much personal motive you had for your work. I think that answers it pretty well. I think, too, that you believe what you are saying. Do you know that people who do things for impersonal motives are as rare as fur on a fish?"

"I hadn't thought about it."

"I believe that, too. Sugar? And milk. I remember. And have you been listening to the radio?"

"Yes. I'm ... a little upset, Jack," said Grenfell, taking the cup.

"I don't know where to time this thing. I'm a technician, not a Machiavelli."

"Visionary, like I said. You don't know if you'll throw this gadget of yours into world history too soon or too late—is that it?"

"Exactly. Jack, the whole world seems to be going crazy. Even fission bombs are too big for humanity to handle."

"What else can you expect," said Jack grimly, "with our dear friends across the water sitting over their push buttons waiting for an excuse to punch them?"

"And we have our own set of buttons, of course."

Jack Roway said: "We've got to defend ourselves."

"Are you kidding?"

Roway glanced at him, his dark brows plotting a V. "Not about this. I seldom kid about anything, but particularly not about this." And he—shuddered.

Grenfell stared amazedly at him and then began to chuckle. "Now," he said, "I've seen everything. My iconoclastic friend Jack Roway, of all people, caught up by a . . . a fashion. A national pastime, fostered by uncertainty and fed by yellow journalism—fear of the enemy."

"This country is not at war."

"You mean, we have no enemy? Are you saying that the gentlemen over the water, with their itching fingertips hovering about the push-buttons, are not our enemies?"

"Well—"

Grenfell came across the room to his friend, and put a hand on his shoulder. "Jack—what's the matter? You can't be so troubled by the news—not *you!*"

Roway stared out at the brazen sun, and shook his head slowly. "International balance is too delicate," he said softly; and if a voice could glaze like eyes, his did. "I see the nations of the world as masses balanced each on its own mathematical point, each with its center of gravity directly above. But the masses are fluid, shifting violently away from the center lines. The opposing trends aren't equal: they can't cancel each other; the phasing is too slow. One or the other is going to topple, and then the whole works is going to go."

"But you've known that for a long time. You've known that ever since Hiroshima. Possibly before. Why should it frighten you now?"

"I didn't think it would happen so soon."

"Oh-ho! So that's it! You have suddenly realized that the explosion is going to come in your lifetime. Hm-m-m? And you can't take that. You're capable of all of your satisfying aesthetic rationalizations as long as you can keep the actualities at arm's length."

"*Whew!*" said Roway, his irrepressible humor passing close enough to nod to him. "Keep it clean, Grenfell!"

Grenfell smiled. "Y'know, Jack, you remind me powerfully of some erstwhile friends of mine who write science-fiction. They had been living very close to atomic power for a long time—years before the man on the street—or the average politician, for that matter—knew an atom from Adam. Atomic power was handy to these specialized word-merchants because it gave them a limitless source of power for background to a limitless source of story material. In the heyday of the Manhattan Project, most of them suspected what was going on, some of them knew—some even worked on it. All of them were quite aware of the terrible potentialities of nuclear energy. Practically all of them were scared silly of the whole idea. They were afraid for humanity, but they themselves were not really afraid, except in a delicious drawing room sort of way, because they couldn't conceive of this Buck Rogers event happening to anything but posterity. But it happened, right smack in the middle of their own sacrosanct lifetimes.

"And I will be dog-goned if you're not doing the same thing. You've gotten quite a bang out of figuring out the doom humanity faces in an atomic war. You've consciously risen above it by calling it inevitable, and in the meantime, leave us gather rosebuds before it rains. You thought you'd be safe home—dead—before the first drops fell. Now social progress has rolled up a thunderhead and you find yourself a mile from home with a crease in your pants and no umbrella. And you're scared."

Roway looked at the floor and said, "It's so soon. It's so soon." He looked up at Grenfell, and his cheekbones seemed too large. He took a deep breath. "You ... we can stop it, Grenfell. The war ...

the ... this thing that's happening to us. The explosion that will come when the strains get too great in the international situation. And it's *got* to be stopped!"

"That's what The Pit is for."

"The Pit!" Roway said scornfully. "I've called you a visionary before. Grenfell, you've got to be more practical! Humanity is not going to learn anything by example. It's got to be kicked and carved. Surgery."

Grenfell's eyes narrowed. "Surgery? What you said a minute ago about my stopping it ... do you mean what I think you mean?"

"Don't you see it?" said Jack urgently. "What you have here—total disruptive energy—the peak of atomic power. One or two wallops with this, in the right place, and we can stop anybody."

"This isn't a weapon. I didn't make this to be a weapon."

"The first rock ever thrown by a prehistoric man wasn't made to be a weapon, either. But it was handy and it was effective, and it was certainly used because it had to be used." He suddenly threw up his hands in a despairing gesture. "You don't understand. Don't you realize that this country is likely to be attacked at any second—that diplomacy is now hopeless and helpless, and the whole world is just waiting for the thing to start? It's probably too late even now but it's the least we can do."

"What, specifically, is the least thing we can do?"

"Turn your work over to the War Department. In a few hours the government can put it where it will do the most good." He drew his finger across his throat. "Anywhere we want to, over the ocean."

There was a taut silence. Roway looked at his watch and licked his lips. Finally Grenfell said, "Turn it over to the government. Use it for a weapon—and what for? To stop war."

"Of course!" blurted Roway. "To show the rest of the world that our way of life ... to scare the daylights out of ... to—"

"*Stop it!*" Grenfell roared. "Nothing of the kind. You think—you hope anyway—that the use of total disruption as a weapon will stall off the inevitable—at least in your lifetime. Don't you?"

"No. I—"

"Don't you?"

"Well, I—"

"You have some more doggerel to write," said Grenfell scathingly. "You have some more blondes to chase. You want to go limp over a few more Bach fugues."

Jack Roway said: "No one knows where the first bomb might hit. It might be anywhere. There's nowhere I ... we ... can go to be safe." He was trembling.

"Are the people in the city quivering like that?" asked Grenfell.

"Riots," breathed Roway, his eyes bright with panic. "The radio won't announce anything about the riots."

"Is that what you came out here for today—to try to get me to give disruptive power to *any* government?"

Jack looked at him guiltily. "It was the only thing to do. I don't know if your bomb will turn the trick, but it has to be tried. It's the only thing left. We've got to be prepared to hit first, and hit harder than anyone else."

"No." Grenfell's one syllable was absolutely unshakable.

"Grenfell—I thought I could argue you into it. Don't make it tough for yourself. You've got to do it. Please do it on your own. Please, Grenfell." He stood up slowly.

"Do it on my own—or what? *Keep away from me!*"

"No ... I—" Roway stiffened suddenly, listening. From far above and to the north came the whir of rotary wings. Roway's fear-slackened lips tightened into a grin, and with two incredibly swift strides he was across to Grenfell. He swept in a handful of the smaller man's shirt front and held him half off the floor.

"Don't try a thing," he gritted. There was not a sound then except their harsh breathing, until Grenfell said wearily: "There was somebody called Judas "

"You can't insult me," said Roway, with a shade of his old cockiness, "And you're flattering yourself."

A helicopter sank into its own roaring dust-cloud outside the building. Men poured out of it and burst in the door. There were three of them. They were not in uniform.

"Dr. Grenfell," said Jack Roway, keeping his grip, "I want you to meet—"

"Never mind that," said the taller of the three in a brisk voice. "You're Roway? Hm-m-m. Dr. Grenfell. I understand you have a nuclear energy device on the premises."

"Why did you come by yourself?" Grenfell asked Roway softly. "Why not just send these stooges?"

"For you, strangely enough. I hoped I could argue you into giving the thing freely. You know what will happen if you resist?"

"I know." Grenfell pursed his lips for a moment, and then turned to the tall man. "Yes. I have some such thing here. Total atomic disruption. Is that what you were looking for?"

"Where is it?"

"Here, in the laboratory, and then there's the pile in the other building. You'll find—" He hesitated. "You'll find two samples of the concentrate. One's over there—" he pointed to a lead case on a shelf behind one of the benches. "And there's another like it in a similar case in the shed back of the pile building."

Roway sighed and released Grenfell. "Good boy. I knew you'd come through."

"Yes," said Grenfell. "Yes—"

"Go get it," said the tall man. One of the others broke away.

"It will take two men to carry it," said Grenfell in a shaken voice. His lips were white.

The tall man pulled out a gun and held it idly. He nodded to the second man. "Go get it. Bring it here and we'll strap the two together and haul 'em to the plane. Snap it up."

The two men went out toward the shed.

"Jack?"

"Yes, Doc."

"You really think humanity can be scared?"

"It will be—now. This thing will be used right."

"I hope so. Oh, I hope so," Grenfell whispered.

The men came back. "Up on the bench," said the leader, nodding toward the case the men carried between them.

As they climbed up on the bench and laid hands on the second case, to swing it down from the shelf, Jack Roway saw Grenfell's face spurt sweat, and a sudden horror swept over him.

"Grenfell!" he said hoarsely. "It's—"

"Of course," Grenfell whispered. "Critical mass."

Then it let go.

It was like Hiroshima, but much bigger. And yet, that explosion did not create The Pit. It was the pile that did—the boron-aluminum lattice which Grenfell had so arduously pieced together from parts bootlegged over the years. Right there at the heart of the fission-explosion, total disruption took place in the pile, for that was its function. This was slower. It took more than an hour for its hellish activity to reach a peak, and in that time a huge crater had been gouged out of the earth, a seething, spewing mass of volatilized elements, raw radiation, and incandescent gases. It was—The Pit. Its activity curve was plotted abruptly—up to peak in an hour and eight minutes, and then a gradual subsidence as it tried to feed further afield with less and less fueling effect; and as it consumed its own flaming wastes in an effort to reach inactivity. Rain would help to blanket it, through energy lost in volatilizing the drops; and each of the many elements involved went through its respective secondary radioactivity, and passed away its successive half-lives. The subsidence of The Pit would take between eight and nine thousand years.

And like Hiroshima, this explosion had effects which reached into history and into men's hearts in places far separated in time from the cataclysm itself.

These things happened:

The explosion could not be concealed; and there was too much hysteria afoot for anything to be confirmed. It was easier to run headlines saying WE ARE ATTACKED. There was an instantaneous and panicky demand for reprisals, and the government acceded, because such "reprisals" suited the policy of certain members who could command emergency powers. And so the First Atomic War was touched off.

And the Second.

There were no more atomic wars after that. The Mutant's War was a barbarous affair, and the mutants defeated the tattered and largely sterile remnants of humanity, because the mutants were strong. And then the mutants died out because they were unfit. For a while there was some very interesting material to be studied on the effects of radiation on heredity, but there was no one to study it.

There were some humans left. The rats got most of them, after increasing in fantastic numbers; and there were three plagues.

After that there were half-stooping, naked things whose twisted heredity could have been traced to humankind; but these could be frightened, as individuals and as a race, so therefore they could not progress. They were certainly not human.

The Pit, in AD 5000, had changed little over the centuries. Still it was an angry memorial to the misuse of great power; and because of it, organized warfare was a forgotten thing. Because of it, the world was free of the wasteful smoke and dirt of industry. The scream and crash of bombs and the soporific beat of marching feet were never heard, and at long last the earth was at peace.

To go near The Pit was slow, certain death, and it was respected and feared, and would be for centuries more. It winked and blinked redly at night, and was surrounded by a bald and broken tract stretching out and away over the horizon; and around it flickered a ghostly blue glow. Nothing lived there. Nothing could.

With such a war memorial, there could only be peace. The earth could never forget the horror that could be loosed by war.

That was Grenfell's dream.

Mewhu's Jet

"We interrupt this program to announce—"

"Jack, don't jump like that! And you've dropped ashes all over your—"

"Aw, Iris, honey, let me listen to—"

"—*at first identified as a comet, the object is pursuing an erratic course through the stratosphere, occasionally dipping as low as*—"

"You make me nervous, Jack. You're an absolute slave to the radio. I wish you paid that much attention to me."

"Darling, I'll argue the point, or pay attention to you, anything in the wide world you like when I've heard this announcement; but please, *please let me listen!*"

"—*dents of the East Coast are warned to watch for the approach of this ob*—"

"Iris, don't—"

Click!

"Well, of all the selfish, inconsiderate, discourteous—"

"That will do, Jack Garry. It's my radio as much as yours, and I have a right to turn it off when I want to."

"Might I ask why you find it necessary to turn it off at this moment?"

"Because I know the announcement will be repeated any number of times if it's important, and you'll shush me every time. Because I'm not interested in that kind of thing and don't see why I should have it rammed down my throat. Because the only thing you ever want to listen to is something which couldn't possibly affect us. But mostly because you yelled at me!"

"I did *not* yell at you!"

"You *did!* And you're yelling now!"

"*Mom!* Daddy!"

297

"Oh. Molly, darling, we woke you up!"

"Poor bratlet. Hey, what about your slippers?"

"It isn't cold tonight, Daddy. What was that on the radio?"

"Something buzzing around in the sky, darling. I didn't hear it all."

"A space ship, I betcha."

"You see? You and your so-called science fiction!"

At which point, something like a giant's fist clouted off the two-room top story of the seaside cottage and scattered it down the beach. The lights winked out, and outside the whole waterfront lit up with a brief, shattering blue glare.

"Jacky darling, are you hurt?"

"Mom, he's bleedin'!"

"Jack, honey, say something. *Please* say something."

"Urrrrgh," said Jack Garry obediently, sitting up with a soft clatter of pieces of falling lath and plaster. He put his hands gently on the sides of his head and whistled. "Something hit the house."

His red-headed wife laughed half-hysterically. "Not really darling." She put her arms around him, whisked some dust out of his hair, and began stroking his neck. "I'm ... frightened, Jack."

"You're frightened!" He looked around shakily in the dim moonlight that filtered in. Radiance from an unfamiliar place caught his bleary gaze, and he clutched Iris' arm. "Upstairs ... it's gone!" he said hoarsely, struggling to his feet. "Molly's room ... Molly—"

"I'm here, Daddy. Hey, you're squeezin'!"

"Happy little family," said Iris, her voice trembling. "Vacationing in a quiet little cottage by the sea, so Daddy can write technical articles while Mummy regains her good disposition—without a phone, without movies within miles, and living in a place where the roof flies away. Jack—what hit us?"

"One of those things you were talking about," said Jack sardonically. "One of the things you refuse to be interested in that couldn't possibly affect us. Remember?"

"The thing the radio was talking about?"

"I wouldn't be surprised. We'd better get out of here. This place may fall in on us, or burn, or something."

"An' we'll all be kilt," crooned Molly.

"Shut up, Molly. Iris, I'm going to poke around. Better go on out and pick us a place to pitch the tent—if I can find the tent."

"Tent?" Iris gasped.

"Boy oh boy," said Molly.

"Jack Garry, I'm not going to go to bed in a tent. Do you realize that this place will be swarming with people in no time flat?"

"O.K., O.K. Only get out from under what's left of the house. Go for a swim. Take a walk. Or g'wan to bed in Molly's room."

"I'm not going out there by myself."

Jack sighed. "I should've asked you to stay in here," he muttered. "If you're not the contrariest woman ever to— Be quiet, Molly."

"I didn't say anything."

Meeew-w-w!

"Aren't you doing that caterwauling?"

"No, Daddy, truly."

Iris said, "I'd say a cat was caught in the wreckage except that cats are smart and no cat would ever come near this place."

Wuh-wuh-wuh-meeee-ew-w-w!

"What a dismal sound!"

"Jack, that isn't a cat."

Mmmmmew. Mmm—m-m-m.

"Whatever it is," Jack said, "it can't be big enough to be afraid of and make a funny little noise like that." He squeezed Iris' arm and, stepping carefully over the rubble, began peering in and around it. Molly scrambled beside him. He was about to caution her against making so much noise, and then thought better of it. What difference would a little racket make?

The noise was not repeated, and five minutes' searching elicited nothing. Garry went back to his wife, who was fumbling around the shambles of a living room, pointlessly setting chairs and coffee tables back on their legs.

"I didn't find anyth—"

"*Yipe!*"

"Molly! What is it?"

Molly was just outside, in the shrubbery. "Daddy, you better come quick!"

Spurred by the urgency of her tone, he went crashing outside. He found Molly standing rigid, trying to cram both her fists in her mouth at the same time. And at her feet was a man with silver-gray skin and a broken arm, who mewed at him.

"—*Guard and Navy Department have withdrawn their warnings. The pilot of a Pan-American transport has reported that the object disappeared into the zenith. It was last seen eighteen miles east of Normandy Beach, New Jersey. Reports from the vicinity describe it as traveling very slowly, with a hissing noise. Although it reached within a few feet of the ground several times, no damage has been reported. Inves—*"

"Think of that," said Iris, switching off the little three-way portable. "No damage."

"Yeah. And if no one saw the thing hit, no one will be out here to investigate. So you can retire to your downy couch in the tent without fear of being interviewed."

"Go to sleep? Are you mad? Sleep in that flimsy tent with that mewing monster lying there?"

"Oh, heck, Mom, he's sick! He wouldn't hurt anybody."

They sat around a cheerful fire, fed by roof shingles. Jack had set up the tent without much trouble. The silver-gray man was stretched out in the shadows, sleeping lightly and emitting an occasional moan.

Jack smiled at Iris. "Y'know, I love your silly chatter, darling. The way you turned to and set his arm was a pleasure to watch. You didn't think of him as a monster while you were tending to him."

"Didn't I, though? Maybe monster was the wrong word to use. Jack, he has only one bone in his forearm!"

"He has what? Oh, nonsense, honey! 'Tain't scientific. He'd have to have a ball-and-socket joint in his wrist."

"He *has* a ball-and-socket joint in his wrist."

"This I have to see," Jack muttered. He picked up a flash lantern and went over to the long prone figure.

Silver eyes blinked up at the light. There was something queer about them. He turned the beam closer. The pupils were not black in that light, but dark green. They all but closed—from the sides, like a cat's. Jack's breath wheezed out. He ran the light over the man's body. It was clad in a bright-blue roomy bathrobe effect, with a yellow sash. The sash had a buckle which apparently consisted of two pieces of yellow metal; there seemed to be nothing to keep them together. They just stayed. When the man had fainted, just as they found him, it had taken almost all Jack's strength to pull them apart.

"Iris."

She got up and came over to him. "Let the poor devil sleep."

"Iris, what color was his robe?"

"Red, with a ... but it's *blue!*"

"Is now. Iris, what on earth have we got here?"

"I don't know. I don't know. Some poor thing that escaped from an institution for—for—"

"For what?"

"How should I know?" she snapped. "There must be some place where they send creatures that get born like that."

"Creatures don't get born like that, he isn't deformed. He's just different."

"I see what you mean. I don't know why I see what you mean, but I'll tell you something." She stopped, and was quiet for so long that he turned to her, surprised. She said slowly, "I ought to be afraid of him, because he's strange, and ugly, but—I'm not."

"Me too."

"Molly, go back to bed."

"He's a leprechaun."

"Maybe you're right. Go on to bed, chicken, and in the morning you can ask him where he keeps his crock of gold."

"Gee." She went off a little way and stood on one foot, drawing a small circle in the sand with the other. "Daddy?"

"Yes, Molly m'love."

"Can I sleep in the tent tomorrow, too?"

"If you're good."

"Daddy obviously means," said Iris acidly, "that if you're not good he'll have a roof on the house by tomorrow night."

"I'll be good." She disappeared into the tent.

The gray man mewed.

"Well, old guy, what is it?"

The man reached over and fumbled at his splinted arm.

"It hurts him," said Iris. She knelt beside him and, taking the wrist of his good arm, lifted it away from the splint, where he was clawing. The man did not resist, but lay and looked at her with pain-filled, slitted eyes.

"He has six fingers," Jack said. "See?" He knelt beside his wife and gently took the man's wrist. He whistled. "It *is* a ball-and-socket."

"Give him some aspirin."

"That's a good . . . wait." Jack stood pulling his lip in puzzlement. "Do you think we should?"

"Why not?"

"We don't know where he comes from. We know nothing of his body chemistry, or what any of our medicines might do to him."

"He . . . what do you mean, where he comes from?"

"Iris, will you open up your mind just a little? In the face of evidence like this, are you going to even attempt to cling to the idea that this man comes from anywhere on this earth?" Jack said with annoyance. "You know your anatomy. Don't tell me you ever saw a human freak with skin and bones like that! That belt buckle, that material in his clothes . . . come on, now. Drop your prejudices and give your brains a chance."

"You're suggesting things that simply don't *happen!*"

"That's what the man in the street said—in Hiroshima. That's what the old-time aeronaut said from the basket of his balloon when they told him about heavier-than-air craft. That's what—"

"All right, all right, Jack. I know the rest of the speech. If you want dialectics instead of what's left of a night's sleep, I might point out that the things you have mentioned have all concerned human endeavors. Show me any new plastic, a new metal, a new kind of engine, and though I may not begin to understand it, I can accept it because it is of human origin. But this, this man, or whatever he is—"

"I know," said Jack, more gently. "It's frightening because it's strange, and away down underneath we feel that anything strange is necessarily dangerous. That's why we wear our best manners for strangers and not for our friends. But I still don't think we should give this character any aspirin."

"He seems to breathe the same air we do. He perspires, he talks ... I think he talks."

"You have a point. Well, if it'll ease his pain at all, it may be worth trying. Give him just one."

Iris went to the pump with a collapsible cup from her first-aid kit, and filled it. Kneeling by the silver-skinned man, she propped up his head, gently put the aspirin between his lips, and brought the cup to his mouth. He sucked the water in greedily, and then went completely limp.

"Oh-oh. I was afraid of that."

Iris put her hand over the man's heart. *"Jack!"*

"Is he ... what is it, Iris?"

"Not dead, if that's what you mean. Will you feel this?"

Jack put his hand beside Iris'. The heart was beating with massive, slow blows, about eight to the minute. Under it, out of phase completely with the main beat, was another, an extremely fast, sharp beat, which felt as if it were going about three hundred.

"He's having some sort of palpitation," Jack said.

"And in two hearts at once!"

Suddenly the man raised his head and uttered a series of ululating shrieks and howls. His eyes opened wide, and across them fluttered a translucent nictitating membrane. He lay perfectly still with his mouth open, shrieking and gargling. Then with a lightning movement he snatched Jack's hand to his mouth. A pointed tongue, light orange and four inches longer than it had any right to be, flicked out and licked Jack's hand. Then the strange eyes closed, the shrieks died to a whimper and faded out, and the man relaxed.

"Sleeping now," said Iris. "Oh, I hope we haven't done anything to him!"

"We've done something. I just hope it isn't serious. Anyhow, his arm isn't bothering him any. That's all we were worried about in the first place."

Iris put a cushion under the man's oddly planed head and touched the beach mattress he was lying on. "He has a beautiful mustache," she said. "Like silver. He looks very old and wise."

"So does an owl. Let's go to bed."

Jack woke early, from a dream in which he had bailed out of a flying motorcycle with an umbrella that turned into a candy cane as he fell. He landed in the middle of some sharp-toothed crags which gave like sponge rubber. He was immediately surrounded by mermaids who looked like Iris and who had hands shaped like spur gears. But nothing frightened him. He awoke smiling, inordinately happy.

Iris was still asleep. Outside somewhere he heard the tinkle of Molly's laugh. He sat up and looked at Molly's camp cot. It was empty. Moving quietly, so as not to disturb his wife, he slid his feet into moccasins and went out.

Molly was on her knees beside their strange visitor, who was squatting on his haunches and—

They were playing patty-cake.

"Molly!"

"Yes, Daddy."

"What are you trying to do? Don't you realize that that man has a broken arm?"

"Oh, gosh, I'm sorry. Do you s'pose I hurt him?"

"I don't know. It's very possible," said Jack Garry testily. He went to the alien, took his good hand.

The man looked up at him and smiled. His smile was peculiarly engaging. All of his teeth were pointed, and they were very widely spaced. "Eeee-yu mow madibu Mewhu," he said.

"That's his name," Molly said excitedly. She leaned forward and tugged at the man's sleeve. "Mewhu. Hey, Mewhu!" And she pointed at her chest.

"Mooly," said Mewhu. "Mooly—Geery."

"See, Daddy?" Molly said ecstatically. "See?" She pointed at her father. "Daddy. Dah—dee."

"Deedy," said Mewhu.

"No, silly. Daddy."

"Dewdy."

"Dah-dy!"

Jack, quite entranced, pointed at himself and said, "Jack."

"Jeek."

"Good enough. Molly, the man can't say 'ah.' He can say 'oo' or 'ee' but not 'ah.' That's good enough."

Jack examined the splints. Iris had done a very competent job. When she realized that instead of the radius-ulna development of a true human, Mewhu had only one bone in his forearm, she had set the arm and laid on two splints instead of one. Jack grinned. Intellectually, Iris would not accept Mewhu's existence even as a possibility; but as a nurse, she not only accepted his body structure but skillfully compensated for its differences.

"I guess he wants to be polite," said Jack to his repentant daughter, "and if you want to play patty-cake he'll go along with you, even if it hurts. Don't take advantage of him, chicken."

"I won't, Daddy."

Jack started up the fire and had a stick crane built and hot water bubbling by the time Iris emerged. "Takes a cataclysm to get you to start breakfast," she grumbled through a pleased smile. "When were you a Boy Scout?"

"Matter of fact," said Garry, "I was once. Will modom now take over?"

"Modom will. How's the patient?"

"Thriving. He and Molly had a patty-cake tournament this morning. His clothes, by the way, are red again."

"Jack, where does he come from?"

"I haven't asked him yet. When I learn to caterwaul, or he learns to talk, perhaps we'll find out. Molly has already elicited the information that his name's Mewhu." Garry grinned. "And he calls me 'Jeek.'"

"Can't pronounce an 'r,' hm?"

"That'll do, woman. Get on with the breakfast."

While Iris busied herself over the fire, Jack went to look at the house. It wasn't as bad as he had thought—a credit to poor construction. Apparently the upper two rooms were a late addition and had just been perched onto the older, comparatively flat-topped lower section. The frame of Molly's bed was bent beyond repair, but the box spring and mattress were intact. The old roof seemed fairly sound, where the removal of the jerrybuilt little top story had exposed it. The living room would be big enough for him and Iris, and Molly's bed could be set up in the study. There were tools and lumber in the garage, the weather was warm and clear, and Jack Garry was very much attracted by the prospect of hard work for which he would not get paid, as long as it wasn't writing. By the time Iris called him for breakfast, he had most of the debris cleared from the roof and a plan of action mapped out. All he would have to do would be to cover the hole where the stairway landing had been and go over the roof for potential leaks. A good rain, he reflected, would search those out for him quickly enough.

"What about Mewhu?" Iris asked as she handed him an aromatic plate of eggs and bacon. "If we feed him any of this, do you think he'll throw another fit?"

Jack looked at their visitor, who sat on the other side of the fire, very close to Molly, gazing big-eyed at their breakfasts.

"I don't know. We could give him a little, I suppose."

Mewhu inhaled his sample and wailed for more. He ate a second helping, and when Iris refused to fry more eggs, he gobbled toast and jam. Each new thing he tasted he would nibble at, then he would blink twice and bolt it down. The only exception was the coffee. One taste was sufficient. He put it down on the ground and very carefully, very delicately overturned it.

"Can you talk to him?" Iris asked suddenly.

"He can talk to me," declared Molly.

"I've heard him," Jack said.

"Oh, no. I don't mean *that*," Molly denied vehemently. "I can't make any sense out of that stuff."

"What do you mean, then?"

"I . . . I dunno, Mommy. He just—talks to me, that's all."

Jack and Iris looked at each other. "Oh," said Iris. Jack shook his head, looking at his daughter carefully, as if he had not really seen her before. He could think of nothing to say, and rose.

"Think the house can be patched up?"

"Oh, sure." He laughed. "You never did like the color of the upstairs rooms, anyway."

"I don't know what's got into me," Iris said thoughtfully "I'd have kicked like a mule at any part of this. I'd have packed up and gone home if, say, just a wall was gone upstairs, or if there were just a hole in the roof, or if this . . . this android phenomenon arrived suddenly. But when it all happens at once—I can take it all."

"Question of perspective. Show me a nagging woman and I'll show you one who hasn't enough to worry about."

"You'll get out of my sight or you'll have this frying pan bounced off your skull," said Iris steadily. Jack got.

Molly and Mewhu trailed after him as he returned to the house— and stood side by side goggling at him as he mounted the ladder.

"Whatsha doing, Daddy?"

"Marking off the edges of this hole where the stairway hits the place where the roof isn't, so I can clean up the edges with a saw."

"Oh."

Jack roughed out the area with a piece of charcoal, lopped off the more manageable rough edges with a hatchet, cast about for his saw. It was still in the garage. He climbed down, got it, climbed up again, and began to saw. Twenty minutes of this, and sweat was streaming down his face. He knocked off, climbed down, doused his head at the pump, lit a cigarette, climbed back up on the roof.

"Why don't you jump off and back?"

The roofing job was looking larger and the day seemed warmer than it had. Jack's enthusiasm was in inverse proportion to these factors. "Don't be funny, Molly."

"Yes, but Mewhu wants to know."

"Oh, he does. Ask him to try it."

He went back to work. A few minutes later, when he paused for a breath, Mewhu and Molly were nowhere to be seen. Probably over by the tent, in Iris' hair, he thought, and went on sawing.

"Daddy!"

Daddy's unaccustomed arm and shoulder were, by this time, yelling for help. The dry softwood alternately cheesed the saw out of line and bound it. He answered impatiently, "Well, what?"

"Mewhu says to come. He wants to show you something."

"Show me what? I haven't time to play now, Molly. I'll attend to Mewhu when we get a roof over our heads again."

"But it's for you."

"What is it?"

"The thing in the tree."

"Oh, all right." Prompted more by laziness than by curiosity, Jack climbed back down the ladder. Molly was waiting. Mewhu was not in sight.

"Where is he?"

"By the tree," she said with exaggerated patience, taking his hand. "Come on. It's not far."

She led him around the house and across the bumpy track that was euphemistically known as a road. There was a tree down on the other side. He looked from it to the house, saw that in line with the felled tree and his damaged roof were more broken trees, where something had come down out of the sky, skimmed the tops of the trees, angling closer to the ground until it wiped the top off his house, and had then risen up and up—to where?

They went deeper into the woods for ten minutes, skirting an occasional branch or fallen treetop, until they came to Mewhu, who was leaning against a young maple. He smiled, pointed up into a tree, pointed to his arm, to the ground. Jack looked at him in puzzlement.

"He fell out of the tree and broke his arm," said Molly.

"How do you know?"

"Well, he just did, Daddy."

"Nice to know. Now can I get back to work?"

"He wants you to get the thing in the tree."

Jack looked upward. Hung on a fork two thirds of the way up the tree was a gleaming object, a stick about five feet long with a streamlined shape on each end, rather like the wingtip tanks of a P-80.

"What on earth is that?"

"I dunno. I can't— He tol' me, but I dunno. Anyway, it's for you, so you don't ... so you don't ... " She looked at Mewhu for a moment. The alien's silver mustache seemed to swell a little. "—so you don't have to climb the ladder so much."

"Molly, how did you know that?"

"He *told* me, that's all. Gosh, Daddy, don't be mad. I don't know how, honest; he just did, that's all."

"I don't get it," muttered Jack. "Anyhow, what's this about that thing in the tree? I'm supposed to break my arm too?"

"It isn't dark."

"What do you mean by that?"

Molly shrugged. "Ask him."

"Oh, I think I catch that. He fell out of the tree because it was dark. He thinks I can get up there and get the whatzit without hurting myself because I can see what I am doing. He also flatters me. Or is it flattery? How close to the apes does he think we are?"

"What are you talking about, Daddy?"

"Never mind. Why am I supposed to get that thing, anyway ?"

"Uh—so's you can jump off the roof."

"That is just silly. However, I do want a look at that thing. Since his ship is gone, that object up there seems to be the only artifact he brought with him except his clothes."

"What's an artifact?"

"Second cousin to an artichoke. Here goes nothin'," and he swung up into the tree. He had not climbed a tree for years, and as he carefully chose his way, it occurred to him that there were probably more efficient ways of gaining altitude.

The tree began to shiver and sway with his weight. He looked down once and decided instantly not to do it again. He looked up and was gratified to see how close he was to the object he was after. He pulled himself up another three feet and was horrified at how far away it was, for the branches were very small up here. He squirmed upward, reached, and his fingers just brushed against the shank of the thing. It had two rings fastened to it, he noticed, each about a foot from the center, large enough to get an arm through. It was one of these which was hung up on a branch. He chinned himself, then, with his unpracticed muscles cracking, took one hand off and reached.

The one-hand chinning didn't come off so well. His arm began to sag. The ring broke off its branch as his weight came on it. He was immediately surrounded by the enthusiastic crackling of breaking shrubbery. He folded his tongue over and got his teeth on it.

309

Since he had a grip on Mewhu's artifact, he held on—even when it came free. He began to fall, tensing himself for the bone-breaking jolt he would get at the bottom.

He didn't get it.

He fell quite fast at first, and then the stick he was holding began to bear him up. He thought it must have caught on a branch, by some miracle—but it hadn't! He was drifting down like a thistle seed, hanging from the rod, which in some impossible fashion was supporting itself in midair. There was a shrill, faint whooshing sound from the two streamlined fixtures at the ends of the rod. He looked down, blinked sweat out of his eyes, and looked again. Mewhu was grinning a broad and happy grin; Molly was slack-jawed with astonishment.

The closer he came to the ground the slower he went. When, after what seemed an eternity, he felt the blessed pressure of earth under his feet, he had to stand and *pull* the rod down. It yielded slowly, like an eddy-current brake. Dry leaves danced and whirled under the end pieces.

"Gee, Daddy, that was wonderful!" He swallowed twice to wet down his dry esophagus, and pulled his eyes back in.

"Yeah. Fun," he said weakly.

Mewhu came and took the rod out of his hand, and dropped it. It stayed perfectly horizontal, and sank slowly down to the ground, where it lay. Mewhu pointed at it, at the tree, and grinned.

"Just like a parachute. Oh, *gee*, Daddy!"

"You keep away from it," said Jack, familiar with youthful intonation. "Heaven knows what it is. It might go off, or something."

He looked fearfully at the object. It lay quietly, the hissing of the end pieces stilled. Mewhu bent suddenly and picked it up, held it over his head with one hand. Then he calmly lifted his feet and hung from it. It lowered him gently, butt first, until he sat on the ground, in a welter of dead leaves; as soon as he picked it up, the streamlined end pieces had begun to blast again.

"That's the silliest thing I ever saw. Here—let me see it." It was floating about waist-high. He leaned over one of the ends. It had a fine round grille over it. He put out a hand. Mewhu reached out and caught his wrist, shaking his head. Apparently it was dangerous to go too near those ends. Garry suddenly saw why. They were tiny, powerful jet motors of some kind. If the jet was powerful enough to support a man's weight, the intake must be drawing like mad— probably enough to snap a hole through a man's hand like a giant ticket-puncher.

But what controlled it? How was the jet strength adjusted to the weight borne by the device, and to the altitude? He remembered without pleasure that when he had fallen with it from the treetop, he had dropped quite fast, and that he went slower and slower as he approached the ground. And yet when Mewhu had held it over his head, it had borne his weight instantly and lowered him very slowly. And besides, how was it so stable? Why didn't it turn upside down and blast itself and passenger down to earth?

He looked at Mewhu with some increase of awe. Obviously he came from a place where the science was really advanced. He wondered if he would ever be able to get any technical information from his visitor—and if he would be able to understand it. Of course, Molly seemed to be able to—

"He wants you to take it back and try it on the roof," said Molly.

"How can that refugee from a Kuttner opus help me?"

Immediately Mewhu took the rod, lifted it, ducked under it, and slipped his arms through the two rings, so that it crossed his back like a water-bucket yoke. Peering around, he turned to face a clearing in the trees, and before their startled eyes he leaped thirty feet in the air, drifted away in a great arc, and came gently to rest twenty yards away.

Molly jumped up and down and clapped her hands, speechless with delight. The only words Garry could find were a reiterated, "Ah, no!"

Mewhu stood where he was, smiling his engaging smile, waiting for them. They walked toward him, and when they were close he leaped again and soared out toward the road.

"What do you do with a thing like this?" breathed Jack. "Who do you go to, and what do you say to him?"

"Le's just keep him for a pet, Daddy."

Jack took her hand, and they followed the bounding, soaring silver man. A pet! A member of some alien race, from some unthinkable civilization—and obviously highly trained, too, for no ordinary individual would be the first to make such a trip. What was his story? Was he an advance guard? Or was he the sole survivor of his people? How far had he come? From Mars? Venus?

They caught up with him at the house. He was standing by the ladder. His strange rod was lying quiet on the ground. He was fascinatedly operating Molly's yo-yo. When he saw them, he threw down the yo-yo, picked up his device, and, slipping it across his shoulders, sprang high in the air and drifted down to the roof. "Eee-yu!" he said, with emphasis, and jumped off backward. So stable was the rod that as he sank through the air his long body swung to and fro.

"Very nice," said Jack. "Also spectacular. And I have to go back to work." He went to the ladder.

Mewhu bounded over to him and caught his arm, whimpering and whistling in his peculiar speech. He took the rod and extended it toward Jack.

"He wants you to use it," said Molly.

"No, thanks," said Jack, a trace of his tree-climbing vertigo returning to him. "I'd just as soon use the ladder." And he put his hand out to it.

Mewhu, hopping with frustration, reached past him and toppled the ladder. It levered over a box as it fell and struck Jack painfully on the shin.

"I guess you better use the flyin' belt, Daddy." Jack looked at Mewhu. The silver man was looking as pleasant as he could with that kind of a face; on the other hand, it might just possibly be wise to humor him a little. Being safely on the ground to begin with, Jack felt that it might not matter if the fantastic thing wouldn't work for him. And if it failed him over the roof—well, the house wasn't *very* tall.

He shrugged his arms through the two rings. Mewhu pointed to the roof, to Jack, made a jumping motion. Jack took a deep breath, aimed carefully, and hoping the gadget wouldn't work, jumped.

He shot up close to the house—too close. The eave caught him a resounding thwack on precisely the spot where the ladder had just hit him. The impact barely checked him. He went sailing up over the roof, hovered for a breathless second, and then began to come down. For a moment he thought his flailing legs would find purchase on the far edge of the roof. He just missed it. All he managed to do was to crack the same shin, in the same place, mightily on the other eave. Trailing clouds of profanity, he landed standing—in Iris' wash basket. Iris, just turning from the clothesline, confronted him.

"Jack! What on earth are you . . . get out of that! You're standing right on my wash with your dirty . . . *oh!*"

"Oh-oh!" said Jack, and stepped backward out of the wash basket. His foot went into Molly's express wagon, which Iris used to carry the heavy basket. To get his balance, he leaped—and immediately rose high in the air. This time his luck was better. He soared completely over the kitchen wing of the house and came to earth near Molly and Mewhu.

"Daddy, you were just like a bird! Me next, huh, Daddy?"

"I'm going to be just like a corpse if your mother's expression means what I think it does. Don't you touch that!" He shucked off the "flyin'-belt" and dived into the house just as Iris rounded the corner. He heard Molly's delighted "He went *that* way" as he plowed through the shambles of the living room and out the front door. As the kitchen door slammed he was rounding the house. He charged up to Mewhu, snatched the gadget from him, slipped it on, and jumped. This time his judgment was faultless. He cleared the house easily although he came very near landing astride the clothesline. When Iris, panting and furious, stormed out of the house, he was busily hanging sheets.

"Just what," said Iris, her voice crackling at the seams, "do you think you're doing?"

"Just giving you a hand with the laundry, m'love," said Jack

"What is that . . . that object on your back?"

"Another evidence of the ubiquity of the devices of science fiction," said Jack blandly. "This is a multilateral, three-dimensional mass adjuster, or pogo-chute. With it I can fly like a gull, evading the cares of the world and the advances of beautiful redheads, at such times as their passions are distasteful to me."

"Sometime in the very near future, you gangling hatrack, I am going to pull the tongue out of your juke box of a head and tie a bowknot in it." Then she laughed.

He heaved a sigh of relief, went and kissed her. "Darling, I am sorry. I was scared silly, dangling from this thing. I didn't see your clothes basket, and if I had I don't know how I'd have steered clear."

"What is it, Jack? How does it work?"

"I dunno. Jets on the ends. They blast hard when there's a lot of weight pushing them toward the earth. They blast harder near the earth than up high. When the weight on them slacks off a bit, they throttle down. What makes them do it, what they use for power—I just wouldn't know. As far as I can see, they suck in air at the top and blow it out through the jets. And, oh yes—they point directly downward no matter which way the rod is turned."

"Where did you get it?"

"Off a tree. It's Mewhu's. Apparently he used it for a parachute. On the way down, a tree branch speared through one of these rings and he slipped out of it and fell and broke his arm."

"What are we going to do with him, Jack?"

"I've been worrying about that myself. We can't sell him to a sideshow." He paused thoughtfully. "There's no doubt that he has a lot that would be of value to humanity. Why, this thing alone would change the face of the earth! Listen—I weigh a hundred and seventy. I *fell* on this thing suddenly, when I lost my grip on a tree, and it bore my weight immediately. Mewhu weighs more than I do, judging from his build. It took his weight when he lifted his feet off the ground while he was holding it over his head. If it can do that, it or a larger version should be able, not only to drive, but to support an aircraft. If for some reason that isn't possible, the power of those little jets certainly could turn a turbine."

"Will it wash clothes?" Iris was glum.

"That's exactly what I mean. Light, portable, and more power than it has any right to have—of course it'll wash clothes. And drive generators, and cars, and ... Iris, what do you do when you have something as big as this?"

"Call a newspaper, I guess."

314

"And have a hundred thousand people peeking and prying all over the place, and Congressional investigations, and what all? Uh-uh!"

"Why not ask Harry Zinsser?"

"Harry? I thought you didn't like him."

"I never said that. It's just that you and he go off in the corner and chatter about mulpitude amputation and debilities of reactance and things like that, and I have to sit, knit—and spit when I want someone's attention. Harry's all right."

"Gosh, honey, you've got it. Harry'll know what to do. I'll go right away!"

"You'll do nothing of the kind. With that hole in the roof? I thought you said you could have it patched up for the night at least. By the time you get back here it'll be dark."

The prospect of sawing out the ragged hole in the roof was suddenly the least appealing thing in the world. But there was logic and an "or else" tone to what she said. He sighed and went off, mumbling something about the greatest single advance in history awaiting the whim of a woman. He forgot that he was wearing Mewhu's armpit altitudinizer. Only his first two paces were on the ground, and Iris hooted with laughter at his clumsy walking on air. When he reached the ground he set his jaw and leaped lightly up to the roof. "Catch me now, you and your piano legs," he taunted cheerfully, ducked the lancelike clothes prop she hurled at him, and went back to work.

As he sawed, he was conscious of a hubbub down below.

"Dah-dee!" "Mr-r-roo ellue—"

He sighed and put down the saw. "What is it?"

"Mewhu wants his flyin' belt!"

Jack looked at the roof, at the lower shed, and decided that his old bones could stand it if he had to get down without a ladder. He took the jet-tipped rod and dropped it. It stayed perfectly horizontal, falling no slower and no faster than it had when he had ridden it down. Mewhu caught it, deftly slipped his splinted arm through it—it was astonishing how careful he was of the arm, and yet how little it inconvenienced him—then the other arm, and sprang up to join Jack on the roof.

"What do you say, fella?"

"Woopen yew weep."

"I know how you feel." He knew the silver man wanted to tell him something, but he couldn't help him out. He grinned and picked up the saw. Mewhu took it out of his hand and tossed it off the roof, being careful to miss Molly, who was dancing back to get a point of vantage.

"What's the big idea?"

"Dellihew hidden," said Mewhu. "Pento deh numinew heh," and he pointed at the flying belt and at the hole in the roof.

"You mean I'd rather fly off in that thing than work? Brother, you got it. But I'm afraid I have to—"

Mewhu circled his arm, pointing all around the hole in the roof, and pointed again to the pogo-chute, indicating one of the jet motors.

"I don't get it," said Jack.

Mewhu apparently understood, and an expression of amazement crossed his mobile face. Kneeling, he placed his good hand around one of the little jet motors, pressed two tiny studs, and the casing popped open. Inside was a compact, sealed, and simple-looking device, the core of the motor itself, apparently. There seemed to be no other fastening. Mewhu lifted it out and handed it to Jack. It was about the size and shape of an electric razor. There was a button on the side. Mewhu pointed at it, pressed the back, and then moved Jack's hand so that the device was pointed away from them both. Jack, expecting anything, from nothing at all to the "blinding bolt of searing, raw energy" so dear to the science-fiction world, pressed the button.

The gadget hissed, and snuggled back into his palm in an easy recoil.

"That's fine," said Jack, "but what do I do with it?" Mewhu pointed at Jack's cut, then at the device.

"Oh," said Jack. He bent close, aimed the thing at the end of the saw cut, and pressed the button. Again the hiss and the slight, steady recoil, and a fine line appeared in the wood. It was a cut, about half as thick as the saw cut, clean and even and, as long as he kept his hand steady, very straight. A fine cloud of pulverized wood rose out of the hole in the roof, carried on a swirl of air.

Jack experimented, holding the jet close to the wood and away from it. He found that it cut finer the closer he got to it. As he drew it away from the wood, the slot got wider and the device cut slower until at about eighteen inches it would not cut at all. Delighted, Jack quickly cut and trimmed the hole. Mewhu watched, grinning. Jack grinned back, knowing how he would feel if he introduced a saw to some primitive who was trying to work wood with a machete.

When he was finished, he handed the jet back to the silver man and slapped his shoulder. "Thanks a million, Mewhu."

"Jeek," said Mewhu, and reached for Jack's neck. One of his thumbs lay on Jack's collarbone, the other on his back, over the scapula. Mewhu squeezed twice, firmly.

"That the way you shake hands back home?" smiled Jack. He thought it likely. Any civilized race was likely to have a manual greeting. The handshake had evolved from a raised palm, indicating that the saluter was unarmed. It was quite possible that this was an extension, in a slightly different direction, of the same sign. It would indeed be an indication of friendliness to have two individuals present their throats to each other.

With three deft motions, Mewhu slipped the tiny jet back into its casing and, holding the rod with one hand, stepped off the roof, letting himself be lowered in that amazing thistledown fashion to the ground. Once there, he tossed the rod back. Jack was startled to see it hurtle upward like any earthly object. He grabbed it and missed. It reached the top of its arc, and as soon as it started down again the jets cut in, and it sank easily to him. He put it on and floated down to join Mewhu.

The silver man followed Jack to the garage, where he kept a few pieces of milled lumber. He selected some one-inch pine boards and dragged them out into the middle of the floor, to measure them and mark them off to the size he wanted to knock together a simple trap door covering for the useless stair well, a process which Mewhu watched with great interest.

Jack took up the flying belt and tried to open the streamlined shell to remove the cutter. It absolutely defied him. He pressed, twisted, wrenched, and pulled. All it did was to hiss gently when he moved it toward the floor.

"Eek, Jeek," said Mewhu. He took the jet from Jack and pressed it. Jack watched closely, then he grinned and took the cutter.

He swiftly cut the lumber up with it, sneering gayly at the rip-saw which hung on the wall. Then he put the whole trap together with a Z-brace, trimmed off the few rough corners, and stood back to admire it. He realized instantly that it was too heavy to carry by himself, let alone lift it to the roof. If Mewhu had two good hands, now— He scratched his head.

"Carry it on the flyin' belt, Daddy."

"Molly! What made you think of that?"

"Mewhu tol' . . . I mean, I sort of—"

"Let's get this straight once and for all. How does Mewhu talk to you?"

"I dunno, Daddy. It's sort of like I remembered something he said, but not the . . . the words he said. I jus' . . . jus' . . . " she faltered, and then said vehemently, "I don't *know*, Daddy. Truly I don't."

"What'd he say this time?"

She looked at Mewhu. Again Jack noticed the peculiar swelling of Mewhu's silver mustache. She said, "Put the door you jus' made on the flyin' belt and lift it. The flyin' belt'll make it fall slow, and you can push it along while . . . it's . . . fallin'."

Jack looked at the door, at the jet device, and got the idea. When he had slipped the jet rod under the door, Mewhu gave him a lift. Up it came; and then Mewhu, steadying it, towed it well outside the garage before it finally sank to the ground. Another lift, another easy tow, and they covered thirty more feet. In this manner they covered the distance to the house, with Molly skipping and laughing behind, pleading for a ride and praising the grinning Mewhu.

At the house, Jack said, "Well, Einstein Junior, how do we get it up on the roof?"

Mewhu picked up Molly's yo-yo and began to operate it deftly. Doing so, he walked around the corner of the house.

"Hey!"

"He don't know, Daddy. You'll have to figger it out."

"You mean he could dream up that slick trick for carrying it out here and now his brains give out?"

"I guess so, Daddy."

Jack Garry looked after the retreating form of the silver man and shook his head. He was already prepared to expect better than human reasoning from Mewhu, even if it was a little different. He couldn't quite phase this with Mewhu's shrugging off a problem in basic logic. Certainly a man with his capabilities would not have reasoned out such an ingenious method of bringing the door out here without realizing that that was only half the problem. He wondered if the solution was so obvious to Mewhu that he couldn't be bothered explaining it.

Shrugging, Jack went back to the garage and got a small block and tackle. He had to put up a big screw hook on the eave, and another on the new trap door; and once he had laboriously hauled the door up until the tackle was two-locked it was a little more than arduous to work it over the edge and drag it into position. Mewhu had apparently quite lost interest. It was two hours later, just as he put the last screw in the tower bolt on the trap door and was calling the job finished, that he heard Mewhu begin to shriek again. He dropped his tools, shrugged into the jet stick, and sailed off the roof.

"Iris! Iris! What's the matter?"

"I don't know, Jack. He's ... "

Jack pounded around to the front of the house. Mewhu was lying on the ground in the midst of some violent, tearing convulsion. He lay on his back, arching it high, digging his heels into the turf, and his head was bent back at an impossible angle, so that his weight was on his heels and his forehead. His good arm pounded the ground though the splinted one lay limp. His lips writhed and he uttered an edgy, gasping series of ululations quite horrible to listen to. He seemed to be able to scream as loudly when inhaling as when exhaling.

Molly stood beside him, watching him hypnotically. She was smiling. Jack knelt beside the writhing form and tried to steady it. "Molly, stop grinning at the poor fellow."

"But—he's happy, Daddy."

"He's what?"

"Can't you see, silly? He feels good, that's all. He's laughing!"

"Iris, what's the matter with him? Do you know?"

"He took some aspirin again, that's all I can tell you."

"He ate four," said Molly. "He loves 'em."

"What can we do, Jack?"

"I don't know, honey," said Jack worriedly. "Better just let him work it out. Any emetic or sedative we give him might be harmful."

The attack slackened and ceased suddenly, and Mewhu went quite limp. Again, with his hand over the man's chest, Jack felt the strange double pulsing.

"Out cold," he said.

Molly said in a strange, quiet voice, "No, Daddy. He's lookin' at dreams."

"Dreams?"

"A place with a or'nge sky," said Molly. He looked up sharply. Her eyes were closed. "Lots of Mewhus. Hunderds an' hunderds—big ones. As big as Mr. Thorndyke." (Thorndyke was an editor whom they knew in the city. He was six feet seven.) "Round houses, an' big airplanes with ... sticks fer wings."

"Molly, you're talking nonsense," her mother said worriedly. Jack shushed her. "Go on, baby."

"A place, a room. It's a ... Mewhu is there and a bunch more. They're in ... in lines. Rows. There's a big one with a yella hat. He keeps them in rows. Here's Mewhu. He's outa the line. He's jumpin' out th' window with a flyin' belt." There was a long silence. Mewhu moaned.

"Well?"

"Nothin', Daddy ... wait! It's ... all ... fuzzy. Now there's a thing, a kinda summarine. Only on the ground, not in the water. The door's open. Mewhu is ... is inside. Knobs, and clocks. Pull on the knobs. Push a— Oh. *Oh!* It hurts!" She put her fists to her temples.

"Molly!"

Molly opened her eyes and said quite calmly, "Oh, I'm all right, Mommy. It was a thing in the dream that hurt, but it didn't hurt me. It was all a bunch of fire an' ... an' a sleepy feeling, only bigger. An' it hurt."

"Jack, he'll harm the child!"

"I doubt it," said Jack.

"So do I," said Iris wonderingly, and then, almost inaudibly, "Now, why did I say that?"

"Mewhu's asleep," said Molly suddenly.

"No more dreams?"

"No more dreams. Gee. That was—funny."

"Come and have some lunch," said Iris. Her voice shook a little. They went into the house. Jack looked down at Mewhu, who was smiling peacefully in his sleep. He thought of putting the strange creature to bed, but the day was warm and the grass was thick and soft where he lay. He shook his head and went into the house.

"Sit down and feed," Iris said.

He looked around. "You've done wonders in here," he said. The litter of lath and plaster was gone, and Iris' triumphant antimacassars blossomed from the upholstery. She curtsied. "Thank you, m'lord."

They sat around the card table and began to do damage to tongue sandwiches. "Jack."

"Mm-m?"

"What was that—telepathy?"

"Think so. Something like that. Oh, wait'll I tell Zinsser! He'll never believe it."

"Are you going down to the airfield this afternoon?"

"You bet. Maybe I'll take Mewhu with me."

"That would be a little rough on the populace, wouldn't it? Mewhu isn't the kind of fellow you can pass off as your cousin Julius."

"Heck, he'd be all right. He could sit in the back seat with Molly while I talked Zinsser into coming out to have a look at him."

"Why not get Zinsser out here?"

"You know that's silly. When we see him in town he's got time off. Out here he's tied to that airport almost every minute."

"Jack, do you think Molly's quite safe with that creature?"

"Of course. Are you worried?"

"I . . . I am, Jack. But not about Mewhu. About me. I'm worried because I think I should worry more, if you see what I mean."

321

Jack leaned over and kissed her. "The good old maternal instinct at work," he chuckled. "Mewhu's new and strange and might be dangerous. At the same time Mewhu's hurt, and he's inoffensive, so something in you wants to mother him, too."

"There you really have something," Iris said thoughtfully. "He's as big and ugly as you are, and unquestionably more intelligent. Yet I don't mother you."

Jack grinned. "You're not kiddin'." He gulped his coffee and stood up. "Eat it up, Molly, and go wash your hands and face. I'm going to have a look at Mewhu."

"You're going into the airport, then?" asked Iris.

"If Mewhu's up to it. There's too much I want to know, too much I haven't the brains to figure out. I don't think I'll get all the answers from Zinsser, by any means; but between us we'll figure out what to do about this thing. Iris, it's *big!*"

Full of wild speculation, he stepped out on the lawn. Mewhu was sitting up, happily contemplating a caterpillar.

"Mewhu."

"Dew?"

"How'd you like to take a ride?"

"Hubilly grees. Jeek?"

"I guess you don't get the idea. C'mon," said Jack, motioning toward the garage. Mewhu very, very carefully set the caterpillar down on a blade of grass and rose to follow; and just then the most unearthly crash issued from the garage. For a frozen moment no one moved, and then Molly's voice set up a hair-raising reiterated screech. Jack was pounding toward the garage before he knew he had moved.

"Molly! What is it?"

At the sound of his voice the child shut up as if she were switch operated.

"Molly!"

"Here I am, Daddy," she said in an extremely small voice. She was standing by the car, her entire being concentrated in her protruding, faintly quivering lower lip. The car was nose-foremost through the back wall of the garage.

"Daddy, I didn't mean to do it; I just wanted to help you get the car out. Are you going to spank me? Please, Daddy, I didn't—"

"*Quiet!*"

She was quiet immediately. "Molly, what on earth possessed you to do a thing like that? You know you're not supposed to touch the starter!"

"I was pretending, Daddy, like it was a summarine that could fly, the way Mewhu did."

Jack threaded his way through this extraordinary shambles of syntax. "Come here," he said sternly. She came, her paces half-size, her feet dragging, her hands behind her where her imagination told her they would do the most good. "I ought to whack you, you know."

"Yeah," she answered tremulously, "I guess you oughta. Not more'n a couple of times, huh, Daddy?"

Jack bit the insides of his cheeks for control, but couldn't make it. He grinned. *You little minx,* he thought. "Tell you what," he said gruffly, looking at the car. The garage was fortunately flimsy, and the few new dents on hood and fenders would blend well with the old ones. "You've got three good whacks coming to you. I'm going to add those on to your next spanking."

"Yes, Daddy," said Molly, her eyes big and chastened. She climbed into the back seat and sat, very straight and small, away back out of sight. Jack cleared away what wreckage he could, and then climbed in, started the old puddle-vaulter, and carefully backed out of the damaged shed.

Mewhu was standing well clear, watching the groaning automobile with startled silver eyes. "Come on in," said Jack, beckoning. Mewhu backed off.

"Mewhu!" cried Molly, putting her head out the rear door. Mewhu said, "Yowk," and came instantly. Molly opened the door and he climbed in, and she shouted with laughter when he crouched down on the floor, and pulled at him until he got up on the seat. Jack drove around the house, stopped, picked up Mewhu's jet rod, blew a kiss through the window to Iris and they were off.

Forty minutes later they wheeled up to the airport after an ecstatic ride during which Molly had kept up a running fire of descriptive commentary on the wonders of a terrestrial countryside. Mewhu had goggled and ogled in a most satisfactory fashion, listening spellbound to the child—sometimes Jack would have sworn that the silver man understood everything she said—and uttering shrieks, exclamatory mewings, and interrogative peeps.

"Now," said Jack, when he had parked at the field boundary, "you two stay in the car for a while. I'm going to speak to Mr. Zinsser and see if he'll come out and meet Mewhu. Molly, do you think you can make Mewhu understand that he's to stay in the car, and out of sight? You see, if other people see him, they'll want to ask a lot of silly questions, and we don't want to embarrass him, do we?"

"No, Daddy. I'll tell him. Mewhu," she said, turning to the silver man. She held his eyes with hers. His mustache swelled, rippled. "You'll be good, won't you, and stay out of sight?"

"Jeek," said Mewhu. "Jeek mereedy."

"He says you're the boss."

Jack laughed, climbing out. "He does, eh?" Did the child really know, or was it mostly a game? "Be good, then. See you soon, Mewhu." Carrying the jet rod, he walked into the building.

Zinsser, as usual, was busy. The field was not large, but it did a great deal of private-plane business, and as traffic manager Zinsser had his hands full. He wrapped one of his pudgy, flexible hands around the phone he was using. "Hi, Garry! What's new out of this world?" he grated cheerfully. "Siddown. With you in a minute." He bumbled cheerfully into the telephone, grinning at Jack as he talked. Jack made himself as comfortable as patience permitted and waited until Zinsser hung up.

"Well, now," said Zinsser, and the phone rang again.

Jack closed his open mouth in annoyance. Zinsser hung up and another bell rang. He picked up a field telephone from its hook on the side of his desk. "Zinsser. Yes—"

"Now that's enough," said Jack to himself. He rose, went to the door, and closed it softly, so that he was alone with the manager. He took the jet rod and, to Zinsser's vast astonishment, stood on his desk, raised the rod high over his head, and stepped off. A hurricane screamed out of the jets. Jack, hanging by his hands from the rod as it lowered him gently through the air, looked over his shoulder. Zinsser's face looked like a red moon in a snow flurry, surrounded as it was by every interoffice memo for the past two weeks.

Anyway, the first thing he did when he could draw a breath was to hang up the phone.

"Thought that would do it," said Jack, grinning.

"You ... you ... what is that thing?"

"It's a dialectical polarizer," said Jack, alighting. "That is, it makes conversations possible with airport managers who won't get off the phone."

Zinsser was out of his chair and around the desk, remarkably light on his feet for a man his size. "Let me see that."

Jack handed it over and began to talk.

"Look, Mewhu! Here comes a plane!" Together they watched the Cub slide in for a landing, and squeaked at the little puffs of dust that were thrown up by the tires and flicked away by the slipstream.

"And there goes another one. It's gonna take off!" The little blue low-wing coupe taxied across the field, braked one wheel, swung in its own length, and roared down toward them, lifting to howl away into the sky far over their heads.

"Eeeeeyow," droned Molly, imitating the sound of the motor as it passed overhead.

"S-s-s-sweeeeee!" hissed Mewhu, exactly duplicating the whine of control surfaces in the prop blast.

Molly clapped her hands and shrieked with delight. Another plane began to circle the field. They watched it avidly.

"Come on out and have a look at him," said Jack.

Zinsser looked at his watch."I can't. All kidding aside, I got to stick by the phone for another half hour at the very least. Will he be all right out there? There's hardly anyone around."

"I think so. Molly's with him, and as I told you, they get along beautifully together. That's one of the things I want to have investigated—that telepathy angle." He laughed suddenly. "That Molly ... know what she did this afternoon?" He told Zinsser about Molly's driving the car through the wrong end of the garage.

"The little hellion," chuckled Zinsser. "They'll all do it, bless 'em. My brother's kid went to work on the front lawn with his mother's vacuum cleaner the other day." He laughed. "To get back to what's-his-name—Mewhu—and this gadget of his. Jack, we've got to hang on to it. Do you realize that he and his clothes and this thing are the only clues we have as to what he is and where he came from?"

"I sure do. But listen, he's very intelligent. I'm sure he'll be able to tell us plenty."

"You can bet he's intelligent," said Zinsser. "He's probably above average on his planet. They wouldn't send just anyone on a trip like that. Jack, what a pity we don't have his ship!"

"Maybe it'll be back. What's your guess as to where he comes from?"

"Mars, maybe."

"Now, you know better than that. We know Mars has an atmosphere, but it's mighty tenuous. An organism the size of Mewhu would have to have enormous lungs to keep him going. No; Mewhu's used to an atmosphere pretty much like ours."

"That would rule Venus out."

"He wears clothes quite comfortably here. His planet must have not only pretty much the same atmosphere, but the same climate. He seems to be able to take most of our foods, though he's revolted by some of them—and aspirin sends him high as a kite. He gets what looks like a laughing drunk when he takes it."

"You don't say. Let's see, it wouldn't be Jupiter, because he isn't built to take a gravity like that. And the outer planets are too cold, and Mercury is too hot." Zinsser leaned back in his chair and absently mopped his bald head. "Jack, this guy doesn't even come from this solar system!"

"Gosh. I guess you're right. Harry, what do you make of this jet gadget?"

"From the way you say it cuts wood . . . can I see that, by the way?" Zinsser asked.

"Sure." Garry went to work on the jet. He found the right studs to press simultaneously. The casing opened smoothly. He lifted out the active core of the device, and, handling it gingerly, sliced a small corner off Zinsser's desk top.

"That is the strangest thing I have ever seen," said Zinsser. "May I see it?"

He took it and turned it over in his hands. "There doesn't seem to be any fuel for it," he said musingly.

"I think it uses air," said Jack.

"But what pushes the air?"

"Air," said Jack. "No, I'm not kidding. I think that in some way it disintegrates part of the air, and uses the energy released to activate a small jet. If you had a shell around this jet, with an intake at one end and a blast tube at the other, it would operate like a high-vacuum pump, dragging more air through."

"Or like an athodyd," said Zinsser. Garry's blood went cold as the manager sighted down into the jet orifice. "For heaven's sake don't push that button."

"I won't. Say—you're right. The tube's concentric. Now, how on earth could a disruption unit be as small and light as that?"

Jack Garry said, "I've been chewing on that all day. I have one answer. Can you take something that sounds really fantastic, so long as it's logical?"

"You know me," grinned Zinsser, waving at a long shelf of back number science-fiction magazines. "Go ahead."

"Well," said Jack carefully. "You know what binding energy is. The stuff that holds the nucleus of an atom together. If I understand my smattering of nuclear theory properly, it seems possible to me that a sphere of binding energy could be produced that would be stable."

"A sphere? With what inside it?"

"Binding energy—or maybe just nothing ... space. Anyhow, if you surround that sphere with another, this one a force-field which is capable of penetrating the inner one, or of allowing matter to penetrate it, it seems to me that anything entering that balance of forces would be disrupted. An explosive pressure would be bottled up inside the inner sphere. Now if you bring your penetrating field in contact with the binding-energy sphere, the pressures inside will come blasting out. Incase the whole rig in a device which controls the amount of matter going in one side of the sphere and the amount of orifice allowed for the escape of energy, and incase that further in an outside shell which will give you a stream of air induced violently through it—like the vacuum pump you mentioned—and you have this," and he rapped on the little jet motor.

"Most ingenious," said Zinsser, wagging his head. "Even if you're wrong, it's an ingenious theory. What you're saying, you know, is that all we have to do to duplicate this device is to discover the nature of binding energy and then find a way to make it stay stably in spherical form. After which we figure out the nature of a field which can penetrate binding energy and allow any matter to do likewise—one way." He spread his hands. "That's all. Just learn to actually use the stuff that the long-hair boys haven't thought of theorizing about yet, and we're all set."

"Shucks," said Garry. "Mewhu will give us all the dope."

"I hope so, Jack. This can revolutionize the entire industrial world."

"You're understating," grinned Jack.

The phone rang. Zinsser looked at his watch again. "There's my call." He sat down, answered the phone, and while he went on at great length to some high-powered character at the other end of the line, about bills of lading and charter service and interstate commerce restrictions, Jack lounged against the cut-off corner of the desk and dreamed. Mewhu—a superior member of a superior race, come to Earth to lead barbaric humanity out of its struggling, wasteful ways. He wondered what Mewhu was like at home among his strange people. Young, but very mature, he decided, and gifted in many ways; the pick of the crop, fit to be ambassador to a new and dynamic civilization like Earth's. And what about the ship? Having dropped Mewhu, had it and its pilot returned to the mysterious corner of the universe from which they had come? Or was it circling about somewhere in space, anxiously awaiting word from the adventurous ambassador?

Zinsser cradled his instrument and stood up with a sigh. "A credit to my will power," he said. "The greatest thing that's ever happened to me, and I stuck by the day's work in spite of it. I feel like a kid on Christmas Eve. Let's go have a look at him."

"*Wheeeeyouwow!*" screamed Mewhu as another rising plane passed over their heads. Molly bounced joyfully up and down on the cushions, for Mewhu was an excellent mimic.

The silver man slipped over the back of the driver's seat in a lithe movement, to see a little better around the corner of a nearby hangar. One of the Cubs had been wheeled into it, and was standing not far away, its prop ticking over.

Molly leaned her elbows on the edge of the seat and stretched her little neck so she could see, too. Mewhu brushed against her head and her hat fell off. He bent to pick it up and bumped his own head on the dashboard, and the glove compartment flew open. His strange pupils narrowed, and the nictitating membranes flickered over his eyes as he reached inside. The next thing Molly knew, he was out of the car and running over the parking area, leaping high in the air, mouthing strange noises, and stopping every few jumps to roll and beat with his good hand on the ground.

Horrified, Molly Garry left the car and ran after him. "Mewhu!" she cried. "Mewhu, come *back!*"

He cavorted toward her, his arms outspread. "W-r-r-row-w!" he shouted, rushing past her. Lowering one arm a little and raising the other like an airplane banking, he ran in a wide arc, leaped the little tarmac retaining wall, and bounded out onto the hangar area.

Molly, panting and sobbing, stopped and stamped her foot. "Mewhu!" she croaked helplessly. "Daddy said—"

Two mechanics standing near the idling Cub looked around at a sound like a civet-cat imitating an Onondaga war whoop. What they saw was a long-legged, silver-gray apparition, with a silver-white mustache and slotted eyes, dressed in a scarlet robe that turned to indigo. Without a sound, moving as one man, they cut and ran. And Mewhu, with one last terrible shriek of joy, leaped to the plane and disappeared inside.

Molly put her hands to her mouth and her eyes bugged. "Oh, Mewhu," she breathed. "Now, you've done it." She heard pounding feet, turned. Her father was racing toward her, with Mr. Zinsser waddling behind. "Molly! Where's Mewhu?"

Wordlessly she pointed at the Cub, and as if it were a signal the little ship throttled up and began to crawl away from the hangar.

"Hey! Wait! Wait!" screamed Jack Garry uselessly, sprinting after the plane. He leaped the wall but misjudged it because of his speed. Hie toe hooked it and he sprawled slitheringly, jarringly on the tarmac. Zinsser and Molly ran to him and helped him up. Jack's nose was bleeding. He whipped out a handkerchief and looked out at the dwindling plane. "Mewhu!"

The little plane waddled across the field, bellowed suddenly with power. The tail came up, and it scooted away from them—crosswind, across the runway. Jack turned to speak to Zinsser and saw the fat man's face absolutely stricken. He followed Zinsser's eyes and there was the other plane, the big six-place cabin job, coming in.

He had never felt so helpless in all his life. Those planes were going to collide. There was nothing anyone could do about it. He watched them, unblinking, almost detachedly. They were hurtling but they seemed to creep; the moment lasted forever. Then, with a twenty-foot altitude, Mewhu cut his gun and dropped a wing. The Cub slowed, leaned into the wind, and *side-slipped* so close under the cabin ship that another coat of paint on either craft would have meant disaster.

Jack didn't know how long he had been holding that breath, but it was agony when he let it out.

"Anyway, he can fly," breathed Zinsser.

"Of course he can fly," snapped Jack. "A prehistoric thing like an airplane would be child's play for him."

"Oh, Daddy, I'm scared."

"I'm not," said Jack hollowly.

"Me, too," said Zinsser with an unconvincing laugh. "The plane's insured."

The Cub arrowed upward. At a hundred feet it went into a skidding turn, harrowing to watch, suddenly winged over, and came shouting down at them. Mewhu buzzed them so close that Zinsser went flat on his face. Jack and Molly simply stood there, wall-eyed. An enormous cloud of dust obscured everything for ninety interminable seconds. When they next saw the plane it was wobbling crazily at a hundred and fifty.

Suddenly Molly screamed piercingly and put her hands over her face.

"Molly! Kiddo, what is it?"

She flung her arms around his neck and sobbed so violently that he knew it was hurting her throat. "Stop it!" he yelled; and then, very gently, he asked, "What's the matter, darling?"

"He's scared. Mewhu's terrible, terrible scared," she said brokenly.

Jack looked up at the plane. It yawed, fell away on one wing.

Zinsser shouted, his voice cracking. "Gun her! Gun her! Throttle up, you idiot!"

Mewhu cut the gun.

Dead stick, the plane winged over and plunged to the ground. The impact was crushing.

Molly said quite calmly, "All Mewhu's pictures have gone out now," and slumped unconscious to the ground.

They got him to the hospital. It was messy, all of it, picking him up, carrying him to the ambulance—

Jack wished fervently that Molly had not seen; but she had sat up and cried as they carried him past. He thought worriedly as he and Zinsser crossed and recrossed in their pacing of the waiting room that he would have his hands full with the child when this thing was all over.

The resident physician came in, wiping his hands. He was a small man with a nose like a walnut meat. "Who brought that plane-crash case in here—you?"

"Both of us," said Zinsser.

"What—who is he?"

"A friend of mine. Is he . . . will he live?"

"How should I know?" snapped the doctor impatiently. "I have never in my experience—" He exhaled through his nostrils. "The man has two circulatory systems. Two *closed* circulatory systems, and a heart for each. All his arterial blood looks veinous—it's purple. How'd he happen to get hurt?"

"He ate half a box of aspirin out of my car," said Jack. "Aspirin makes him drunk. He swiped a plane and piled it up."

"Aspirin makes him—" The doctor looked at each of them in turn. "I won't ask if you're kidding me. Just to see that . . . that thing in there is enough to kid any doctor. How long has that splint been on his arm?"

Zinsser looked at Jack and Jack said, "About eighteen hours."

"Eighteen *hours?*" The doctor shook his head. "It's so well knitted that I'd say eighteen days." Before Jack could say anything he added, "He needs a transfusion."

"But you can't! I mean, his blood—"

"I know. Took a sample to type it. I have two technicians trying to blend chemicals into plasma so we can approximate it. Both of 'em called me a liar. But he's got to have the transfusion. I'll let you know." He strode out of the room.

"There goes one bewildered medico."

"He's O.K." said Zinsser. "I know him well. Can you blame him?"

"For feeling that way? Gosh no. Harry, I don't know what I'll do if Mewhu checks out."

"That fond of him?"

"Oh, it isn't only that. But to come so close to meeting a new culture, and then have it slip from our fingers like this, it's too much."

"That jet—Jack, without Mewhu to explain it, I don't think any scientist will be able to build another. It would be like . . . like giving a Damascus sword-smith some tungsten and asking him to draw it into filaments. There the jet would be, hissing when you shove it toward the ground, sneering at you."

"And that telepathy—what J. B. Rhine wouldn't give to be able to study it!"

"Yeah, and what about his origin?" Zinsser asked excitedly. "He isn't from this system. It means that he used an interstellar drive of some kind, or even that space-time warp the boys write about."

"He's got to live," said Jack. "He's got to, or there ain't no justice. There are too many things we've got to know, Harry! Look—he's here. That must mean that some more of his people will come some day."

"Yeah. Why haven't they come before now?"

"Maybe they have. Charles Fort—"

"Aw, look," said Zinsser, "don't let's get this thing out of hand."

The doctor came back. "I think he'll make it."

"Really?"

"Not really. Nothing real about that character. But from all indications, he'll be O.K. Responded very strongly. What does he eat?"

"Pretty much the same as we do, I think."

"You think. You don't seem to know much about him."

"I don't. He only just got here. No—don't ask me where from," said Jack. "You'll have to ask him."

The doctor scratched his head. "He's out of this world. I can tell you that. Obviously adult, but every fracture but one is a green stick break; kind of thing you see on a three-year old. Transparent membranes over his— What are you laughing at?" he asked suddenly.

Jack had started easily, with a chuckle, but it got out of control. He roared.

Zinsser said, "Jack! Cut it out. This is a hosp—"

Jack shoved his hand away. "I got to," he said helplessly and went off on another peal.

"You've got to what?"

"Laugh," said Jack, gasping. He sobered, he more than sobered. "It has to be funny, Harry. I won't let it be anything else."

"What the devil do you—"

"Look, Harry. We assumed a lot about Mewhu, his culture, his technology, his origin. We'll never know anything about it!"

"Why? You mean he won't tell us?"

"He won't tell us. I'm wrong. He'll tell us plenty. But it won't do any good. Here's what I mean. Because he's our size, because he obviously arrived in a space ship, because he brought a gadget or two that's obviously the product of a highly advanced civilization, we believe that *he* produced the civilization, that he's a superior individual in his own place."

"Well, he must be."

"He must be? Harry, did Molly invent the automobile?"

"No, but—"

333

"But she drove one through the back of the garage."

Light began to dawn on Zinsser's moon face. "You mean—"

"It all fits! Remember when Mewhu figured out how to carry that heavy trap door of mine on the jet stick, and then left the problem half-finished? Remember his fascination with Molly's yo-yo? What about that peculiar rapport he has with Molly? Doesn't that begin to look reasonable? Look at Iris' reaction to him—almost maternal, though she didn't know why."

"The poor little fellow," breathed Zinsser. "I wonder if he thought he was home when he landed?"

"Poor little fellow—sure," said Jack, and began to laugh again. "Can Molly tell you how an internal combustion engine works? Can she explain laminar flow on an airfoil?" He shook his head. "You wait and see. Mewhu will be able to tell us the equivalent of Molly's 'I rode in the car with Daddy and we went sixty miles an hour.'"

"But how did he get here?"

"How did Molly get through the back of my garage?"

The doctor shrugged his shoulders helplessly. "His biological reactions do look like those of a child—and if he is a child, then his rate of tissue restoration will be high, and I'll guarantee he'll live."

Zinsser groaned. "Much good will it do us—and him, poor kid. With a kid's faith in any intelligent adult, he's probably been sure we'd get him home somehow. Well, we haven't got what it takes, and won't have for a long, long time. We don't even know enough to start duplicating that jet of his—and that was just a little kid's toy on his world."

Story Notes

by Paul Williams

The first period in Theodore Sturgeon's writing career began in December 1937 and ended in June 1941 when he and his wife and child moved from New York City to the British West Indies. The first five stories in this volume date from late in that first period. He then did no writing of any sort until April-May 1944, when he wrote the novella "Killdozer!" The rest of the stories included here were written between 1944 and early 1946.

In an interview at the 1972 World Science Fiction Convention in Los Angeles, David Hartwell asked TS why he stopped writing for that long stretch in the West Indies. Sturgeon replied:

Well, the tropics is funny. The sun's going to shine tomorrow the way it's shining today, and you can put it off; and also I was running a hotel and I was extremely busy. I'd been very recently married and had a baby by that time and, uh, I don't know, it just got lost. But anyway, I couldn't write successfully in the tropics. I had one more session of that, in the late 50's, when I went down to the West Indies again, and again the same thing happened. And I will never go down to the West Indies again, or any tropical clime like that, without an assured income of some sort, because really it terrifies—something clicks off as soon as I go down there, and I don't know what it is or whether that indeed is it. But I wouldn't risk it again.

"Blabbermouth": first published in *Amazing Stories*, February 1947. Very likely written before June 1941. Sturgeon's papers contain an untitled 2½ page manuscript, written between August 1940 and June 1941, which is identical to the first thirteen paragraphs of "Blabbermouth" with the exception of a few word changes. Separately his surviving papers contain a half-page unfinished story idea, from the same period or possibly earlier, which starts: *Introduce Blabbermouth by an incident—past tense. Guy is irresistibly led to mischief-making. Consciously (at first reluctantly) imparts false information to total strangers—accosts an aging woman and tells her that her boss is about to replace her with a younger woman, and that her son will also lose his job.* Apart from the "blabbermouth" being male, this fragment demonstrates that the core idea of the story has not yet occurred to Sturgeon, because the information is described as "false." So it was later in the story-creating process that he came up with the notion of a person compelled, under certain circumstances, to blab the truth.

It is possible that story-opening and story idea were not combined and developed until after the War, but much more likely that the story was written by 1941, rejected, and resubmitted when Sturgeon returned to active writing in 1946.

Sturgeon's "in one sentence" summary of "Blabbermouth"'s message, in a 1954 exercise, was: *Any "haunted" individual expression can be circumvented.* Presumably this refers to the curse-turned-into-a-blessing resolution of the story, which is similar in this respect to his earlier fantasy "Derm Fool." It also strikes me that this one-liner could result from confusing "Blabbermouth" with "Ghost of a Chance" (both written around the same time, both included in Sturgeon's 1955 collection *Caviar*). Whether or not this is the case, I am struck by the way the phrase "'haunted' individual expression" points to the ghost story as an allegorical representation of a psychological condition. In fact, in "Ghost of a Chance" one of the characters is a psychologist who is unable to help the "haunted" girl because of his scientific skepticism.

To me the central idea in "Blabbermouth"—not well-developed but still a powerful, original, stimulating insight—is that something synergistic occurs when one person's mood—suspicion—meets another's mood—specifically, guilt. Sturgeon, as a very young (and attractive, charming) husband, presumably drew this insight from personal experience. And what he observes (and it is his treatment of this sort of insight that makes Sturgeon close to unique among fiction writers, sf or otherwise) is that something tangible is created, an energy being which is not matter but nonetheless measurably, experientially real. In this case it's referred to as a poltergeist, and its reality is measured by its impact on one of the characters in the story (who happens also to be the love object, as in "Ghost of a Chance"). In other Sturgeon stories the (psychologically created) energy being evolves to the level of a kind of life form ("The Perfect Host"), or manifests as an emotional field (doubt in "The Pod and the Barrier," guilt in "Rule of Three," fear in "Mr. Costello, Hero") with the measurable physical power to paralyze or otherwise dominate an entire planet or civilization. This is genuine psychological science fiction, containing insights arguably as original and worthwhile as those of Erickson or Jung or Freud. And because of the uneasy status of psychology (shamanism, science, art form?) in the twentieth century, Sturgeon's fiction of this sort mixes science fiction, fantasy, and so-called mainstream or literary fiction in a very unusual way.

Because psychology is not a "hard" science, and also because Sturgeon chooses not to develop his idea in a pseudoscientific psychological framework (something he does do, effectively and appropriately, in his 1956 story "The Other Man"), it's easy to understand editor John Campbell rejecting "Blabbermouth" for *Astounding Science-Fiction*; and it is also not too hard to imagine him concluding, perhaps regretfully, that the fantastic element is not strong enough for the story to fit in his other magazine, *Unknown*. On the other hand, such a story was then and probably is still today too idea-driven to be published as literary or mainstream popular fiction. (In this case it is also not a very strong story outside of its idea. But many first-rate Sturgeon tales fall between the cracks in precisely the same way, notably "And Now the News," in my opinion one of the finest short stories ever written by an American writer.)

For readers from other countries or eras, be it noted that the last lines of "Blabbermouth" were presumably universally recognized by readers at the time as a reference to Walter Winchell.

The blurb above the story in its original pulp magazine publication read: SHE WAS POSSESSED—OR SO SHE SAID—AND A LITTLE IMP WHISPERED TO HER ...THINGS SHE HAD TO REPEAT!

"Medusa": first published in *Astounding Science-Fiction,* February 1942, and certainly written before June 1941. The concept of a spaceship of fools (on a dangerous and vital mission), each of whom has been told there's only one sane man aboard the ship, is a memorable one. Eminent science fiction critic Damon Knight later wrote a groundbreaking essay on Robert A. Heinlein entitled "One Sane Man."

As with so many stories from this period (and very few from later in Sturgeon's career), a related false start can be found in the Sturgeon papers. This untitled, unfinished eight-page manuscript is about a man brought before a panel of distinguished "psychoscientists," one of eight men who has been intentionally rendered insane and who will now crew a space cruiser on a special mission against a mysterious galactic enemy. In other details it's quite a different story: it's told in the third person, the enemy are seemingly friendly galactic traders similar to the Artnans in "Artnan Process," etc.

Sturgeon's 1957 story "The Pod and the Barrier" can be considered an extremely sophisticated rewrite of "Medusa."

TS's introduction to "Medusa" in his 1984 collection *Alien Cargo: This is fun too, but of a whole different order of magnitude. Some fun is, by its nature, trivial. This kind, however, is at base deeply thoughtful, though it masquerades as a comedy. It is, in short—metaphor.*

Magazine blurb (title page): "YOU," SAID THE HEADQUARTERS MEN, "WILL BE THE ONLY SANE MAN IN THE CREW. THE REST ARE MADMEN BUT DON'T KNOW IT, OF COURSE—"

"Ghost of a Chance": first published in *Unknown Worlds,* June 1943, under the title "The Green-Eyed Monster." The title was changed, probably by Sturgeon, when the story was reprinted in a magazine entitled *Suspense* in 1951, and the title change was retained in 1955 when the story appeared in Sturgeon's collection *Caviar.*

See related comments under "Blabbermouth." Sturgeon wrote a number of stories in which the hero falls in love with a beautiful woman at first sight, after a chance encounter, and then must do battle with a mysterious circumstance that makes her unavailable.

Magazine blurb (contents page): SHOOING OFF A JEALOUS

LOVER IS ORDINARILY SOMETHING OF A PROBLEM, BUT
WHEN THE JEALOUS ONE IS A GHOST, AND A GHOST WITH
A NASTY HABIT OF HAUNTING MOST UNPLEASANTLY HIS
MORE SOLID RIVALS—

"The Bones": by Theodore Sturgeon and James H. Beard; first published in *Unknown Worlds,* August 1943. Beard, according to Sam Moskowitz in his book *Seekers of Tomorrow,* was "a crippled old man who had submitted several stories to [John] Campbell which were strongly plotted but inadequately written. Campbell asked Sturgeon if he would take Beard's plots and turn them into stories." How closely Sturgeon followed Beard's original plot-line is not known. "The Bones" was jointly credited to Sturgeon and Beard when it appeared in *Unknown Worlds,* but Beard's credit was omitted when the story was reprinted in Sturgeon's 1960 collection *Beyond.*

I was a great one for crystal [radio] *sets, made them all sorts of ways,* Sturgeon said in a childhood reminiscence written for his therapist in 1965 (and later published as *Argyll*).

Magazine blurb (contents page): THE INTENTION WAS TO MAKE A SUPER-RADIO. IT NEVER GLEANED A MESSAGE FROM THE AIR-WAVES, BUT IT "HEARD"—BONES TALK!

"The Hag Séleen": by Theodore Sturgeon and James H. Beard; first published in *Unknown Worlds,* December 1942. When the story was included in D.R. Bensen's 1964 anthology *The Unknown Five,* Sturgeon was given sole credit. The editor noted that the story had been credited in the magazine to Sturgeon and Beard, but added: "All the same, it's a Sturgeon story—Beard, who collaborated sometimes with Sturgeon on other pieces, supplied the background information for this one, and Sturgeon did the writing." In the 1978 Sturgeon collection *Visions and Venturers,* the story title is followed by the line "(written with James H. Beard)".

In a letter dated March 22, 1941, Beard wrote to Sturgeon:

"In case you elect to do the River Spider story, I think you had better have a copy of the rune used by devotees of the spider when launching their tiny canoes on the river.

"These canoes by the way are often delicately and beautifully made, sometimes carved of cedar or cypress, sometimes made of bark, brightly colored with dyes which are prepared from various plants growing in the swamp.

"The rune follows:

> River Spider, black and strong
> Folks round here have done me wrong.
> Three fat flies I'm sending you
> Human blood, they've all been through.
> First fly, he named Willie Brown,
> River Spider, drag him down!
> Second fly, she is Alice Jones,
> River Spider, crack her bones.
> Third fly, he named Willie Flood,
> River Spider, drink his blood."

Beard in the letter invites Sturgeon to visit him, and in a letter to his mother dated April 6, 1941, Sturgeon mentions that in the next week he and Dorothe have plans to: *drive forty miles to Suffern, N.Y., where lives Captain Beard, my collaborator on a new series for* Unknown.

In the Sturgeon Papers at the Spencer Library at the University of Kansas there is an incomplete manuscript of a longer version of this story, typed by Sturgeon, and an attached letter from TS asking his wife to edit it down from 13,500 words to 6,000 (presumably at Campbell's request), retyping and rewriting as necessary. He asks her to drop the first 9½ pages and suggests a couple of other possible cuts, but leaves the decision-making to her discretion. He also provides instructions on how to mail it to the magazine when she's finished.

The missing manuscript pages (14–19, 29–33, and 40 to end) are probably absent because they weren't rewritten and could be included as is in the final manuscript. If Dorothe did in fact cut and edit the story from the surviving manuscript (we don't know for certain that Sturgeon didn't do the job himself in the end), she did an extraordinary job. Whole paragraphs of exposition have been added, plus connecting sentences here and there, that sound very much like Sturgeon, and indeed the finished work is one of his better-written stories of the period.

As for the circumstances of his asking her to do the edit (without even his final review), he may have been traveling for a few days, though from what I know of his biography it's not easy to imagine where or why. More likely is that he had been awake for days, finishing up writing assignments to get the money to pay for their trip to Jamaica (this writing was done sometime between April 1941 and the end of June, when they left New York), and he was giving her this assignment to carry out while he collapsed into ten hours' sleep. There's no reason Campbell would have been in a rush to have the story; but Sturgeon was always in a rush to collect his payment, and all the more so if this was done just before their departure.

The story was significantly improved by being shortened. The published version is between 7,500 and 8,000 words (evidently 6,000 was not possible).

The narrator says of Séleen, "She looked like a Cartier illustration." Edd Cartier was one of the finest fantasy artists of the era, and did many of the interior illustrations for *Unknown* (which changed its name to *Unknown Worlds* in late '41); ultimately he did illustrate this story.

Patty in the story has the same name as Dorothe and Ted's first child, who was no more than six months old when "The Hag Séleen" was written.

Magazine blurb (contents page): THE DARK, DANK MAGIC OF THE BAYOUS WAS BEYOND THE UNDERSTANDING OF MODERN ADULTS. IT TOOK A CHILD WITH A GIFT FOR RHYMING TO HANDLE THE HAG SÉLEEN.

"**Killdozer!**": First published in *Astounding Science-Fiction*, November 1944. Written early May, 1944. Later adapted for an ABC-TV "Suspense Movie," directed by Jerry London and starring Clint Walker, first aired on February 2, 1974.

The purpose of these story notes is to make readily available to readers useful information about each story's writing and publication, including biographical and other influences that may be reflected in its content, comments the author has made about a story, at the time of writing or since, and the context of the story's writing within the events of the author's life and career. With this in mind, there is much that must be said about "Killdozer!" It draws heavily, of course, from Sturgeon's experience as a bulldozer operator in the tropics in 1942 and 1943. In terms of money and acclaim, it was arguably the most successful story of the first decade of his career. And in Sturgeon's own telling of his life story, it punctuates his longest bout of "writer's block," usually described by him (in interviews, and in the foreword to his 1971 collection *Sturgeon Is Alive and Well...*) as lasting for six years, 1940 to 1946, with "Killdozer!" a solitary interruption in the middle, 1943.

Close examination of documentary evidence, primarily copies of letters to and from Sturgeon during and after this period, allows a more accurate dating. He did continue to write as long as he was still in New York, which he left (in order to manage his uncle's hotel at Treasure Beach on the island of Jamaica) on June 28, 1941. Although he and his wife expected that the hotel job and change of scene would make it easier for him to go on writing fiction, he did not do any writing until April of 1944, on St. Croix in the Virgin Islands, when he wrote a (probably mainstream, i.e. not aimed at the science fiction or fantasy market) short story *propagandizing in favor of the much misunderstood Nisei, or American-born Japs.* (Italicized phrases are quotes from Sturgeon, in this case from a letter writen to his mother on May 8, 1944.) This story immediately went to a new agent, Nannine Joseph, who was unable to sell it; the manuscript does not survive among Sturgeon's papers.

The first week of May, 1944, while still completing "the Nisei story," TS began "Killdozer!", which he wrote in nine days and immediately sent to the science fiction editor who had published him regularly between 1939 and 1943. From a letter to his mother, Christine Hamilton Sturgeon, July 8, 1944: *When we were right at the end of the rope, in comes a check and a letter from Jack Campbell. The check was a godsend, but the letter is something that I'll treasure for the rest of my life. I must have sold him thirty-five or* *forty stories and never have I had such a missive from him. "I don't know how I can place it or when I'll be able to use it, but there, my friend, you have a hunk of story. I'm giving you our highest rate, which brings the check to $542.50. I'm glad you're back in the field, and if you have any more with anything like this level of tenseness, send 'em along. I want 'em."*

In May or June Sturgeon wrote and sent his agent another story, "Operator—Please!", *a slick-style woman's angle number about a USO singer in the South Pacific who was walking on a cleared track by herself deep in the jungle and came on the bulldozer that was doing the work; argued* [with] *the operator because he wouldn't let her ride; jumped on the machine when his back was turned; dropped the blade on him by accident, pinning his legs.* This story also didn't sell and has been lost. Sturgeon's frustration with his agent was the primary reason for his trip back to New York in October 1944; he subsequently found himself unable to sell or to write satisfactorily. He didn't return to his family on St. Croix, or send them money, and in June 1945 Dorothe divorced him.

Although TS did write a few more stories in 1944 and early '45, the breakthrough as he remembered it came with the next story he sold, "The Chromium Helmet," completed at the end of 1945. So what he thought of as his "writer's block" lasted from July '41 to December '45, punctuated by only one story that sold close to the time when it was written: "Killdozer!" in 1944.

How Ted became a 'dozer driver (abbreviated from a conversation between TS and Paul Williams, December 6, 1975): *So while we were in Jamaica, along came December the 7th, and Pearl Harbor, and here we were at the hotel, ninety miles away from Kingston, with gasoline supplies cut off and no chance of getting any guests out there at all. The Americans started building a very large base at Fort Simonds, and we went down there and applied for jobs. I ended up on the Jamaican payroll, handling mess halls and barracks, and a food warehouse. And finally a man came along, clearing up ground around the housing area, and driving a bulldozer. And I fell in love with that machine. So he let me get up on it, and I learned an awful lot. Then I was transferred from quarters and barracks to a gasoline station.*

We serviced all kinds of equipment, and I got to know some of the American operators, and finally I got hired as a bulldozer operator. I was making more money than I'd ever seen in my life. Then when the base began to fold up, a guy came around recruiting for another job, in Puerto Rico at a place called Ensenada Honda, where they were building an enormous shipfitting plant, and a dry dock, and a landing field. And ultimately we moved over to St. Croix and I settled down to write. Sturgeon worked in Puerto Rico as a bulldozer operator from August '42 to December '43, after which he worked for the Navy for a few months as a supply clerk and cost analyst. In April he and Dorothe and their two daughters moved to St. Croix.

The manuscript title of "Killdozer!" was "Daisy Etta." In August 1945, recalling the experience of writing this story as *Worked like hell for nine days, wrote something after two and a half years of being dried up,* Sturgeon described it to his mother as *Complete justification for everything.* In a letter to his father, Edward Waldo, Feb. 27, 1946, he further reported: *The thing wrote itself! It was called KILLDOZER and after it I could write nothing else. It sold on sight for $542.50, and the editor thought so well of it that he cancelled his production schedule and had it in print within weeks, as the lead novel in his magazine, with a cover illustration. (The original oil painting for that cover now hangs in my living room.) The magazine hit the stands just as I arrived back in the States, and apparently caused quite a stir in the science-fiction crowd. Through this I met many people who have become valuable friends—including* [his roommate] *Stanton. Crown Publishing Co. released a new anthology of science-fiction last week.* [*The Best of Science Fiction.*] *A month ago, an advance copy was read by a science editor out in California who, on seeing KILLDOZER leading its section in the book, wrote me and asked me if I would take on this series of juveniles.* [A "novel series" called *Bob Haley of the Atomic Police,* that employed Sturgeon as a "for hire" writer in spring 1946.] *And Crown has just sent me a check for $155 for the reprint rights! In other words, what seemed like a mere temporary alleviation of my circumstances down in St. Croix and nothing more, has proved to be the focal point of a whole series of fine breaks.* And in two more letters to his mother: March 25, 1946: *The original oil painting from the cover...is my proudest possession. Through that yarn I got in really solid with John Campbell, editor of* Astounding *and now an increasingly important man.* April 25, 1946: *By the way, got a call from a screen agent who has high hopes for KILLDOZER in Hollywood. Good ol' KILLDOZER!*

So the story also brought Sturgeon the first of what was to be a lifelong series of tantalizing (and, usually, disappointing) flirtations with the money and glory of Hollywood, in regard to his stories and novels and original scripts. In July 1970 (after Sturgeon had already seen two of his scripts become well-known Star Trek episodes) he wrote to Tom Snell at Columbia Studios, apparently a producer who'd expressed interest to a director who told Sturgeon he wanted to film this story: *I have been called a "visual" writer; KILLDOZER is far and away the most cinematographic piece of prose I have ever done. It has been optioned before, over the years. The last time was CBS' Cinema 100. Just before first-draft screenplay it became a victim of Sen. Pastore's famous speech on violence in TV. The people out here were all for going ahead, but back east CBS got cold feet and killed every one of their works-in-progress that might possibly be called violent. I honestly do not think that the kind of violence which occurs in KILLDOZER is the sort of thing the good Senator had in mind. KILLDOZER is a fable about man vs the machine, and it ends in a fine climax of victory for man. But you can't argue with cold feet—not in television-land, anyway.*

Later in this letter Sturgeon said, *We've even got a class-A heavy equipment operator who knows construction machinery as well as he does a script—especially this script. Namely, me.* And then he provided a compact treatment: *KILLDOZER is the story of eight men alone on an island with a million dollars' worth of heavy earth-moving equipment and the assignment of carving an airstrip in ten days' time. One of the machines—an 18-ton Caterpillar D-7—gets a life of its own, vast intelligence, and the obsessive desire to kill men. It gets five of them; the survivors "kill" it.*

The 1974 TV movie that did get made was commemorated in the April 1974 issue of a Marvel Comics comic book called *Worlds*

Unknown presents the Thing Called KILLDOZER. ("based on the spine-tingling shocker by Theodore Sturgeon, author of 'It!' ") The story and film have since given their name to at least one rock and roll group.

In 1972 actor Anthony Quinn called TS to ask if screen rights to "Killdozer!" were available—but he had just sold it to Universal Television. On 4/4/78 Sturgeon wrote to Quinn, saying, *They finally rejected my first draft* [screenplay] *and produced one of the worst "Movies of the Week" I have ever seen.*

Editor's blurb from the original magazine publication: STURGEON'S BEEN MISSING FOR A LONG TIME NOW; HE'S BEEN DOING HEAVY CONSTRUCTION WORK. THIS YARN HE GOT OUT OF THAT EXPERIENCE; IT WILL, CERTAINLY, BE LONG REMEMBERED.

In 1959 "Killdozer!" was first included in a book of Sturgeon stories, a paperback, *Aliens 4*. At first the publisher was going to call the book *Killdozer* but they changed their mind, and Sturgeon expressed his chagrin to his agent at the time, Sterling Lord, in a letter dated 2/25/59: *Not too bad a title, but it irritates me on two counts. They say the title must categorize the book; now, that's just stupid. There are more impulse-buyers who can't stand s-f than those who look for it. They say KILLDOZER sounds like a detective novel. Well, dandy. What's wrong with that? In addition, the only similarity between my stuff and what is usually called s-f is that my stuff has appeared mostly in s-f magazines—not a subtle distinction at all when you think about it. If it's the real s-f cognoscenti they're after, the much-lauded KILLDOZER will pull 'em in better than any new title.* (Sturgeon had tried unsuccessfully in 1947 to get Simon & Schuster to publish "Killdozer!" as "a separate novel.")

Sept. 23, 1958, Sturgeon wrote his agent: *I would like to correct galleys on the collection called KILLDOZER. One reason . . .has to do with the title story, which has been talked about for films ever since it was written. It is a World War II story and needn't be; a very little invisible mending will take care of that. It also needs a touch here and there in characterization and dialogue—for example, Street & Smith's editing "damn" into "care" every time they saw it, so that your bulldozer operators keep saying "I don't give a care ..." and one or two other small repairs.*

So Sturgeon did rewrite the last eight paragraphs. In cases like this, this series chooses to assume that the last revision the author chose to make for publication is the proper text for his Collected Stories. So our text has been set from the book that reflects Sturgeon's 1959 corrections and revisions. For the readers' interest, we do include in these notes the text of the original ending, as published in *Astounding* in 1944 and *The Best of Science Fiction* in 1946.

Text of the original ending of "Killdozer!":

This is the story of Daisy Etta, *the bulldozer that went mad and had a life of its own, and not the story of the flat-top* Marokuru *of the Imperial Japanese Navy, which has been told elsewhere. But there is a connection. You will remember how the* Marokuru *was cut off from its base by the concentrated attack on Truk, how it slipped far to the south and east and was sunk nearer to our shores than any other Jap warship in the whole course of the war. And you will remember how a squadron of five planes, having been separated by three vertical miles of water from their flight deck, turned east with their bomb-loads and droned away for a suicide mission. You read that they bombed a minor airfield in the outside of Panama's far-flung defenses, and all hands crashed in the best sacrificial fashion.*

Well, that was no airfield, no matter what it might have looked like from the air. It was simply a roughly graded runway, white marl against brown scrub-grass.

The planes came two days after the death of Daisy Etta, *as Tom and Kelly sat in the shadow of the pile of fuel drums, down in the coolth of the swag that* Daisy *had dug there to fuel herself. They were poring over paper and pencil, trying to complete the impossible task of making a written statement of what had happened on the island, and why they and their company had failed to complete their contract. They had found Chub and Harris, and had buried them next to the other three. Al Knowles was tied up in the camp, because they had heard him raving in his sleep, and it seemed he could not believe that* Daisy *was dead and he still wanted to go around killing operators for her. They knew that there must be an investigation, and they knew just how far their story would go; and having escaped a monster like* Daisy Etta, *life was far too sweet for them to want to be shot for sabotage. And murder.*

The first stick of bombs struck three hundred yards behind them at the edge of the camp, and at the same instant a plane whistled low over their heads, and that was the first they knew about it. They ran to Al Knowles and untied his feet and the three of them headed for the bush. They found refuge, strangely enough, inside the mound where Daisy Etta *had first met her possessor.*

"Bless their black little hearts," said Kelly as he and Tom stood on the bluff and looked at the flaming wreckage of a camp and five medium bombers below them. And he took the statement they had been sweating out and tore it across.

"But what about him?" said Tom, pointing at Al Knowles, who was sitting on the ground, playing with his fingers. "He'll still spill the whole thing, no matter if we do try to blame it all on the bombing."

"What's the matter with that?" said Kelly.

Tom thought a minute, then grinned. "Why, nothing! That's just the sort of thing they'll expect from him!"

"Abreaction": first published in *Weird Tales*, July 1948. Written between July and October 1944. In a letter to TS dated Dec. 19, 1944, his friend Art Kohn said, "What cooks on the literary front? By now maybe comes words of acceptance from *Colliers* of one or two stories—but howzabout the ones you had already prepared— to wit 'Poor Yorick,' 'Crossfire,' 'Abreaction' et all. Surely must be a market for 'em somewheres. Also and to wit the Campbell inspired yarn anent polarized fields of rotators or some such." In context, this seems to refer to stories Sturgeon told Kohn he had written (or showed him) before he left St. Croix.

Sturgeon was a gymnast in high school and may well have fallen off the parallel bars.

Magazine blurb: HE WANTED TO GO BACK TO A PLACE HE'D SURELY NEVER VISITED!

"Poor Yorick": unpublished. A handwritten note on the manuscript says "submitted—NJ [agent's initials] 8–2–44." Manuscript is untitled, probably a rough draft, but surely is the "Poor Yorick" referred to in Kohn's 12/44 letter. Some pages of "synopses," ideas for stories he might try to write, survive from this era (dated by a reference to "NJ" in one of the notes). One of the 32 entries reads as follows:

Wicked little short short—and I dare you sell it. Girl gets present from boy-friend in the South Pacific of Japanese skull. Is a little queasy but proud. Some character—friend of the family, Lionel Barrymore type, gives deep pronouncements on the basic fellowship of man and so forth, and rather deplores the gift. Family dentist drops around, takes one look at it, and then what you will. It's the manhandled skull of her own brother, picked up already sunbleached and to an expert not recognizable as caucasian.

"Crossfire": unpublished. Another single-spaced rough draft, probably written in summer '44. No title on ms., but quite possibly the "Crossfire" Kohn refers to.

"Noon Gun": first published in *Playboy*, September 1963. The existence of a manuscript with Sturgeon's St. Croix address on the top sheet alongside the name of the agent he got in late '44 to replace Nannine Joseph, dates it as having been written in the second half of 1944 or the early months of 1945. Never included in a Sturgeon book until now, this was scheduled for a collection called *Slow Sculpture* that was cancelled by the publisher sometime after TS wrote an introduction and rubrics for it in 1980. The "Noon Gun" rubric:

I've been very fortunate; what I write, I sell. There have been just two stories I couldn't even give away for years: "Bianca's Hands," which ultimately won a prestigious literary award in England and the first check I had ever seen for over a thousand dollars, and this one, written in 1946 and sold in 1962 to Playboy *for $100 per typed page. It's a highly autobiographical tale.*

On Feb. 9, 1947 Sturgeon wrote to his mother about his new association with still another agent, Scott Meredith: *In my files was one 5000 worder called NOON GUN, written during that desperate period in early '45 when I was starving in New York and my family likewise in St. Croix. Scott was mightily pleased with it. I had given it to my current agent, a sweet old has-been called Ed Bodin, and he had mismarketed it dreadfully. Since its one or two submissions it had lain in the files. (Two others he had had, I sold instantly when I picked up my stuff from him last spring.) So I rewrote NOON GUN, making only slight changes in the dialogue which referred to the war (the magazines don't know there was a war any more!) and gave it to him. It's been out for quite a few weeks, and Scott says that's good.*

Wouldn't it be ironic if that story, of all stories, should be my first slick sale! If it had sold when written, I wouldn't have been stuck in New York. I'd have been home (St. Croix) for Christmas with my pockets bulging and my faith in myself (which later took such a dreadful fall) intact and blooming!

Magazine blurb: AS THEY WALKED, HE TRIED TO ENVISION THE BIG GUY GROVELING—BUT ALL HE COULD SEE WAS THAT KID WAITING FOR THE CANNON TO FIRE.

"Bulldozer Is a Noun": unpublished. Again, the St. Croix address on the manuscript shows it was written before June 1945, perhaps in spring '45 when Sturgeon briefly held the first office job of his life. On August 3, 1945, TS wrote his mother: *Finally in March met some people in the Biltmore Bar and found myself Copy Director of Advertising Division of a big electronics firm. $85. [ellipses his] ... something happened. I didn't send any money south. I didn't know why. Fifty bucks just then would have saved the whole situation. I went psychotic over food. I couldn't get enough to eat. I ate five, six meals a day; cost me $30, $40 a week to eat. I put money into insurance, things like that.*

No title on surviving manuscript; this title assigned by PW.

"August Sixth 1945": unpublished. Probably written soon after. The authorial address in the upper right corner of the first page suggests TS did consider this something to be submitted for possible publication; whether and where it was submitted is not known.

"The Chromium Helmet": first published in *Astounding Science-Fiction*, June 1946. Written at the end of 1945. Sam Moskowitz in *Seekers of Tomorrow* reports what TS told him in a 1961 interview: "Sturgeon returned to New York . . . He was in a daze for months. John Campbell befriended him, inviting him as a house guest for periods as prolonged as two weeks at a stretch. Gradually, Campbell coaxed him out of his depression, until one day, in the basement of the editor's home, Sturgeon sat down at a typewriter and wrote 'The Chromium Helmet.' Campbell read the first draft straight from the typewriter and accepted the story." In 1972 TS told David Hartwell, *I was really in a zombieish condition. Gradually I began to write again, and finally I wrote a story called "The Chromium Helmet" in John's cellar out in Westfield, New Jersey. And that was really the first of these so-called "therapeutic" or optimum humanity stories. And they just went on from there.* However, an undated (probably mid-'46) fragment of a letter from TS to a friend found in Sturgeon's papers complicates things by saying, *. . .began to write again, and sold "The Chromium Helmet," four thousand words of which had been done for a year or more. That broke the ice, and I began to pull out of it.* Could this possibly be "the Campbell inspired yarn anent polarized fields of rotators" Art Kohn mentioned in his 12/44 letter (see "Crossfire" note)? Regardless of when Sturgeon began it, finishing and *selling* the story in Campbell's cellar was certainly an event, a breakthrough, TS long remembered and recounted.

Your editor, who's done much of the research for these notes in Sturgeon's daughter's cellar, wishes to report that he now considers "The Chromium Helmet" a major and surprising and visionary story, even though other readers including the estimable Mr. Silverberg, and myself two decades ago when I first read it, have failed to appreciate it. Sturgeon almost alone among modern writers seems to have some insight into the psychological and cultural significance of the technological advances being made in the realm of "wish fulfillment" in the Media Age. I missed this story's allegorical power until now, even though TS told me in 1975: *"The Chromium Helmet," according to that man I told you about* [a renegade therapist who treated Sturgeon with LSD in 1965 at the therapist's country home over a period of weeks, just like a character in a Pynchon novel] *is the first of my "therapy" stories—it's not too exceptionable as a story, but it does have that component, as does everything else that I've ever written since then. And from then on, I started turning out a tremendous amount of stuff, and finally busted it wide open.*

He was able to point out to me that the nature of my work changed so drastically between 1940 and 1946, that they were not wasted years, that clearly something was going on all the time. There was an evolution towards something infinitely more important and infinitely more serious than anything I'd ever done before. And that there was no break, there were no "wasted years." This was a tremendous comfort to me, it is to this day as a matter of fact. And now, when I go through long periods, which I do, when I'm not writing anything, I don't panic.

Hartwell ('72): "You've said that love is the principal theme of practically everything you've ever written. Have you ever written anything that it wasn't?" Sturgeon: *No, except that my preoccupation in a larger sense is the optimum man. The question of establishing an internal ecology, where the optimum liver works with the optimum spleen and the optimum eyeball and so forth. Now, when you get to the mind—not the brain, but the optimum mind—then you have the whole inner space idea; my conviction is that there's more room there than there is in outer space, in each individual human being. Love of course has a great deal to do with that, as a necessary coloration and adjunct to everything that we do—to love oneself, to love the parts of oneself, to love the interaction of the parts of oneself, and then the interaction of that whole organism with those of another person. Which is as good a definition of love as you can get, I think.*

And to PW in 1975: *It wasn't until comparatively recently, before I discovered that there is a common denominator in all my stories, and that is, the search for the optimum human being. This was pointed out to me by a therapist many years ago, when I was bemoaning the fact of a time when I would let six years go by without writing anything. He said that the stories I'd written before that hiatus were good enough in their way, and brilliant in some ways, but they were entertainments. And the ones I wrote* after *that six year period were all—well, we all take our own specialty, you know, and graft it onto what we're talking about—but he said they're all* therapy *stories. In the sense that they are almost always about somebody who is no good who gets good, somebody who is good who gets better, somebody who is sick and gets well, somebody who gets well and turns into a super-person, and so on. "The Other Man," "Maturity" and all these different stories are very much obsessed with the search for the optimum human being. Not the superman* ... PW: "We're talking here about human potential." TS: *That's right. And everything that I've ever done since then has been—well, the one that I won all those awards for, "Slow Sculpture," is purely and simply a description of that search. Not only for the optimum human being but for* human acceptance *of the optimum human being.*

Magazine blurb: THIS ISN'T THE BEST OF ALL POSSIBLE WORLDS—BUT IT WAS NO HELP TO FIVE REASONABLY COMFORTABLE PEOPLE TO ENCOUNTER THE STRANGE EFFECTS OF THE 'CORMIUM HEMLET.'

"Memorial": first published in *Astounding Science-Fiction,* April 1946. Written January '46?

Sturgeon's story introduction from *Without Sorcery* (1948):

It could happen. it really could.
It might happen. It really might.
It can be stopped. It's up to you.

On the Science Fiction Radio Show in 1983, Sturgeon made a comment on "Thunder and Roses" (written or finished 1947) that seems more applicable to "Memorial": *It's probably the first "atomic doom" story that was written after the bomb was dropped. It was written in late 1945 and was looked at with considerable passion. There wasn't anybody in the world who understood what had happened, except the people in the science fiction fraternity and one or two rather forward-thinking scientists at Oak Ridge and in the state of Washington. The rest of the world thought it was just another big bang. In science fiction, John Campbell had been publishing atomic power and atomic war stories for fifteen years before that. We all understood what had happened; every single person who had been writing or reading science fiction understood precisely what had happened and what it meant to the world. Now, of course, it is very much in the forefront. But we all saw it coming, a very bad and ugly situation.*

"Memorial" was translated into the proposed "world language" Esperanto by Forrest J. Ackerman, and published in *Heraldo de Esperanto*, a newspaper published in the Netherlands, May 25, 1946. Magazine blurb (from *Astounding*): HIS PLAN WAS TO CREATE A CRATER THAT WOULD WARN ALL MEN TO AVOID ATOMIC WAR FOR FIVE THOUSAND YEARS TO COME, A MEMORIAL THAT WOULD SPIT LAVA AND DEADLY RAYS FOR FIVE MILLENIA. PART OF HIS PLAN WAS FULFILLED— THE WRONG PART.

"Mewhu's Jet": first published in *Astounding Science-Fiction*, November 1946 (cover story). Written early 1946.

Although I don't know of Sturgeon ever commenting on the subject, it's hard not to think that "Mewhu's Jet" was a significant forerunner of and inspiration for Steven Spielberg's 1982 film *E.T.*

TS to his mother, July 4, 1947: *Now, about kids in general. You, and quite a few other people, keep spotting my kids in my stories. Not so. I can't explain it at all. One of the big reasons for kids appearing at all is that when a story dies in my arms, I can invariably inject a kid and make it go again. I not only don't know why this is, I don't know how I do it; for never in my life have I been associated with the seven-to-ten-year-old girl children who pop up in my copy. I have been told repeatedly that they are real in action and in dialogue, but so help me, I don't know where they come from. I should mention one other phenomenon: when I use a kid in a story this way, for this reason, the little devil invariably takes the bit in her teeth and walks off with the plot, turning out to be the kind of character who would under no circumstances act the way I have laid the narrative course. So, after writing six or eight thousand words, which I'll be damned if I'll do again, I have to figure out some way to rationalize the plot with the characterization. It comes to me eventually, and accounts for the readability of much of my stuff—the reader can't possibly know how it's going to turn out because the author didn't . . .*

Magazine blurb: MEWHU CAME FROM—SOMEWHERE. HE WRECKED HIS SPACESHIP ON LANDING, BUT THE 'PARA-CHUTE' HE HAD WAS SOMETHING DECIDEDLY SUPER—AN ATOMIC JET JOB! THE PROBLEM WAS TO GET INTO COM-MUNICATION—THEY THOUGHT.

I found six pages stapled together among Sturgeon's papers left in Woodstock, numbered 46 to 51 that give every appearance of being the last pages of a 51–page manuscript. It seems reasonable to assume that they are the original manuscript ending of "Mewhu's Jet" that was cut by the author because he ran out of inspiration (the bottom two-thirds of the last page is blank, and does not say "end"), or by the editor to strengthen the story.

Text of the unpublished original ending of "Mewhu's Jet":

The following three weeks were the fullest, the most exciting, and the most infuriating of Jack Garry's life. Jack was a family man, and in his own argumentative, bull-headed way he loved his wife. Mewhu's arrival had completely turned over and shaken up his way of life—even his thinking. He had enough to do to adjust himself to this fantastic series of events, and to worry about Molly and her new strangeness, and to worry even more about Iris. Iris was outraged at the change in Molly, and at the same time was deeply troubled about Mewhu. Iris wanted, with everything in her vitriolic nature, to blame someone, but her native intelligence made it impossible for her to hang the culpability on anyone, except for brief periods.

Yes indeed, it was enough to drive any man frantic; but Jack Garry was not permitted to stay home and let things there get him frantic. He was suddenly a public figure. "Do you realize," strange voices would say to him over the telephone in his city apartment, "that Zincus' No-Phlegm Trokeys are the only product which contains every palliative and preventive against the common cold?"

And Jack would roll his eyes up and say, "No, I hadn't realized. So what?"

And the voice would say, "Since you have gone on the record as wanting to protect the Man from Mars in every possible way, you cannot afford to overlook this remarkable—"

And Jack would say, "Exactly what do you want?"

And the voice would say, "Would you consider five thousand dollars to sign a small testimonial?" and Jack would bang down the receiver; and the phone would ring again . . .

There were people outside. There were always people outside, hanging around in the lobby of the apartment house when they could get in, lounging outside. Autographs. Sometimes pickets carrying signs denouncing him for bringing new terror to the world. Once somebody shot at him. Most of the loungers just gawked.

And the mail! Checks and dollar bills. Threats. Appeals for money, made apparently for no other reason than that Jack had had his name in the papers. "Dear Mr. Garry, at last I know that there is a man alive with enough foresight, enough breadth of vision, to understand me and my work, for only such a man would have been chosen to receive a distinguished visitor from another world. I have a theory for the development of a space-warp generator, and if you can get backing to the extent of fifty thousand dollars, we can collaborate on the beginnings of this amazing—" "Dear Sir you are a crimnell and a thief you shud of kild that monster insted of takin him into your midst. aint we got trubl enough." "Dear Mr. Garry, Let us face it. Small considerations, magnified by the conventions, are not important to people like you and me. It is our duty to found a super-race together. My background of deep study into esoteric matters has convinced me that the only thing that can save the race is to people the world with the superior strain evident in both of us. I enclose a nude photograph of myself and will appreciate it if you will do likewise. I am thirty three years old and have kept myself sacrosanct awaiting this great moment." "Dear sir: My most sincere congratulations to you and your co-workers on your execution of the most magnificent hoax since the Cardiff Giant. It is evident from the extent of the publicity you are receiving that you have the backing of the Jews and the international bankers. I hereby serve notice on you that you are being carefully watched by the Blood-

Brotherhood of the Sons of Caesar. You will not get away with it."

And yet Jack Garry stayed by the telephone, leafed through all the mail, went out constantly to get any possible reports of Mewhu. For Mewhu was alive.

It was incredible. A human being could not possibly have survived that crash. If Mewhu had not cut the ignition, he would not have lived either. The list of his injuries was frightening, and, due to his alien structure, it was impossible to determine their true extent. As for treatment, that had to be a guess-and-prayer operation. He lost a good deal of his purplish blood before they dared to give him a transfusion. Two Red Cross surgeons and an Army man had a violent altercation over the first-aid substitutions in plasma which they had concocted to approximate the first rough analysis of Mewhu's blood. They chanced it, finally, because they had to. Jack Garry, in one of the few moments he had to reflect about anything, was amused by the attitude of the medical mind. Like Iris, when she had used her nurse's training to set Mewhu's broken arm while refusing to admit Mewhu's existence, these doctors had done everything in their power to save Mewhu's life without daring to cogitate on what he really was.

But after he was whisked away to a Naval hospital, under careful guard, the controversies started. Mewhu was accused of being a Russian, a Japanese, a Turk, an Atlantean, and the Devil. He was credited with being homo superior, a secret weapon, and the Messiah. The one thing that infuriated Garry the most was that the newspapers called him "the Man from Mars," the public insisted that he was from Mars, newspapers whose editorial policy included headlines in red published diagrams of the orbit of Mars and monosyllable rewrites of weighty words on the subject of Mars originally composed years ago by theoreticians specializing in Mars. The careful series of tests of Mewhu's blood, bones, nerves and organs which was conducted for the purpose of saving his life, was violently attacked in the press by the anti-vivisection bloc, who took the position that the Man from Mars should be permitted to die in the established Martian fashion. Garry reached a point where he would have given anything in the world to feel free to run down the street shouting "He's not *from Mars!*" But he had family considerations ...

When they had first returned to the city, Iris had stood over Molly like a tigress, refusing to let the child be questioned by anyone, including Jack.

"But honey," he pleaded, "Molly may know things that can change the face of the Earth! She's been subject to a degree of telepathy unheard of before. She's had the chance to see, through Mewhu's eyes, a totally new civilization, infinitely farther advanced than ours. She has the only key to it, and you won't let us get to it."

"As long as she cries when she's questioned— no! Let Mewhu do his own press-agentry."

"He can't even talk yet—not even in his own language. You wouldn't either, with a busted jaw. He might even die before we can get anything out of him."

"Molly's going to have trouble enough getting over this," said Iris firmly. "Better drop the subject, Jack."

Mild words, but the set of her red head and the tied-in look of her mouth told him that she was right—it would be better to drop it.

When he could, he dropped in to see the child. She had a three-quarter size bed, and she looked very tiny in it. Iris would stand just inside the room, leaning easily against the door, her arms folded, deftly keeping the conversation where she thought it should be kept.

"How do you feel, chicken?"

Her face was almost as white as the sheet, and her eyes were as dark as her hair against it. Her freckles were startling.

"Okay, daddy."

"What you been doing?"

"Helpin' Mewhu get better."

"Tell daddy about the book I got you today, Molly," said Iris too quickly, too loud.

And Molly would smile and say that the book was fine.

The doctors couldn't find anything wrong with her. She simply didn't have all of her vitality. She didn't lack a dangerous amount of it, and it didn't vary. She didn't move much when they first came back to the city; she didn't try. She was apparently very contented. Only she seemed to know something. It was there in her face all the time, but particularly when she smiled.

And as the weeks passed she got better—slowly, evenly, without relapses. It was not a cyclic thing at all. She ate well, and she slept well; and, devastatingly, she always did exactly as she was told.

It was midwinter when Mewhu walked again. Jack had not been permitted to see him in all that time, not only because the silver man had been such a nine-days wonder that armed guards had had to surround the hospital, but because Congress had appointed a committee to study Mewhu—a committee which, by the way, included no psychologists, no physicians, no sociologists, anthropologists, physicists or astronomers. The Army and the Navy were represented, however. After a due period of polysyllabic ponderment, the committee tabled the matter until such time as the alien was in a position to speak for himself. He was to be taught the language if possible and otherwise kept incommunicado.

Afterword

by Robert A. Heinlein

(Excerpted from "Agape and Eros: The Art of Theodore Sturgeon," first published as an introduction to Sturgeon's last novel, Godbody)

Again and again for half a century Theodore Sturgeon has given us one message—a message that was ancient before he was born but which he made his own, then spoke it and sang it and shouted it and sometimes scolded us with it:

"Love one another."

Simple. Ancient. Difficult.

Seldom attained.

Early this century, before World War I, I was taught in Sunday school that Jesus loves us, you and me and everyone, saint and sinner alike. Then the Kaiser raped poor innocent Belgium, and never again did the world seem sweet and warm and safe. Today I cannot promise you that Jesus loves you, but I can assure you that Ted Sturgeon loves you ... did love you and does today—"does," present tense, because what I still hold of my childhood faith includes a conviction that Ted did not cease to be when his worn-out body stopped breathing. It may be that villains die utterly. But not saints.

In fifty years of storytelling Sturgeon spoke to us of love, again and again and yet again, without ever repeating himself. One of the marks of his art was his unique talent for looking at an old situation from a new angle, one that no one else had ever noticed. He did not imitate (and could not be imitated) ... and each of his stories was a love story.

Examples:

"Bianca's Hands." (That one? A story so horrible that editors not only bounced it but blacklisted the author? Yes, that one.)

"The World Well Lost." (A love story, obviously—one about homosexuals. But please note that the copyright on it is 1953, many years before "gay pride" was even whispered, much less shouted. And Ted was not speaking in defense of himself but out of empathy for others. Ted was not even mildly homosexual. You can check this for yourself if you wish. I have no need to; I knew him intimately for more than forty years.)

"Some of Your Blood." (Go back and read it again. Yes, George Smith makes Count Dracula look like a tenderfoot Scout. But Sturgeon invites you to look at it from George Smith's angle.)

And so on, story after story for half a century. Some of Sturgeon's yarns had adventure trappings, or science-fiction gadgets, or fantasy/weird/horror props, or whodunnit gimmicks or other McGuffins, but in each, tucked away or displayed openly, you will find some searching comment on love, a new statement, not something borrowed from another writer.

In addition to this prime interest Ted was alive to every facet of the world around him: He had a lifelong passion for machinery; his interest in music was intense and professional; he delighted in travel; he relished teaching others what he had learned—but above all and at all times, waking and sleeping, he loved his fellow humans and expressed it in all aspects of his life.

I first met Theodore Sturgeon in 1944. He had just returned from the Caribbean, where he had been a heavy-machinery operator building airstrips for the U.S. Army Air Force. That job played out in '44; no more airfields were being built in the Antilles; the emphasis was shifting to the Pacific Theater. Ted was 4-F, a waste of skin; his draft board laughed at him. He was not even eligible for limited service. Rheumatic fever in his high-school days had left him with a heart so disabled that simply staying alive through each day was a separate miracle.

That damaged heart not only kept Ted out of military service;

ten years earlier it had robbed him of his dearest ambition: to be a circus acrobat. In high school, by grueling daily practice, he had transformed himself from that fabled ninety-pound weakling into a heavily muscled and highly skilled tumbler, one who could reasonably hope to join someday the "Greatest Show on Earth." Then one morning he woke up ill.

He recovered . . . but with a badly damaged heart. A circus career was out of the question, and many other pursuits were foreclosed. Eventually his disability forced him into the one career open to anyone whose body is warm and mind still functioning: free-lance writing.

I once collected notes for an essay—the relation between physical disability and the literary pursuit; or Shakespeare was 4-F and so was Lord Byron and Julius Caesar and Somerset Maugham—and what's your excuse, brother? Was it a queasy itch to see your name in print and a distaste for hard work? Or was it diabetes (polio, consumption, heart trouble) and a pressing need to pay the rent?

If we limit the discussion to science fiction, I can recall offhand several writers who got into the business not from choice but from physical disability coupled with financial necessity: Theodore Sturgeon, Robert A. Heinlein, Cleve Cartmill, H. G. Wells, Fletcher Pratt, Daniel F. Galouye, J. T. McIntosh. Each on this list wound up as a free-lance writer through physical limitations that crowded him into it . . . and I am sure that the list could be much longer, if we but knew.

So what was Sturgeon doing running bulldozers and backhoes and power shovels? Driving a Daisy Eight is not as easy as driving a car; rassling a dozer is no job for a man with a bad heart.

The answer is simple: Ted never paid any more attention to his physical limitations than he was forced to, and in wartime the physical examination for a civilian employee of the army or navy consisted of walking past the surgeon, who would then mark the prospect "fit for heavy manual labor." I am not joking. In World War II, I hired many civilians for the Navy Field Service; the Army Field Service was not more demanding than we were—or we would have snatched their prospects away from them. This was a time when any warm body would do. A typist was a girl who could tell a typewriter from a washing machine. (Later we took out the washing machine.)

So Ted built airstrips in broiling sun and 120-degree heat and failed to drop dead. He outlasted the job and then came to New York.

I think Ted worked for a while for the University of California, in the Empire State Building, with John W. Campbell, Jr., the editor of *Astounding Science Fiction,* as his supervisor. No, I have not jumped my trolley; at that time the University of California occupied one entire floor in the Empire State Building. Campbell was supervisor in a classified section that wrote radar operation and maintenance manuals—and even the word "radar" was classified; one did not say that word. (And didn't even *think* the word "uranium," not even in one's sleep.)

I am not certain what work Ted did, because in 1944 one did not poke into another man's classified work. I knew a trifle about this radar project because I had a radar project of my own, with a touch of overlap. But Campbell is dead now, and so is George O. Smith and so is Ted; I can't check. (Ted's wife Jayne can't be certain; I am speaking of the year she was born.)

As may be, Ted was writing at night for Campbell and sharing lodging with Jay Stanton, who was both Campbell's assistant supervisor on the radar writing project and Campbell's assistant editor at Street and Smith . . . and all three men were part of another project I ran for OpNav-23, a brainstorming job on antikamikaze measures. (I was wearing three hats, not unusual then. One tended to live on aspirin and soothing syrup.)

I had been ordered to round up science-fiction writers for this crash project—the wildest brains I could find, so Ted was a welcome recruit. Some of the others were George O. Smith, John W. Campbell, Jr., Murray Leinster, L. Ron Hubbard, Sprague de Camp, and Fletcher Pratt. On Saturday nights and Sundays this group usually gathered at my apartment in downtown Philadelphia.

At my request Campbell brought Sturgeon there. My first impression of Sturgeon was that no male had any business being that pretty. He was a golden boy, one that caused comparisons with Michelangelo's David. Or Baldur. He was twenty-six but looked about twenty. He was tall, straight, broad-shouldered, and carried himself with the grace of a tightwire artist. He had a crown of golden curls, classic features and a sweet, permanent smile.

All this would have been inexcusable had it not been that he was honestly humble and warmly charming. When others spoke, Sturgeon listened with full attention. His interest in others caused one to forget his physical beauty.

My flat was about three hundred yards from the Broad Street Station; people came to these meetings from Washington, Scarsdale, Princeton, the Main Line, Manhattan, Arlington, etc.; my place was the most convenient rendezvous for most of the group. No one could drive a car (war restrictions), but the trains every thirty minutes on the Pennsylvania Railroad could get any member of the group there in two hours or less. It was a good neutral ground, too, for meetings that might include several officers (lieutenant to admiral), a corporal from OSS, a State Department officer, one sergeant, civil servants ranging from P-1 to P-6, contractors' employees with clearances up to "top secret" but limited by "need to know," and civilians with no official status and no clearance. I never worried about security because there was always one member of naval intelligence invariably present.

On Saturday nights there would be two or three in my bed, a couple on the couch and the rest on the living-room floor. If there was still overflow, I sent them a block down the street to a friend with more floor space if not beds. Hotel rooms? Let's not be silly; this was 1944.

The first weekend Sturgeon was there he slept on the hall rug, a choice spot, while both L. Ron Hubbard and George O. Smith were in the overflow who had to walk down the street. In retrospect that seems like a wrong decision; Hubbard should not have been asked to walk, as both of his feet had been broken (drumhead-type injury) when his last ship was bombed. Ron had had a busy war—sunk four times and wounded again and again—and at that time was on limited duty at Princeton, attending military governors' school.

On Sunday afternoon the working meeting was over, and we were sitting around in my living room. Ron and Ted had been swapping stories and horrible puns and harmonizing on songs—both were fine vocalists, one baritone, one tenor. I think it was the first time they had met, and they obviously enjoyed each other's company.

Ron had run through a burlesque skit, playing all the parts; then Ted got up and made a speech "explaining" Marxism and featuring puns such as "Engels with dirty faces" (groan), and ending with "then comes the Revolution!" At that last word he jumped straight up into the air and into a full revolution—a back flip. His heels missed the ceiling by a scant inch, and he landed as perfectly as Mary Lou Retton on the exact spot on which he had been standing.

This with no warning—which is how I learned that Ted was a tumbler. This in a crowded room. This with no windup. I don't think he could have done it in a phone booth but he did not have much more room.

Ron Hubbard leaned toward me, said quietly into my ear, "Uh huh, I can see him now, a skinny kid in a clown suit too big for him, piling out of that little car with the other clowns and bouncing straight into his routine."

Ron was almost right.

I think it was a later weekend that we learned of Ted's incredible ability to produce just from his vocal cords, no props, any sound he had ever heard—traffic noises, train noises, shipboard noises, animals, birds, machinery, any accent whatever.

Here is the first one I asked for: A frosty morning, a buzzsaw powered by a two-cycle engine cranked by a line. Start the engine despite the freezing weather, then use the saw to cut firewood. The saw hits a nail in the wood.

I'm sorry I can't offer you a tape. Ted scored a cold four-oh.

Thirty-three years later, in front of a large audience at San Diego ComiCon, I asked Sturgeon to repeat that buzzsaw routine, defining it again for him, as he had forgotten ever doing it. He thought for a few seconds, then did it. Another four-oh.

The second one I demanded was this: A hen lays an egg, then announces it. The farm wife shoos her off the nest long enough to grab the egg and replace it with a china egg.

Another perfect score—I do not know when or where Sturgeon coped with cranky two-cycle engines or with temperamental hens'

... but this farm boy now speaking can testify that Ted had been there in each case and could reproduce the sounds as exactly as any equipment from Sony or Mitsubishi.

I hope that someone somewhere has taped and preserved some of Sturgeon's jokes in dialect. I would like to hear again the one about the pub in London where one could get a bit of bread, a bit of cheese, a pint of bitter, a gammon of Yorkshire ham, a bit of pudding and a go with the barmaid, all for two and six. Try to imagine all *that*. Was anyone running a recorder?

Ted's ear was phenomenal and not limited to parlor tricks. Mark Twain said that the difference between the right word and almost the right word was the difference between lightning and a lightning bug.

Sturgeon did not deal in lightning bugs.

Robert A. Heinlein
September 1985